The
Sorcerers
Of
Caramine

To
Freia

Happy
Reading

Luke Brady

First published in Great Britain in 2017
Luke Brady Publishing

The moral right of the author has been asserted
A CIP catalogue record of this book is available from the British
Library

ISBN: 9

ISBN-13: 978-1527220492

To Dad

Luke Brady

CHAPTER ONE

Each subject of study came with its own unique odour. As Perin made his way from the chemistry laboratory, with its smells of gas flames, ammonia and an intangible sweet vapour that had always given him a headache, he progressed towards the history study. He had made this trip many times before, and knew this would be one of the last. He took in the details more sincerely and precisely than ever before.

The walls of the Great Academy wore their pristine paint with silent solemnity and unsmiling tutors paced the corridors. Each teaching room was vast. although they had a uniform construction, each room seemed to harbour something of the personality of the subject taught there.

The study of words and literature was accompanied by the smell of dried ink and chalk. The study of mathematics had a metallic aroma, due to the compasses, protractors, steel counting strips and slide edges.

As Perin progressed through the heavy, grand oak doors to the history study, he breathed in deeply. He smelled stories. To most other people this was simply the smell of books and paper. To Perin, however, they were much more. These papers carried the tales of long-dead people and largely forgotten events, and they fascinated him beyond measure.

It would be the height of rudeness and vulgarity for Perin to publicly take enjoyment in this subject. His tutor would never forgive him for treating it with such disrespect. That level of frivolity was simply unheard of in the Academy. Deep down though, he relished hearing of the battles, the missions, the political intrigue, the marriages of convenience and the men and women who had carried them all out. It was with this knowledge that he stared around the room for the last time.

There was a raised dais on one side of the room with a large bench stood in front in dark oak. A black scroll, the width of the room, lined the side of the wall behind the bench from roof to floor so that the tutors could inscribe swathes of text and then raise the words up via a winch beside the door, that a random student was selected to operate each lesson.

The top of the room reached as high as some houses, and Perin had often left with pains in his neck having been so enthralled by the top most tale that he had never ventured further down for the full length of a lesson. He would often sneak back to the room later to enjoy the next story alone, and then the next, and next, until all the light had disappeared. At the height of summer, when light could last almost through one day and into the next, he had survived on hardly any sleep at all. The stories sustained him.

The circular style of the amphitheater in a rectangular room left two vestibules behind the seating area. This was where the tomes were kept. These were the records of the history of Caramine that were relayed to the students. It was unknown who had first recorded the information in these volumes, but Perin was extremely grateful that they had. If he reached the end of the tutors' scratching on the wall, and there was still sufficient light, he would often start to peruse the dusty but intriguing manuscripts.

On this day Perin was the first to arrive. This was not

unusual. Many of his fellow students had always found history to be a dull and wordy subject, and preferred to be constructing, brewing, mixing, baking, or some such laborious pastime. The very thought made Perin's veins cool to winter water. He was not a gifted athlete. Competent? Perhaps, but certainly not gifted.

Now, he considered, *Where would be the best spot for today?* As he looked around the room he took in the different options. *Close to the door perhaps, for a quick escape? In the centre, where it was easiest to become lost in the sea of humanity? In the uppermost seats where all the good students sat to get the best view?* For this reason, the uppermost seats were often referred to as 'the angels'. It was a term of deep disparagement that usually caused Perin to avoid sitting there, even if it would save his neck.

No, he thought, *If this is to be my last story, I want to savour every moment of it.* He climbed the sloping central wooden staircase, which had been rubbed smooth by thousands of reluctant feet, to the uppermost level. He took the seat furthest away from the door. Perin had been the first to come into the room, and from this position he would likely be the last to leave.

It did not take long before other students arrived. Although they had been in the same educational groupings for all of Perin's sixteen years, he knew few of their names. He recognised Pym, a tall clever boy with a knack for using words to relay his point. He was closely followed by Acci, a long straight-haired girl with a short flat nose that caused her round reading spectacles to slip off. Behind her was Gruff, a broad-shouldered hulk of mass who had all the intelligence and sense of a moth flying into a flame. He was, however, an exceptional athlete.

These three, amongst the almost three hundred that were soon streaming into his class, were the ones who could be considered his comrades. He knew a few more names, but these three were somehow closer. They stayed in adjacent rooms and had therefore seen each other more than any of the other students. Each one in turn spied Perin sitting in his upper sanctuary, and with a wide-eyed amazement resolutely took the decision not to venture up the staircase to join him. They all opted for the centre of the room, where it was easiest to be missed.

As Perin looked around the room, he considered how he compared to the rest of his classmates. He was relatively short. As he did not have any inclination towards athletic pursuits this had always seemed rather unimportant to him. His waistline was rather large, and his hair rather greasy. Although these sorts of things often made his life more difficult, he certainly wouldn't swap one fact, story or piece of information at his recall to be more like Gruff.

What Perin did possess, that he had always enjoyed and been secretly proud of, was his voice. Although Pym had a use of words that Perin couldn't match, Perin seemed to be able to convince people with greater ease. He conveyed sincerity and an inner strength of conviction that, at least in conversation, brought people to his side in almost any dispute. His comrades had often just referred to this as luck – luck that would one day run out. They suggested that when that happened, Perin would come crashing down without his dignity and perhaps without some of his teeth. Perin had never cared much for his teeth either, so considered this to be no great loss.

With the study now nearly full, the large wooden entrance doors swung open and their tutor made his entrance. The room fell silent as the sound of approaching footsteps betrayed his approach. As they grew louder they drew all attention to the door as their tutor arrived.

Professor Roth approached the bench at the front of the study. He was a slight man in long black robes. A rather imperious figure, he had a long thin nose that turned up slightly at its end, giving him a constant expression of disdain, as well as a rather unpleasant continuous view of his nostrils. On top of his prominent nose he wore a pair of thin rimless spectacles. These seemed to be more for effect than to correct his vision as, for the most part, he looked over the top of the glasses to communicate. It was in this manner that he addressed the class:

"Good afternoon gentlemen and ladies," he boomed. The acoustics of the hall amplified his voice several times and gave the impression that the sound was coming from the walls themselves. "As some of you may know, I am a man of history myself." With an air of superiority he began to pace back and forth across the front of the study. "You will also be aware that tomorrow, you all take the Grand Committee exam."

A murmur of tension rippled across the chamber. There had indeed been little else on the minds of the assembled company apart from the exam they were all about to take the next day.

"I therefore decided some time ago to take it upon myself to give the final history lecture to all students on their final day."

He paused at this point, presumably expecting a reaction from the assembled company. After a few moments a polite, if somewhat lacklustre, ripple of appreciative applause broke out from some of the more eager students inclined to ingratiate themselves upon the faculty. Perin enjoyed a little smirk at this. The truth was that the following day, whatever it would bring, would mark the end of the tutor's power over the students. The day after that the people surrounding him would be farmers, soldiers or perhaps even tutors themselves. Perin knew it would be a culture shock to him, and every student as they adjusted to a new life, but this was the first time he had considered that the tutors might also have a culture shock when their favourites, or indeed their least favourite students went forth after the exam, their power over them, and their authority completely broken. What he was witnessing was the old man's last hurrah with this group of young men and women. He probably deserved a smattering of applause, so Perin joined in.

"Thank you ladies and gentlemen," the Dean continued as he raised his arms to silence them all. "I do, however, have a lesson to teach you and a final lecture to give."

The applause instantly died away. Some of the students had clearly hoped that this was to be a wish of good luck and fortune and then an early finish. The old man had dashed their hopes.

"So our subject for today will be the history and background of the Great Committee examination itself."

The room seemed to relax a little. The students had doubtless been concerned that some new last minute topic was to be presented to them that they would have to master within a day. Thankfully, it seemed to be more of an exercise in self-justification for the dean. Perin did find that he was interested in the background and context. He already knew the basic principles, but from an academic perspective more than a historical one.

"In the days before the Great Committee, our society was anarchic." He dramatically raised his arms again. The long sleeves of his gown, when combined with his flared nostrils made him look like an ageing bat. "All parents were free to raise their children individually with their own beliefs and their own styles. They refused to ensure their children served the needs of society, but served their own needs and pursued their own passions."

Looking around the room, Perin could see the feelings of repulsion emanating from the crowd. As far as they were concerned, what the dean suggested could only have been employed by savages. He somewhat liked the idea, but how could the world work without the Great Committee deciding how many people were needed for each role in society and who was best suited to fill it?

"The governmental committee of the time attempted to organise society as best they could but a degree of anarchy was accepted as the norm. At least until –" he paused, ensuring the room was completely engaged in his lecture, "The discovery of sorcery."

The mood in the room instantly changed. Perin leaned forward in his seat. The existence of magic was no secret, but its practice, and even its discussion, was regulated by the Great Committee itself. This lecture had suddenly become very important because the text would have had to have been cleared, if not written by the Committee itself for public dissemination. Perin quickly realised that this was why the dean was giving the lecture. There was no way he would allow someone of a lesser position to speak for the Committee itself. He had been around the longest and in society, put simply, longevity mattered more than anything else.

"When the first embers of sorcery were discovered there was great concern. People were primitive back in those days. Many clung to religious and other senseless beliefs and saw the end of the world ahead of them through magic. Their fears could have been justified, and anarchy could have overtaken the fragile beginnings of our great society. The Committee immediately took action to investigate the extent to which magic could be used and to record, formalise and control its usage. This led to the full and complete control of the dissemination of all materials relating to magical education and knowledge. It was a success. The Committee soon applied this rationalisation towards the study of all subjects and fields and gradually society became more civilised and controlled."

A sense of warm contentment flowed over the crowd. They were obviously very comfortable with this. Perin knew the alternative was anarchy, but he did consider the thought that it would perhaps be a more interesting world.

"Although magic proved positive for the country," the Dean continued, "it proved difficult for members of industries that had been fundamentally changed by its discovery. The Committee stepped forward to ensure that everyone was trained in a skill or subject that would be of use of society. This was the beginning of the Great Academy."

He paused at this point, spreading his arms wide again. He slowly rotated on the spot as if to encourage everyone to drink in the sight of this one classroom. The truth was that the room had provided most of the students interminable boredom. History was not considered a subject with much potential by the student populace. Perhaps sensing he was losing his audience, the dean quickly continued.

"From that point, all children have been educated here until they reach the age where they take the Great Committee exam, which will lead them into the career that will best serve them, the Great Committee and society."

The room seemed to lose its tension and attention. This was language that everyone in the room had heard before. The notion that 'The Great Committee' looks after you and society is one that every student had learned from their very first lessons in speech. These were some of the first words that everyone in the room had been taught. At this point Perin and the rest of the assembled company had completely tuned out of the lecture. They had heard it all before.

As an alternative, Perin enjoyed looking round the room at the wooden seats, the high arched windows and the old blackboard. From his vantage point in the back row, he could even look down on tomes in awe and longing at the knowledge on display there.

Soon enough though, the old man had come to the conclusion of his speech.

"So as you go forth onto the next stage of your own journey, remember that you will always have the lessons you have learned here, all on behalf of the Great Committee who loves you and cares for you. This academy was here for those before you, it was here for you and it will be here for your children, should the Great Committee find you worthy of them in the future. Go now, do yourself and this academy proud, as you serve the Great Committee with your life and your talents."

With this undeniable and somewhat unseemly crescendo, he raised his arm once more, swept around and was out of the room before the first of the students in the first row had even left his seat. As the door closed and it was clear that the lecture was over a cheer went up from the students.

"It's over!" shouted a student from the front of the room. It was met with a cheer from the assembled company.

"Oh no," Perin said to himself, "It's just beginning!"

CHAPTER TWO

"What the hells were you doing up in the Angels?" Gruff demanded with a scowl.

Not long after Perin had left the lecture hall, he had been ushered to one side by his giant acquaintance and pleasantly escorted, though not without insistence, to their hostelry of choice.

"Just taking in the overall scene," replied Perin indignantly. "After all, it's the last time any of us will be in that room."

"Exactly!" Acci said. "It was the last time for all of us and it would have been appropriate for us to sit together, as we have done thousands of times before! It's the last time we will be here as well." The young woman gestured around at the busy tavern as if it were a cathedral or other religious retreat from days gone by. Perin had read about religious iconography, however, and did not consider the cracked bar stools, stale beer and discoloured floors to be good examples of it.

He did feel a pang of regret. Acci was obviously hurt, and sitting together for their final lecture would have been a kind thing for comrades to do. They had faced all sorts of different trials together over the years. Perin was an unnatural and clumsy athlete, so Gruff had taken care of him and compensated for his inability in the regular team competitions. Gruff in turn was fairly useless when it came to more word-based subjects. In fact, his worst was probably language itself, where his writing was constantly checked and corrected by the rest of the group. All their lives, they had all aided each other in their weaker areas. Perin understood their disappointment at being abandoned on their final day, but he wasn't ready to concede the point just yet. This was to be a battle of wits, and one that Perin had little intention of losing.

"You are all quite right," he said with a chaste expression and repentant tone. "I should have sat with my longest-serving comrades. I should have known intuitively through some unlearned magic where you wished to sit. I should have suspected that you would not join me in the Angels. I should have known that your disappointment at my absence would not have been enough to inspire you to climb a set of stairs to join me." He paused briefly, looking each of them in the eye in turn. "I should've known that I'm not that important to you."

Gruff looked completely defeated. He now believed he had done something terribly wrong. Acci looked defeated, but not upset. Hers was the look of someone who had been bested. Pym alone looked unrepentant, his arms folded and his brow furrowed. *Ah*, thought Perin, *this isn't going to be as straightforward as I thought.*

"Come off it, Perin," Pym began, nostrils flaring. "It's not as if any of us has ever had any desire to sit up in the Angels, particularly in that class. You knew fine well that we wouldn't want to go up there. You knew that when you made the decision, but your own desire for grandeur and sentiment outweighed our opinions or worth to you."

Poor Gruff now looked very confused, and Acci was rubbing her temples. This was a dance she had seen them engage in several hundred times. For his part, Perin suppressed a small smile. Pym was right, and he was indeed regretful for neglecting to consider his friends. There was, however, no way he was going to let Pym get a final verbal victory over him, though he knew he would be forced to make a small concession to achieve the greater victory.

"I did neglect to consider your opinions, and for that I apologise. Just as you neglected to consider my opinions and feelings regarding…" he looked at him through squinted eyes, "what was it you called it? Grandeur and sentiment? You clearly know me so well, you knew how important such things would be to me, but you took no notice of them when deciding where you should sit, any more than I thought of you when deciding for myself."

The pace of his speech had increased as he spoke, and it was clear from Gruff's bemused expression that he had lost track of the conversation. Acci clearly just wanted to move on. Pym still looked determined, but Perin had his killer blow prepared.

"But are you absolutely sure," he continued, "that continuing this argument is how we should spend our last evening together?" His tone was now one of imploring comradeship. "Does our history count for so little that you are determined to persist with disagreement and disappointment on our final night together as living mates? I thought better of you," he finished with a downcast look he felt was thoroughly realistic.

"Shut up and get a drink!" Pym retorted with undeniable resignation.

Victory, thought Perin. He decided it would be best to be magnanimous in his triumph to ensure that the evening went as amiably as possible. To that end, he rose from his chair and headed towards the bar to order a round of drinks. This also allowed him to turn away from the other three as a wide smile threatened to spread across his face.

There was nothing remarkable about the establishment. It was a typical watering hole. The smooth surface of the bar had absorbed so much alcohol and so many sugary beverages that it was now constantly tacky to touch, regardless of how well it had been cleaned. As Perin stood with his elbow on the sticky wood he surveyed the room. Hunters had furnished the walls with antlers and horns from their various kills. After they had sold the meat, the trophies may have been exchanged for a few drinks to be used as decoration. The armchairs were mismatched and in various degrees of disrepair. There were some holes burnt into the arms by patrons who smoked tobacco sticks. The leather was worn through in many cases, and the springs had obviously given way in others due to decades of use by heavy customers. That said, when all this was combined with the roaring fire, its light bouncing off the copper fireplace, and the friendly if somewhat unpolished service, the place seemed more enticing rather than less.

A large bartender with red hair only a few shades brighter than his face worked his way through the customers lining the bar. When he came to Perin, he addressed him in his well-practised, affable boom.

"What'll it be?"

"A glass of shine, a shot of fire and two glasses of spirit water," Perin recited. This had been the standard round for the quartet of comrades since they had reached the age where their stomachs could handle the alcohol.

As the barman prepared the drinks, Perin looked back at the table where his friends continued to talk. He wondered where the exams tomorrow would lead them, and if he would still have contact with any of them. He didn't hold out much hope for Gruff; his talents were very different from Perin's. Acci was less academic than he and Pym were, but intelligent nonetheless. It was likely that Perin would end up in a similar profession to Pym. They were fairly well matched in academic subjects, although Perin considered himself to have a slight edge. He conceded that, although not exceptional, Pym had the edge when it came to practical subjects. Although not physical like Gruff, who could throw a wooden barrel further than either of them, Pym excelled in physical experimentation, combining chemicals and other such things.

The bartender returned with the drinks on a tray to make it easier for Perin to carry them. The bar had become more crowded and he was forced to weave his way back to the table to avoid spilling the drinks.

He returned to the table and received a smile from Acci. "Many thanks," she said.

"You are most welcome," replied Perin.

Gruff and Pym had already retrieved their drinks and raised them to show their gratitude before taking a sup. Perin returned the gesture and drank a mouthful himself. As one, they relaxed into their chairs, ready for a final night of amicable conversation before the exam.

"So," started Pym, "assuming all goes well tomorrow, what do you think would be the ideal assignment for us?"

"The Great Committee will see us right, more than we could ever know," recited Acci.

It was considered the height of rudeness to second-guess the actions of the Committee. To do so suggested you had ambitions beyond your abilities, and believed you knew better than those in charge. As with all such things, these taboo subjects became the staples of private conversation amongst young comrades. The truth was that Acci had no problem with the conversation. This was simply a preface that she always employed to make herself feel more comfortable, and in order to give the impression that she was a virtuous and upright member of the Grand Committee's society. It was an aspect of her character that Perin found endearing, but he knew it drove Pym to distraction. This only added to its appeal as far as Perin was concerned.

"Yes," Perin interjected, "but accepting that the Great Committee will take no notice of our wishes, and that what will happen will happen, there's no harm in a bit of conjecture."

This was also a part of this unwritten ritual: Perin

would be the one to talk Acci into the conversation. Tonight she did not seem to be in the mood for putting up much of a fight, as she was the first to make her opinion known.

"I think I'm best suited for having children. I've always hated those books of yours, Perin, and if I never have to run round that damned athletic track again with you, Gruff, I won't feel that there is something missing from my life."

Perin noticed that Pym had narrowed his eyes and taken another slow drink from his glass. 'Books of yours, Perin,' she'd said, not 'Books of yours, Pym.' That must have hurt. Perin felt a flash of guilt at this, but it soon faded; after all, it wasn't him who had said it.

Pym had no difficulty in making himself known, as became evident when he put down his glass and cleared his throat. His every statement was like a declaration.

"You say that the Great Committee will know better than us, but I intend to join it."

Acci looked at him, dumbfounded. "You're not serious?"

"I am," he replied. "And why not?"

"Well," said Acci, who was never comfortable justifying herself. This was obviously Pym's way of getting back at her, but she soldiered on, "no one joins the Great Committee, you are simply selected, but it will be because you excel at what you do in life, and I don't think being a student counts towards that."

"Yes, well," Pym replied with a superior and defensive air, "I'm sure that's true for most people, but it is entirely possible that a protégé of the Academy could go straight onto the Committee to learn from the great minds that sit upon it."

"How do you know?"

The voice came from behind Gruff's glass, which had just left his lips. Normally he wouldn't have contributed to this sort of conversation. He would simply look at the person talking, laugh when appropriate and enjoy his drink in relative silence.

"Well, of course a person could go straight onto the Committee in exceptional circumstances. Why couldn't they?" spat Pym.

"That's not what I meant," said Gruff. "I meant, how do you know the people on the Great Committee have great minds? Could be that they are all strong warriors instead."

Perin suddenly understood. Everyone believes those at the top are, by and large, like them, simply better at it. For Gruff that meant they were physical, not mental beings.

"Don't be so dense," laughed Pym. "The Committee decide what everyone's role will be in society based on the results of the tests they set. Weren't you listening this afternoon? They are the ones who discovered, control and regulate the use of magic. They civilised our society and set up this very Academy! That's not the job of warriors and athletes!"

"But they have also kept the peace and avoided war by staying strong," Gruff countered. "What's that if not the job of a warrior?"

Good grief, thought Perin, *Gruff is holding his own. This must be quite important to him.* It was at that point, despite agreeing entirely with Pym's point of view, that he decided to take Gruff's side. In all the years they had known each other, in terms of discussion, Gruff had never bested anyone. It would be quite the way to end their friendship.

"It seems to me," Perin said, "that since the Great Committee represents all the various aspects of society – the physical, mental, domestic and mystical – it stands to reason that all these matters must be somewhat represented on the Committee, otherwise it would be a rather ineffectual and certainly an unjust entity. Is that what you are suggesting, Pym?" He grinned wickedly.

Pym seemed taken aback by the suggestion. Suggesting that the Committee could be unjust or working against the good of society was strictly taboo.

"Of course not!" he said, abashed.

"Then you must concede," Perin continued, "that the most likely scenario is that the heads of enforcement and military must be on the Committee, and they are far more likely to possess qualities like those Gruff excels in than either you or I."

"That's certainly the most likely scenario," Pym agreed, "but who are we to question or speculate on the make-up of our Great Committee?"

This was a blatant attempt to change the subject, and having accepted his victory on behalf of Gruff, who was now beaming into his glass, Perin was happy to drop the subject.

At some point during the conversation Acci must have slipped away to get the next round of drinks, because she now returned carrying the same tray that Perin had used earlier. Distracted by the additional libations, the conversation rambled on for some time about the classes they would miss and the tutors they would be happy not to see again.

During this part of the night, Perin was fairly quiet as his mind replayed many of the stories he had heard in the history hall that he would now likely never hear again.

"Perin?" Acci said inquisitively, but Perin was so involved in his own thoughts that she had to touch the top of his arm to get him to break out of his reverie.

"Huh? Sorry, what?" Perin said with a start.

"You never told us what you might consider an appropriate place for you after tomorrow."

"I'm not sure," Perin replied with a shrug. "The truth is, I've never given it much thought. There are parts of studying here that have really come quite naturally to me, and we all know that no one wishes to consider leaving what feels natural. I suppose thinking about what I might do after it's over is too much of a reminder that as of tomorrow, it will be over."

Luke Brady

Sadness came over him. His entire life had been in the Academy, and although most students didn't feel at ease there, Perin always had.

"You must be joking," Pym said mockingly. "You want to stay? I can't wait to get out of here!"

"Me neither," agreed Gruff.

"I can't say I disagree," said Acci apologetically.

"I understand that," explained Perin. "I haven't realised it till now, but the pursuit of knowledge and new information is what intrigues me, and I'm not ready to give that up."

"You're cracked!" said Pym. "You've got all the information you'll need. The damn test is tomorrow!"

"This conversation isn't about what we need, though; it's about what we want!" Perin explained. "If I had to choose a role, I'd probably be a history tutor. That way, I could record events, read accounts of ones that have already occurred, and convey information to other people preparing for the exam."

When he looked around, he saw that all three of his comrades were smiling.

"That would fit you like a skinny man's suit!" Gruff exclaimed, raising his glass.

"If the Great Committee has any sense, then that's what you'll be doing," said Acci.

"If I do find myself on the Grand Committee by tomorrow evening," Pym intoned with renewed superiority, "then I shall make it my first suggestion that my new colleagues give you that position." Slowly, he raised his glass to Perin and toasted him and all the others. "In fact, I shall endeavour to ensure that Gruff here is made captain of my personal guard as well."

"You do that and I'll kill you in your sleep," Gruff stated, with less humour than Perin hoped he intended.

"My good fellow," Pym replied, "I'll only do it so that you are close at hand when the one in charge of the military or enforcement dies or disgraces himself. Then I can have you brought in to join me on the Committee itself!"

"Well, in that case," Gruff considered, "I'd wait till after I was in post and then kill you in your sleep!"

Perin had been taking a drink. Gruff was not known for his wit, so this caught him totally off guard. He choked hard on his drink, and laughed and coughed in equal measure. He may very well have underestimated this hulking lout over the past sixteen years. He glanced over at Acci, who was laughing heartily too, before interjecting.

"All right then, Pym, so what am I to be granted in your grand utopian future?!"

"Oh, Acci, you want to be a mother. That's fair enough. How about you be mother to the Great Committee itself, and you can have children for all the men sitting on it and continue their legacies?"

Acci looked at Pym with intrigue and suspicion before her face broke into a wide grin.

"You're a cad, Pym!" she said with a mischievous laugh.

"Mine own self?" Pym replied with mock sincerity. "What do you mean?!"

"So you want to get yourself and Gruff on the Committee, and then me to have your children?" Acci continued.

It was a long-standing criticism Perin had of Pym: not so much that he wanted to mate with her; there was nothing wrong with that, but Acci had always held him off, just at the edge of affection. During their education, anything else would have been a bit unseemly. This did not, however, stop Pym bringing it up in a backhanded manner at every opportunity. Acci often shone light on it, and Pym seemed to think this was her way of encouraging him, but Perin suspected she was trying to kill the conversation. *I better stop this*, he thought. *It's not really how I want one of our last conversations to go.*

"I think we should probably turn in for the night!" he

said. "It's not as if tomorrow is an unimportant day." Perin rose from the table, picked up his glass and emptied the remaining contents into his mouth.

"Aye," said Gruff, following his lead.

"Indeed," said Acci, also rising.

"I suppose it is time." Pym was noticeably perturbed at the ending of the conversation, but conceded, finally rising from his chair.

The four companions exited the tavern into the cold night air. The freezing temperature hit them all the more harshly coming out of the oppressive warmth that had been generated by the fire inside. Acci linked arms with Perin and Pym, and Gruff walked in step on Perin's other side. They began their walk back to their four-person dormitory, and they had had enough to drink for the cobbled streets to pose more of a challenge than they would have if they had stuck to water. This was made worse by the fact that a thin layer of frost was forming on the stones. About halfway home, Acci slipped but was held up by Perin and Pym on either side.

"My heroes," she exclaimed.

Perin laughed, but Pym stayed quiet. He was still sulking.

"Oh, Pym, come on," Acci continued. "The truth is, there was one part of your idea that I really very much enjoyed." She held the two of them a bit closer and tighter.

"Oh yes?" Pym replied. "And what would that be?"

"You suggested that most of us should stay together. I would quite like that."

"Thank heaven for small mercies," Pym replied sarcastically.

"In fact, all it would take to make it perfect would be if Perin stayed with us too." Acci gave Perin's arm a subtle squeeze and drew a bit closer to him.

Oh God, thought Perin – *well, that's it. Pym's never going to stop sulking now!*

He was right. Pym never said another word throughout the rest of the walk home. Arriving at the simple dormitory, they all headed to their own rooms and wished each other goodnight, except Pym, who was in his room with the door closed before anyone could speak.

"I really hope that whatever we end up doing, we can see each other again," Acci said as she closed her door for the night.

Perin had no idea what the next day, or day after that, would bring. All he was fairly sure of was that Acci would not likely receive her wish. The thought preoccupied him as he lay down in his bed to go to sleep for his last night as a student of the Great Academy.

CHAPTER THREE

"Up!" roared Gruff through Perin's bedroom door.

Perin's return to consciousness was unceremonious to say the least. The assault on his senses left him with an instantaneous headache. There had actually been several attempts beforehand to raise him from his slumber. Acci's soft whispers had done very little to rouse him, and the door banging as Pym went out to start his trials had not even registered. Three loud bangs on the strong, dark wooden door by Gruff had also failed, but his voice, when raised to an animalistic roar, was exactly what was called for.

Perin's world was not quite in focus as yet. Being woken up too quickly always seemed rather like expecting a kettle to boil on command. Certain things take time, and waking up is one of them. This was probably why Perin did not instantly realise the urgency with which he needed to emerge from his room.

"Time?" he shouted, his mouth dry and his throat sore.

"Sunrise was two hours ago," came Gruff's reply.

Devil's teeth! thought Perin. He should have been up with the sun. He was late.

The exam varied with each candidate. There was no requirement to sit subjects you did not feel you had sufficient knowledge of to be able to do well. The decision about what exams to attend was treated as a partial exam in itself. Those a candidate set themselves and those they did not told as much about their character as anything else. Most people rose with the sunrise and took as many as they could in the day. This was, Perin realised, why Acci and Pym had already left. Gruff was probably only still there because he had elected to participate in athletic and physical examinations only. These required good light, and therefore those examinations did not start till later.

Perin felt a pang of guilt and regret at not rising earlier, not just because he had lost valuable examination time, but because he would not see his comrades one final time before leaving. At the conclusion of the day it was customary for candidates to stand in a colossal queue of students to await their results in a building known as Admissions and Demissions. Students would only set foot in that building twice: once when they were processed and led to their cabins as young students, and once to be told where they were to go next. Perin couldn't remember arriving at the Academy; it was likely this happened before he could walk. The thought made him smile. Cradled by an educator, clad in swaddling clothes, his mind would have been untouched, a clean slate to be filled with knowledge. Now he was about to find out how full it had become.

Perin emerged from his room having dressed hurriedly. His eyes were still having trouble focusing. He wore two odd socks, one of which had his left trouser leg tucked into the top. His cream shirt was crumpled and only partially tucked into the top of his trousers. His hair stood up at the back where he had been sleeping, and he had no time to attempt to flatten it down with water. Perin had never understood the tendency for students to attempt to look impressive on examination day. As far as he was concerned, if a pressed suit and white teeth took in an assessor, then they lacked the intelligence for the role.

Gruff stood in front of him in his black athletic vest and shorts. They were skintight and not flattering to someone so broad. They would be even less so to someone who was, like Perin, rather broad across his stomach as well as his shoulders.

"Best of luck," Gruff said, sticking out his hand.

"And you," replied Perin, "whatever the future may bring." He clasped Gruff's hand, gave it a firm shake, then barrelled towards the door in a vague attempt to make up for some lost time.

He stopped before he reached the door and turned back. Gruff still stood in the narrow hallway. The broad-shouldered youth filled the space in front of him, but his head was somewhat downcast. He was either nervous or melancholy about the approaching change. Perin knew he didn't have much time, but Gruff had always been such a positive and pleasant person. He felt the need to comfort him in some way.

"Gruff?" said Perin, causing him to look back towards him. "You're the best of us, remember that."

The big man smiled, and tears appeared in his eyes.

Perin knew he would be embarrassed about that, so as he reached for the door, he finished by saying, "As long as you don't screw it up!" As he walked along the corridor towards the main entrance, he could hear Gruff laughing.

Once he reached the street, he walked as briskly as he could. He didn't run – that was not something Perin had ever possessed a talent for – but he hurried as fast as he could to the main complex. He passed the clock tower that marked the centre of the island on which the Great Academy stood. It was even later than Perin had thought. He would only have time to focus on the subjects he was strongest in, mainly language and history. Numbers had always been relatively simple for him too, and he decided to add this to the list to provide diversity. He also decided on geography, as he had managed to combine in his mind the places with historical events that had occurred there. This meant he could conjure up an image of the whole continent in his mind's eye. *Four will have to be enough,* he thought. He was also a competent astrological plotter, but that examination had been before dawn. That, along with reading of runes, archaeology, and theoretical logic, would have to fall by the wayside.

He turned into the mathematics building and charged up the stairs towards one of the examination rooms. *I'm sure if I can show logic in my answers, and bring astrology, runes and archaeology into some of my history answers, then I will show enough of my skills there to forgo the exam.*

A long corridor of stone, lined with identical doors, marked the rooms that were set aside for the mathematics examination. The doors were windowless and plain, except for a sliding brass plaque that covered up the words *Examination in Progress* if it was swiped to the left. Perin walked along the corridor in search of a vacant room, but they were all occupied, presumably by some poor attendee being grilled. As he approached the far end of the corridor, he started to encounter nervous-looking students waiting outside. At this point, he stopped looking for a vacant room; if students had to wait to be admitted, then they were all clearly full. He returned to the top of the corridor and sat down in front of the first door. *Closest to the exit,* he thought. *That way he could get out of the building and to one of his other exams quickly.* In his head, he started to plot a route that would allow him to get from one building to the next with minimal time and effort.

After a while, when no other students had emerged from the doors that he could see, Perin began to worry that he was losing some of his precious time and would have to cut out another exam. *What can I afford to lose?* he thought. As far as he was concerned, he had already cut his itinerary down to the bare minimum. *Am I approaching this the right way? Is mathematics worth the time I am spending on it now? Probably not. I should probably consider what is the most important exam for me to take.*

That was without a doubt history, but the building was one of the furthest away. Perin did not know how long it would take when he arrived. He decided the best course of action was to go and take the history exam and see what time was left after that.

With that decision made, he got to his feet, angry at having wasted his time. He left the mathematics building and walked the length of the complex. The Great Academy occupied an entire island. Children were brought there almost directly from their mother's labour bed and raised in the Infantoretum, then passed to various parts of the island specialising in different levels of education. Once they were old enough to be self-sufficient (approximately ten years), they were moved into the main academic complex through which Perin now walked.

Each building housed a different subject and contained specialised teaching equipment. This had the side effect that the building often took on something of the personality of its subject. As Perin passed the domesticity building, he noticed that it seemed portly and welcoming in nature; like a domesticated bearer of children it gave the sense of large mixing bowls, sweet smells and clean clothes. Acci was probably in there now, displaying her prowess for sewing, cooking, cleaning and other domestic skills.

As he continued further, he passed the astronomy building with its large dome gleaming brightly in the reflected sunlight. The great telescope sat protruding from the top. The building reminded Perin of a giant brass owl waking up each night and gazing into the sky.

The athletics building stank of sweat that could be smelled from the street, and no matter what time of day you passed by, there tended to be the sound of a whistle piercing the air around it.

The chemistry building was awash with various

chimneys, each producing a gas or vapour of a different colour. The purples, pinks, oranges, greens and yellows pooled together in the sky directly above the building in a giant brown cloud. Occasionally flashes of lightning and rumbles of thunder could be heard from inside this nebulous assortment. Thankfully, this was not the case on this day, as it usually precipitated a downpour of rain. Perin was most relieved. The sun was beating down on the pavement. Under other circumstances, it would be a day to do very little.

He eventually arrived at the history building, which must have been one of the first constructed in the Great Academy, as it gave the impression of being both old and unchanging. Its stone facings were weather-worn and the roof displayed signs of having been fixed with many different materials over the years. This structural instability meant that for as long as Perin could remember, there had been scaffolding erected on different parts of the building whilst burly men, not unlike Gruff, worked to shore it up. At the moment, this scaffolding was right over the main entrance, which was covered by a canopy balcony for the office above. The slates on the front of the canopy had started to work their way free, and it was entirely possible that one had fallen off and seriously hurt someone. Perin had the impression that a member of staff had probably been injured. One student concussion wouldn't likely justify the impressive archway of scaffolding he now walked underneath at speed.

As soon as he entered the dimly lit foyer of the building, he felt serenity pass over him. This was his place, and he would not be shamed or undervalued here. He had a passionate grasp on this subject. If he achieved his desire of teaching here, then he may never have to leave.

He walked up the marble staircase, which began at the centre of the room and split up to encompass both sides, then flowed onto a balcony that encircled the room and looked back down on the entrance hall. Corridors broke off from the balcony like the spokes of a wheel. Perin walked around the perimeter, searching for the corridor that contained the room set aside for history examinations. At the far side, there was a corridor that Perin could see had a row of chairs along one wall that had not been there the previous day. Judging from his experience in the mathematics building, this was his destination.

As he approached the corridor, he could see the same *Examination in Progress* plaques on the doors. Although the rooms he passed all stated they had an exam in progress, there was no one waiting outside to go in next. The further he journeyed down the corridor, the fainter the noises of the vestibule, which had been quite busy, became. The temperature also dropped, and Perin shivered slightly.

The corridor came to a dead end and Perin saw that the plaque on the door of the final room was blank: there was no exam in progress inside. He took a deep breath. Well, he thought, this is it. He straightened himself up and knocked on the door.

"Come," came the disembodied voice from behind.

Perin laid his hand on the knob and turned it. The door opened with a creak, and light from the window inside poured into the otherwise dark corridor.

Perin walked into the room, and the first thing he noticed was the heat. There was a large, functional stone fireplace on the right-hand wall of the room. This had been lit and stoked, and now a roaring fire crackled and spat against the black iron grate, causing strange shadows to dance around the floor. Directly opposite the door was a high stained-glass window depicting an army descending a hill towards a water well. Underneath would be the date and name of the window, but these had been covered with a cloth, presumably to avoid helping a student with the answer to an exam question. The rest of the room was clear except for four desks that had been stacked against the remaining wall, and one wheeled desk chair in the centre of the room facing the fire.

Standing in front of the fire was the examiner. He was a stern-looking man who stood imperiously tall. He wore a black wig, not unlike the white ones that Perin would have expected a legal expert to wear. Apart from the colour, the only other difference was that on top of his wig was a black academic cap. He wore a jet-black cloak that covered his shoulders and buttoned up the front. It cascaded all the way to the floor. Along with standing as straight as a steel pole, this gave the impression that the examiner may have been bolted to the floor.

"Sit," he said. Perin obeyed. "This exam will take the following format. I will ask you questions and you will answer them if you have an answer to give. Once you are satisfied with your answer, you will tell me it is complete and then I will move on to the next question. The more questions you answer, the more obscure the subject matter shall become. You can end the exam whenever you wish by leaving the room. Do you understand?"

"Yes," Perin replied. He knew these words well; they were the introduction to every exam in each verbal subject.

The examiner hadn't made eye contact with him, and continued to look off into the middle distance. He stood in silence. Perin waited. A full minute passed, then two. By the third minute, Perin had started to panic. *What's going on?* he thought. He considered asking the examiner...until he realised. The exam had already begun.

"My answer is complete," Perin said, slightly embarrassed.

"Give a brief account of the First Farmers' War," intoned the examiner.

From here, Perin was on firm ground; these were the stories he had heard and learned from an early age, and had shown great interest in. That interest had led to easy memorisation. He dealt with each question without any trouble and was able to go into an exacting amount of detail on the First and Second Farmers' Wars, the first

Great Committee, the establishment of the Great Academy, the trade disputes, and even a description of the fisherman's picket, a subject found so boring by his fellow classmates many had fallen asleep when lectured on it. Perin was supremely confident and even managed to make the subject vaguely interesting.

"Give a full and detailed account of the effects of the discovery of magic," drawled the examiner.

Hah! thought Perin. The dean touched on that yesterday. He then went on to give a full and detailed history that he had read several times from various tomes.

When he was finished, he used the stock refrain: "My answer is complete."

"Having given an account of the effects of the discovery of magic, please give an account of the discovery of magic itself."

Perin felt as though his momentum had met a brick wall. "Excuse me?"

The examiner stood impassively, continuing to stare ahead.

Perin stood up and started to pace, racking his brains. The subject of how magic had been discovered was not discussed in polite company, and he was fairly sure that he had never read anything on it. The effects of magic on the social and governmental structures of Caramine were well known and documented, but its discovery was not discussed.

Perin knew that this was it: he would have to leave the room and concede that this was as far as he could take the exam. He headed towards the door, but something made him stop.

As he turned back to face the examiner, still passively looking forward, he heard himself say, "The discovery of magic involved a man being lost in the desert and deprived of food and water for over three weeks. He approached a ditch, and as he looked into it, it filled with water, as was his desire. He drank his fill, but the more he drank, the more water appeared in the ditch, until it was as large as a lake…"

He continued for at least another twenty minutes, adding embellishment, suspense and true artistry to his oration. It was complete nonsense, of course, but it struck Perin that logically he should make a guess rather than just leave the room. By the time his story came to a conclusion it had included two epic battles, a change of government, several love interests and comrades-in-arms feasting over their victorious discovery. Perin had begun to sweat. He was throwing his arms around wildly in excitement and emotion, and dashing around the room with nervous tension. Although this was a truly terrifying moment in his life, he had never felt this kind of elation before. He was smiling, a broad, tooth-filled grin, and his eyes were wild and alive. He knew that he must have looked as if he had lost his mind. For some reason, this seemed to add to the delight of the experience.

As his story reached its crescendo, he needed to finish his answer in some way. With a truly unseemly flourish, he concluded, "My answer is thoroughly, resolutely, emphatically, completely and utterly complete!"

He looked at the examiner, who for the first time was looking directly at him. He looked surprised, aghast and perhaps a little angry.

"The exam is concluded. You are to report to the Academic Faculty Building at once." There was a distinct hint of irritation in the examiner's voice, and the look on his face was evolving into something quite unpleasant. *This must be the first time someone has passed his exam with full marks*, thought Perin. He must have given the right answer, or sufficiently close to it.

He left the office and walked down the corridor with a spring in his step. He failed to notice his return to the cold outside the exam room; nor did he notice, as he descended the staircase and exited the door, that some of the men and women in the building were staring at him, as if he were a different kind of person to anyone they had seen before.

Maybe the examiner is allowed to select my role on behalf of the Committee, thought Perin. *Yes, that's what it must be. That's why I'm heading to the Academic Faculty. I'm about to join them.* He quickened his step and began to swing his arms.

The look on the examiner's face had been slightly concerning, but Perin put this down to sour grapes at having been bested in intellectual combat. He couldn't suppress a smile at the thought.

The Academic Faculty Building was a rather stark building, not unlike the simple dormitories that the students inhabited. Bare, angular walls with identical windows lined each floor. The main difference was that the Faculty Building was connected to each of the other academic buildings by a spider's web of copper wires that branched from a large pole on the roof. This was so that messages could be sent from the other buildings, conveying messages or news. Perin smiled at the thought that the history examiner now had to go to the machine and notify the Faculty Building that a truly exceptional student was on his way.

Visitors to this building were extremely rare. As such, it had no public entrance. Only people who lived inside had a key to enter directly, so Perin had no other choice than to knock on the door. It was opened by a doorman in uniform.

"I was sent here direct from my exam," announced Perin.

"Direct?" said the doorman, raising an eyebrow.

"Indeed," replied Perin with pride.

"Please wait here," said the doorman resignedly. He shut the door.

I suppose this is to be expected – they have probably never had someone rise directly to the teaching staff.

Perin revelled for a few minutes before realising that it

had grown dark outside. The sun had set during his exam and he had not noticed it; come to think of it, he had no idea what time it was. He hoped he had not woken anyone up.

The door flew open, causing him to jump back in surprise, and the dean himself appeared on the threshold. He was wearing casual clothes, and judging from the crumbs scattered across them, he had been disturbed during his dinner.

"Come in, my dear boy – Perin, isn't it?" he said with an affable air, quite different from his formal lecture the day before.

"Thank you very much, sir," replied Perin. He walked over the threshold.

As much as the Academic Faculty Building had resembled the student housing complex from the outside, there was absolutely no resemblance inside the building, which was comfortable to the point of opulence. Tapestries hung on the walls, and thick carpets lined the floors. There were well-maintained fires in every room Perin and the dean passed as he led him further into the building.

"I imagine you could do with something to eat, Perin?" the dean said with a grin.

"Well, I did have to skip breakfast, and it appears I've missed lunch as well," Perin replied. "It also looks like I may have disturbed you at your dinner, for which I'm most sorry!"

"Oh, my dear fellow, please be at your ease – it is a great honour and privilege to have you here!" gushed the dean. He displayed his teeth, which were yellowing and contained pieces of greenery, presumably from his half-consumed dinner.

He opened a side door that led down a steep flight of stone steps. Although the staircase was dark and cold, there were fabulous smells coming from the bottom. *They have their own kitchens,* thought Perin. The students had to go to a separate dining complex to eat. The thought of domesticaters making his meals to order every day was tantalising in the extreme. *The day just kept getting better.*

As they descended the steps, the smells grew stronger and the unmistakable heat of a kitchen rose to meet them. The dean stopped and opened another side door.

"Here we are," he said, and gestured inside.

The smell was sweet, like cakes or fruit bread.

"Thank you very much," said Perin, extending his hand.

"A pleasure," replied the dean, shaking it enthusiastically.

Then in one swift movement, he pulled hard on Perin's arm, swinging him inside the room. As sweet as it smelled, there was no light inside. Before Perin had time to react, the dean slammed the door and all was dark. As Perin's senses adjusted to their sudden change in circumstances, he heard one sound very clearly, the unmistakable and ominous click of the key in the lock.

CHAPTER FOUR

Perin stood in rigid, blackened silence for a few moments, struck dumb by the sheer unexpectedness of this turn of events. He was not afraid exactly; simply confused. First of all, he was not entirely convinced that he was alone in the room. The sheer rush of activity and confusion meant that he was unsure whether the dean had entered the room as well. Perin held his breath and listened carefully to ascertain if he could hear anyone else breathing. As far as he could tell, there was nothing.

He moved tentatively forward towards what he thought was the door, his arms outstretched to avoid bumping into anything. This plan failed almost immediately. The pain shooting up his shin and the high, piercing shriek of wood being scraped across cold stone told him that he had just bumped into a desk or a chair. Instinctively, he quickly reached down to rub the feeling back into his leg. This caused greater confusion as it resulted in a sharp pain to the top of his head. In leaning over too quickly, he had inadvertently struck his head hard against something. As white stars pierced the blackness in Perin's vision, he staggered backwards, caught his foot on something on the ground and crumpled over the piece of furniture he had just bumped into. He lay on the floor, momentarily unable to move and feeling like he had been assaulted.

"I hope there isn't anyone else in here," he said out loud to the darkness, *because if there is, I've made a total and complete ass of myself.*

The floor was ice-cold, but having bumped his head and hurt his back, he found it oddly comforting. He lay there for a few minutes until his senses returned to him.

This is ridiculous, he thought. *It must be part of the exam process. Yes, that's it: I'm still being tested, and given my current state of affairs, I'm probably not doing particularly well.*

With that notion in his head, he rolled onto his hands and knees and shuffled forward at a slow pace, feeling in front of him with his hands as he went. He quickly found a wall, which he believed must have been what he had hit his head on. Keeping his hands to the cold stone, he hoisted himself back up to standing. He then started to feel his way along, attempting to find the door. He was flushed with relief and success when the texture beneath his fingertips changed from stone to wood. He then used an approximate idea of what the door would look like in a bid to locate the handle. It wasn't there. There was a hole where a handle could have been, but the actual turning mechanism had been broken off.

Perin tried to work his finger into the hole to get some kind of grip to pull the door open, but only succeeded in cutting his finger. He tried knocking on the door.

"Excuse me? I'd like to be let out now. I think I'm through with this question," he shouted through the door. After a small pause, he added, slightly pathetically, "My answer is complete?"

There was no reply, and the door did not open.

Perin pushed his ear to the wood. He had a vague idea that there were people on the other side – he could hear heavy breathing and the sound of footsteps. *Why won't they help me? he thought to himself.*

This moment marked the first time in Perin's entire life when he suspected that he was no longer safe within the confines of the Great Academy, and that perhaps something or someone here was working against him. He began to panic. As a young man who had spent his whole existence wrapped in a cocoon of safety and conformity, to be imprisoned by the man in charge of that cocoon was profoundly terrifying.

He hammered his fists against the door. "Help! Someone help me!" he bellowed. The sound was painfully loud and amplified in what must have been a rather small room, but he was totally unaware of how well it would carry out into the corridor, if at all.

There was no reply.

"Please!" he continued. "I apologise, I repent, I recant, I'll work, I'll pay, I'll do anything, just let me go!"

He collapsed to his knees against the door and sobbed. He continued to beat the door from this position for a few more moments, each strike less forceful as the energy drained out of him. Then there was a sudden and surprising crash against the door a foot or a knee was slammed into it in response.

"You'll shut up and you'll do it now!"

Perin had been leaning against the door, and the sudden sound was ear-splitting. He fell back into the darkness of the room, then sat with his knees against his chest and his head resting forward.

I don't understand, he thought. *What have I done to justify this?*

"What have I done?" he repeated, this time shouting at the door, but again there was no reply.

Is this all because I only sat one exam? he wondered. *No, it can't be — the examiner would never have known that. It must be something I did in the room. Perhaps I was too clever, perhaps I got too many questions right. Perhaps I got too many questions wrong. Perhaps...*

It was obvious: for the last question, he had created an

answer. It hadn't been a guess based on historical knowledge and fact; it had been a creation, a fiction dreamed up from his own imagination. He hadn't realised it at the time, but this was beyond offensive. Creating new things was introducing the unplanned into the Great Committee's system, and was frowned upon. Creating a story in answer to a history question was at best lying and at worst a challenge to the established history of the Great Committee itself. He deserved to be locked up like this – although he hadn't realised it and hadn't acted out of malice, he was a criminal and deserved punishment. In despair, he curled up into a ball and sobbed against the cold, hard floor.

He wasn't sure how long he lay there. He was unsure if time was passing slowly or quickly. He was alone with no changing light to guide him. The most peculiar thing was that he felt as if he had gone to sleep, but couldn't be quite sure. After a time he couldn't even be sure if his eyes were shut or open. He had also lost all concept of what was a thought and what was a dream. He started to fear that he was going mad.

Why am I here? he thought. Not so much as an existential question – given the circumstances, he thought it best to cling to logic and exercise his potentially slipping mind. *Transgression must happen relatively frequently in some manner or other, given the number of Students at the Great Academy, but this is in no way a holding cell or prison.* It was so dark he couldn't see anything to confirm this, but it struck Perin as odd that a holding cell would be placed in the living area of the Academy tutors. *Why would it be adjacent to the kitchens? If it were, then why would it resemble – by feel, at least – an oversized cupboard? This must not be part of any plan or system.*

As this idea sunk in, he realised what a truly terrifying notion it was. The Great Committee was supposed to be all-seeing and all-knowing. If it couldn't directly avoid something happening, it was nonetheless meant to be intelligent enough to foresee it. If, as he suspected, his transgression was one of creativity, then surely he was not the first? *Surely,* he thought, *there must be several of us a year at exam time who decide that a wild guess is better than no answer at all?* Then as he examined it further, he began to ask himself, *Is that the case? Should I have walked away from the question? There is certainly a level of logic to that – if you know nothing, you say nothing – but there is a contrary logic that would suggest that if you may be right, you speak out, even if there is a very small chance of success.*

At this point, he was distracted by hunger. He had actually been quite hungry when he arrived, but events had somewhat overtaken that desire. Now he was ravenous. He stood up, careful not to collide with anything he had already discerned was in the room, and felt his way to the door.

He balled his hand into a fist and slammed three times at head height before shouting, "I need food and water! Please, or I may faint!"

He waited a few seconds before the reply came back: "If you faint, you'll shut up!"

Perin considered his reply. "If I faint, I will fall. If I fall, I will hit my head and may die, and I imagine I'm being imprisoned for a reason, not as capital punishment."

This thought cheered him up, but only momentarily.

"Aye," the voice came back. "You're right, you're not to die – well, not yet at any rate."

The bottom fell out of Perin's stomach. Not only was this a truly terrifying threat, but he was taken aback by the tone of relish. This man wanted him dead, and looked forward to that eventuality. Perin decided he no longer wanted to eat anything; he did, however, know that his body needed food. He decided to pluck up his courage and continue the conversation.

"Well, perhaps you could help keep me alive until the person who makes the judgement arrives?" He attempted to say this with more dignity than it perhaps deserved, but could not tell how successful he had been.

"We left bread and a pitcher of water in there before you arrived! Now shut up!" came the terse and impatient reply.

We? thought Perin. He had only heard one voice, but this suggested there was more than one man behind the door. They didn't sound like faculty. They sounded like soldiers or hired mercenaries. Who were they afraid would let him out? Perin knew he had no chance of escape, so could not fathom why those men were outside.

However, he had more pressing concerns. He started to feel along the walls into areas of the darkness that he thought he had not been to before. It was extremely difficult to tell. In complete darkness, there is a sense of staying still. Perin eventually found a table, and as he very carefully ran his hands over it, he found the plate of bread and the pitcher of water. There was no glass, so he would have to drink directly from the pitcher. As he searched the table, his foot touched something wooden that moved. He reached down and felt a bucket under the table, and inside was a folded soft cloth that Perin thought must be a blanket. So the intention is for me to be here for some time, then. As he thought about that, he stopped drinking the water and decided to ration it. He did, however, eat all the bread.

After this meagre feast, he crawled back to what he thought was the centre of the room, unfolded the blanket and lay down. Although he now had some protection from the cold floor, it still made him shiver. It took him a very long time to fall asleep.

Judging from the depth of sleep that Perin had come out of, he knew he must have been asleep for some time. His eyes shot open, but he was still enveloped by blackness. Now there was activity outside. He strained his ears for clues as to what was going on. There was the distinctive sound of steel clashing upon steel, and footfalls rushing past where Perin now knew the door was.

"You stay here, we'll head them off." He heard a disembodied voice from the other side, presumably a conversation between two or possibly three guards that had been posted there.

If someone is trying to break in here and needs to be headed off, perhaps it's me they've come for, Perin thought. He was hesitant as there was always the chance that it was not a rescue mission, but an attempt to drag him into an even more unsavoury situation. *Oh, come off it, Perin,* he thought to himself – *how much worse are things likely to get? The damn guard has already told you you're going to be killed!*

With his mind made up, he made his way towards the door and started to hammer and bellow for help at the top of his lungs.

"Devil's teeth," he heard one of the guards say. "If that lot actually catch his voice they'll be here in a shake!"

This encouraged Perin to bang and crash even harder. "Here!" he screamed. "I'm in here!"

He wasn't sure how long he had been shouting, but he thought he could hear thunder rumbling around him. Not in the distance like a far-off cloud, but actually surrounding the room. Perin found it quite comforting and reassuring. He knew it must be a trick of the acoustics and maybe his hearing being sharpened by the darkness, but to him it was as if a storm had itself endeavoured to help him. He continued to shout until his voice grew hoarse and he couldn't shout any more, then kept bashing his hands against the door.

"Have you got the key? We've got to shut him up!" came the ominous voice of the guard from outside the door.

"You will do no such thing!"

Perin immediately stopped banging. The unknown voice had silenced him, it had silenced the thunder, and it appeared to have silenced the guards. The only person it hadn't silenced was a second unknown voice.

"Enough of the dramatics, Occidens – you get the child, I'll deal with these gentlemen!"

It was a female voice, quite formal. If Perin hadn't known better, he would have thought it was a tutor who had spoken. It did have a mysterious quality that set it apart from the voices he had heard all of his life. The first unknown voice had also been female, and had conveyed a power not unlike that the dean had tried to convey at his last lecture, but multiplied by several magnitudes.

"Oh no you don't, old woman!" the first voice replied. "I've waited for this for a long time, and I'm not giving up this scrap for anything!"

"Who the hell do you think you're calling old, Occidens? You're twice my age!"

"Excuse me, ladies," interrupted one of the guards, "but clear off. This is the Great Academy. It's not a place for dried-up old prunes."

There was silence for a few seconds until the formal voice said simply, "You…interrupted…us."

There was a sound of clashing steel, the blunt force of fists against guts, and cries of pain coming from the distinctly male voices. The formal voice spoke again, but this time with more urgency.

"I'm not kidding…*get the boy*!"

There was a flash, and the door burst open. For a second Perin was blinded by the light pouring into the room, then he was struck in the face by the door. He had been leaning down to listen as closely as he could, and had been hit full force. He was aware of being on the floor, but couldn't see anything clearly: his eyes had not adjusted to the light. He also found that he was unable to move due to the force of the impact.

"Oh, good grief!" he heard a voice above him saying to herself. "You come all this way, after all this time, and what do you discover?! The damn boy's a klutz!"

Perin could just make out the shape of the woman standing in the doorway. The light behind her and Perin's still-adjusting eyes meant that she was little more than a silhouette. She was not tall, her back had a stoop and she leaned heavily on a stick. She turned back out of the door and called behind her.

"Are you finished out there, Rienta?"

"Don't rush me – there's a skill to this, you know!" came the reply, swiftly followed by, "Cloth-headed moron!" Though this seemed to be aimed at someone else as it was accented by a sharp, metallic clang and a very definite thud.

Perin was falling out of consciousness, he could tell. His head was splitting and he couldn't stay awake or keep his eyes in focus. He was vaguely aware that the second woman had entered the room and that she was very much taller and more straight-backed than her companion.

"What a mess of a boy," he heard the short one say.

"Are you sure about this, Occidens?"

"I know what I'm doing, Rienta," the short one said in a knowing tone.

"The last time you said that was with that ridiculous business with the squid!" Rienta complained. "Stim needed a whole new set of clothes!"

"Do you genuinely think this is the time to criticise my decision-making?" Occidens asked irritably.

"Oh, if I had a rowboat for every time I heard that, I'd have a navy!"

"Well, as pleasant as this is, I think we should probably get on with things, don't you? Now, let's get out of here!"

Perin was aware of movement, and then the strangest thing occurred. He felt as if he were floating. He could no longer feel himself lying on the ground. His head no longer rested upon the stone, and it fell back, giving him a pain in his neck, yet he still felt unable to control his limbs. He was aware of movement around him, the shapes of the furniture and the sources of light, making him dizzy. He could also feel the movement of air. Yet he still couldn't move himself, or see properly, and the pain was overwhelming. He couldn't feel anything underneath him holding him up, or tied to him, pulling him along.

I don't understand, Perin thought. This confusion was the last thing he remembered before he lost consciousness completely.

CHAPTER FIVE

Perin woke with a start and an ache. He had trouble locating the source of the pain because, in truth, everything seemed to hurt. His head was throbbing, his neck ached, his back spasmed, his hands were all bruised, and there was blood seeping from his shins through his trousers. All in all, he must have looked as he felt: a mess.

Not a dream, then, he thought. This was something of a disappointment, as it would have avoided any further complications. His mouth was dry, so he couldn't ask any questions of the numerous passers-by, who seemed to take absolutely no notice of him at all.

On the positive side, he was able to see again: his eyes had readjusted to the light and the pain in his head had subsided enough that his brain could now understand the images he saw. They were truly unexpected and awe inspiring images at that.

The sky was clear blue and cloudless, and the sun shined down. It was a warm and bright day. Perin was entangled in a seemingly endless coil of rough rope that had been curled and piled upon itself. It was coarse against his skin and fairly unyielding, which probably explained the pain in his neck and his back if he had been lying there for some time.

He was in a harbour. That was the only explanation for what he saw around him. There were stalls where merchants and sailors sold and haggled. The sound of hard-heeled boots against the wooden pier reminded Perin of the thunder he had heard the previous night. There was a distinctive salty smell to the air. Perin had never been to the sea before, as it lay on the far side of the island from the Great Academy. He had read about the salt water, though; that on long sea voyages salted and smoked fish was the delicacy of choice. This he had tried and enjoyed, and now the scent of it filled his nostrils. *Gods, I'm hungry!* he thought.

He tried to get to his feet, but found that two lengths of the rope had been tied around his ankles. As Perin tried to free himself, he realised that he had not been tied to one end of the rope or the other, but appeared to be bound in the middle. He tried to pry his legs out, but the knots were cleverer than he was and each struggle seemed to lead to a tighter grip. He would need help to extricate himself.

Do I want to escape? he asked himself. *If I do, where will I go? My life as a student is over anyway. Perhaps I'm better here.* But even if that were the case, he couldn't live his life entangled in harbour rope.

Although he couldn't get his legs untangled, after some trying he was able to push himself up onto his feet and get a more panoramic view of the harbour. It was a large semi-circular cove, with high cliffs on either side. There were lighthouses positioned high atop both cliffs; *a truly exceptional defensive position*, he thought. The harbour itself consisted of three moorings jutting out into the sea like the tines of a trident. A large vessel could dock on either side of each mooring, giving the harbour a capacity of six boats. At present, there were only three vessels moored. One was a pleasure boat; it looked very grand next to the fishing vessel beside it. The remaining ship was a trade vessel; much larger, tall and with a vast hold. The side of the ship contained a removable panel, which had been lowered to reveal stalls within. It was a sort of floating marketplace.

This was the source of the commotion within the port, and why the passers-by were paying Perin in his tangle of rope no mind. People had obviously come to do trade with this vessel, and other local merchants had dotted themselves around the harbour to pick up some business from the influx of people. Any one of them could be here to take him back to the Academy. His mind returned to his predicament.

"Awake and upright? That's a good start."

As he turned around, Perin momentarily forgot that his feet were bound together and overbalanced and fell to the ground in a tangle of limbs and rope.

"Occidens was clearly right. You, my dear boy, are a klutz."

Perin managed to hoist himself back up to face the source of the voice. He recognised it as coming from the taller of the two assailants from the previous night, but this was the first time he had had a chance to see her properly.

She was actually only of medium height, which suggested her companion had been extremely short. She was a slender woman who stood ramrod-straight. Short grey hair tied in a severe bun. Her stern features were contradicted by extremely blue eyes, which matched the water in front of him and the sky above. Her eyes did not lack warmth and, contradictory to the rest of her appearance, seemed to smile despite the fact that her mouth did not. Her clothes were smart: a pair of grey trousers with a cutlass in a scabbard hung loosely at her side, and a burgundy blouse that ruffled at the chest. It looked very warm for the day, but she gave no sign of discomfort.

"My name," she said, "is Rienta." She stood with her arms behind her back, but inclined her head as some form of greeting.

"My name is Perin," replied Perin. "Forgive me for not standing to greet you, but I'm somewhat indisposed."

Rienta looked down at Perin, and this time a small smile did reach the corner of her mouth.

"Simply a precaution to avoid you being whisked away, or whisking yourself away." She withdrew her sword and, as quick as lightning, made a swiping motion that Perin was convinced almost lost him an ear. In a blink, the sword was back in its scabbard. Perin was amazed to find that his feet had been freed, and that the rope had been severed cleanly and efficiently in about five places.

"You have a talent for swordplay," he said, impressed.

"I have talent, dear boy, that is certainly true, but I would advise that this be the one and only time you assign me any of your narrow labels. They will simply make you look foolish where you are going."

Where I am going? Perin finally began to lose patience. He had been able to tolerate much of what had happened because his life was due to change in an unexpected way anyway. He wasn't going to put up with being told he was foolish.

"I don't think I need to go with you anywhere," he said. "I don't know who you are, where you intend to take me, how you intend us to get there, or for what purpose." He stamped his newly released foot. "In the past day, I have been tested, judged, detained, attacked, threatened and abducted. Until the world makes a little more sense, I don't see why I should take a single step with you!"

Rienta stared at him impassively. "All certainly true, and I'm afraid I don't intend to explain it all at the moment. What I will tell you is that my title is actually Captain Rienta, and I intend to take you on board my vessel. More will be become clear from there."

Perin was taken aback. He had been given, at least partially, a direct answer to a query, and Rienta had been honest about not answering the rest. She must have noticed the change in his demeanour, because she seemed, almost imperceptibly, to soften hers slightly as well.

"Look, boy, I'm not going to lie to you. Things are about to get very strange in your life. Very dangerous. My crew and I intend to defend you and assist you. You must know by now that I and my colleague helped you last night by rescuing you and bringing you to the other side of the island."

Perin was starting to get even more confused. Although he was grateful for Rienta's little explanation, in truth it only raised more questions. He decided to give voice to them.

"What is the cause of all this?" he pleaded. "Why me? Who are you defending me against? Assist me to do what? How did you know to rescue me? Why come to this side of the island?"

Rienta looked over Perin's head, as if retrieving something from her memory, or perhaps suppressing a biting comment.

"You see, this is why I shouldn't have said anything – I should just have knocked you out and carried you." She looked at Perin. "I'm not going into all of that, mainly because I don't have the time and we aren't entirely safe here yet. What I will say is that you were brought here because we required a safe harbour to privately and quietly get you aboard the *Muta*."

"What's the *Muta*?" he asked.

"The *Muta* is my vessel, soon to be our home and method of transport. It fired its guns at the Academy last night while my colleague and I smuggled you out. The *Muta* managed to pick up my colleague, who then drew away some of our potential pursuers while we made a run for it in the opposite direction. We have come here to rendezvous."

Perin looked towards the trading galleon. "It's a fine vessel."

Rienta started to laugh. A peculiar sight for someone so

49

stern, the laughter escaped her mouth almost as if it were against her will. It did not last long, and she regained her composure quickly.

"None of these ships is the *Muta*. None could hold a candle to her." She lowered her voice. "The *Muta* is on the far side to the right of the cove. There is a blind spot there that was used by smugglers, years ago. It can only be seen from the lighthouse up there, but the occupant has been dealt with and we will be away before it becomes an issue."

Perin was taken aback. "Murder?" The pit of his stomach gave a lurch. Although he had heard the sounds of combat the previous evening, he had not truly considered the results of such a thing until this moment. He felt ill.

Rienta bent down and locked eyes with him, her nose mere inches from his own, before saying in a very soft voice, "Yes, and I would get used to that sort of thing if I were you."

The colour drained from Perin's face. "I'm not a killer. Whatever it is you have in mind, that's not going to change." The steely resolve he displayed surprised even himself. He could see it had surprised Rienta as well, as she arched a tidy, slender eyebrow at him.

"That's as maybe," she said. "Regardless, we'd better get out of here. It won't be long before they send someone after you."

Perin felt himself losing his temper. "Who are 'they'?" he asked, exasperated.

Rienta rubbed her temples with the thumb and index finger of one hand. "Look, my boy, I promise you will get all these answers in due course, but we need to get out of here. Come on."

She reached out and took him by the hand, and with uncanny strength pulled him to his feet and led him towards the ships in the port.

"How are we going to get to the *Muta*?" Perin asked.

"We are going to steal the pleasure boat," replied

Rienta matter-of-factly.

Perin was rapidly forming an opinion of Rienta as a well-meaning scoundrel. He knew he should be suspicious, resentful and perhaps a little terrified of her, but somehow she gave him a feeling of security and straightforwardness that he found refreshing, and needed at this point.

As they headed towards the boats, he asked, "Why the pleasure boat and not the fishing boat? Wouldn't that be less conspicuous?"

Without turning around, Rienta replied, "You're probably right, but the pleasure boat belongs to the dean, and I rather enjoy the idea of escaping in his own boat."

Perin stopped about five metres away from the pleasure boat before saying, "We're going to steal the dean's yacht? The man who locked me in a cupboard with an armed guard?"

"That's the general idea," replied Rienta. "Why, do you have a problem with that?"

Perin thought for a moment. "Not entirely," he said. "Though I do have one condition."

Rienta turned to face him with a raised eyebrow. "And that would be…?"

"When we're finished with it, we sink the damn thing."

"Hah!" exclaimed Rienta. "My dear boy, for the first time since meeting you, you've given me reason to like you. All aboard."

She stretched out her hand, inviting Perin to board the pleasure craft. He jumped on, ignoring the aches and pains he still felt. He was followed by Rienta, who, with a swift movement, turned and sliced through the rope that held the boat to the mooring.

"Unfurl the sail, and I'll steer us out of here. If I stick to the back end of that trading ship we will be away before anyone notices."

Perin did as he was instructed and found that he was starting to enjoy this adventure. He turned to look at Rienta behind the wheel of the boat. She was probably in her seventies, but once she was at the helm of a vessel the years seemed to drop away and she was freshly invigorated.

The craft took sail and picked up speed easily. As Rienta had suggested, before there was any chance of being seen they were past the trading galleon. Once they were clear of it, though, it was open water until the end of the cove. Here it was impossible to remain unseen.

"Could get bumpy from here, dear boy. Keep your head down," shouted Rienta.

On the dock, a bell started to ring, followed by three successive loud bangs. A moment of eerie stillness, and then a spray of water over the side of the boat. A cannonball had landed no more than six feet away from them on the right. This was followed, moments later, by another to their left. Perin looked up and saw a third cannonball heading straight for them.

'Incoming!" he shouted, and in a flash Rienta was beside him, her sword unsheathed. She swung it through the air and there was an ear-splitting crack. Perin looked on in amazement as Rienta cut the cannonball in half and the two pieces fell with a dramatic splash into the sea on either side of the vessel. He looked, open-mouthed, at the water for a few moments.

When he turned back, Rienta was at the helm again as if nothing had happened, and they were passing the end of the cove. Behind, though, was another disturbing sight.

"Captain," said Perin, as this seemed a sensible way to address Rienta whilst at the helm, "I think we have company."

Rienta turned and saw what he had seen: the fishing vessel and four rowing boats from the trading galleon were all in pursuit.

"Oh, I wouldn't worry – our own help is about to arrive."

Perin turned back to the open water and beheld an incredible sight. A war galleon was appearing from beyond the right side of the cove. It dwarfed the trading galleon, and whereas the trader was made of dark wood, the warship was made of warm-coloured oak. This made it look less imposing than the average war galleon, but the sight of it was still enough to cause the pursuing craft to break off their chase.

Out of range of the dock cannons and free from pursuit, Perin was able to focus on the ship now growing in size in front of him as they approached. It had six gun ports, three facing straight across and three slightly higher in the air, presumably for better distance. The sail was currently furled to keep the ship stationary in the water, and there were holes in the side where oars could be used for rowing. It wasn't as long as some war galleons Perin had read about, but what it lacked in length, it made up for in height. The stern and bow of the boat were almost the same height as the mast. It gave the galleon a squat look, but it also looked strong. It gave an impression of safety and security, not unlike Rienta.

As they approached the side of the galleon, Rienta called out, "Stim! Drop ladders!"

A wooden ladder was thrown over the side, landing with a soft, satisfying splash nearby. Rienta pulled the bottom of the ladder from the water, tied the dripping end to the pleasure craft and then turned to Perin.

"Here we go, it's time to start. Up you go!"

Although he knew he should be nervous, he felt a sincere sense of anticipation as he began his climb. Upon reaching the zenith, a strong hand appeared to pull him onto the deck. It belonged to a large, broad man. His skin was tanned very dark, which served to accent his muscles. He had a bushy moustache that stretched down the sides of his mouth.

A few moments later, Rienta followed. As she leapt over the side of the boat, the assembled crew of the *Muta* let out a cheer of delight and solidarity.

"Hang on," she shouted. "I have a promise to keep

first, before any celebration! Stim?"

"Yes, Captain?" replied the rough-faced man who had helped Perin.

"Bring me a cannonball," she said.

"Captain?" replied Stim, plainly confused.

"You heard me."

Stim obeyed and retrieved a cannonball, about the size of a large fist. He brought it to Rienta as if it weighed nothing.

"If you'd do the honours, sink that damn barge," she said.

A smile spread across Stim's face as he walked to the side of the galleon and looked down at the deck of the dean's pleasure yacht. As many of the crew as could fit, including Perin, lined the side of the *Muta* to watch as Stim raised the cannonball above his head and threw it at full force. It went straight through the deck, splitting it wide open. Water poured through and enveloped the boat in a swirling mass of water as it descended into the deep.

"If you have finished, Stim…?" said a voice from a doorway behind them. Everyone turned, and Perin was faced with the other woman from his rescue party the previous evening.

She was indeed short and stooped. She walked with a stick and had white hair in a tight bun at the back of her head. She was not thin, and had rather protruding teeth. Her eyes were jet-black and piercing. Perin instinctively stepped forward.

"Hello, Perin," the woman said. "I am Lady Occidens. I am here for one purpose, and one purpose only."

"Me?" asked Perin.

"That's absolutely right," replied Occidens with a toothy smile. "Particularly, I am here to train you."

This made Perin rather confused, and not unsurprised – as far as he knew, his training had been completed the previous day. Though, he supposed, a great many things had changed in that time.

"If it's not a rude question, what can you train me in?" Perin enquired.

"I can train you to be what I am," replied Occidens. She took a step forward and lowered her head even further so she was eye to eye with Perin. "And what I am is the last true Sorcerer of Caramine, at least until now!!"

Another cheer went up from the crew of the *Muta*, all for Perin, who found all of this impossible to believe.

CHAPTER SIX

Amongst the celebrating crew, Perin found himself bemused and uncomfortable. Coming from a life under the Great Academy's tutelage, he found such a public display of celebration unseemly. This didn't even take into account that this old crone had just claimed to be a sorcerer, and that she intended to pass on this knowledge to Perin. He found the very notion ridiculous. Magic may exist in Caramine within the confines of the Great Committee but it certainly wasn't known by old women on galleons and certainly not taught to Academy exiles. Perin had to admit, it clearly was not so outlandish to this crew of rejoicing vagabonds. He found himself unable to speak.

Captain Rienta stepped forward and put her hand on Perin's shoulder. It was reassuring but firm. She leaned towards him.

"You look like you could use a seat, dear boy," she whispered.

Returning to the crew, she raised her hands in the air, silencing them. "As happy as we all are, are we going to sit here and wait to be attacked? Yes, we have the boy, but the *Muta* is hardly unknown to the Great Committee and I'm fairly certain someone on the dock will know who to tell that we were here."

"Heading, Captain?" Stim enquired.

"Open water please, Stim," Rienta replied casually. "We can decide where to go from there. At the moment, just buy me time!"

Lady Occidens had sidled up to Perin and taken him by the arm. "I imagine you have a few questions?" she said with a toothy smile. "And I don't deny that I have a lot of explaining to do as well."

She smelled of alcohol and perfume, and generated a warmth that reassured Perin, giving the impression of warm-blooded kindness. She gestured towards an open door situated at the top of a dual set of wooden stairs that flanked the helm. It looked from the deck as if it led into a study or captain's quarters. The rest of the crew had quickly assumed their duties, following Rienta's orders. Rienta herself was talking to Stim. There was something amusing about a large man towering over this elderly woman. Stim looked as though he could tear Rienta in half, but he was clearly intimidated by and filled with respect for the captain. Despite being significantly shorter than him, she was very much in charge. This gave Perin hope.

As he headed towards the study, Perin was still dumbstruck and could not deny that he could do with getting away from the crowd. Closely followed by Occidens, he climbed the stairs and walked through into the study. As he entered, his breath caught in his chest.

The change in atmosphere was instant. The walls muffled the sound from outside to a murmur. It was peaceful, homely and comfortable. There were two overstuffed sofas in a deep burgundy leather, with a few cuts where white wool protruded. Directly opposite the door was a lavish writing desk against the wall, which was otherwise covered with dark wooden bookcases. Thick, ornately decorated rugs covered the floor and golden candelabra sat on several surfaces, giving the room an eerie, mystical glow.

Occidens shuffled into the room and lowered herself to the creaking swivel chair that sat at the writing desk. Like all the other pieces of furniture it appeared to be bolted to the deck to avoid it moving around during heavy weather – *or attack*, thought Perin.

"First things first," Occidens announced. "Let's get you, and me a drink." She swivelled the chair around to the desk and opened a side drawer. With a clink, she removed two bottles with one hand and two glasses with the other. The liquid in both bottles was clear, but there was obviously a distinction that Perin could not discern. Occidens poured a small amount of one liquid into each glass, then topped it up with the other. Then with a wry smile, she looked at Perin, tapped the side of her nose, then put a second dash of the original liquid in the top of each glass.

"We have both had a rather interesting couple of days. I think we could use a bit of a stiffener."

She handed Perin the glass. He sniffed it and tried to identify the unfamiliar scent. It smelled of bitter berries. When he drank, there was a burning sensation, not unlike that he got from fire wine, but more refreshing. It was far from an unenjoyable experience, and the old woman was right: it had been an interesting few days.

Occidens took a long draught from her glass and seemed to sink further into her seat. "Now," she said, "I'm not entirely sure where to begin."

"How about at the start?" suggested Perin.

Occidens smiled, then began to shake, and laughed a hearty, open-mouthed laugh from deep within her throat that seemed to brighten the room. Perin found himself laughing too.

"My dear boy, maybe you're not just a klutz, maybe you are a smart-arse too! I hope you never lose that, because it will endear you to some and distance you from others, and that's probably an excellent way to judge who you should and shouldn't associate with!" She continued to chuckle until she took another drink.

Perin, for once in his life, decided to stay quiet. He hung upon Occidens' words as if there were meaning to her every inflection.

"I was the original Sorcerer of Caramine. I discovered magic by stumbling off a cliff. I flew through the air and landed like a feather on the ground." She looked down at her more-than-ample frame filling the chair. "Nowadays I would probably look more like a galleon in full sail, though flight is a power I haven't had in a long time."

Perin had to fight the urge to be overwhelmed by the matter-of-fact way in which Occidens spoke about magic. It may exist, but it was not something encountered by ordinary people. Despite the extraordinary circumstances, Perin still considered himself to be thoroughly ordinary. This didn't mean he couldn't ask questions for the sake of understanding or clarification, though.

"You mean you can lose magic once you have it?" Perin said.

"In a manner of speaking," Occidens replied. "Magic requires the use of the mind and the imagination. These things are affected by age and experience. Sometimes this is for the better, and sometimes for the worse. I am no longer able to fly, but my overall strength has increased."

"Strength to do what precisely?" Perin asked, keen to understand the extent of magic's capabilities.

"Let's not get ahead of ourselves, – I'm actually trying to explain why you are here!" Occidens said with a hint of irritation. Perin fell silent and decided to stay that way until she had finished telling her story.

"When it became clear to my village that I had supernatural powers, they wanted to burn me," she said with a dismissive wave of her hand. "They found that I could make myself immune to burning and call upon rains to extinguish their fire, even indoors. They then tried to drown me, but found I could breathe underwater. Their attempts to hang me or rack me, poison me or behead me all met with similar failure. Your first and most important lesson of the day is this: only magic can kill magic. Only another sorcerer could possibly dispatch me.

"Now, at this time, as I was the only sorcerer, the village gave up its quest to kill me and we continued for quite some time without incident. Then after a while, news of my abilities travelled and I became a sort of lightning conductor for people, young and old, with similar abilities."

Perin's curiosity and enthusiasm for the story was mounting with each passing word, and he couldn't resist the temptation to speak any longer. "What causes magical ability to occur?"

Occidens looked at him for a long while before taking another drink and answering. "Well, I suppose now is as good a time as any. Magic was formed in our world because creativity had reached a climax in Caramine. You see, the telling of a story or painting of a picture or playing of music is creating something that wasn't there before. This is only a small step from changing the world around us to fit in with our creative wishes. In other words, the mind has the power to create new circumstances, objects or natures. Take my original state, for instance. I believed it was possible for me to fly, I imagined it was so, and the circumstances conspired to allow it to happen in that moment. That, dear boy is the essence of magic: the ultimate expression of the creative mind."

Perin was dumbfounded. He had never before heard anything even close to this. He had been conditioned through his every experience in the Great Academy to shun creativity and to find it distasteful and rude. It was this indoctrination that caused his suspension of disbelief to break, and he challenged the old woman.

"That," he said, "is the most fantastical poppycock I have ever heard in my admittedly short life."

Occidens smiled, which Perin had not expected.

"I know," she said. "That is actually the very reason why all this is occurring."

"In what way?" Perin asked. He was becoming confused again. The truth was, he was becoming fairly accustomed to the feeling, though he would still rather it went away.

"The best way for me to explain that is actually to continue with my story," she said. "As I mentioned, I had become something of a figurehead for other extremely creative fledgling sorcerers to gather around. For a time, this all worked very well and magic started to find its natural home in society. It kept the peace, aided in the harvest and other such routine things. The problem occurred some years later when a group of young sorcerers decided to write a book."

"I like books," Perin heard himself say.

"As do I," replied Occidens. "A book is a splendid thing: it can feed the creative spirit and enhance a person in ways that they had no idea of before they dived into its pages."

She looked down at her glass. Sadness had crept across her features, and she looked older for it.

"This book, however, was entitled *The Manual*, and it was an attempt to catalogue how magic could be studied and what it could be used for. As part of their 'research,' this group assumed control of the village, then a nearby village, and gradually spread throughout society. They used their findings and instructions to increase the prevalence of magic in daily life. When they decided that particular pairings would increase the chances of magical offspring, in the name of efficiency, they decided who could marry, who could breed, and what job everyone would do based on their aptitude. This was the genesis of—"

"…the Great Committee," Perin finished.

"The Great Committee," Occidens repeated, "and then in turn, the Great Academy."

Perin had picked up from Occidens' tone that she disapproved of the Great Committee's approach, but he saw little problem with it.

"Hasn't the Great Committee provided stability and prosperity through these methods?" he asked.

"Of course not!" Occidens replied, standing up. "This is what you must understand. First of all, the prosperity you speak of is bunk and bull! There is no prosperity, simply continuity, and there is no peace, only conformity. Look no further than yourself. You created one new story based upon your own creativity and you ended up locked in a cupboard for summary execution."

"Execution?" Perin asked. Although he had suspected something like that after his conversation with the guard in the Academy part of him had hoped that he had been lying. "What for?"

"Well, dear boy, if you stopped interrupting me, then perhaps I would get to the end of my story." Occidens sat back down in her chair, and Perin was quiet once again. "The Great Committee did indeed formalise all aspects of society, but this created an unexpected and, at first, unwelcome side effect. You see, these people considered creativity a negative thing. They liked formalisation and information, and viewed creativity as introducing an unknown and uncontrollable element. That was why they wrote the manual, but in doing so, in many ways they sealed their own fate. You see, when magic was written down and catalogued, it became inaccessible. Sorcery ceased to be a creative experience, and therefore could not be successful. In attempting to make magic something more people could do, they made it disappear entirely."

Perin had an epiphany. This explained the Academy's approach to society; it explained the very existence of the Academy!

"Although at the heart of the first Great Committee's activities there was a desire to formalise magic to make it more widespread, this did not remain the case for long.

Once they realised that magic was no longer spreading, their view quickly changed to one where existing magic had to be protected and defended for themselves alone."

Perin knew this before Occidens had even said it. That was why creativity and displays of emotion were frowned upon by society.

"I, along with some friends, fled and started to search for a new, true creative, whilst also avoiding the advancing power of the Great Committee. This ship has been our home ever since, although I am the last of the original crew. Welcome Perin, to *The Muta*."

"Hang on," Perin interjected. "The years don't work here – you would have to be older than—"

"…than living memory," Occidens interrupted. "You are quite right. I told you: only magic can kill magic. I, like any other sorcerer you might meet, am over a hundred years old."

"Good grief," Perin said. He stared at the old woman with even greater wonderment.

"Now, I have to admit that the Committee has done a fine job of reducing living memory to a fraction of what it should be," she said scornfully. "By taking babies from their parents and raising them as they want, it took only a single generation to completely change society. I will be the only person you are likely to meet that will remember first-hand how things used to be."

As Perin struggled to come to terms with this, a thought occurred to him. "But where do I fit into this? How did you find me?" he asked.

"Well," said Occidens, swirling what was left in her glass, "the Great Committee watch what goes on in the Academy very closely, as do I. They decided some time ago that if someone with creative prowess showed himself or herself, then they should be dispatched as an anomaly. After all, if they were to develop magical powers then they may not subscribe to the Committee's way of thinking, in which case they would be a threat and would have to be dealt with. Once a person has magical powers, that becomes more difficult."

"You think I'm going to develop magical powers?" Perin asked.

"You must," said Occidens. "Put bluntly, I need help. There are four sorcerers on the Great Committee and only one of me. I have stayed ahead of them for almost a hundred years, but to combat them, I need new blood. I need you, a young, creative mind with a fresh discovery of magic."

Warmth enveloped Perin. The idea of new, forbidden learning excited him. "I hope I can do you proud," he said.

Occidens broke into a wide grin and leapt to her feet with an energy Perin did not expect from her squat, elderly frame. "Excellent, dear boy. Though you may not maintain that level of enthusiasm as we try and get that magic out of you!"

"I've never had a lesson of the mind I did not like!" stated Perin proudly.

Occidens didn't answer; she just laughed. But there was one other question that was bothering Perin, and he felt he should ask it before they went any further.

"I do have to ask," he said, "how did you know to come looking for me? I mean, I guess that the Great Committee has ways of overseeing the work at the Academy, but how did you know what happened in my exam? Also, how on Caramine did you get there before the Committee?"

Occidens looked at him with a wry smile. "Well, I will answer your second question first. We didn't arrive there before the Committee. There was a warship deploying troops into the Academy grounds. Stim led the crew against the troops already grounded whilst the *Muta* engaged the enemy ship."

"So that was the *Muta* I heard firing cannons. I thought it was thunder," Perin recalled.

"Ah, well, there was a bit of thunder – you see, to save

some time I called down a bit of lightning to deal with some trouble we ran into, but yes, it could have been cannon fire you heard."

"You can control lightning?" Perin said, his eyes wide.

"Yes, but it's a tricky one, you won't get to that till much later," she said. She then walked to a corner table that had a plain white silk cloth draped over it. "To answer your first question, how I knew you were there – well, that is down to this." She lifted the cloth to reveal a brass compass that pointed towards where Perin was sitting. He walked closer and found that the point of the compass followed him wherever he went in the room.

"Now you see," said Occidens, "up until a couple of days ago, the point of this compass simply spun round continually, not giving any heading at all. Then, presumably at the moment you started to spin your yarn in that history exam, it pointed directly towards the Academy. We set sail immediately to your rescue."

The mention of setting sail drew Perin's mind to the ship they were sailing on. His curiosity started to spread to the rest of the vessel.

"Do you mind if I go and have a look round the ship now?" he asked. "I'd quite like to meet some more of the crew, have a bite to eat, maybe get some sleep?"

Occidens' eyes flashed, as if she had just realised how long she had been monopolising the young hero of the crew. "Yes, yes, of course – you will need your strength and resolve for tomorrow when we kick off your training."

Smiling, Perin headed towards the door. Just as he reached it, one final thing occurred to him.

"Lady Occidens?"

"Hmmmm?" she replied, without looking up.

"I never told you about sitting my exam. How did you know?" he asked.

"You saw Captain Rienta being rather impressive with a sword, didn't you?" Occidens replied.

"Oh yes," said Perin.

"So did the dean of the Academy on our way in. He became most enthusiastic in his wish to tell us as much as he could."

This made Perin smile from ear to ear as he exited the study and walked back out into the salty sea air. Stim was raising the sail single-handed, observed by a group of crewmen who seemed to consider this a normal activity. Captain Rienta stood firmly at the helm, guiding the ship to some as yet unknown location. Occidens appeared at Perin's side and put a hand on his shoulder.

"Well, dear boy," she said, "will this do all right for you as home?"

Perin looked around and smiled, and it came as a surprise even to himself as he heard himself say, "You know, I think this will do very nicely indeed."

CHAPTER SEVEN

Perin looked around the deck and surveyed the people going about their duties. Occidens continued to stand by his shoulder. She had a smile on her face, and was staring off into the middle distance in a way that suggested her mind was elsewhere.

"Are all these people sorcerers?" he asked.

Occidens was brought out of her revelry and looked at him with startled confusion. "Weren't you listening to me, boy? I'm the only one here, and that's why I need you!" she said indignantly. "Life will go much smoother if you just listen to me the first time!"

"Sorry," replied Perin. "What I meant was, why are these people here serving you?"

"Loyalty, dear boy," Occidens said, rocking back and forward on her heels. "I was probably slightly incorrect when I said I was the only one here who commanded magic. You see, Rienta up there?" She gestured to the imperious figure at the helm. "She has a knack of inspiring loyalty amongst her crew. Our mission has often seemed rather hopeless till now. We've been relegated to simple pirates and, generally speaking, that's not a mission that many noble men and women wish to take up. Rienta convinces them of the nobility of the cause through sheer example and power of personality. That's a magic all of its own."

Perin thought of his own ability to use words to win arguments. He had never considered it in the noble terms that Occidens had just used, but they were effectively the same thing. *Perhaps I shouldn't use this 'power' for trivial means and should use my ability to convince people for good,* he thought. As he looked towards the captain he had a growing feeling of affection and respect. He then remembered her cleaving the cannonball in half as they made their escape.

"I think Captain Rienta has another form of magic," he said.

"I think I'd know!" said Occidens. "Don't be ignorant, Perin."

"I'm not!" Perin stamped his foot. "As we were escaping from the port, Rienta managed to cut a cannonball in half in mid-air with one swipe of her sword. If that's not magic I don't know what is."

"Oh, I see," said Occidens with patronising sympathy. "I'm afraid you've gotten the wrong end of the stick, dear boy, or rather the sword. You see, in order to make them as effective as possible, I have the ability to imbue some people with magical properties. Now, Rienta is a skilled fighter with exceptional abilities of her own, but that particular power was one that I gave her. She would find it difficult to do it a second time, and impossible a third, without a bit of a recharge."

"So people have a magical fuel tank? Like on mechanical vehicles or large ships?" Perin asked.

"Yes, I suppose you could say that, and the ability you give them is, like all magic, based on your own imagination, so it tends to be some form of accent to their natural ability. Look over there, for example." She gestured towards Stim. "Stim is a strong man, strongest on the ship, and when I give him a charge he could take on a whole legion of the Great Committee's finest warriors, and any steel they might land on him wouldn't even leave a scratch. It takes his natural abilities and my imagination, and creativity amplifies it."

That made sense to Perin, and he started to understand how imperative it was that another sorcerer be trained and found. Stim had looked across and realised that he was being watched, and made his way over to them.

"Anything I can do for you, Lady Occidens?" he said in a respectful tone.

"Not directly, Stimmy," she replied sweetly. "But if you could see to the young master here – he deserves a good night's sleep and a good meal to prepare him for the lessons tomorrow."

With that she turned and headed back into her study and closed the door behind her. Stim looked down at Perin. He stood head and shoulders over the short, overweight boy, making him feel thoroughly inadequate.

"How're you doing, little man?" he asked pleasantly.

"A bit…" he hesitated as he found the right word, "lost."

"Well, maybe if we take you to your quarters, you can look at getting found?"

He led Perin down the steep wooden staircase into the lower hull of the *Muta*. There were more levels than Perin had realised. The first level down was a gun deck with dark iron cannons across the wall, protruding out of the boat. There was a smell of gunpowder and burnt matches in this room, as if the wood had taken on the smell of a thousand fired cannons. The stairwell continued downwards to the next level, which was a bunk deck with hammocks strung between strong wooden supports that ran from floor to ceiling. Each of the hammocks had a few personal items scattered around it: in some cases books, in others a mirror and small vanity trunk. One even had a half-completed woodwork project with shavings surrounding the area. Perin could only imagine what this place would be like

Luke Brady

when it was full of tired crewmen. He looked around to see which hammock was empty. He couldn't see one.

"Is one of these bunks mine?" he asked.

"Oh no," said Stim with a knowing smile. "You're a bit more special than that. We have some more high-class accommodation in mind for you, with some added protection."

They continued down to a third level that contained more cannons and a complex engine for powering oars that stood unused. The oars lay in place across the benches that would be occupied by crewmen when in use, but at the end of each was a mechanical contraption that, when powered, would rotate the oar in synchrony with all the others.

"This has got to be more efficient than having the guys row when the wind drops," Perin said.

Stim shrugged and smirked. "If it worked! A technician joined the crew some years ago and invented, designed and built this monstrosity. The problem was, we've never found anything that can provide enough power to get all the gears working at once. As it is, all it's done is make it impossible for my boys to get in here to row themselves. We just go with the wind." He lowered his voice and looked from side to side before continuing, "A fact that we need to keep from the Committee, or they would just send a rowing galleon downwind of us and catch us unawares!"

Perin started to feel nervous that there was such a fundamental weakness in the *Muta*. He had been quite good at design, and with alchemical studies into transferring and creating power. He decided that as soon as he had the opportunity, he would look at getting this system working.

They continued down to the final basement level, and it was far less cluttered than the other three: an empty room with fairly steep, curved sides, as they had reached the bottom of the vessel. At either end was a door; one to the

70

fore of the boat and one to the aft. On either side of the door towards the rear of the vessel were two large levers that looked like they would take three men each (or perhaps just Stim) to lower them.

"Welcome to the best rooms in the house," Stim said grandly. "To the fore of the vessel, your neighbour will be the one and only Captain Rienta. She doesn't usually entertain guests, and is generally a silent neighbour." He gestured towards the aft door. "This room is yours." He walked towards it and turned the handle.

Before entering, Perin had to ask about the levers on either side. "What are those for?" he said, pointing at them.

Stim looked at them and rubbed his forehead. Perin got the impression that explanation was not one of his talents.

"You are very important," said Stim, "more important than even the *Muta* itself. If we're attacked and can't win, can't defend you, then at least we can save you."

Perin was confused. "How?"

"This room is safe, it's not part of the ship. It's held in place in the hull by large chains. In an emergency, with you inside, we can pull these levers and send you off safely to be collected later." He looked tremendously proud of this feature.

"How far would it float away?" asked Perin.

"Not float, sink!" explained Stim with a grin. "If you floated you would be found. If you sink, only we can find you!"

Perin started to panic. "How much air is in there?!"

"Oh," said Stim, "lots of tanks at the back, maybe three or four weeks' worth. When they are empty there's an automatic float that will bring you back to the top."

This calmed Perin down slightly and he appreciated the defence, but looking at the solid boat and the excellent crew, he felt safe enough.

Stim walked into the room, and gestured for Perin to follow. Entering, he was stunned by its opulence. A beautiful four-poster bed was ornately carved into the rear bulkhead curving up into the ceiling. A bookcase carved into the corner was stacked full of old tomes. A quick glance revealed that these were not books that Perin had ever seen at the Great Academy. He could feel his mouth begin to salivate at the idea of sitting and reading these books, though then again, this may have had more to do with the aroma from a platter of roast pork that was sitting on a beautiful carved table. As Perin walked towards it, he saw that a map of Caramine had been carved into the tabletop. He sat down and looked around again.

"Is everything OK?" asked Stim, who was visibly uncomfortable with having to stoop to accommodate himself beneath the room's relatively low ceiling. Perin got the impression he really wanted out of there, and was rather uncomfortable with the opulence of the room as well. Stim did look like the kind of man who preferred rustic over comfortable.

To answer his question, he said, "Yes, it's absolutely wonderful. If you don't mind, though, I think I'd like to grab a bite to eat and then get some sleep."

"I think that's for the best. You have a big day tomorrow," Stim replied with a smile, obviously relieved.

"I had a big day today," Perin chuckled.

"There's more to come," Stim said with a knowing look. "Good night."

He smiled once more and then left. Perin closed the door and exhaled a long slow breath. He sat down at his table and picked up a little meat from the plate. As he ate, he grew more and more tired. His muscles had begun to ache in protest and seize up as he sat. As he finished eating and washing the food down with a light red wine, he felt thoroughly exhausted. He walked over to the bed and, without taking off his clothes or peeling the bedclothes back, flopped forward onto the mattress. It was incredibly soft.

This will do nicely, he thought, as he fell into a deep sleep.

Perin was woken by a sharp knock on his door. Even though he had been brought back to consciousness rather abruptly, he felt well rested. For an instant he was back in his room at the Great Academy, and could have sworn that it was Gruff knocking on the door. Acci would be making food, and Pym would be complaining about something. The thought made him smile. After a few moments, he returned to reality, and as he opened his eyes the room around him could not have borne less resemblance to his simple quarters in what had been his home for so many years. He was so comfortable, and still recovering from being woken so abruptly. He wasn't keen on leaving the bed, but the second sharp knock forced his hand. As he walked to the door, he wondered if Occidens or Stim had come to get him up.

Opening the door, he took a step back. Framed in the doorway, looking imperious, was Captain Rienta. She looked at the newly awoken young man in his two-day-old clothes standing in front of her.

"I believe it's about time you began your training." After looking him up and down, she added, "Though I think some time can be afforded for you to wash and dress. There should be some clothes in your size in the chest of drawers in your room."

"How do you have things in my size?" Perin asked.

"You were unconscious when we rescued you, and we had some time in port and were surrounded by traders. It was easy enough, and a good opportunity for me to blend in and not arouse immediate suspicion. I will expect you up on deck in half an hour." With that, she turned and left.

Efficient and logical, Perin thought. He liked the captain more the more he spoke to her.

He quickly stripped off his clothes and washed using a basin of fresh water from under his bed. He opened the chest of drawers and removed a pair of light tan-coloured trousers and a baggy shirt with a string lace in the front.

He slipped them on and headed towards the door, then paused briefly, grabbed a piece of leftover pork from the table and ate it as he headed out of the door and up towards the deck. It was dry and slightly stale, and he usually preferred something sweet in the mornings to freshen his breath, but this would have to do.

As he emerged, he took in the beautiful day. The blue of the sky mirrored the ocean. There was a slight breeze, but the sails were not unfurled so the ship was relatively stationary, just rocking gently from side to side. The calm and stillness created an almost disconcerting level of quiet. The only distinguishable sound was the gentle lapping of the water against the hull. Occidens stood at the door to her study with Stim next to her. Rienta stood at her post at the helm. Perin walked towards Occidens and smiled.

"Well, are we ready?" he asked pleasantly.

"I'm afraid that's not the question," she replied. "I would suggest that you, rather than we, had better be ready, because this is not going to be an easy ride."

Perin was a little surprised – *that almost sounded like a threat.* He decided to try to take all this in his stride, pulled himself up to his full height and said, "I'm ready."

"Good," Occidens replied, then turned to the large man at her side. "Stim?"

Without warning, Stim grabbed Perin around the waist and hoisted him into the air. Perin was too shocked to respond at first, but when Stim walked toward the side of the vessel he started to panic, kick and shout at Stim to let him go.

"It's for your own good, little master," Stim said, hoisting him high above his head. He then deposited him over the side of the deck, standing on a plank extending over the crystal blue water. Perin was shaking with disbelief, confusion and fear.

"Now, dear boy," he heard Occidens say, "imagine yourself flying, as you fall from the side of the boat."

"I'm not falling, I'm standing on the plank and I have no intention of—"

"Stim," interrupted Occidens, and the large man gave Perin the most powerful shove he had ever felt in his life; it was like being hit by a gust of wind. For a moment Perin thought he had been successful as he flew through the air, but he soon realised he was picking up speed, not height, descending towards the water.

The impact hurt like he had run into a brick wall. Perin had no experience of or talent for diving, and landed in the water in a horizontal position with a sickening slap. He thought he might lose consciousness. At the speed at which he had hit the surface of the water, there was little difference between liquid and solid ground. He found himself unable to move. He was sinking, drowning. Then, as quick as his descent had been, he felt his stomach heave as he ascended through the water. This wasn't through his own power; he felt as if he were inside a ball of water that was heading towards the surface.

The ball burst, the sound of water splashing against wood could be heard, and Perin found himself, coughing and spluttering, back on the deck of the *Muta*. Occidens had her arms outstretched in front of her. She had raised a small portion of the ocean in the shape of a ball, containing Perin and lifting him back onto the deck.

As he gasped for air he attempted to thank her for saving him, but before he could utter a word, Occidens looked at him coldly and said, "Again."

Perin lost count of the times he was thrown overboard that day. He found that with each successive throw, his brain got more muddled and he couldn't focus to imagine himself flying through the air. He had tried, but it was very difficult when his mind was preoccupied with fear and dread. Occidens never failed to save him and did not seem to make any judgements on his performance; this helped Perin maintain composure, but any enthusiasm he'd had for learning evaporated by the third time Stim launched him from the side of the ship.

As time wore on, Perin's body was giving in to the pain of impact against the water. Eventually he tried pointing his head downwards in a dive, and however sloppy it may have been, it negated some of the pain. This time when Occidens brought him up from the depths she had a look of resignation on her face.

"We are done for the day," she said, and without another word she walked into her study and closed the door.

Perin's clothes were soaked, his eyes stung from the salt water and his lungs burned. As he looked around, he saw sadness and disappointment on the faces of the crew. Stim looked regretful and somewhat ashamed; Perin assumed for his complicity in throwing him overboard all day. Rienta had not moved from her spot at the helm. Since he didn't know what else to do with himself, Perin walked down to his quarters.

As he opened the door, he was met with the smell of seared beef. Turning towards the map table, he saw a freshly cooked side of beef – it had appeared as if by magic, still sizzling, clear grease escaping from its pores. There was a sealed note beside it. He picked it up and opened it.

Eat well, sleep well, and don't lose heart.
There's always tomorrow.
Regards,
O

Perin collapsed into the chair and put his head into his hands. Hot tears stung his cheeks. He wanted to be a success at this, he wanted to be a sorcerer and unlock his imagination so he could do incredible things like those Occidens had described. She had flown through the air as her first magical act, and had done so without knowing that magic even existed. Perin wanted this, but his body kept betraying him. He considered that this may all have been a big mistake, and perhaps he wasn't destined to be the first of a new generation of sorcerers. Perhaps he was the very definition of a disappointment and a waste of time, energy and resources.

He was interrupted in his self-pity by a sharp knock on the door. He realised that he was still in his soaking wet clothes and his face was still flushed from his tears.

"I'm sorry, could you come back later?" he shouted.

"Perhaps a better idea would be if you came to my quarters when you are ready." It was Rienta. This would have stunned Perin on its own, but what struck him in particular was the feeling in her voice. There was genuine concern and compassion in her usually steely tone.

"I won't be long," Perin replied.

"Very good." Then came the sound of her boots walking off towards her own quarters.

He dressed as quickly as he could and washed his face again. He took a few bites of the beef and then headed across the deck to dine with the captain. As he reached the door, he knocked on it tentatively.

"In," came the reply.

Perin pushed the door and walked in. The room was a mirror image of his own, but slightly larger, presumably because the ejection mechanism in his room occupied some of the space.

Rienta stood ramrod-straight and looked at Perin with piercing blue eyes.

"I'm sure that wasn't very much to your taste today," she said matter-of-factly. She gestured towards the table where two glasses of wine had already been poured. Perin took one and drank deeply, as the salt water had left him with a dry throat and terrible thirst. The burning in his lungs had not subsided, though, and the alcohol caused him to cough and splutter.

"I thought you might want to talk about the day's events," she said, ignoring his hacking and spluttering.

Perin looked her in the eye, and welled up with tears. "I don't know how to do this, I don't know what is required of me. No one has done it in over a hundred years. How am I supposed to discover the secret?"

Rienta looked at him for a minute, then drew breath. "First of all, I think this display of genuine emotion is the most productive thing I've seen from you since we rescued you from the Academy. If you don't have access to your emotions, you won't be able to tap into them."

Perin tried to compose himself, and nodded.

"Occidens made an error today, in my opinion. After the first time Stim threw you from the ship, you knew that she would save you. There was no real peril. How could you possibly tap into your emotions and creativity?" She took a long drink from her glass. "One thing that did worry me was that on your final attempt, you turned your exercise into a dive."

"I was trying to save myself a bit of pain," Perin complained.

"True, but taking off and flying around the ship would also have done that. When you committed to taking a dive, you gave up all hope of being successful. That's why Occidens ended the day's tutoring."

Perin hadn't realised, but she was, of course, right.

"How should I proceed?" he asked.

"I really can't help you there." She sighed. "Though I would suggest that whatever your approach was today, you should probably change it tomorrow when you try again."

CHAPTER EIGHT

Perin woke the next morning feeling unexpectedly well. Despite his numerous dips in the sea, his body did not ache nearly as much as it should and he felt exceptionally well rested. He could not hear a great deal of movement on the decks above. The ship was swaying with more purpose, making his stomach churn and suggesting that the *Muta* was moving at quite a speed. *A few moments' peace,* he thought. He took a more leisurely approach to getting up and dressed, sat down at his table and ate a few more pieces of beef. It was as delicious cold as it had been hot.

He couldn't help feeling bitter towards Occidens, despite her having sent him the food. *Why can't she be more civilised and humane?* he thought. *Rienta seemed to understand last night. I wish she were the one training me.*

The more he thought it through, however, the more that attitude in itself seemed to exemplify his problem. Rienta was not a sorcerer. She lacked a quality that was required. She couldn't wield magic that wasn't gifted to her by Occidens to enhance her natural abilities. She couldn't create the magic herself. That must have been the key word: *create*. Rienta did not strike Perin as having a great deal of imagination or creativity. Her logic and pragmatism made her a good captain, but must have held her back from being a sorcerer. Perin wondered if Occidens had ever tried to train her in magic. Perhaps she had once been a protégée and then failed. This made him consider what would happen if he were unable to succeed. Would he join the crew of the *Muta*? Would he become yesterday's man and journey with the crew to find the next best hope? He didn't think he could stand the idea or the disappointment. He resolved to go forward that day and put himself through whatever trials Occidens had in mind. It was all for the best.

He rose from his chair and left the cabin. As he climbed up towards the deck he was astounded to find almost the entire crew still in their bunks. Not asleep, but while judging from the noises outside it was clearly daytime, they were relaxing in their hammocks, reading, laughing, whittling, snoozing or chatting. As Perin continued up the stairs a hush came over them. Perin was embarrassed. *They must consider me such a waste of effort.*

As he was just about to disappear from view, he heard the voice of a sailor he had yet to have a conversation with. "Good luck out there today, lad, we're all with you."

Perin continued up the stairs, though his eyes were filling with tears. When he read stories of history it was not the tales of loss, sadness or tragedy that moved him to tears, but loyalty and triumph against adversity. He had never considered that such support would ever be shown to him, particularly when he had, as yet, done nothing to deserve it. His resolve to knuckle down and accomplish something today hardened.

There was a peculiar eeriness on deck. The absence of the crew, with their background chatter and noise, made every creak of the mast and floorboards echo in the emptiness of the ocean. The sail was unfurled and the *Muta* was gliding across fairly calm waters. The sky was a clear blue and the sun beat down upon the water. It was warm, and although the sun was strong, there was a pleasant breeze. Perin had assumed he was going to be taking more dives into the ocean today, so had worn another loose shirt and tan trousers to be as comfortable as possible.

There were only two people to be seen. Stim stood at the helm, his giant hands clamped to the wheel, guiding the vessel. This struck Perin as slightly odd, as he had only seen Rienta manning this position till now. *I suppose she has to sleep,* he thought, *and someone has to be in charge of our direction when she does. Besides, there's no reason why she should be the only one at the helm all the time.*

Standing on the deck directly in front of him was Occidens. She was smiling and looked to be in a pleasant enough mood.

"Good morning, Perin," she said.

"Morning, Lady Occidens," Perin replied formally. There was obviously some lingering sourness over his treatment yesterday. He tried to push it from his mind.

"I hope you have recovered from your endeavours yesterday." Occidens continued swaying on her heels. "I know it can't have been easy for you, and you may think me cruel but—"

"If it is what has to be done, then it is what has to be done," interrupted Perin.

Occidens raised an eyebrow. "If? Do you consider there to be another way? Do you consider my actions unfair, unjust?"

"No," Perin said, "it's just that I don't know if it is unjust or not, I have no frame of reference for this kind of teaching."

"Nor does anyone else," countered Occidens, "so you won't be able to find verification from anyone else. You will just have to trust me."

Perin looked at her and considered his next words. The truth was, he didn't know if he did trust the sorcerer .

"That being said," the old woman continued, "you are not the first I have had to defend my methods to today. It was brought to my attention that after I rescued you for the first time yesterday, you knew you were really, in essence, safe and therefore could not tap into the emotions you needed to be creative. What do you think of that?"

"Captain Rienta did make that case to me as well. I suspect she is trying to protect me, but I'm tougher than I look."

Occidens laughed at this, and gave him a grin wide enough to display some gaps in her teeth that Perin had not noticed before.

"My dear boy, I believe you judge the captain's enthusiasm that you make progress correctly, but I think your assessment of your robustness is misjudged."

"What do you mean?" Perin asked, perplexed.

"I mean that the good captain told me this morning that I should have let you lose consciousness in the water before rescuing you in order to put you in genuine peril. Now, Rienta can be a bit vicious, but she wouldn't suggest I wait till you conk out before being resuscitated, then thrown in the drink again if she doubted your ability to cope with it."

Perin was confused. The idea was horrible, and he realised how much worse the previous day could have been if that had been Occidens' plan from the beginning.

"Is that the plan for today, then?" he said, looking at Stim, who was resolutely avoiding eye contact. "Did you send everyone away so they couldn't see my humiliation?"

Occidens shook her head. "Nothing as dramatic as that. I simply think that today's exercise would be better served by your solitude."

Perin looked at Stim again, then turned back to Occidens. "Am I to throw myself over the side this time?"

"No, that won't be necessary – that's not our lesson for today. I actually thought you might enjoy some time to yourself." She gestured upwards towards the crow's nest.

Perin looked up at the oversized barrel positioned above the sail and sighed. He wasn't relieved at being sent to climb a pole higher than the tallest building he could think of, but he was certainly relieved that he wouldn't be getting wet today.

"When do I get to come down?" he asked.

"When it is time," said Occidens dismissively. "Now off you go!"

Perin sighed and headed towards the mast. He had not been close to it before, and was amazed to think that this colossal pole had been carved from the trunk of a tree. It seemed simply too large to be from any tree he had seen. Stim probably had the widest arm span of anyone he had met, and he would only be able to reach around little over halfway. Perhaps Stim and Gruff together would just be able to fit their arms around it.

It also seemed a great deal further to climb up than he would have anticipated. The ladder was made of knotted rope, and it wasn't secured against the pole. He would have to hold tight to avoid being swung clean off the mast. He drew in a short breath in order to calm himself. *If I fall,* he thought*, at least Occidens is here to catch me.*

As if reading his mind, Occidens called out, "Today, Perin, the only action I will take is to defend this ship. I will not save you should you fall or do anything foolish. Do you understand?"

Perin nodded, and with his emergency lifeline removed, his hands started to shake. This was not ideal for climbing. He balled a hand into a fist and remembered the sailor who had wished him luck as he came up to deck, and his hand stopped shaking for long enough for him to start his climb.

It was hard work; he had to repeatedly relax and tense his entire body in order to move with the ladder or against it to avoid it twisting around and throwing him off. It would also have been much easier if the *Muta* was not moving. Every wave the bow struck sent a shudder up the mast that threatened to shake Perin from his perch. His resolve held and he eventually, foot by foot and hand by hand, made it to the top of the mast and into the crow's nest.

He looked around and knew why he had been tasked with finding his way here. The view from the top of the ship was magnificent: endless ocean surrounding him in gorgeous shades of blue and green. The tranquillity and solitude would do him good.

After a while, he found he was hungry. There was no access to food or water up here, but it was worth a day's hunger in order to enjoy the view and the solitude. He lay on his back with his feet up against the inside of the nest and created stories in his head based on the history lessons he had enjoyed at the Great Academy. He considered what would have happened had the victor in particular battles been different, and what that may have led to. It was an exceptionally pleasant way to pass the day.

He was then blinded by the sun directly above the ship as he faced the sky. It was getting exceptionally hot in the nest. He was glad of his light clothes. He unlaced his shirt and pulled it up slightly to give his head a degree of cover. As the sun reached its zenith, Perin realised he had absolutely no idea how long he had been lying in the nest. He rolled over and stood up. Occidens was now sitting, or perhaps lying down would be more accurate, on a reclining deckchair. She wore dark-lensed spectacles to shield her eyes, and a ridiculous straw hat. She looked like she may be asleep.

Perin thought it was time to come back down to the deck, so he reached over the side of the nest only to find that the rope ladder was gone. He could feel short, frayed stumps attached to the side, but could no longer see any ladder. It hadn't been cut, and the weather had not been sufficient for it to break away. *There's magic afoot here,* Perin thought. He looked back down for Occidens, but she was gone. Stim was still navigating, and even from this far above, his frame looked impressive.

Perin yelled down to him, but received no reply. At first he thought that it was because his voice wasn't carrying, but then he had the sneaking suspicion that he was actually being ignored.

So this is my test, Perin thought. *I have to find my way down from the crow's nest without the ladder. I have to jump, fly, float or whatever else without splattering myself against the deck and smashing the ship to splinters.*

The sky went dark. A black cloud had formed out of nowhere at incredible speed. It blocked out the sun and plunged the *Muta* and the surrounding water into a sinister twilight. The wind turned cold, and a light rain began to fall, making Perin shiver. The wind picked up, deafening him. This was getting out of hand. The rain grew heavier and Perin was soaked from head to toe; his tan shirt had turned a darker shade of brown and was plastered to his skin.

He leaned over the side of the nest, his knuckles turning white as he gripped the wooden rail with all his strength. Below, Stim continued to man the helm. Perin imagined he could see his arms strain holding the wheel steady. He looked around again for Occidens, but she was still nowhere to be seen. Had she gone inside when she saw the storm coming? *No,* Perin thought, *I would have seen it before she did.* Then the truth dawned on him, and froze him to the spot. *This storm is her doing. That's why Stim is at the wheel: he's the only one with the strength to hold the ship in place. Damn her!*

He leaned down and screamed Stim's name at the top of his lungs. Not only could Stim not hear him (and he had probably been ordered not to react), but Perin could not hear his own voice over the howl of the wind. His shivering turned to shaking as the cold began to bite. He tried to imagine himself blowing the clouds away with the power of his lungs. He stood to face them and took a deep breath in, closed his eyes and pictured the rolling darkness evaporating before him as he blew it away from the *Muta*. He opened his mouth and blew out with all his might.

Nothing happened. At least, nothing constructive. The storm's response was a bolt of lightning arcing out of the cloud to strike the sail of the ship. It ignited in red flame, spreading outwards. Perin could feel the heat on his face and smell the acrid smoke. He watched in horror as it turned black and start to disintegrate. He suddenly spotted Occidens hurrying out from her study below. She raised her hands, and Perin felt the wind change. Occidens waved her arms as if swatting flies, and eventually he could discern a pattern: with each swipe of her hand, a gust of wind, accompanied by a sheet of rain, was directed towards the burning sail. Perin watched as the flames were extinguished and only a blackened stain remained around the hole in the sail.

Another arc of lightning came streaking from the cloud. Occidens thrust her arms to the left, and the lightning bolt seemed to bend through the air and struck the water to the port side of the *Muta*. It had passed within three feet of the crow's nest. Perin's nerve and courage gave way. He sat hugging his knees, soaking wet and terrified. It was only a matter of time before lightning exploded the crow's nest and cooked him to a cinder.

Then his fear turned to rage and disbelief. *She said she would defend the ship only, and not me. I'm going to die up here. She doesn't care.* His anger seemed to slow time around him. He still knew it was raining, and that the boat was under assault from the electric-blue lightning that Occidens created and controlled. He had to show her that he wasn't afraid, even if he was.

Perin stood up in the crow's nest. Another bolt of lightning had struck the side of the ship; Occidens had not been able to direct it all the way into the water. It had started a small fire, and she was making a scooping motion with her arms, bringing water from the ocean in unnatural waves to put out the flames.

Perin looked up towards the sky and the dark, ominous cloud. He saw a flash deep within the cloud, and then a blue bolt headed directly for the crow's nest. He instinctively raised his hands to his face. He knew it would give no actual protection, but it was a reflex. He closed his eyes, expecting oblivion.

Then he thought he must be dead. The wind was gone, the rain was gone, and the *Muta* itself seemed to be gone. As he opened his eyes, he realised that he was not dead. He was a sorcerer.

His hands glowed with a red light and it distorted the air around him, shimmering outwards from his palms. The red light fed into an electrical orb that had enveloped the crow's nest and blocked out sound, wind, rain and, he was relieved to discover, lightning. It crackled and sizzled with energy where the bolts had hit it. Perin had created a shield that had absorbed the impact of the lightning. He could no longer see the deck of the ship, and could not really make out if the storm outside continued. He very slowly closed his hands into fists. The light subsided and the red orb faded, and Perin was plunged back into the chaos of the world that he had left behind.

Lightning continued to come from the centre of the cloud. The sound of thunder was constant. It was as if the cloud itself had been angered by the defence Perin had raised. He looked down at his clenched hands, then up at the cloud. Without thinking, he threw his arms above his head, released an angry, frustrated scream, and extended his fingers. Blood-red lightning streaked up from them towards the cloud, striking it in the centre. White flashes pierced the dark cloud and the smell of burning was overpowering. He was doing something truly impossible, truly fantastic, truly magical, but in that moment, he didn't think about it in those terms. He imagined his victory, imagined the lightning he created destroying the storm Occidens had used to torment him. He relished the idea of finally succeeding, and the response this would get from the crew, Occidens, Rienta and even Stim. He felt wonderful, and not a little mad.

From the point where the red lightning had struck the cloud, it had started to change colour from black and grey to pink, red and then a deep burgundy. The world around the *Muta* took on a reddish hue as the sun started to shine through this eerie, magical cloud. The wind had stopped, as had the rain. Perin brought his hands downwards and the lightning halted. He was covered in sweat, and fell to his knees, exhausted. The silence was deafening. Perin was aware of the blood pounding in his ears, accompanied by the ringing the continual clashes of thunder had caused.

After a few minutes, he stood up and looked over the side of the crow's nest. A tremendous cheer rose from the entire crew of the *Muta*, who had come back up onto the deck. Occidens was at the fore, her arms outstretched towards the crow's nest. Perin could make out her beaming smile, and his animosity and anger towards her evaporated instantly. He leapt from his perch.

There were screams below as he plummeted from the crow's nest, and Perin himself started to panic. He put his hands out towards the deck as if to brace for impact, and the air distorted in front of them. Some buckets and loose timber flew across the deck with the rush of air, and crewmen who had not anchored themselves with a wide stance stumbled back a few paces. The speed of his fall decreased, and the world came into sharper focus. His hands shook with the pressure, and Perin realised he did not have as complete control of his descent as he would have liked. He landed on his feet a little harder than intended which caused him to overbalance and fall over. He was caught by two members of the crew, who helped him up. The ordeal had been almost too much for Perin, and they had to keep hold of him.

Occidens walked towards him, applauding. "Well, dear boy, I must say that was—"

"Out of the way!" Stim shouted from behind.

Perin was hoisted into the air. Stim had wrapped his tree-trunk arms around his waist and was hugging him tightly whilst spinning him round and round. Perin couldn't quite tell if this was congratulation or torture.

"You did it, little master, you did it, you did it!"

The rest of the crew were laughing, and Perin smiled.

"Stim, enough!" said a formal voice that Perin recognised as Rienta's. "We are all glad that Perin has proved his worth, but before you break any of his bones, could you let him down?"

Stim stopped spinning and put Perin back down. He was facing Captain Rienta and Occidens. The latter was smiling; the former was not.

"That was very advanced magic!" said Occidens.

"Most impressive," said Rienta, "but it has left us not without problems."

"Oh, for goodness' sake," exclaimed Occidens. "I will see the sail mended, and a few scorched beams—"

"As inconvenient as those things are," Rienta interrupted, "that is not what I had in mind. I was referring to that." She pointed a long, slender finger up towards the cloud that still loomed overhead, now turning blood-red. "We know the Committee are looking for us, and I think we may have just given away our location."

The bottom fell out of Perin's stomach. Had he put them all in danger?

"Ah," said Occidens with a sheepish look. "That may be true, and we aren't really in a position to mount much of a defence with a charred sail. Rienta, my dear, can you get us to a port? As quickly as possible?"

Perin looked at the deck. He felt as though his greatest triumph might have endangered everything the crew had worked for for years.

"I can't get us to a port, but this crew can and will," Rienta declared, raising her voice. "That is, after we give three cheers for Perin, the newest Sorcerer of Caramine."

CHAPTER NINE

Following the elation, there was an uncomfortable stillness on deck. Everyone knew that what Rienta had said was true. They *had* given away their position, so it was imperative that they make the best possible speed to port. Occidens, Stim, Rienta and Perin stood at the door of Occidens' study and surveyed the crew going about their duties.

In the first instance, this meant patching up the sail as best as was possible. The issue was that although the hole itself was relatively small, there was a large charred area surrounding it that was exceptionally fragile. As the wind blew through the remains of the material, more blackened flakes rained down on the deck.

"No way you could have stopped that, was there?" Rienta said to Occidens, gesturing towards the ruined sail with a hint of annoyance.

"Collateral damage, my dear, worth every charred inch," Occidens replied.

"Well, is there anything you can do to get us moving?"

"I could whip us up a gale at our backs in a second, but looking at that," she raised her hand to the remains of the sail, "I don't think it could hold up to it."

"Right then," Rienta said firmly. "Stim, Occidens, Perin, with me please." She headed for the stairwell that led down to the lower decks, then stopped on the second deck that housed the out-of-order rowing mechanism.

"Occi," she said gently, "it was a fine idea, but this contraption does not work and now it is putting us in harm's way."

"We may still be able to get it working. It's just beyond my particular gifts. If we *could* get it up and running, then we would be the fastest ship on the oceans," Occidens whined.

"If, buts and maybes!" implored Rienta. "Stim, rip out these girders."

As the huge man moved towards the gears, Perin spoke up.

"Wait a minute, wait a minute."

He was surprised when the other three fell silent. He surveyed the deck. There were four long benches that ran the width of the deck, save for a small gap in the centre that formed a corridor of sorts. A long oar was suspended above each of the eight sections. Running along the central corridor were two iron girders, one on each side, with a solid brass gear attached to the end of each oar. These were all held together by thick, dark, oiled leather belts that fed along the deck and into a main engine at the end of the room. Perin walked over to it and studied the central mechanism. As far as he could tell from his engineering and chemistry classes at the Great Academy, this machine should work, if a power source large enough could be found.

"Why can't you use your magic to make this work?" he asked Occidens.

For the first time since he had met her, she looked thoroughly uncomfortable. "The truth is, that it is beyond my imagination. During my formative years, contraptions such as these did not exist. They were created as magic subsided from society to make life easier without it. I don't really understand what this is, so how can I imagine it working?"

A smile crept across Perin's face, and an idea formed in his head. "I might be able to help you there," he said. "You see, I think I know how this works, and I think I can imagine it working. Could you come round here?"

What followed was almost comical. Rienta, Occidens and Stim made their way, eyes wide with curiosity, to the far side of the deck where the engine was stationed. Perin pointed to a cylindrical valve that was built into the structure, leading deep into the workings of the engine.

"That is where the fuel has to go. It will have to be very potent in order to power something of this size."

He looked at the faces of the other three. Occidens looked puzzled, Stim had an expression that suggested Perin might have spoken a foreign language, and Rienta looked stoical, which Perin considered was probably as close to confused as she could muster.

"I'm afraid we don't know what constitutes 'fuel', Perin," she said simply. "We know that fuel for humans is the food we eat and the drink we drink, but I assume that is not the case for something like this."

Perin laughed. He quickly realised that this was insensitive and regretted it. It suddenly struck him that in many ways he had been incredibly ignorant of the world around him when he had come aboard the ship, but he had never been deliberately treated like a fool, which was how he was now treating his only three friends in the world he was ever likely to see again.

"I'm sorry," he said, though only Stim looked hurt. "Engines like this are powered by combustion – so we need a liquid that can be burned to create heat energy."

"Lamp oil?" suggested Rienta.

"That's it, exactly," said Perin excitedly. "Though I don't think that would provide the power required in this case. You would need that oil before it's refined. We should be able to get some in port. The key is that it needs to burn with great heat and for a long time."

"That doesn't help us right now," said Rienta. "Would something that burns fast, giving off great heat, serve us as a stopgap measure?"

"Yeah, I guess so," said Perin. "You'll just use a hell of a lot of it."

Rienta slowly turned and looked at Stim, who at first looked at her pleasantly, but a look of horror crossed his face as the realisation struck him.

"No," he said.

"Yes," said Rienta.

"Not my fire wine! You can't just burn it!"

"It can save our lives," Perin said, realising that Rienta was on to something.

"It's vintage!" pleaded Stim.

"Stimmy," Occidens interjected sympathetically, "I will personally help you rebuild your collection once we get out of this, but it has to be done."

Stim looked at the floor, where dark spots appeared on the wood as silent tears fell from his eyes. "For the crew of the *Muta*, I'll do it."

"Attaboy," Occidens said.

Stim then stalked up the stairs, all the while staring glumly at the floor. From above, they could hear the clink of bottles and Stim's sniffling.

"What is the nearest port?" Occidens asked.

"The Gardens of Kenadia," Rienta replied. "Good for taking on food and cloth, not so much for oil and alcohol."

"Oh, I'm sure we will find a way," Occidens said with a smirk.

As if in reply, the clinking of bottles approached. Stim had brought great armfuls back with him. Perin held out his hands to take one of the bottles, but Stim pulled away.

"No – these are mine, if you don't mind. You show me what to do and I'll get this ship going."

Perin understood and pointed out the valve into which the fire wine had to be poured. Stim uncorked one of the bottles and took a swallow from it, then poured the rest into the valve. It only filled the tank by about a third, so he repeated the process twice more. Perin showed him how to work a small pump lever three times to prime the engine, and then pull a starting cord. As Stim pulled once, the engine creaked into life and then died, with a second yank it gave a further objection, but with the third the engine growled into life. It was working.

Something was wrong, though. The gears had not moved in so long that they screeched in protest.

"They need oil!" shouted Perin over the horrible, high-pitched noise.

"Leave that one to me," replied Occidens, and she proceeded down the narrow corridor. She rubbed her thumb and forefinger together above each separate gear, as if adding a pinch of salt to a recipe, but it wasn't a white, granular substance that fell from her fingers; it was black oil.

The boards moved beneath their feet as the ship started to shift with the momentum of the engine moving the oars.

"The helm!" Rienta exclaimed as she headed towards the stairwell.

Stim sobbed as he uncorked another bottle and Occidens cackled wildly, hitching up her skirts and dancing in the small corridor between the benches. Perin looked at the three of them and felt a sense of what he imagined family must have been like, in the days when that was how children were raised.

A day later, they reached their destination. Perin couldn't deny that the Gardens of Kenadia were beautiful. Although there were cliffs surrounding the docks, they were not the dusty brown of stone, or the white of snow-covered peaks – they were a vivid green as the slopes were covered with productive farms for grazing livestock. One of the results of this local agriculture, Perin discovered as the *Muta* glided into port, was that the whole area smelled strongly of flowers, soil and grass. He found it tremendously pleasant.

On arriving, he was keen to explore this new land so, after checking with Occidens and Rienta, he disembarked and walked beside Stim along the cobbled streets. Market stalls lined the pavement on either side, selling everything from flowers, fruit and vegetables to jewelry, livestock and woodwork. Rienta was dealing with replacing the damaged sail and finding unfiltered oil that would run the rowing engine more efficiently, which she thought she could do at the docks. Stim, on the other hand, had been sent to find a watering hole in which he could nurse his sorrows as well as barter for food like whole legs of beef, lamb and pork. Occidens was finding an apothecary for some lotions and potions she required, as well as picking up fruit and vegetables for the crew.

Stim's pace quickened, and as Perin followed his line of vision he realised that Stim had spotted his drinking establishment of choice. Perin had to almost run to keep up with the huge man; it took four steps to match every stride that Stim took.

The entrance to the unnamed drinking hole was down a few steps. There was no natural light in the room, and the air smelled stale and didn't seem to be circulating. A haze of smoke drifted around the ceiling. It was not busy, but smelled as though it had been the previous night. The aroma of stale sweat and tobacco, as well as a cocktail of spilled drinks and perhaps even bodily fluids, took some getting used to. Perin had to forcibly unwrinkle his nose.

The bar was a round, central island, with a tall set of glass shelves in the middle. A few patrons sat on stools around it. On one side, a woman who wore her face as if she had had a tough life was serving drinks, and on the other a man with a lined face and several scars did likewise.

He wore an eye patch. Perin got the impression that this was rather a rough establishment. He was glad he was with Stim, and noticed that he looked rather at home here.

"Three home brews," Stim said.

"Three for two?" asked the barman, looking at Perin.

"Sorry," Stim said, turning to Perin, "you want something?"

"No, I'm fine," he replied.

Stim turned back to the barman and said, "In that case, three will do."

The barman looked confused, but started to pour three large flagons of dark brown liquid. He understood, though, when after pouring the second glass, the first was returned empty, then the second as he poured the third.

Stim nursed his final drink a little longer. With his thirst quenched, he got down to business.

"In the market for some provisions," he said. "This the place?"

"Aye," said the barman, a little suspiciously.

Perin had to suppress a smile. The past few days, indeed his entire life, had been built upon words. In many ways, the more words were used the better, and here he was witnessing negotiations in monosyllabic sentences of five words or fewer. In a strange way, it was humbling. Perin couldn't help thinking of Gruff. He had always considered himself, and been considered by others, as a bit of a failure for his lack of eloquence. But it seemed that maybe outside the Academy, this wasn't as big an issue as everyone thought.

"Fish, beef, lamb, pork, month's worth, thirty crew," Stim said. "Two months of fire wine, vintage."

"Aye," said the barman. He then reached under the bar and withdrew a pad and pencil, scrawled the price down and handed it to Stim.

Perin couldn't see the amount, and strangely enough, he didn't know what the crew of the *Muta* would use for currency. Actual coins and notes were not really used any more, ports like these existed through a barter system. This was how the economy of Caramine had worked since the reforms of the Great Committee. What was plain was that however Stim had intended to pay, he had not expected the price that was written on the piece of paper.

"Too high," he said with a sigh.

"It's what I'll get when you leave," the barman replied.

Perin raised an eyebrow. The conversation was taking a peculiar turn. "What do you mean?" he asked.

The barman looked down at him as if he had just realised that Perin had witnessed the conversation. "Big ship coming in tomorrow sent word ahead. Needs a complete restock and will pay full price."

Stim laughed. "No one pays full price, even if they say they will."

"Great Committee does," the barman replied.

Perin felt Stim go rigid beside him.

"Which ship?" he asked in a strangled voice. This was no longer a casual conversation; there was a distinct urgency, almost panic in his tone. Perin started to sweat.

"*Formalite*," said the barman.

Stim grabbed the pencil out of the barman's hand, scored out the number he had written and wrote his own number. He handed it back.

"Just for the fish, beef, lamb and pork – forget the fire wine. To be delivered to the *Muta* at the dock in one hour, and to be paid in sail silk."

The barman looked taken aback. Perin thought it was distinctly possible that Stim was paying over the odds to get them out of there. The barman nodded and shook Stim's hand, and before he had even broken the handshake, Stim turned to Perin.

"Out, now!"

Together they headed as quickly as they could back towards the dock. Perin had to run flat out. As they arrived, they were met with a sight that Stim clearly didn't want to see: the new sail was being fitted on the *Muta*. This looked like it would take some time, and certainly more than Stim wanted to spend. Perin had not made it onto the boarding plank before the great hulk was at the helm, talking to Rienta. The effect of their conversation was instant. Rienta urgently gesticulated towards all the crew that were not helping with the sail, encouraging them to join in. She was obviously keen to get out of the port as well.

"What's the hubbub?" Turning, Perin came face-to-face with Occidens. She was followed by three men hauling heavy wooden carts laden with vegetables. The carts of meat had arrived too, and the parts of the old sail that remained uncharred were being cut up to be used as currency.

"There's a Great Committee ship on the way," Perin said.

"Oh, is that all?" Occidens said dismissively. "I imagine Stim and Rienta are going quite round the twist," she added with a grin.

"Aren't you concerned?" asked Perin in disbelief. "What if we don't get away?"

"Then we will stand and fight, as we have done several times before," Occidens said with steely resolve. "Now, I imagine we are waiting for that sail to be raised." Without waiting for a reply, she raised her hands and the sail lifted itself into place and tied itself to the mast. She then turned to the men with carts. "Get all that aboard now," she barked. The men gave her a curt nod and started to unload the carts.

Occidens and Perin boarded the *Muta* and approached Stim and Rienta.

"We must be quite close to leaving," Occidens said pleasantly.

"This is not the time for a laid-back approach," said Rienta sternly, "I want us out of here. All the crew is aboard, so as soon as the supplies are on board then we will make a hasty exit. Once we are in open water we can start up the engines as well as using the sails and be halfway across the ocean before the *Formalite'* arrives."

"Oh, it's the *Formalite'*," said Occidens. "The flagship. Well, that's a well-armed barge indeed, but still something we can deal with."

Stim looked uncomfortable, but Rienta's face filled with rage.

"You overconfident fool!" she fumed. "You may be a sorceress, but my crew would be in terrible danger and I'm determined to get them out of here."

"I am fully capable of defending the *Muta*, its crew and its captain, if it comes to it. You are also forgetting that I now have some help in that regard." Occidens gestured towards Perin, who felt suddenly inadequate. He was not sure he could summon up magic again now that the moment had passed. Even if he could, he didn't think he could do so in any helpful way.

A crew member came forward, but looked as if he didn't want to interrupt. Rienta turned to him. "Speak," she snapped.

"All supplies are now on board," the crewman reported. Rienta nodded and turned away from him, and he backed away.

"Stim, get down and start up the engines." She climbed the steps to the helm and ordered the anchor to be raised. As the *Muta* pulled away from the dock, Perin heard a splash. The boarding ramp had not been pulled in, and had slipped into the water. This was a quick escape.

Not quick enough, though. No sooner had they cleared the loading docks than a jet-black galleon, equal in size to the *Muta*, appeared on the horizon, heading directly for them. The shape of the port made it impossible for them to turn in any other direction. They were trapped.

A confrontation was inevitable, and Perin was about to have his first direct experience of the officers of the Great Committee.

CHAPTER TEN

The most impressive and striking feature of the warship on the horizon was its armaments. It had taken a flanking position, its broadside facing the *Muta*, which had its bow facing the *Formalite'*. As Perin looked at the galleon, he could make out four rows of cannons, which he assumed were repeated on the other side. At the moment, all of them were drawn and facing the *Muta*. Although too far away to strike at present, if they tried to flee, the only route ahead would see them blasted to splinters before they could get past.

"Suggestions welcome," said Rienta. Amazingly, Perin thought there was an absence of any real concern in her voice. He assumed that she was simply cool under pressure. As far as he could see, there was no easy way out of this.

"They're heavy," said Stim thickly. "All those cannons and no oars. It can't be the fastest ship on the waves, and we have the engines."

"Very helpful," said Occidens absently, looking at her nails. "But I suspect that the getaway will come rather later."

"Indeed," agreed Rienta, "so how do we get away from them?"

"Magic," Perin found himself saying. "Surely Occidens can pull some trick…"

"Trick?" Occidens enquired, looking somewhat put out. "I hope you haven't just disparaged my sorcery as 'tricks', dear boy?"

"No, no, that's not what I mean—"

"I know, I know," Occidens interrupted. "In fact they are tricks, but as you are yourself a trainee in this area, what would you suggest?"

"Well…" Perin thought, attempting to flex his fledgling imagination. "You could make the ship invisible? Or make it fly? Or shield us from the cannon fire while we escape?"

"There are merits to those suggestions," Rienta reasoned.

Occidens raised her hand and counted on her fingers. "If I made the ship invisible, they would have to be extremely stupid to not fire some exploratory shots. They would sink us anyway."

Perin had to admit this was true.

"Making the ship fly is a novel thought, but would take far too much in the way of imagination. I would have to picture each person, each piece of cargo, each loaf of bread in the hold, otherwise the ship would take off without them – you could end up flying but without your boots, and with half the planks and the bottom level of the ship left behind. The *Formalite'* is probably already set to destroy the *Muta*, and I would rather not help it."

"What about the shield idea?" Rienta enquired. "It's something you've done before."

"We could try that," said Occidens, "but I can only envisage each cannonball I see being deflected by a shield. If I don't see it, or can't keep track of them all, then a shield would fail. It's fairly simple with a ship with a standard armament of four cannons but this amount of firepower would be hard to defend against."

"Could you buy us enough time to escape that way?" Stim asked.

Occidens seemed to mull it over, and stole another glance at the *Formalite'*, which had not moved from its position just at the end of the cove.

"Possibly," she said, "although, I have a much simpler solution." She walked to the bow of the boat and extended her arms. Her hands started to glow with an electric-blue aura. Sparks flew from her fingers until balls of light glowed in each hand. She raised them above her head and the light arced from each palm, meeting directly above the old woman's head, creating an ominous sphere of white-blue light about the size of a cannonball. It bathed her in a terrifying glow.

As Perin watched, it was the first time he had felt truly afraid of Occidens. She looked like an otherworldly demon, as the light almost made her transparent. Where it met above her head, the ball grew to the size of a cargo barrel, and continued to grow until it was the size of Occidens herself. The light from her palms intensified, and a flash emanated from the ball of power above her head. A bolt of lightning darted towards the *Formalite'*.

"She's going to destroy it?" Perin asked.

"It's toast!" replied Stim with a hint of satisfaction.

"An efficient strategy," conceded Rienta.

The electrical charge had dissipated from the ball of light above Occidens and was streaking towards the *Formalite'*. It darted back and forth as it progressed, like an eel or rodent; it did not use a straight route, but its ultimate destination was assured. With a flash, the lightning struck.

The world turned green. The crew of the *Muta* were momentarily blinded by the flash that lit up the sky from the direction of the *Formalite'*.

"Toast," said Stim with satisfaction.

"Oh hell," said Rienta in a tone that Perin did not recognise.

As his eyes adjusted, he looked out towards the enemy

ship, expecting to see a smouldering wreck. What he saw took his breath away. A glowing orb had encased the enemy vessel and absorbed Occidens' attack. The orb appeared to be made of a similar electrical charge to that Occidens had used, although it was a bright and sinister shade of green. It looked like hundreds of interlinking strands of lightning had been woven together around the ship, giving the effect of surrounding it with shattered glass.

Perin turned towards Occidens and saw her looking silently out at the protected galleon. She no longer looked otherworldly or intimidating. In fact, it occurred to Perin that he had never seen her look so old. Rienta, Stim and Perin watched her for some time, but she didn't seem to have any inclination to move.

Rienta swore – *another first,* Perin thought – then proceeded up the steps towards the bow. She took Occidens' arm and appeared to whisper something to her, then led her, like the frail old woman that, Perin supposed, she was, down the steps. Occidens' eyes were fixed upon the deck. She looked nervous and a little nauseous. This, above all else, terrified Perin.

"Perin, would you accompany Occidens and I to her study?" Rienta asked. "We have a couple of things to discuss." She turned to Stim. "Keep us away from that ship. If she advances, you retreat back into the port – I don't care if you run the *Muta* aground." Without another word, she led Occidens and Perin into the study that sat at the rear of the helm.

As they entered the room, Rienta proceeded towards the desk and mixed a concoction of the two clear liquids. It seemed to be a much more even mixture than it had been when Occidens had poured them. Rienta handed a glass to Occidens. For a moment, she looked at it as if she had no idea what she was supposed to do with it. Then in one swift movement she emptied the entire contents down her throat and gave a rasping cough.

"Well, let's get down to business!" she said, with guile and a boundless energy in her voice.

Rienta rolled her eyes. "Good to have you back with us. Now, I think we need a more serious discussion about what is going on. I've brought the boy in, since he's going to need to hear all of this sooner or later."

"True enough," Occidens said. "Perin, sit." She clearly had some pent-up energy, so was not indulging in fanciful language.

"I am not a dog," Perin objected, but did as he was told.

"There is a sorcerer on the *Formalite'*," said Occidens. "That's the only way they could have put up a defence." A glimmer of failure passed across her face. "As I've said to you before, there are only a small number of sorcerers, so I must know the person over there. There is no chance it is the leader of the Great Committee, he never leaves his capital citadel. That leaves three others."

"Can you tell from the magic which one it is?" Rienta asked.

"Not entirely," explained Occidens. "One of them is more partial to green, in the same way I gravitate towards blue and Perin towards red, but I could very easily imagine a green bolt of lightning to strike across there. It's just not what I would naturally do. It's possible one of the other two would use green magic to vex me."

"Why would green magic vex you?" asked Perin, causing a look of panic to burst over Rienta's face.

"That is perhaps a subject for another—"

"I personally taught one of the members of the Great Committee," said Occidens. "Viri was her name, and she had a partiality for green in her magic." She held out her glass and Rienta sighed, stood up, took it and started the process of refilling it.

"If it is Viri, then we are going to have to fight our way out. She is exceptionally violent." She took the glass from Rienta. "That being the case, though, I don't know why she would have them hold their position. That is not her style at all."

"So if it's not Viri, who is more likely – Seus?"

"Seus?" Occidens repeated in a measured tone. "Unlikely! That syrupy cow wouldn't travel on a galleon, even the flagship!"

"That leaves Rudrum," said Rienta. Perin could tell from her tone of voice that this was the most undesirable of the available options.

"What's special about this Rudrum?" he asked.

"Rudrum is a complicated individual," said Occidens, settling into her chair. "She is actually the least magically capable of the Great Committee, though what she can do she does well, and that shield would be well within her capabilities."

"So she's the least bad?" Perin suggested.

"Oh goodness, no," explained Occidens. "In many ways, Rudrum is the source of everything we are fighting against. Yes, the Great Committee decided that society should shun creativity and become formalised, organised and sanitised to the point of almost destroying personal interaction and magic itself, but how on earth do you approach doing that?"

"I don't know," said Perin, a little irked to be covering this old ground again.

"Exactly," said Occidens, "but Rudrum does, and did. She designed the society that the Great Committee implemented. She founded the Academy, decided what would be taught there and how students would be assessed."

Perin shuddered at the thought. It sounded as if this woman was the epitome of evil.

"So," Rienta interjected, "assuming it is one of the three, how do we deal with them?"

"If it's Viri, then we fight and we win. She's like a dog with a bone and we won't be able to shake her off in any other way than incapacitating her and her ship."

"It's not just her on the ship, though," Perin said. "It looks like the kind of ship that has a big crew."

"The Great Committee flagship will have a crew of at least a hundred. It limits its range and increases its weight if we get into a chase, but in a direct assault it will be a close fight."

"Close?!" gasped Perin. "We only have about forty on the *Muta*, that's more than a two-to-one advantage."

"Stim," said Occidens by way of explanation. "If it's Seus, then if we threaten to attack, she'll assume we have some plot up our sleeves, and will make a mistake."

"In other words," said Rienta, "she'll blink first?"

Occidens nodded.

"And if it's Rudrum?" asked Perin.

"If it's Rudrum," Occidens said with a downcast look, "then there's not much we can do."

"If it's Rudrum then we'll blink, you mean?" Perin said.

"I can't say that's an inaccurate statement," replied Occidens with more than a hint of shame. "Well, Captain," she said, turning towards Rienta, "taking all of this into account, my dear, you are the head of this vessel, and whatever you decide today you will have both my full support, and any magic I can muster to help you."

Rienta pulled herself up to her full, authoritative height as Occidens finished, "So what's it to be?"

"To be honest," the captain said, "on one level this has all been just semantics. I don't think we have any other option but to fight. The question is just whether we should attempt to get past them and then fight to flee, or take them on and fight to win."

Occidens nodded. "I repeat, though, what's it to be?"

Rienta smiled. "Well, I see no reason why we can't fight to win. If we do then we can flee later, and if we don't then fleeing becomes less important, and I'm sure this crew would rather go down attempting to win a fight than avoiding one."

"Well said," agreed Occidens with a smile. "Now, just

for information, Stim has been listening at the door since approximately thirty seconds after we came in here."

A crash followed by a distinct "Damn it!" could be heard.

Rienta sighed. "So if I want to inform my crew of the plan, then I suppose I'd better do so with some urgency."

"Not to mention a sorcerer-led galleon bearing down on us," said Perin. "That provides a sort of urgency in itself."

"Leave the jokes to me, boy," said Occidens. "Your creativity shows promise, but your wit is still only half grown." She stood up with a groan and followed Rienta out of the study. Perin took up the rear.

Rienta made her way to the helm. The crew was assembled on the deck. They fell silent as she raised her arms.

"As you have seen, this ship is threatened not just by the strength of arms, but by magic that may equal our own. That ship is the flag-bearer, for the Great Committee. The same Great Committee we have all shunned, or fled from, or been rescued from." She gestured to various members of the crew, singling them out as examples of each different reason for joining the *Muta*'s ranks.

"We have before us," she continued, "only two options. Fight, or flee. You all know that I consider my position as captain of this ship to be more of a service to the *Muta* and you as her crew than one that requires you to follow my orders. I hope that I have inspired you all by never leading you astray, and by leading you well."

There was a strong murmur of agreement from the crew.

"Today, we must put aside keeping each other from harm. There comes a time in everyone's life when they must fight for what they believe in. Will you fight?"

A roar in the affirmative rose from the crew. Perin stood in awe of the captain of the *Muta*. Rienta already had the respect and obedience of the crew under her command, but now she had inspired them to take action, and they would fight harder and faster for it.

At the moment, she appeared to be soaking up the adulation with dignity, her hands clasped behind her back and staring off into the distance. Once the roar had died down, she continued.

"That being the case, Mr Stim, set the sail and let's give them hell."

The crew roared again and Stim pulled on the thick, rough ropes that raised the sail. As it ascended and unfurled, Perin could not help looking beyond it and seeing the dark and ominous galleon in the distance, with its shining cannons and fading green honeycomb shield that seemed to crackle and glisten in the sunlight. He found himself preoccupied with the question of who was over there, and how they would shape the events that were about to follow. He glanced to his side and saw that Occidens too was staring out towards the *Formalite'*. Perin was fairly sure that she was preoccupied with similar thoughts.

CHAPTER ELEVEN

As the sails expanded like a giant's chest the image of the *Formalite'* started to grow in front of them like a black cancer on the horizon drawing closer. It was an undeniably ominous sight. Perin was sure that if he listened with all his might he could hear war drums beating out a steady rhythm that was increasing ever so slightly in tempo. He realised that he wasn't breathing, and took in a gulp of air. The beat of those war drums had not come from the *Formalite'* but had been the sound of his own blood pumping in his ears. As the *Muta* picked up speed, the *Formalite'* began to slowly turn to face them bow to bow.

"Arm yourselves," Rienta cried from the helm behind them; she hadn't taken her eyes off the approaching ship. It suddenly occurred to Perin that he had no weapons, no armour and no discernible skill with a bow or sword if he were given one. He turned to Occidens, who had adopted a wide stance with her arms behind her back, not unlike that Rienta would have used had she not been grasping the helm to keep the course steady. Occidens had her eyes shut as if in silent meditation or contemplation. Perin didn't know if it would be appropriate to interrupt her.

"What is it, boy?" she asked without opening her eyes. Her voice had a monotone to it, as if she were speaking from within a trance.

"I'm sorry, I don't want to interrupt—"

"You are not interrupting," she said with a slight shake of her head. Perin could see her eyes moving around underneath her eyelids. It was as if she were having a waking dream. "I am simply using my powers to give us as much of an advantage as I can."

"In what way?" Perin asked.

"The ocean beneath us will play its part in any battle that is to come. The currents, the tides, the waves – I would prefer them to be in our favour. That does, however, take quite a degree of visualisation." She opened her eyes and looked directly at Perin. She seemed incredibly calm, which was even more disconcerting when there were forty crew members rushing around them manning defensible positions, strapping on leather armour and barking at their crew mates. As Perin locked eyes with the old woman all of this seemed to drain away.

"Why don't you try?" she said.

"Are you sure this is quite the moment—"

"I am," she interrupted with a smile.

Perin did as he was told, or at least he tried to. He closed his eyes and envisaged himself lowered beneath the waves surrounding the *Muta*. He imagined the wildlife, the tides and the currents. He tried to bend them to his will, but he couldn't quite picture it. It was such an impossible task; there were simply too many variables. Perin had never been confident in the water. Swimming lessons were a large part of the physical curriculum at the Great Academy but it was never something he had displayed a talent for. He started to picture the water currents dragging him down into the deep dark water. It was so cold. He started to shiver and break out in a cold sweat. He found he couldn't breathe. Panic set in as he realised that his imagination had led him into a waking nightmare. He felt as if his lungs were full of seawater; he could taste the salt. The burning pain in his chest was starting to overcome him when suddenly a sharp pain across his face caused him to cough up a throat full of seawater over the deck. He turned to find Occidens looking at him with some concern. All Perin could do was gasp.

"Are you all right, dear boy?" Occidens said, patting his shoulder.

"I think so," Perin said between great gasps and coughs. "I think that sort of magic is beyond me."

"Maybe for now, but it looks as if you imagined yourself into a perilous situation. That takes strong magic in itself. We obviously need to work on levels of control with you, but that can come."

Perin looked out towards the oncoming *Formalite'*. It was now clear that it was a bigger vessel than the *Muta*. "If we manage to live that long," he said.

Occidens leaned in towards Perin and whispered, "Your survival is imperative. It can be assured."

"What?"

"Why don't you go and wait in your quarters?" Occidens said with emphasis on the word 'quarters'. Perin understood: *the ejection mechanism*. He had to admit that there was a degree of sound logic to the idea, but on a deeper, more visceral level he knew that he couldn't possibly allow himself to be bundled off the ship whilst others put themselves in danger for his sake. He had heard Rienta's speech as well and the truth was it had had an effect.

"I can't do that," Perin said. "I'm as much a member of this crew as any other and I couldn't possibly abandon them. Especially since they are fighting for me."

Occidens smiled her toothy grin and slapped Perin on the shoulder. "You know, dear boy, if we are about to go into a fight, that's just what I needed to hear."

"What do you mean?" he asked.

"You just proved you are worth it, my boy." She then adopted her wide-footed stance, put her hands behind her back and closed her eyes again. It may have been his imagination but Perin swore he could detect a change, barely perceptible in the way the *Muta* was moving through the water. It was just a little bit smoother.

A quick guess suggested that the *Muta* and the *Formalite'* would meet in about three minutes. Perin was aware of a large presence behind him. He turned to find Stim looking out over the water. He seemed to lack his usual level of confidence.

"Lady Occidens?" he said enquiringly. "If I may be so bold?"

The old woman was brought out of her trancelike state and seemed a tad flustered, not at being interrupted but giving the impression of having forgotten something.

"My dear chap," she exclaimed, "of course!" She extended one hand and a shimmer of blue light disrupted the air in front of her and spread outward towards Stim's chest. He was encapsulated in the blue shimmering light. He spread his arms outwards and lifted his head to the sky as if accepting a divine gift. He had a look of true contentment on his face, the kind of look a person has when lying down in a hot bath after having developed sore muscles. The process only took a few seconds and Occidens' hand lightly drifted back down to her side and she looked at Stim expectantly. As he lowered his head back to their level and opened his eyes his expression had completely changed. He now had a look of confidence plus a slight sense of impish glee to his smile.

"Let's send them bastards packing," he said with resolve.

"Attaboy," replied Occidens. "Perin, if you'd accompany me to the helm. Stim, you should probably put yourself in the vanguard, try and keep them off this ship." Stim nodded and Occidens made her way slowly and deliberately up the stairs to the helm at the stern. Perin followed behind, although he kept glancing over his shoulder. The *Formalite'* was almost upon them.

"Rienta?" said Occidens to the stoic-looking captain

who still had her eyes locked on the oncoming ship. "Top up, my dear?"

"I've been thinking about that," she replied without moving her eyes. "I think it may be sending a dangerous message to the crew, that their captain needs this sort of performance enhancement to defend them."

Occidens seemed exasperated.

"Oh hell, not this again!" she flapped. "You couldn't possibly have picked a worse time to—"

"If only you could find a way," Rienta interrupted, "to administer your gifts with a smaller degree of flamboyance than that ecclesiastical bestowing you just demonstrated on Stim." She paused. "In front of the entire crew."

Occidens looked a little chastened. Perin thought he understood. Occidens did not bestow these gifts to everyone. In fact, the only two on the ship that she provided magic to were Stim and Rienta. This could very easily lead to jealousy and division among such a small crew.

"You know I don't agree with that," argued Occidens. "I think showing off your best weapons heartens the crew."

"That's as maybe," Rienta replied, "but not for the captain."

Occidens rubbed her forehead as if Rienta were giving her a headache. "All right, my dear, if you want to face this one with your own guile and skill, they cannot be matched." She extended her hand. Rienta's eyes flashed towards it as if she was reluctant to take her hands off the wheel. She decided it was worth the risk and shook the woman's hand firmly, and as their eyes met, the two old women smiled. There was clearly a huge amount of respect between them both. They gave the impression of being old warriors who had fought alongside each other for a long time. Perin wondered how they had met and made a mental note to ask later when this was all over.

With a deep intake of breath Rienta grabbed the wheel

again and raised her voice to the crew, telling them which positions needed more men and ensuring everyone was primed. Perin realised that many of them had been watching the proceedings between the two ladies very closely. *Ship gossip trumps an impending battle,* thought Perin with a smile.

"This won't be a cannon battle," she shouted. "Either of our ships could have turned and made the first shot by now. Prepare to repel boarders." A battle cry rose from the forty brave sailors in response. Perin saw the flash of a smile on Rienta's face. *You're allowed that,* he thought.

The *Formalite'* was closing in on them. Almost simultaneously both ships dropped their sails to slow their momentum. Rienta turned the helm slightly so as to avoid the two vessels crashing into each other. Occidens had returned to her trancelike state, presumably helping Rienta with the tight control of the ship.

The *Formalite'* was much bigger than the *Muta* in every conceivable way. It was longer, taller and wider. The decks of both ships did not match evenly. This would be a tactical disadvantage to the *Muta*, who would have to fight upwards. Perin was just relieved that the first row of cannons on the side of the colossal ship was still beneath the line of the *Muta*'s deck, otherwise they would all be slaughtered in seconds. As it was, the black form of the *Formalite'* had placed itself between the *Muta* and the sun, covering them all in shadow and causing the passing wind to chill the sweat on their skins and make them shiver.

As the bow of the *Formalite'* drew up in line with the stern of the *Muta* it began. A horn sounded from somewhere on board the enemy vessel. A deep battle cry sounded on their decks. Countless ropes swung from their yardarms high up in the air, each holding one if not two darkly clad warriors. They looked far more like soldiers than sailors. They were dressed from head to toe in heavy black leather and each wore a tight-fitting leather helmet on their head. It gave the impression that they were bald and hid their features as a metal guard protruded down over their nose to protect it. It was an efficient and intimidating uniform.

"Fire!" shouted Rienta from the helm, which was now locked in place. Archers from the opposite end of the deck raised their bows and took aim with stunning quickness. Perin counted seven hits that resulted in enemy combatants tumbling to the water between the two ships in a mass of flailing legs and arms.

Stim had caught two of the boarders in mid-air and flung them hard back against the hull of the *Formalite'*. The wood creaked in protest and they too fell, lifeless, into the water.

About half a dozen of the enemy had made it to the *Muta*'s deck and were now in close combat with the crew. Perin could tell from their stance and movements that they were exceptionally well trained. Another horn sounded and the ropes appeared with a new batch of enemies. This time they had simple wooden shields held across their fronts. This would largely defend them from the *Muta*'s arrows.

"I think not," shouted Occidens. Her arms flashed up from her side. A wall of water rose between the two ships, knocking most of the new boarders off their ropes and dragging them back down as the wall receded back into the ocean, spraying the startled combatants already on deck from behind and allowing the *Muta*'s crew member's a few moments to take back the offensive. A few new attackers had made it through the wall of water and joined the fight with their comrades clumsily, clearly stunned by the manner of their arrival. Perin, safe for now up at the helm, noticed that there was a formulaic style to their combat that allowed the best fighters amongst the *Muta*'s crew to overcome them easily. *Another argument for creativity over technique*, he thought.

Stim grabbed two more of the leather-clad enemies and with one arm each threw them back towards the hull of the *Formalite'*. This time he used so much force that the hull gave way and with a sickening crunch they disappeared from view as splinters and cracked wood gave way to darkness inside. Archers appeared in the dark holes Stim had created and began firing at the *Muta*'s defenders. Stim picked up a nearby cannonball in each hand and threw it inside each hole. He put his complete weight behind it. There was a crashing sound from within the *Formalite'* as whatever the cannonball had collided with was obliterated. The arrows stopped.

There were a few moments of silence from the *Formalite'* and as the *Muta*'s crew pushed the attackers back to the side of the ship, for a second Perin thought that perhaps the battle was over and the *Formalite'* had given up. The remainder of the crew stood poised, waiting for a third horn to blow and the assault that would follow. It didn't come, and crew members glanced at each other nervously. It was Stim who broke the silence.

"What the hell are you waiting for!?" he bellowed at the decks of the enemy ship.

As if in response ropes soared through the air towards the decks of the *Muta*. There was something different this time though. The ropes were not being swung from the ships beams to carry men to the decks. They had come from the decks of the *Formalite'* itself. The type of rope was different as well – this was the kind the farmers would use on horseback to capture running bulls or oxen. The crew was thrown into confusion. Although most of the whips did not find purchase on anything and snaked back towards the *Formalite'*, one landed around Stim's arm and pulled tight around his bicep. He looked at it, first with confusion, then with amusement.

"Oh dear," he said with mock concern. "They've got me!" He pulled firmly and the whip came loose from whoever or whatever was holding it. He then tried to rip free the end that had tied itself round his arm. Another volley of the ropes followed but this time they were all firmly aimed at Stim. The whips caught him around his

waist, several on both arms and one around his neck. He
looked like a distressed, distended marionette. For a brief
second there was a look of fear on his face before he
tensed his muscles and all of the whips went taut with the
tension.

"Stim, no!" screamed Rienta, but it was too late.

The world lurched sideways, sending most of the crew,
including Perin, to their knees. Occidens and Rienta held
their feet but they were two of the few that did. Pain
erupted up Perin's knees as he crashed into the deck. He
looked up to see that the ropes Stim had pulled against
were not giving way. They couldn't be being held by men
on the other end, they must have been tied against the hull
of the *Formalite'*. Both ships were now being dragged
together and tipping towards each other. Stim tried to stop
pulling, but now the whips were being pulled in the
opposite direction and if Stim did not pull against them he
would be hauled over the side of the *Muta* and either end
up dragged beneath the waves or smashed between the
hulls of both ships.

With a splintering crunch and the sound of ripping
material, Perin looked up to see that the ships had collided.
The tips of the sails and masts were the first things to
entangle, and the whole ship vibrated as they ground
against one another. The ships continued to move closer
and a worrying groaning overpowered everyone's ears as
the hulls met.

Three horns sounded. These were of a higher pitch
than before. Perin instinctively looked up to the entangled
masts, but then heard the sounds of a dozen or more rope
ladders being swung over the side of the *Formalite'* and
down to the deck of the *Muta*.

"Archers!" Rienta screamed. "Bows down, swords out,
prepare for hand-to-hand combat." The archers who were
still in disarray from their fall to the deck quickly formed
ranks and joined their comrades waiting at the foot of the
ladders. Stim was working to free himself from the ropes.

Rienta had abandoned the helm and joined the archers in their advance, drawing her own sword.

"What should we do?" Perin asked Occidens, who had remained with him at the helm.

"We will hold fast for the moment," she replied.

Then they came, with shields over their backs to parry any potential attacks. Perin was astounded at the sheer number of them. The thirty or so sailors of the *Muta* looked quite impressive until they were dwarfed by more and more soldiers coming from the decks of the *Formalite'*. The *Muta*'s crew tried to keep them surrounded by forming a semicircle around the ladders but there were still too many of them and they could easily have broken through the hastily made ranks through numbers alone. No one was fighting yet though. Stim and Rienta stood towards the back of the crowd in the centre of the ship, standing on either side of the mast which afforded them a higher vantage point.

Having established a two-to-one advantage in numbers, Perin watched as a plank was raised forming a walking platform between the *Formalite'* and the *Muta*. A moment later, a striking woman appeared dramatically at the top of the plank and descended towards them. Her arrogance gave the impression that she herself had conquered the *Muta*. She wore a deep velvet green bodice with translucent sleeves showing thin floating arms and a flowing ragged skirt. Heeled boots signalled her approach, giving a militaristic clack with each step. Her eyes were as green as her clothes and her grey hair was cut short. It appeared that the natural position of her thin-lipped mouth was not so much a smile or frown but a sneer.

"Viri," Occidens said under her breath. Then she started to walk towards the steps leading down to the deck. Perin saw Occidens and Rienta meet each other's eyes. There was a flash from Rienta that suggested Occidens should stay back. Occidens held her ground, until Rienta made a slow nod and Occidens continued towards the advancing woman.

As Viri reached the front of her own ranks the crew of the *Muta* made an instinctive retreat back a few steps, creating a gap between the two forces. Occidens walked through her own lines and the two women stood face to face between the two.

"Occidens," said Viri. Her voice was high and harsh. It had an accent that Perin had never heard before. This was a voice that could be used as a weapon.

"Viri, my dear," Occidens replied, her voice dripping with sarcasm. "It's been so long since we've spoken! How have you been?"

"Oh, very well," she replied in kind. "Running the nation, you understand. Difficult work, rewarding yet time-consuming." Her eyebrows flared as her level of sarcasm rose to match that of her old tutor. "Though I'm sure that's not a concept you find easy to understand, having given up your life to mindless frivolity."

Occidens took a step forward. Perin was glad to see that Viri took a step back. *Good, still a measure of fear there.*

"Frivolity, my dear?" Occidens said with amusement. "You always did enjoy that word. You use it to describe everything that you dislike or disapprove of."

"My recollection is that there was a great deal that I had good cause to disapprove of," spat Viri.

Occidens looked to be tiring of the conversation, as if it were one she had had a number of times before. She kept shooting glances over her shoulder towards Stim and Rienta. She turned back to Viri and concluded, "Your own lack of intelligence and judgement have no place here, Madame Viri – now please state your business so we can all get on with our lives." Viri turned her eyes towards Perin and smiled. Her teeth were too white and perfect to be genuine – obviously replacements – but this did, however, make it look like she had fangs.

"I'm here for the boy," she said simply. "The Great Committee has business with him."

"He's busy," replied Occidens equally simply. "Indeed I'm afraid his schedule is awfully full for some considerable time. If only you had arrived to pick him up a little earlier from the Great Academy."

"The Committee won't stand to allow someone with potential gifts to be nurtured by you," Viri said matter-of-factly. "Not only would it be dangerous for the Committee but I don't believe it's in the boy's best interests either."

"The boy's best interests?" Occidens shouted with a sudden vigour that made Viri, and indeed her entire line of troops, step back. "You expect anyone to believe that you have Perin," she stopped briefly then smiled, "that's his name by the way," and restarted, "that you have Perin's interests at heart."

"I certainly do," she retorted. Then she turned directly to Perin. He did not like her having her eyes on him. He was still relatively safe up next to the helm. *Though if she can call down lightning like Occidens, there wouldn't be much I could do.* This was not a pleasant thought and he tried to push it from his mind.

"Perin," Viri called out to him, "if you come with me, then you will not be pressured into some form of crusade or paraded around as some form of false messiah against a society that has nothing but the best interests of its people at heart." Her tone of voice had changed entirely. It was now almost saccharine sweet with none of the abrasiveness of mere moments ago during her confrontation with Occidens.

"No, no!" shouted Occidens, also addressing Perin. "You won't be doing much of anything, because you'll be dead and buried!"

"That is not the case," Viri said, appearing mortally offended. "The current plan is for him to become a junior member of the Committee, but as there are only five of our number, that makes it rather an important role. You would then be trained by the four true sorcerers of Caramine so that you could take your place in the running of society." Perin was astounded. *If only Pym had heard that.* He found himself smiling. Not only that, he found himself tempted. He didn't trust this woman though. There was something about her that Perin was instinctively fearful of. Also, the way Viri had said 'current plan' made him nervous.

"What if I agree with Occidens, and this crew's beliefs on how society should be?" he asked from his perch. She seemed a little taken aback that Perin was proud or perhaps stupid enough to say anything.

"Then your voice will be heard, and you will have a chance to persuade the rest of us as to the validity of your argument." She smiled her sweetest and therefore most threatening smile. "We are a democracy, Perin. With you on the Great Committee there would be five. That means to change all of society all you need do is convince another two members."

Perin thought about it, took a deep breath and said, "I am glad to hear it, and I accept your proposal!"

There was immediate uproar. Occidens whirled to face him. Viri began to laugh, along with her troops. The crew of the *Muta* were split fairly evenly in condemnation of Perin and shouts to convince him to change his mind. Stim looked like he may cry, and Rienta's face had begun to twitch. He was unsure if her natural instinct would be to convince or condemn.

Viri brought silence to the crowd by shouting, "Enough!" with a voice that thundered around them and managed to ripple the ocean around the still-entwined boats, which gave a dangerous creak in response. When she opened her mouth again it was to address Perin and there was a distinct triumph in her saccharine tone this time.

"It appears as if our business is very much concluded. Perin, if you would like to come on board the *Formalite'* we can set this all in motion and—" Perin raised his hand and to his surprise Viri fell quiet.

"I'm afraid you may have misunderstood me," Perin said, smiling. "I said I accepted your offer of a post on the Great Committee. I'm afraid though that I have no intention of filling it myself. I am too young and inexperienced, but at least have the intelligence to know that much. I am, however, perfectly prepared to appoint a proxy in my stead. For that position, I can think of no one better than…Lady Occidens."

Anarchy ruled once more. This time the crew of the *Muta* cheered and those wearing hats threw them in the air. The *Formalite*'s crew looked confused and glanced at their leader to take her lead. Occidens had begun to cackle wildly, Rienta nodded approvingly, and Stim still looked like he was going to cry, but Perin assumed it was for rather a different reason.

"Enough," Viri boomed again, and once more the world around them creaked. "That is not an option. This offer is for you – you cannot appoint a proxy." Although she attempted to hold on to her syrupy voice, there was an intense irritation starting to push through.

"That's quite a shame," said Perin. "I guess I will just have to stay on board the *Muta* then." He was now completely playing to the crowd. He was thoroughly enjoying the cheers and applause he was gaining from the crew members.

"Not an option," Viri stated with growing impatience, "Guards, slaughter everyone on this ship and bring the boy. If he raises magic against you, run a spear through his stomach."

Occidens had raised her hand as if to ask permission to speak in a children's class. "Excuse me, dear—"

"And furthermore" Viri continued, "I would like the heads of the old woman, the strongman and the stone-faced captain brought to me at once."

"I really do think—"

"What is it, old woman?!" she shrieked with fire in her eyes.

"I think you need to stop for just a moment," said Occidens urgently, "and listen…" She looked off into the middle distance, concentrating fiercely on this invisible sound. Viri understood that something rather important was happening and started to listen carefully as well, along with the troops on both sides of the fight and Perin.

"I don't hear anything," Viri whispered. Occidens looked at her with bewilderment.

"That could be," she replied in a barely audible whisper, "because this was a distraction. NOW!" Her last word was bellowed with the booming amplification that Viri had used earlier. Even as Perin covered his ears he thought it another example of how a skill or ability is enhanced further when using it creatively. Viri had fallen to the ground clasping her ears – she was the closest to Occidens at the time. The guards were distracted for a moment but it was all that was required.

Rienta had drawn her sword and whirled on the spot in one fluid motion with her sword outstretched. She had moved so fast it was almost impossible to see what she had done. Perin smiled – Occidens must have surreptitiously recharged Rienta's powers. *But what for?* Perin wondered. She came to a stop almost exactly where she had started but now she was smiling.

She locked eyes with Perin and shouted, "Engine room!" Perin was confused until the ear-splitting creak behind her made him realise what she had done: Rienta had cut the mast of the *Muta* clean in half. As it started to fall forward Stim wrapped his giant arms around it and held it in place. Then with a rotation of his hips and a swing of his body he hurled the mast, still attached to that of the *Formalite'* at the hull of the enemy ship. The two masts came unstuck with an echoing crack. Luckily the upper part of the *Formalite*'s mast fell into the ocean. It created more confusion as both ships started to rock with the change of weight and movement of the water.

As Perin headed towards the downward staircase that

went to the engine room he saw the mast of the *Muta* crash into the deck of the *Formalite'*, the brown wood of the mast splintering the black of the deck. It was as if a giant oak tree had not just fallen but thrown itself on a house. It was glorious. The force of the impact broke the two ships away from each other.

Viri was incensed. Her arms flashed out in every direction, taking down her own men as well as *Muta* crewmen. When she caught sight of Perin, her eyes themselves flashed with electricity and her voice had taken on a frightening power.

"This ends now, boy!" she boomed, and raised her hands in front of her.

"I quite agree!" Perin heard, and he turned to see Occidens surrounded by a shimmering blue light. It was an orb that she had encased herself in, sustained by the lights from her hands. It was the same kind of light that Perin had seen her use to transfer power to Stim. Viri shot a bolt of green lightning at the old woman, but when the arc struck the blue orb it crackled but did not give way. Then, without warning, the blue orb surrounding her expanded in a whoosh to encase the whole ship, Occidens roaring with the effort. As its outer edges reached Viri she was thrown backwards in a whirl of green fabric, sending her clear of the *Muta* to land with a splash in the ocean. She was not alone: Occidens' field of energy had pushed every one of the *Formalite'* crew from the decks. Only then did the blue light that had surrounded them all dissipate. Perin looked towards Occidens with amazement. She met his eye, smiled, and fainted dead away.

"Perin!" screamed Rienta over the commotion. "Engine room, now!"

Not hesitating this time, Perin leapt down the stairs taking three and four at a time till he reached the deck that housed the rowing apparatus. He started up the engines with as much fire wine as Stim had left lying around and the gears turned slowly at first but then hurried their pace to match Perin's desperation. *We have engines but no mast. They have no mast or engines but perhaps oars. We need to get out of here.*

With the *Muta* moving ahead he returned to the deck. The *Muta* had indeed pulled away from the *Formalite'* which stood in disarray behind them. Perin could make out Viri's green form making a rather undignified climb up a cargo net along with some of her troops to get back aboard. Rienta was back at the helm of the *Muta* manning the getaway. Stim had picked up Occidens and was taking her into her study. She was lifeless as far as Perin could tell. Other crew members were dealing with those that had been wounded in the battle. Perin had not seen anyone killed, but now he could hear the undeniable sound of mourning from crew members who had gone looking for their friends and found them silent.

Although they had been victorious, there was no celebrating. This victory had come at a cost. A cost, Perin realised, that was entirely because of him. His heart sank.

CHAPTER TWELVE

The ship was awash with an eerie silence. The crew themselves were ashen and downcast from the loss of seven crew members and were deeply concerned for the six more who had been injured. The *Muta* did not have a sickbay as such. Many of the crew had rudimentary field medic abilities that allowed them to stabilise or patch up wounded soldiers, but there were little to no medical supplies like bandages, pain relieving chemicals or tonics on board.

Perin walked along the crew deck and saw the injured men. Some were conscious but in clear pain. One with a sword wound to the shoulder seemed in high spirits, but his grey pallor and sunken eyes suggested that the wound might have become infected. Perin had not excelled at biological sciences but he had keen memories of the scare tactics employed by the tutors when it came to the hazards of failing to sterilise or clean cuts and scrapes. This man was going to develop a series of worsening symptoms before dying a death that would be unquestionably worse than those inflicted on the crew members who had already died. Perin found he couldn't look the man in the eye.

At the far end of the deck were the silent patients. They had lost consciousness, in most cases due to blood loss. As Perin continued past these patients he started to feel nauseous. He was directly responsible for this. He knew that he couldn't be held responsible for the Great Committee seeking him, and he wasn't even particularly guilty about these people being hurt in his defence. What made him feel as though his stomach was about to collapse was that he had failed to play any physical role in the battle. *Some future of sorcery you are*, he thought to himself.

As he walked up the stairs towards the main deck, Stim was walking down. He looked almost in a trance. He had been taking direct care of Occidens since she collapsed, half a day ago now.

Rienta had refused to relinquish the helm as they made their escape. She made random course changes to shake off the *Formalite'*. There was no sign of them taking chase – not surprising given the close to ruined state the *Muta* had left them in – but Perin had become concerned by the maddened glint in the normally passive eyes of the captain. He was on his way to speak to her, perhaps to figure out what would happen from here. As he trudged his way up the steps he saw that Rienta had clearly still refused to relinquish the helm. Her knuckles were white against the spokes of the ship's wheel. Her short hair had started to become unkempt and her bright blue eyes were darting across the skyline as if picking out potential targets.

"Captain?" Perin asked tentatively. He was not entirely sure that the woman knew he was there. Her eyes darted to him for a fraction of a second then returned to their previous position.

"Yes, boy?" she said. It was curt, though not dismissive. She appeared happy to speak with him, though obviously preoccupied.

"I was just wondering," Perin said with caution, "if you had any thoughts on what we should be doing from here?"

"Exactly what we are doing!" she replied. "Staying focused, staying vigilant and staying ahead." That very much seemed to Perin to be a mantra that Rienta lived by, but it didn't really address his question.

"So how are we going to do that?" Perin enquired, trying to make his voice sound casual so as not to inspire any ire from the clearly stressed captain. She turned away from the skyline to look him directly in the eye. This approach had clearly not been successful.

"How we are going to do that, Perin, is we are going to keep going at full pace until one of three things happens. The first is that Occidens wakes up and is able to heal our crew and defend our ship. The second is that we run out of ocean. The third is that the Great Committee unleashes another ship, or ships, manned by their other sorcerers, to find us."

"How long do you think it will be before Occidens wakes up?" Perin asked.

"I have no idea," she replied. "This has not happened before. Being unable to wake her has left this ship completely at the Great Committee's mercy."

"What can I do?" Perin asked.

"You've done enough," she replied, looking back towards the skyline, the hint of blame in her voice undeniable and inescapable. *She knows this is my fault too.* This felt like a dagger through Perin's heart. The guilt he felt had been bad enough, but to have it justified by Rienta almost caused him to bend over double in physical pain.

"She's awake," came a familiar voice from the stairs. Rienta and Perin both turned to see Stim. He still looked exhausted both mentally and physically. *The magic is wearing off,* Perin thought. The big man did, however, look relieved at the news he had just delivered. Perin also noticed that Rienta's shoulders had released slightly. Perhaps he had imagined it though. Some of the knot in his stomach had loosened, but his face still felt flush and his eyes were red with suppressed tears at what Rienta had said. *Because she's right,* Perin concluded grimly.

He moved to join Stim, presuming they would climb down the steps to see Occidens, but neither Stim nor Rienta had moved. Perin stopped just short of Stim's mammoth chest.

"Shouldn't we go and speak to her?" Perin asked.

"She's not very strong," Stim said in a measured tone.

"What has she said to you?" Rienta asked Stim.

"Not very much I can make sense of. I think she's done something to her mind," he said, welling up with tears.

Perin was no longer thinking and darted past Stim. He was down the stairs in three leaps. "Hey!" Stim cried and made a grab but he missed Perin by a few inches. In mere seconds he was at the door; he turned the handle and darted in.

There was a strong smell of incense in the room from several burning sticks in small glass vials on many of the surfaces. They created little wisps of smoke that looked like snakes creeping up into the air before they dissipated.

There was a low couch in worn soft burgundy leather that had been moved into the centre of the room and the old woman was lying upon it, her wrinkled hands clasped together on her lap. Her eyes were only half open and she mumbled what seemed to Perin to be gibberish.

"One to the left, three scuffs on left boot. Two to the left, cut on the right trouser leg. Three to the left…"

And so it continued in some nonsensical list. Perin approached her and was shocked by the change that had come over her. As she lay on the couch the pull of gravity caused her skin to sag in unnatural ways.

"Occidens," he whispered. "Can you hear me?"

"Pass through, Perin," she replied. "Pass through." *Well at least she can understand me,* he thought.

"I have decided that I am going to turn myself over to the Great Committee," he said. "I can't be a danger to this crew. People have died for me." He didn't realise he was convinced to take this action until the words were out of his mouth.

Occidens became supremely agitated. "Pass through, Stim, pass through, Rienta, pass through, all!" Perin took a step back and he welled up with tears. *She wants me to speak to Stim and Rienta.*

"I can't talk to them about this," he said. "They will try to stop me."

"Skirts over head," she mumbled. Perin assumed this meant that Occidens had accused him of losing his senses. Maybe she was right. All Perin could do was head towards the door of the study. As he reached the door and his hand stretched out for the handle he heard her speak again through her mumbling.

"Perin," She sounded more lucid and direct.

"Yes?"

"If you want to do this damn stupid thing, don't do it in this damn stupid way."

He returned to her quickly but she seemed to have fallen back into unconsciousness. Perin left as quietly as he could. He suspected their brief confused conversation had only made matters worse for her, but he had needed to speak to someone, and Rienta would not have been appropriate. Given her reaction to Perin at the helm, he thought she might be glad to be rid of him. As he left the room he almost walked straight into the captain. She had been waiting outside of Occidens' study for him.

"Perin," she said in a conciliatory tone. "I feel that I owe you an apology."

Enough is enough, Perin thought, and his temper gave way. "No, Captain Rienta, you were absolutely right. I have done quite enough. I could complain at being abducted from my home after my examinations—"

"—rescued," Rienta interjected.

"I could complain at being thrown off the ship, forced to walk the plank, stranded on the crow's nest." Rienta had gone extremely quiet. "I should apologise for unleashing that damn lightning bolt and changing the colour of that cloud, but I thought it was a good thing to have done, until I saw those bodies, until I saw those poor injured and dead bodies."

"They did what they chose to do," Rienta said with purpose. "I'm not attempting to coddle you. It is indeed true that those men, injured and dead, would be alive today if you had never been born, but that is not the point. The point is that they are still glad you are here and glad that you may find a way to help us bring about a brighter and more just future free of the Great Committee."

"And how am I going to do that?" Perin fumed. "That's never been explained to me! I'm to learn how to use magic, like Occidens. That's fine, but why isn't she the one changing this world of ours? Why isn't she the one responsible for all those deaths? You haven't seen her in there yet," he pointed wildly behind him towards her door. "She's babbling, her mind may be broken, the poor old woman, and it was because she had too much faith in me, but I still don't know what I was supposed to have done!"

Rienta looked at him with a mixture of sympathy and regret. "You are quite right," she said. "Your purpose was never truly explained to you. We were afraid it would frighten you off."

Perin looked into her face, the face he had had an instant respect for, and now that façade had fallen away and she was simply another old woman. "Well, I'm frightened now, but still here, so come on!"

Rienta took a deep breath, adding to her height. "You are to depose the master of the Great Committee and take his place. Occidens does not have the strength to do this alone."

Perin was dumbstruck. "One lightning bolt and you have me conquering Caramine?" He laughed. "Let's be serious, you don't really know me – you know nothing of my character, of my opinions on governance and democracy. I could be an even greater autocrat than the current Great Committee."

"We had hoped to have longer alone with you before being subjected to their assault so that you could be trained and prepared, not just in magic but in fairness and ethics. Other arts that have sadly disappeared under the current regime."

"That's another thing! What makes you consider yourself and this crew to be so enlightened," Perin fumed, "when you are so quick to take up arms and kill other people with opposing beliefs? Even if the Committee are as bad as you say, what makes you any better than them? I'm starting to think you're just as bad!"

He felt a strong slap across his face. Perin had no idea what had happened at first. The movement had been too quick to comprehend. As his eyes refocused and locked with Rienta's it was clear that it had been she who had slapped him. The look in her eyes was not one of anger. It was one of panic. Not just panic alone though – panic and a great sadness.

"You have no idea," she breathed. "Everyone on this ship has lost so much to the Committee. Their way of life is lost, so of course they lose their way, lose their ethos, their compassion or ethics." Her voice cracked, but she swallowed and continued. "Perin, I understand what you are trying to say, and there is truth in it. In order to fight a foe as big and strong as we face, you have to stoop to their level sometimes. Yes, we compromise even our greatest principles, but there comes a time when all reasonable men and women must act against the unreasonable even if that is what they themselves must become."

Perin was not interested in a philosophical ethics lesson right now. As far as he was concerned, he had heard enough and made up his mind.

"I'm done here," he said, and walked past Rienta. She put her hands behind her back and lowered her head as if respectfully resigned. As he was about to walk down the stairs towards his own quarters, he turned and saw her standing a few feet from Occidens' door. She seemed to be considering whether or not to enter. After a few moments she turned and walked back up the staircase towards the helm where Perin noticed Stim had taken temporary command. Despite their current divisions and cross words, Perin was determined that they would not be hurt or pursued on his account. He decided that he would steal a life raft during the night and row a reverse course. It may take some time for him to find the *Formalite'* as Rienta had been changing courses wildly, but if he could find land then he could signal for them or pass word through some official channel or other. Once the *Formalite'* had him it would call of any pursuit. The *Muta* could escape and would hopefully be safe for a long time to come. Their safety would be a condition of Perin's cooperation.

Perhaps Viri was right, he considered. *If I am to join the Great Committee itself then that will mark a huge power shift from within. There must be moderate elements. One of the sorcerers must have more reasonable leanings that he can align himself with and hopefully turn into practice.*

As he considered this, a point that Viri had mentioned earlier fell into focus for him. She had said that there were four members of the Great Committee at present. This must mean that a tie in any vote would be rather easy and must be quite common. The head of the Great Committee must hold the deciding vote to break any tie.

That gives him a lot of power, Perin thought. *Power that Viri seems to say the Committee are willing to pass over to me.* As he reached his study, even though it was barely midday, he lay down on his bed and tried to sleep. He would need his wits about him later in the evening.

Lying there he started to consider the possibilities he had if he were to accept the position as Viri had suggested. He would be able to act as the power broker, the voice of reason and the swing vote in any case that provided the rest of the Committee with even the slightest bit of controversy. He pictured the head of the Great Committee as some grand old man, very much past his prime. He was sort of a male version of Occidens to Perin's mind but with a cruelty and malice that the old woman could never muster. Very quickly, he imagined, he would prove to be the power behind the throne and he could lead the Committee to allow Caramine to be the democratic and creative society that the crew of the *Muta* really wanted. The truth was that despite what he had said to Rienta, as he listened to the crew speak he had become convinced that they were right. His words to the captain had been for the sake of shock, scare and petulance. Truthfully he was on their side and also wanted to achieve what they wanted to achieve. It worried him that Rienta felt this could only be accomplished through force. Surely this was an approach the Committee would take and not the more enlightened crew that the *Muta* considered themselves to be?

As he lapsed into unconsciousness his last thought was a question. He wondered if he still had much to learn from Occidens, Rienta and the crew of the *Muta*, or if he instead had a lot he could teach them and the Great Committee itself.

CHAPTER THIRTEEN

When Perin woke he had a lump in his throat and a knot in his stomach. After sleeping on his anger and his frustration with Rienta and the crew it had dissipated a little. He still held on to some of it, particularly the unreasonableness of the expectations placed on him, but he started to doubt his planned course of action would solve anything. It would also be a dangerous course of action. There was, after all, no guarantee that he would not simply be run through by a guard the moment he stepped on board the *Formalite'* – if he was even able to survive until he found it.

He lay in the bed for some time, staring at the dark ceiling above and feeling the motion of the ship move him from side to side. It was not unlike a baby's cradle. It would be so easy to simply close his eyes, abandon the plan and go back to sleep. He would be safe, at least for now, defended by the *Muta* and its crew.

Ironically, it was this very thought which brought him out of his indecision and raised him to his feet. He thought of those injured and dead crewmen. He could not allow that to happen to any others regardless of their keenness to defend him. By being here, he was putting them all at risk. That was unacceptable. He would abandon ship for the *Formalite'* so that everyone else on board could live. That was it. Regardless of whatever else had come into his mind, or been considered with regards to the Great Committee or what Viri had said, Perin decided that this would be his inspiration and motivation to push him onwards in his escape.

He dressed quickly, found a satchel in one of the drawers and filled it with as many useful scraps as he could find a use for. This included leftover meat from his table and two large glass bottles of fresh water, separated in the bag by some clothes to avoid them clinking and signalling his escape to the whole ship. He slid the sharp meat knife from the table and put it in his boot.

As he looked around the room he felt a wistful sadness. This would be the last time he saw this room, his room. Despite having only lived in it for a relatively short time, it was very homely and comforting. He would miss it. He briefly considered simply trying to pull the levers outside the doors to jettison the room from the ship, with him in it, though he remembered it would likely sink and the *Muta* would just pick him up again. *A pity*, he thought, but that's how it was.

He was careful not to make any noise as he closed his door and walked with slow deliberate steps, avoiding any creaking boards as he approached the staircase. The only other room on the floor was Rienta's but it wasn't her he was most afraid of disturbing. He made his way up to the top deck. There were some who were still awake, playing cards by candlelight, or talking to the wounded who could not get to sleep due to their discomfort. This simply pushed Perin onwards and hardened his resolve to leave. It was for those brave men that he had taken this decision.

As he reached the top deck, he peered up to the helm.

There was no sign of Rienta. *Thank goodness,* Perin thought. He did not have confidence that he could fool the captain if she had been on watch. There was a crewman on duty, but he was distracted and not standing at the helm itself but several steps behind it. He had a telescope in hand and was looking behind the *Muta*. Perin thought it likely he was seeing if they were being pursued by the *Formalite'*. He realised he had no idea what heading they were on, or what heading he should take. In the opposite direction from the *Muta* seemed obvious, so he decided that was his best option.

Getting on deck was the first part of his plan. The second was trickier. He wanted to make sure there was no way the *Muta* could quickly turn round and follow him. For this, he needed to perform a little light sabotage. The wheel of the *Muta*'s helm turned a mechanism at the rear of the deck. This mechanism turned a great horizontal wheel that in turn rotated the rudder of the ship to control the direction. If Perin managed to stop the horizontal wheel from turning, then the ship would be stuck on its current course. He looked in front of him into the night. He hoped there was no land directly ahead, but found it hard to believe that Rienta would bring them close to land whilst trying to flee.

He slowly approached the cannon closest to the rear of the ship. There were several cannonballs there for loading into the weapon. Perin tried to lift the cannonball, and with both hands and the full strength of his back he could, but there was no way he could walk with it. He managed to put the ball on the deck without it making a sound and very slowly rolled it towards the stern on his hands and knees. Luckily there was no reason anyone would be near this part of the *Muta*, particularly in the middle of the night, but it was still important that he not make enough noise that the watchmen at the helm would become suspicious.

After what seemed like an exceptionally long time,

Perin had the ball in position at the foot of the mechanism. Putting his back into it, he managed to lift the cannonball up onto the wheel. It was indented with triangular slats so that all parts of the mechanism fit into one another. This also meant the wheel was not smooth and the cannonball would not roll off. Perin placed the ball on the disk and against the rod that came down from the helm. The rudder could now no longer be turned left.

Perin repeated the process and put the cannonball on the other side of the mechanism, stopping it from moving right. The wheel above was now jammed into place. As an extra precaution Perin removed three leather belts that had been in his quarters and tied them around both cannonballs and the mechanism. There was no way anything would move now. No permanent damage had been done, and this could all be undone in a few minutes, but it should be enough time to get himself a little further away.

Perin then continued to the nearest lifeboat. This was part three of his plan, and the easiest to go wrong. The lifeboats were not intended for one person. They were attached to the deck of the *Muta* by two lengths of sturdy rope. The idea was that these could be released gradually and simultaneously by two crewmen. Perin did not have another crewman so would have to do it himself, but the boat would be too heavy for him to take the weight of both lengths of rope. With his knife from his boot, he slowly shaved a little of the rope away, holding one side of the craft. He stopped when it started to creak and fray of its own accord under the weight. The plan was that the boat would come loose and smash against the side of the *Muta*, creating an awful racket.

Perin then made his way to a second life raft, and waited. He would have to time his escape very carefully. He tied a leather belt to each of the rope winches and then tied them together in the middle where he sat. With one tug now he could release the boat and it would drop into the water. Hopefully it would survive the fall. It would create a large splash, but he hoped the smashing boat on the other side of the *Muta* would cause enough of a distraction that he could get away unseen. It was a risk.

He waited what seemed like an eternity. The rope on the decoy boat was taking far too long to fray. It had obviously regained purchase and stabilised itself. He peered over the side of his escape craft and willed it to fall, willed it to go. He imagined it falling, imagined the sound of it splintering and everyone running up on deck to see what the commotion was and to pull up the remains. It wasn't happening. Perin closed his eyes and imagined the rope on the decoy giving way. Subconsciously, instinctively, he pulled on the leather belt and released his escape craft.

Everything rushed from his view into a blur as his boat plummeted towards the water. He heard a crash and the distinct sound of splintering wood. *This is it, he thought, I'm dead.* This proved to be both premature and inaccurate. Not only was he not dead, he was also unharmed and remarkably dry. His eyes focused and his boat was free and clear on the water at the side of the hulking wooden frame of the *Muta*. As the vessel continued forward leaving Perin's ship behind, he saw that the other lifeboat had indeed broken free at exactly the same time as Perin's and created just the distraction he was looking for. As quick as he could, he took out the oars and started to row away from the *Muta*. He could hear shouted orders for a while coming from the *Muta*.

"Stop the bloody engines!" had certainly come from Stim.

"Bring it up!" shouted Rienta.

As he sailed further away from the galleon the sound faded to silence. It was still incredibly dark and Perin had no oil lamps. As the *Muta* faded into the pitch darkness of the night it became apparent that it had been the only source of light. Perin rowed for as long as he felt he was physically able and then he raised the small wooden mast. It had no sail attached; it had probably been cannibalised for repairs. Perin made do by attaching three of his shirts to it. They billowed outwards, filling with air, and Perin felt his little escape ship lurch forward into the darkness. There was very little else he could do at this point, so he decided he would be best served by going to sleep. As he closed his eyes, the rock of the boat was rougher than it had been on the *Muta*. *This child-raiser isn't as caring or protective as the last,* he thought. It was a stark reminder that he had given up his protection and given up his supposed destiny, as outlined by Rienta and Occidens.

Perin didn't really know how he felt about that yet. The importance he had been given on the *Muta* had been empowering. He felt he would probably still be treated with some importance on the *Formalite'*. It may just be with a negative kind of importance. That scared him, but he knew he was doing the right thing. *My friends are safe,* he thought. *I've defended them, the same way they defended me.* This thought led him into an uneasy sleep. He did not dream; in truth he did not really rest. He merely closed his eyes to pass the time till daylight.

Daylight came, and Perin did not wake straight away. He had managed to pull the rough cargo cover that was in the lifeboat over his head and it had blocked out all light. A very insistent knocking woke him up. At first, from the blackness underneath the cover, he forgot where he was and thought someone was knocking on the door of his quarters back on the *Muta*. When the feeling came back to him and his muscles complained at the hard wood floor and his skin itched from the rough spun cover he sat bolt upright and threw the cover from his face.

He stared into the black. Not the black night, but black wood. He had set out to find the *Formalite'* but it had found him. He was now facing the side of its hull. As he looked around himself he saw four sinister-looking punctures in the side of his small boat's hull. Arrows attached to thin metal wires had been fired at the boat. There was another knock and another arrow appeared dangerously close to him. The arrows were made of blackened wood as well. They looked quite strong. He realised this was a method of mooring the boat to the side of the *Formalite'*. He was at a disadvantage in terms of perspective. All he could see was the hull of the boat, but that black hull made it very distinctive. This was the Great Committee's flagship he had set out to find. It was still afloat and still intimidating.

He was immediately worried. He could not have travelled very far, which meant that the ship had managed to track the *Muta* and was quite close. His mind flooded with questions and queries. *How had they managed to travel so far so fast? Their mast was broken in two!* Perin thought. *Even if they managed to mend it, how had they known where to go with Rienta's constant course corrections?* Despite these queries, Perin was even more convinced that he had done the right thing by coming here. Regardless of how it had happened, the *Formalite'* had caught up with *Muta* and had it not stopped now to pick him up it would catch up with them even sooner. A quick calculation in his head of how far this little boat could realistically have come suggested that the *Formalite'* would have caught up with the *Muta* later that same day. Occidens was far from her usual self, if she ever would be again, and a conflict on this day would probably have led to a slaughter of all hands. Perin managed to feel a sense of pride and vindication in fleeing. He had almost definitely saved his friends.

This feeling faded somewhat when a large rope ladder, exactly like those used to board the *Muta*, descended to his little craft. This was what he came here for but his hands shook as he grabbed hold of the ladder. He tied it to his little ship, avoiding the spider web of wires that had been created to hold it in place. He picked up his bag and slung it over his shoulder, then reached out to take hold of the rope ladder. He noticed his hands were shaking. He didn't know if he was doing the right thing anymore; a great deal of his bravery had deserted him. By this point though, there really was no other option; he would simply have to ascend this ladder and see what happened when he reached the top. He put his foot on the bottom rung of the ladder and began to climb.

CHAPTER FOURTEEN

As Perin climbed higher his hands began to sweat and redden. Beads of the salty water ran down his face and his lungs started to burn. He still lacked the athletic skills or muscle to be very good at that sort of thing, but he pulled himself further and further upward until he could see where the ladder curved over onto the deck of the *Formalite'*. He could hear voices and footsteps above him. He was proud of his motives but intensely scared about what he was going to face. Perin paused with one more rung of the ladder to go before climbing over the top. He breathed deeply into his stinging lungs and tried to swallow down his fear. He could only make one entrance onto the deck of the *Formalite'* and he wanted to make it count. He counted to ten in his head, and then hauled himself over the top as elegantly as he could. He even managed to land on his feet. He smiled at that, and couldn't help but think that the smile would also make him look both unafraid and impressive.

The contrast to the deck of the *Muta* could not have been starker. The deck of the *Formalite'* was as dark as the hull; the black wood had been polished meticulously, the shine making it look closer to coal than it did to wood. That was with the exception of the portions of the hull that had been hastily spliced together with all sorts of materials. These scars from the confrontation with the *Muta* showed it had been repaired with everything from wooden cabinets to leather and shaped steel. Without a forge on board these repairs must have been conducted by Viri. A shiver ran up Perin's spine – he had never considered shaping metal as a potential power. The idea of a metal prison springing up around him made him even more nervous.

It wouldn't have been necessary though. He was surrounded. A tightly packed line of troops with their trademark black leather outfits and helmets formed a semicircle around Perin. Right at the centre of it was Viri, dressed in her identical green that she had when she had boarded the *Muta*. She had a sinister smile on her face and her arms outstretched. This time it wasn't with any magical intent, but a display of supposed welcome. It made Perin's blood run cold.

"Welcome," she proclaimed. "Welcome, welcome." As she walked forward she clasped her hands together and shook them in front of herself in delight. "I can't deny that I was more than a little surprised that your boat appeared on our horizon," she said, licking her lips. Perin looked towards her and locked his eyes with hers; they were also green and reminded him of some carnivorous lizard.

"I won't have anyone else die for me," Perin stated with as much dignity as he could muster. "I am here to cooperate with you, but only if the crew of the *Muta* are no longer pursued and are forgiven any crime you may hold against them."

There was a ripple of discontent from the crew. This was not a popular notion. Viri had not taken her eyes away from Perin and she waited for the ripple of noise amongst the crew to die down.

"I'm afraid," Viri said with insincere sympathy, "that

may simply not be possible." The crew in the rear ranks of the makeshift semicircle who were carrying spears banged the hilt of their weapons against the deck in support. "The crimes of the *Muta* are well known and simply impossible for the Great Committee to turn a blind eye to. They have attacked Great Committee facilities, they have preached seditious and traitorous propaganda against the wishes of the Committee and therefore against the best interests of society. They are criminals and must be treated as such." A cheer began to rise around Viri from rumble to roar. Somehow her voice could still be heard above the cheers. "To do anything else would be to encourage these traits in others!"

One of the soldiers to Viri's left said something along the lines of, "Pirate scum," though Perin was unable to make it out precisely. In the event it didn't matter as Viri outstretched her hand and picked the soldier up by his throat with her long thin fingers. She didn't appear to even strain a muscle in her thin arms. She looked into the soldier's eyes above her. Perin could see that they were terrified even through the leather helmet that covered the majority of his face. Still holding him there, Viri turned back to Perin.

"You see, this soldier is loyal, and preached an opinion I wholeheartedly agree with, but there is to be no talking in my ranks and he spoke. Therefore…"

Her arm became encased in green electricity which snaked up her arm and into the throat of the soldier. It then spread up around his face and down his chest towards his heart. Viri let go, and the soldier crumpled to the floor. There were no signs of life and the rest of the soldiers on deck had fallen into obedient silence.

Despite his fear at the sudden, cruel and emotionless way in which Viri had just turned on her own man, Perin fought to keep his emotions from his face and maintain his attempted show of inner strength. He suspected it may be cracking to those watching but he fought valiantly none the less.

"That may be," he said, gesturing towards the crumpled, smouldering corpse at his feet. He had to fight against coughing at the stench of fried flesh. "This man's death, although dramatic, is not really relevant to the situation." He walked around the corpse and started pacing back and forth as if it were not there. His insides had begun to churn, and he feared he might vomit. "I have broken many of the rules you attribute to the crew of the *Muta*, but I stand here apparently not in any immediate danger—"

"Oh?" Viri said. "Whatever gave you that impression?" The same green electricity began to dance between her fingers as if she were toying with it. Now was the time that Perin knew he had to hold his nerve and make his show or he would be dead in short order.

"Firstly," he began, "because I am still alive and you could have killed me. Secondly," he counted off on his fingers, "because my existence can no longer be denied. The *Muta* will exist long enough to ensure that." Viri's face had begun to fall. "Finally," he concluded, "the offer of my cooperation is on the table. If that is less important to you than the detaining and punishment of a gaggle of pirates and a senile sorcerer, then I do not think you appreciate the potential of your situation." He stood looking directly into those electric green eyes and slowly, Viri nodded.

"We shall continue this discussion in my war room." Turning on her heel she walked to a stairwell leading up towards the rear of the vessel. The troops sprang away from her, clearing a path. Perin quickly, with his hands clasped behind him, walked behind her and followed her up the stairs.

She led him to a large rectangular room. The walls were lined with glass cabinets, inside of which were several heavy glass jars with different coloured transparent liquids or gels and some specimens being preserved. There were skulls of what looked like feline and canine subjects as well as human hands, eyeballs, tails from lizards and various other cuttings from unidentifiable animals. A large table of polished brass with leather edging dominated the centre of the room. There was a green fire crackling in a fireplace at the far end of the room. Perin briefly considered the intelligence behind installing a fireplace on a wooden vessel, but since the flames were green he decided there must be some of Viri's sorcery involved to avoid the fire spreading. The green flames created an eerie macabre light that bounced and reflected off the brass of the table and gave the room, panelled with the same black wood of the rest of the ship, the feel of an underground cave or bunker. Viri looked at home in these surroundings and seated herself at the head of the table. She gestured towards one of the other empty seats.

"Sit," she said. It was definitely an order, but there was still an attempt at pleasantness in her voice. Perin saw no reason to obey directly so chose a different seat. The chair was also lined with brass and was cold to the touch. It made Perin shiver. This made Viri smile.

"Explain to me," she said with a simper, "what you mean exactly by your 'cooperation'." Perin gulped.

"I mean that I will agree to join the Great Committee, as you suggested at our last meeting."

Viri smiled so widely Perin thought it might be magically enhanced. The green light from the fire bouncing off her teeth made it look as if they dripped with an ungodly green blood.

"Really?" she asked. "Perhaps something has changed and you are no longer required on the Committee. Why would we want you? What can you bring?"

Perin began to panic. His entire plan and reasoning for coming to this ship hinged upon his ability to do some good from within the Great Committee – if that opportunity was no longer available then he really was as good as dead.

"I am willing to be tutored in the use of magic by you and the other members of the Committee."

Viri leaned over and opened a hidden drawer that was available on her side of the table. She withdrew a glass and a long thin bottle. She uncorked it and poured a measure of thick amber liquid into her glass. She picked up the glass and swirled the contents. It seemed to thin them out slightly and she took a drink before answering.

"Your willingness is certainly refreshing," she said in a relaxed tone of voice, "but that simply goes without saying. I highly suspect your training is barely in its infancy. Tell me, the large red cloud that led us directly to the *Muta*. Was that Occidens or you?"

"That was me." Viri raised an eyebrow.

"Well I don't deny that that's impressive. What exactly did Occidens do to unlock that power within you?" She leaned forward and folded her elbows on the table in front of her. Perin did not know whether it was prudent to tell Viri what Occidens' methods had entailed. It was entirely possible she had no idea how to teach sorcery and this was a way of convincing Perin to reveal the secret.

"You don't need to worry," she said dismissively, as if reading his mind. "I'm sure Occidens told you that she was the source of my own magical education. At least to start."

Perin considered this and then decided that if he was to continue the conversation and convince Viri that he was amenable to staying here, he would have to answer.

"She sent me up into the crow's nest then created a storm directly above me. I evaporated the cloud with a lightning bolt of my own." He stated this in a factual manner, the way the Great Academy had taught him was the proper way to answer an enquiry. Perhaps if he had stuck to this notion he would never have ended up in this mess.

"That's clever," admitted Viri. "It is true that negative emotion is a good way to inspire the victim to consider all options to discover a method of escape. This inspires creativity which would then, in your case, lead to the igniting of your magical mind. Yes, I have to applaud her for that strategy and if we judge by the red cloud that sprang across the ocean and could be seen from Capital Island, it was a very effective strategy."

"I'm glad you approve," said Perin. He couldn't completely keep the bitterness out of his voice.

"You sound angry about it," Viri said sympathetically. "And of course you should be." She stood up and began pacing her side of the table. "You see, my methods would be somewhat different. The Great Committee is not in the business of making your life, or anyone else's, unnecessarily unpleasant. If your spark could be ignited through negative emotion and self-preservation, it stands to reason that it could also be ignited by the opposite. Extreme pleasure and confidence could also lead to its use."

"If that's true, why wouldn't Occidens have done that?" Perin asked disbelievingly.

"Well," Viri said with a slightly pouted lip, "not to be cruel, but we have better resources at our command. If you are to learn magic with us you will be treated to the finest gold, clothes, servants and all manner of…" she smiled, "stimuli a young man could desire."

Perin was well aware what she was offering and he was tempted by the idea but still couldn't get the notion out of his head that this was all too good to be true.

"What if it's not effective? Would you go back to the more negative methods?" Perin asked. Viri pursed her lips as if considering her reply.

"No, the truth is that even if your magical abilities do not come to fruition, the idea that a new Sorcerer of Caramine has come to us will still be a strong facility for maintaining our power base. The truth is we would likely create the myth that you are a sorcerer even if you turned out not to be so. You would still live in the lap of luxury for your cooperation."

"But I would not be a member of the Great Committee?" Perin asked.

"Not really," she replied. "You would be a member in name alone and for display purposes only." Although Perin liked the idea of relative comfort and ease in life, he realised that this meant complicity in the Great Committee's actions with no chance of changing them. He was being bought off.

"What if I refused that offer?" he asked. Viri put her glass down and looked at Perin with a sinister smile. The flames in the fire turned red, which changed the complexion of the room entirely.

"Then you would be killed, in some very painful and public way as a heretic and a criminal," she said simply. "Anything else?"

It was at this moment that Perin realised he had made a tremendous mistake and wished that he could take his actions back and return to the *Muta*.

As if in response, the world turned upside down. At first Perin thought he had been overcome with dizziness or had fallen from his chair, but the chair had in fact fallen from the deck. Perin and Viri had been thrown to the floor as the room itself had lurched sideways. The table slid across the room and crashed into the glass cabinets on the left wall. Perin was drenched in the bitter-smelling chemicals from the broken jars and he felt the prickling of pain on his skin as the shards of glass struck him and pierced his arms and face. He tried to get to his feet but the floor was no longer where it should be. The ship was not resting the way it should; it had partially capsized. As he got to his feet at the opposite end of the room Viri emerged from beneath her own pile of broken apparel. She was incandescent with fury. She had a cut on her head and the red of her blood ran down her face towards the green neckline of her blouse.

"You!" she screamed. "You appear to have more magic in you than you led me to believe! I think you need to be dealt with now!"

Perin attempted to shout that this was not his doing, but Viri had extended her hand towards the green fire and siphoned the flames off into her own hand. The fire moved as if pulled by some precise wind under Viri's control, the flames not hurting her but seeming to answer to her command. She raised her arm to throw them at Perin, but once again the world shifted beneath their feet, this time in the opposite direction, and threw them, the remains of the glass cabinets and the table into the right-hand wall. More glass shattered and more horrible-smelling chemicals and animal remains rained down upon them.

"This is not me!" Perin screamed from the floor. "We must be under attack!"

"That damned old woman!" Viri exclaimed. "This must be your friends from the *Muta*. You planned this all along! I'll kill them, and then Committee be damned, I'm going to kill you!"

As she scrambled to get to her feet her skirts which had tangled around her legs, caused her to stumble. Perin was closer to the door and crawled in agony across the broken glass to stay ahead of Viri. *Could she be right? Is the* Muta *outside? I didn't want them to rescue me,* he thought as he proceeded to the door. As he reached the deck he heard Viri scream and the war room become engulfed in green flames. *The flames must have ignited one of the chemicals,* he thought. *She must be dead.* He was horrified to see the flames part and Viri walked out with evil intentions burning in her eyes. At that moment Perin changed his mind and began to hope that the *Muta* had come to rescue him.

CHAPTER FIFTEEN

The rage in Viri's face was incandescent, the very shape of her features changed and contorted. Her cheekbones were higher and more pointed, the teeth that had smiled at Perin earlier were now bared in fury, and the green light that danced in her hands lit her face from below and made her look like a terrible demon. Her eyes bore down on Perin preparing for the kill like some enraged bird of prey.

Perin realised it was dark outside and a storm had gathered, blotting out the sun. Viri's chaotic anger had stirred the elements as violently as Occidens' storm had done, perhaps even more so.

"You," she shrieked, "will pay with blood for this attempted ruse of yours!" She sent a blast from her hand towards Perin who was still on his hands and knees. He rolled out of the way but felt the heat scorch the wood where he had been. "Your sincerity in there impressed me!" she said, as she sent another bolt of fire, Perin rolling again and scrambling backwards to try and escape. "I thought for a moment you actually intended to join us!" Sparks joined the flames in her hand as she sent another volley at Perin's head; he ducked but this time the fire grazed his arm and he felt a searing pain. The fire was no longer just green flame, but white lightning coursed within it, sizzling the air around them. Perin screamed and held his arm to his chest as Viri bore down on him. "You are nothing but a little fool if you thought that I had any intention of allowing you to be part of our great society!" she fumed. "We have fought for generations to stamp out the anarchic origins of those fledgling little powers of yours and now you will be snuffed out as if you never existed!"

She raised her hands to make a final strike. Perin closed his eyes. He knew his only chance was to summon a shield like Occidens had created to block out her assault, but when he pictured Viri in his mind's eye all he could imagine was her fearsome face and the pain in his arm and how it was about to spread to the rest of his body. The crack of thunder and the rush of fire and electricity came and Perin waited for oblivion, but nothing happened. For a second he considered that he might have been successful and defended himself with a blue sphere of light as Occidens had, but as he opened his eyes what he saw was even more fantastic.

Rienta stood in between Viri and Perin, her legs a wide stance apart. She held her sword outstretched horizontally in front of her at chest height. It was absorbing Viri's attack. The flames and electricity seemed to be soaked up by the sword, which vibrated in her hand and shone a comforting blue light. She wore a tight-fitting leather burgundy jacket and leather trousers. This was combat attire of a much younger woman than the captain. Her face was still as old as it had been when they first met, with many lines and her short white hair slightly thinning. It was lit by a combination of the green light of the flames and the blue light coming from her sword. She had a look of determination in her blue eyes and Viri's brow was furrowed in intense concentration. Rienta took a step forward which seemed to increase the pressure of the fire and light that crackled between the two women.

"Perin, don't you recognise a rescue when you see one?" Rienta shouted. "Get out of here!" Not needing to be told again Perin got up and searched the ocean for the *Muta*. He didn't see it. That was a surprise.

"Don't you need any help?" he shouted towards the captain.

"Against this weedy little witch," she said with a smile, "I should think not!" With that, and what appeared to be a great strain, she took another step forward that pushed Viri back through the door of her ruined study. She then pulled her sword upwards which caused the lightning and fire to hit the roof of the room, causing it to explode in flame and crackling energy. Although Viri could clearly withstand fire, Perin thought that the collapse of so much rubble on top of her should be the end of it. Rienta fell to one knee, gasping for breath. Perin rushed over to help but she held out her hand to stop him.

"I said get out of here! I'll take care of Viri if she comes out."

The crew of the *Formalite'* were still attempting to gather and right themselves from the attempted capsizing of the ship. Many had lost their weapons along with their footing or had been injured. At the opposite end of the ship, at the bow, Perin noticed one other recognisable figure amongst the chaos on deck. Stim was battling a dozen of the *Formalite's* crew. He was using one of them held by the legs as a clubbing weapon. The poor crew member was still conscious and wailed as he was flung around into his friends and comrades.

"Stim!" shouted Perin, attempting to get the giant man's attention. He did not cease his assault but did smile as he continued to rotate his makeshift club around his head.

"Perin, my lad!" Stim said with enthusiasm. "Sorry it took us so long! Occidens took some time to come round and tell us why you'd left!"

"I'm so glad to see you," he said, and he meant it. He couldn't help but smile despite the chaos. "But the whole point was to keep you all out of any more danger!"

"Yeah, about that," he said, throwing the now limp crewman into the few remaining enemies standing and making his way to Perin. "The Great Committee being bloodthirsty morons ain't your fault," he said, putting his giant hands on Perin's shoulders, "and what we do with ourselves is our own business!"

"But—"

"We did, however, think you would appreciate as little risk as possible in your rescue, so it's just me and the captain over there!" he said and punched an approaching crew member so hard he was thrown backwards and knocked six remaining attackers overboard with one shot.

"Just the two of you?" Perin was confused. "Then what happened when you boarded?"

Stim looked a little sheepish. "I'm afraid things didn't go entirely according to plan." He looked at his hands. "I was supposed to tip the boat over from the dingy, but I only got halfway before our little boat collapsed and we had to climb on board."

That explained the chaos, but Perin had to admit, as far as distractions went it had been exceptionally effective.

"Where's the captain?" Stim asked, glancing around.

"She buried Viri in a mountain of smouldering wood," Perin replied with satisfaction. "She was waiting to see if she came out."

Stim looked concerned. "We have to go and help her!"

"She seemed to have matters well in hand."

"Don't you remember what Occidens taught you?" Stim urged. "Only magic can kill magic! Rienta may have a charged-up sword, but its charge will wear out long before Viri's magic does!" He started to take great strides towards the shattered rear of the vessel where Perin had left the old woman.

As they made their way to where Perin had left Rienta,

across broken shards of wood and bodies that Stim had knocked unconscious, they could see that although Viri had not reappeared from the rubble of her study the captain was engaged with seven of the *Formalite*'s crew, all armed with swords of their own. Perin had never seen anything so impressive. There was a faint whistle in the air as Rienta's blade flashed so quickly that although Perin could make out its arc it no longer looked like a blade, but like lightning flashing around the old woman who was twirling and striking. Although it was fast, it was elegant. It was what Perin imagined dancing must have looked like. Stim approached from the rear and knocked two of the attackers' heads together as if he was doing nothing more than throwing aside a used chicken bone. This was less elegant but undeniably effective. Rienta slashed at one of the assailants and he looked down at his torso to see what had happened. He then fell to the deck and blood seeped through his dark leather. Rienta vaulted over the body and kicked another assailant in the chest. They had worked their way close to the side of the boat and with a straight kick she sent another assailant over the side with a satisfying splash. As two more headed towards her, Stim lifted the final assailant up over his head and threw him towards them. All three fell to the deck in a tangle of flailing limbs.

Perin could hear commotion from below the deck as presumably the other members of the crew were preparing to join the fray.

"Stim," he shouted. "Below decks!" He signalled towards the opening that led to the crew cabins. Stim started towards it as if to jump down and take them all in closed quarters.

"No!" shouted Rienta. "Just cut them off so we can get out of here!" Stim nodded and went looking for a large barrel or piece of debris that could be used to cover the hatch. Perin and Rienta stood together in the first moment of calm since they arrived. The old woman was a little out of breath but held her composure.

"I must apologise to you, Perin," she said with sincere feeling.

"No, you don't need to. I ran away," he replied, dropping his head.

"You ran because of what I said," she continued, "and because you wished to protect your friends and the crew. That's understandable and laudable." She smiled at him. "I'm very proud of you for those actions."

Perin welled up with tears and respect for the captain. Occidens had been right. She had a magic of her own in inspiring loyalty.

"That being said," she had changed her tone of voice and Perin expected reproach, "it was an undeniably stupid thing to attempt to do. What did you hope to accomplish, other than suicide?"

"I thought I could join the Committee and change things from the inside like Viri said," he admitted, lowering his head.

"Oh, Perin," Rienta said, shaking her head. "That has been tried before."

Perin was aghast. He had no idea. "Someone joined the Committee to change things? What happened?"

"He became the worst of them. He was corrupted by their ideas and their methods and he eventually became their leader." She fixed Perin with her blue eyes. "The head of the Great Committee started out life exactly the same way as you."

Perin was astounded and found it too hard to fathom. No one had really spoken about the leader of the Great Committee before now.

"Why tell me this now?"

"Because you are not a child, and you both deserve and can handle the truth of all these matters. You are the future, and I am determined to defend it."

"That is where you are wrong," came a shrill and venomous voice. Both Rienta and Perin turned to see Viri emerging from the rubble, bringing herself from one knee to full height. She was bleeding from her temple and her skirt was badly torn and stained with blood. She held her arm to her stomach. It looked to be broken.

"He is the future, and you are the past," Rienta said, facing up to the injured sorcerer. "In fact, I would say your time is just about done."

"Old woman," Viri shook her head, eyes still blazing with green fury, "you don't know what you are talking about. This boy cannot be the future because he will be stopped. He will be diverted and if that fails he will be killed! I know this because I will do it myself!"

She was clearly badly wounded. As she moved around one of her feet was dragging and as she spoke blood spattered her teeth. Far from making her seem less threatening though, Perin felt more intimidated than he had when she was in her regal finery.

"You are a spent force," Rienta said as she gestured towards Viri. "Look at you – bruised, battered and holding on through sheer stubbornness. You're no threat to Perin. We will move him forward. We will keep him on course. He won't be killed because my entire crew will lay down their lives to defend him."

"Is that so?" Viri asked, then in one swift movement she pulled a dagger that had been hidden in the sleeve of her injured arm and threw it directly at Perin. It was so fast, he couldn't have moved out of the way of the throw and he covered his face instinctively and shut his eyes.

He waited for the pain, for the oblivion to take him, but for the second time it didn't come. He opened his eyes, and what he saw made him wish the dagger had struck him clean in the chest.

Rienta stood in between Perin and Viri with the silver hilt of the dagger protruding from above her heart. She looked down at the weapon and put her hand on the blade; with a wince she pulled it out of her body and threw it to the ground. Her breathing was wheezy and she was struggling to maintain her balance. Perin moved forward to hold her up but she held her arm out to indicate that he should stay back.

"Yes, Viri," she said with breathless gasps. "We will all lay down our lives for Perin."

"Good to know," snarled Viri and she thrust her uninjured hand forward. There was a gust of air and Rienta was lifted from her feet and thrown backwards. Her legs hit the side of the deck and she tumbled silently over the side of the ship like a child's toy falling from a shelf. It was followed by the inevitable splash. The sound took some of Perin's soul with it. He felt numb. He couldn't take his eyes away from the spot where Rienta had fallen. At least, not until the pain came. He was overcome with a white pain that made him open his mouth to scream but no sound came forward. Viri had ignited her hand with green electricity and had struck Perin in the side of the head with it. She now stood over him, lit with a terrifying green light.

"Who is going to keep you moving forward now?" she shrieked at him mockingly. She struck him directly in the face. Perin lost control of his limbs. They no longer responded to his brain with the electric shot. He couldn't see, but he could tell Viri was still bearing down on him.

"Who is going to keep you on course?" she screamed, hitting him in the face again. This time he lost control of his body completely, vomiting onto the deck as Viri cackled over him.

"Well, there's still me!" came the roaring reply from somewhere to Perin's right. As his eyes came back into focus, he saw Stim standing square in front of Viri ready for a conflict. *He knows he can't win,* thought Perin. *Only magic can kill magic.* Hot tears streamed down his face as he tried to push himself up from the deck. Viri had turned her back on the fallen Perin and was bearing down on her new prey, Stim. She looked like a hawk circling. The light still shone from her uninjured hand. It flashed outward and sent a flaming crackle of green-white electricity at the hulking mass. Stim screamed an animalistic scream but stayed on his feet.

"Impressive," said Viri, "but I think I can burn through the rest of Occidens' magic in quick order. At least then you can go and join the old captain without delay."

"Rienta?" Stim said. He obviously had not realised she had been killed and some of the fight seemed to go out of him as he stood there. As Perin managed to get to one knee he thought that Stim had actually shrunk in front of him.

"She died defending your precious future," Viri snarled. "I'm going to kill you, and then put an end to him and this whole nasty business."

"No more," Perin said. He had managed to get to his feet, though it would take nothing more than a feather to knock him down again. Viri turned and the smile she had been holding on her face faded a little when she saw he was up.

"It seems you are not without your talents," she observed, though some of the confidence had gone.

"No more," Perin repeated. He could feel the anger swelling in him. The anger, loss and grief were all swirling together inside him to form an incandescent blood-red rage.

"You can't possibly understand what you are dealing with," she said, though there was definitely a tone of concern to her voice now.

"No MORE!" Perin screamed. This time he threw his hands in the air and red lightning exploded from them, as it had done when he had fought the storm. As the clouds above turned blood red and burned off, allowing the sun to break through again, Perin looked at Viri, who looked at him with fear. Perin had never felt so powerful, but his own feelings scared him. This was the woman who had killed Rienta and there was only one thing that he wanted to do in that moment. He pointed his hand towards the sorcerer and red lightning erupted from the tips of his fingers towards her heart. His imagination had been incredibly vivid: he wanted to watch her writhe in the pain that he had felt at her hand and then burn a hole straight through her where her knife had pierced his friend.

It wasn't quite meant to be though. Viri threw her hand across her chest, creating a cross. A green electrical shield sprung up between her and Perin. Her arm was still injured and had not had quite the desired effect. Although she had deflected the blast it ripped through her shield and struck home on the mainsail of the *Formalite'*. The material burst into flames and quickly spread to the crow's nest and the beams that held up the sails.

Viri lay on the ground unconscious. The force of the blast that ripped through her defences had thrown her to the deck. Perin stood bathed in the warmth from the inferno he had helped create. He was brought back to reality when he was picked up by Stim, who barrelled towards the side of the boat and leaped into the air.

For a brief second Perin considered that Stim may have the ability to fly, but it was simply that the power in his legs was able to launch them further in the air than any normal man could possibly have jumped. They landed with a thud and Perin realised they were in one of the ship's rowboats, which must have either been cut loose or shaken free.

"We gotta get outta here," he panted. "There's gunpowder on that thing, enough to blow up half the ocean." He set two oars up on the rowboat and sat down to begin the work of their escape. With each row the small craft lurched forward and within a few short minutes the *Formalite'* was simply a red stain on the horizon as it burned. As Perin looked back and couldn't help thinking that somewhere under the water was the lifeless body of the captain of the *Muta*. The woman who had come to save him. Now he would have to go back to the ship and explain why it no longer had its captain. Making matters worse, the explosion that would signal the end of the

Formalite' never came.

    Perin put his head in his hands and wept.

CHAPTER SIXTEEN

Hot tears streamed down Stim's face. As Perin looked at the hulking yet broken man rowing them forward with such strength while his eyes showed nothing but devastating loss, it only resulted in heightening his own pain. The contrast between the tension in his muscles pulling against the oars and the release of despair flowing down his face and matting his beard with salty teardrops made it impossible for Perin to do anything else but join him. He couldn't even comfort Stim with an arm or a hand as he was still rowing them to safety.

"How am I going to tell Occidens?" Stim managed to mumble between sobs. Perin hesitated a second. He knew that Occidens had let Rienta and Stim know about Perin's reasons for leaving the *Muta* but he didn't know to what extent she was otherwise lucid.

"How was Occidens when you left the *Muta*?" Perin enquired, wiping away the tears from his face. Perhaps changing the subject to something else would help them both focus. Stim looked confused for a moment and then Perin's query seemed to make sense to him.

"Oh, she's all right. She came out of her stupor. She

was just mentally frazzled," he said with a sniff. "She had to picture each of the attackers well enough that she could imagine them being thrown off the decks by her shield. That takes an incredible amount of concentration and her mind isn't as young and springy as it used to be." He looked as though he was about to quote Rienta but had stopped himself. He looked away and closed his eyes to the tears and continued to row. Perin was amazed by the feat that Occidens had pulled off and was relieved that she had made a full recovery. Somehow, his face simply refused to show it at that moment.

"Why didn't she just imagine a lightning bolt or a tornado?" he asked. "That would have done the same job." He tried to imagine how he could have saved the ship in the way Occidens had and this seemed the only feasible option to him. There was no way he could picture the attackers, distinguishing one from the other but he could probably conjure the image of a lightning strike, fire bolt or some other destructive force.

Stim looked at him with some confusion. "Occidens' shield passed through the rest of us – she only pictured the people she wanted to harm. A tornado would have just ripped through the whole ship."

Perin understood and that brought the conversation to something of an impasse. The two simply sat in each other's silent company. Perin could see Stim's mind linger on thoughts of his fallen captain. Perhaps that was what was written on his own face as well.

The water was clear and relatively calm. Perin's throat was dry, making him thirsty, and the sun overhead was making him sweat. Stim looked to be wilting under the sun as well. Given his exertion on the *Formalite'* and the time he had been rowing it was entirely possible he was running out of his magical charge. Perin had no idea how long a full charge would last and didn't know if Occidens had revived him fully before the rescue mission. For some reason it seemed impolite to ask. It would only draw attention to his waning strength. As time wore further on the giant's head began to drop and his hair became drenched in sweat. His level of exertion had started to rise. Perin was afraid he would have to take over the rowing soon once Stim's breathing started to wheeze.

As the sun receded from its zenith at midday, Perin saw a form appearing on the horizon. He couldn't make it out and Stim turned to see if he would have better luck. He let out a tired and relieved, "Ahhhh." Moments later Perin was filled with indescribable relief as the welcoming form of the *Muta* grew up out of the ocean. It started with the mast. When Perin left, it had been missing in action, having been cut in half by Rienta. It was an impressive memory but gave him a stab of pain and guilt to remember the captain at her finest and fullest powers.

"Where did you get the mast?" Perin asked, intrigued. Stim had taken on a little more colour, presumably because the end was in sight for his labours. He had started to row harder again but it took considerable visible effort.

"Fished the old one out the sea," he said breathlessly. "Curved some steel round it and Occidens used magic to bolt it in place." He was taking gaps in between words, each time making another row with the oars. "It's not at a hundred per cent, but it'll hold till we get to a port."

The *Muta* had noticed their approach and was turning to meet them. As it looked close to them the knot in Perin's stomach tightened. In minutes he would have to tell the crew and Occidens that their friend and captain had been slain defending him. He didn't know how he could cope with the guilt or even how they would react. *If I were them I'd throw me right back into the water. They've lost so much because of me.* He then gave himself a shake. Those thoughts had led to matters being worse, not better. Rienta had told him so herself and she had also made clear that everyone on the *Muta* was choosing their own path. Perin wanted to help them with their mission. He wanted to help them create a world where everyone could have that choice, even if that did mean slaying the leader of the Great Committee, the last failed hope. He was determined not to repeat those mistakes.

They drew the boat up against the side of the *Muta*. Its wooden panel was a pleasing shade of brown in comparison to the *Formalite'*, the colour of milk chocolate. The wood looked fabulous in the sunlight, and made the Muta feel warm and welcoming. A long rope ladder descended to meet them and Stim tied it off against the boat. He put one foot onto the bottom rung and then hung his head and breathed in deeply. Perin watched him. He had known this crew and indeed Rienta for so much longer than Perin. *This must be destroying him.* Perin moved forward and, with a stretch, put a hand on Stim's broad shoulder. Without looking up to face him, Stim moved his other hand across and placed it on top of Perin's. It was rough and calloused but warm and gentle in equal measure.

"The captain liked you," he said. "She respected us all, and we all loved her, and by the devil we are going to miss her as a captain and a friend."

"I'm sorry," was all Perin could find to say as tears welled up in his eyes. He had meant it to sound comforting – he was trying to apologise for Stim's loss – but as the words came out of his mouth he found that he was apologising again for this all being his fault.

"My point is," Stim continued, still not looking up, "I think it's unfair how much pressure you've been put under, being treated like a saviour." He turned to face him, "but that's how it is, you don't have any control over that, no more than I do. What you do have control over is the kind of person you are, with that hand being dealt to you, and as I see it, you played that hand the way the boss liked." He smiled at him. "You could do worse but not much better."

Perin lost all sense of composure and threw his arms around the big man. His speech was always plain but he had a kindness to his voice. Perin had never considered he would show wisdom and compassion of that kind, particularly at a time of such pain and loss. Stim put a hand on the young man's shoulder before straightening up and looking up the ladder towards the deck above.

"The next bit ain't gonna be fun," he said. Straightening up he continued, "The captain would never have run away from something because it wasn't fun, and we won't either!" Without another word he started to climb. Perin felt a warmth inside him that hadn't been there before. It couldn't undo the horrible knot he still felt in his gut but it gave him the courage to continue. He followed Stim up the ladder.

As they reached the top Stim went over first and a cheer went up from the crowd. The pit of Perin's stomach dropped a little at that. He hesitated and took a breath before he vaulted over too. He would not have been able to do that when he first arrived but he appeared to be developing some muscle and losing some weight.

He was met with complete silence when his feet hit the ground. One look at Stim's face had already conveyed that there was bad news to the crew. There was a noticeable feeling of relief when Perin followed Stim over; obviously many had considered that they had found him already dead or that it was he who had been killed in the escape. A few silent, horrible moments passed as the crew looked towards the point from where Stim and Perin had just returned. No one followed.

"How?" croaked a voice from one side. It was Occidens. She looked a little more worn than before her ordeal, but a hundred thousand times better than directly following it. She had always walked with a stick but Perin thought she leaned on it a bit harder now. In fact, as dawning realisation crept into the old woman's eyes it appeared to be the only thing holding her up.

"Viri," answered Stim. "Got her with a throwing knife." The confirmation sent a wave of despair through the crew. Grown men were so stunned they dropped their weapons in disbelief. Some cried in each other's arms. Perin needed to help in some way, but he also felt they needed and deserved the true and full story.

"Rienta died the most honourable death she could imagine," he stated, and the despairing crowd silenced. "She died defending me. Viri threw her dagger at me and she stood in front of it so that the hope she believed in could continue to live." The crew looked towards him, and Perin knew that their despair could easily turn into anger against him. "Up until that point I did not know how I felt about that belief," he explained. "Now I do. I will be the person that Rienta thought I could be. I shall do this to honour her and to defend you. She will never be forgotten as long as I am here to remember her."

The crew did something Perin could never have expected. Through their grief, they cheered. With tears in their eyes and new pain still forming inside them, they threw their arms in the air and cheered. Perin was shocked by the display but felt glad that he seemed to have comforted them. One person who did not cheer was Occidens. She looked at Perin as if she had seen him for the first time. She looked kindly towards him but her eyes still had the deadened expression that can only be brought on by an intense loss. When the commotion had died down she stepped forward.

"How did you escape?" she asked. Stim appeared to take it upon himself to relay the next part of the story.

"Perin unleashed a torrent of red lightning at the witch. It burst through her defences and set fire to every inch of the mast. It blazed like an inferno, like—"

"Wait a minute," Occidens interrupted, turning to Perin, her eyes momentarily dancing alive again. "You blasted through a shield she conjured?"

"Yes," Perin said, "though her arm was injured so it wasn't as strong as it could have been."

"My dear boy," Occidens beamed. "Magic is not decided by the strength of one's arm! Did you imagine breaking through her shield?" She was frantically excited.

"No, she didn't conjure it until after I had created the bolt." He hesitated before adding, "I was envisaging blasting her." He was a bit guilty about his admitted bloodlust so added, "But she had just killed the captain."

"Perin," Occidens said gravely, "I don't think anyone here would begrudge you a little retribution, particularly if you remember that the witch was attempting to also kill you at the time!" The crew nodded in agreement and murmured their consent. "My point is, dear boy, that your will shattered hers. That's a breakthrough I could never have taught you!"

"I was really angry," Perin said, a little confused, "Perhaps that played a part in it."

"I don't think you realise the significance of this, Perin," Occidens said, her eyes glowing. "You had seen your friend murdered, that is definitely a source of huge emotion and would lead to a very vivid image of you destroying that smug green little face clean from the face of the planet, but you overcame the will and imagination of a lifetime sorcerer, who was acting in defence of her own life! That is serious magic, even if she did partially succeed in deflecting the bolt!"

"I suppose," Perin said tentatively.

"Don't you understand, dear boy?" she implored. "*They* will be absolutely terrified! We now have a weapon. Yes untrained and untested, but that just makes you even more dangerous in their eyes! They now think, they now *know,* we are winning!"

The crew, who had been listening intently, erupted in a passionate fervour. They were still devastated by the loss of Rienta but this news, along with a little bloodlust, had given them new hope and purpose. Perin felt vindication and acceptance again. He had finally put the guilt he felt over the original attack to bed. He would, however, have to continue to deal with the guilt over the captain's death. Occidens stepped forward to address the crew directly. If

Perin wasn't mistaken she was attempting to stand as Rienta would have stood and speak like Rienta would have spoken. A big part of their mission going forward would be attempting to keep the morale and spirits of the crew high.

"Rienta would not want us to stand around here waiting for something to happen," Occidens announced. "If you don't mind, I will take Perin and Stim into private counsel and we will decide how to proceed. We are dangerously close to Capital Island and our first priority must be to put some safe distance between it and us." She turned back to Perin and Stim, who looked so exhausted he might fall over. "If you gentlemen wouldn't mind joining me in my study." She hobbled off towards the door of her sanctum. As Perin looked around at the crew he realised that the talk of being in danger and close to the capital had scared the crew and made them nervous. It had deflated the energy, not enhanced it. Perin remembered the conversation with Occidens where she had described Rienta's ability to inspire and motivate those under her command. Perin realised that Occidens did not have this power, at least not with words. The more he considered it the more he thought *he* might.

Words have always been my friends, he thought. *Perhaps they can also be my tools.* He stepped forward to the nervous crowd.

"Friends," he started with arms wide. "Captain Rienta would also have wanted us to go forward without fear, without hesitation and without doubt. I know what it's like to have wrestled with this. After the initial assault when we lost long-time friends and colleagues, I was overcome with guilt and doubt at my own worth to you. That is why I decided to leave you." There was a murmur of objection from the crew and Perin knew he was doing the right thing. "The captain came to me during the rescue and reminded me of something very important." The mention of Rienta had silenced the crowd. "She reminded me that all men and women on this ship choose to give their loyalty and service. You are all loyal and courageous people whom I am honoured to serve with. I will do everything I can to be worthy of the trust and faith you have placed in me. Together, we shall succeed." He paused. *That was enough substance – time to finish with a theatrical flourish.* "Those bastards won't know what hit them!" he said with a raised voice.

The response was instant and miraculous. The crew cheered once again and chanted Perin's name. As that naturally faded the crew dispersed and busied themselves readying the ship, checking everything was in good shape should it be called upon. Perin felt a hand upon his shoulder. It was a large, heavy hand. Stim had remained behind him the whole time.

"You did well," he said. "The boss would have been proud of you." He looked as if he were about to collapse. Perin realised that placing his hand on his shoulder wasn't just a show of affection – he was in fear of collapsing and needed Perin's help to get to Occidens' study. Perin allowed his shoulder to be used as a crutch and they very slowly made their way across the deck as inconspicuously as possible. It was not easy with someone so large and who weighed as much as Stim but they did eventually reach the door, which Occidens had left open, and entered to plan their next move.

Luke Brady

CHAPTER SEVENTEEN

As soon as they had made their way through the door Stim collapsed into the closest chair he could find. A cloud of dust rose from the chair as it creaked violently in protest. The old woman was busying herself at her desk making something to drink.

"Occidens," called Stim, his voice thinner than Stim had ever heard it. "If you would be so kind, I'm dying over here." Occidens turned round with a steaming clay cup in her hands. Perin didn't think she looked particularly sympathetic towards the big man. She walked forward and handed him the cup.

"Drink this and stop being a baby," she said, with a smile creeping to the edge of her mouth. "You think if I don't have you magic-infused to the gills all the time you are going to fall apart." She leaned down towards him. "What you are feeling right now is simple fatigue. You've had an ordeal and haven't slept. You're tired, you lummox!"

Stim looked chastened as he drank from the steaming cup. "What's this?"

"It's tea." Occidens sighed. "A restorative infusion of

172

hot water through some plant leaves. If it is truly a revelation to you then you're dimmer than I thought."

Perin instinctively started to laugh. He loved both of these people and he had missed them. He was also intensely relieved to see Occidens back to her old self. Without warning though, his laughter turned to tears as his thoughts came to Rienta. She would have watched the conversation between Stim and Occidens with a fold of her arms and a roll of her eyes. Perin missed that too. Occidens made her way over to him and put her arms around the young man. She smelled like heavily scented flowers. Once Perin's nose adapted to the initial burn it was oddly comforting.

"We miss her too," said Occidens with soft understanding. "But we must look at getting the ship out of danger." Perin nodded and breathed in deeply with a sniff and then fought successfully to regain his composure. Occidens looked at him with a piercing stare and then nodded. Straightening up with the hint of a groan she made her way to her desk and picked up a long roll of worn, fragile parchment. She brought it to her copper-coloured desk and spread it out and placed a clay mug on each corner to stop it springing back. Perin recognised it immediately; it was a larger, more detailed version of the maps he had seen at the Great Academy and was moulded into his desk in his quarters below deck. This was Caramine in all its splendour.

The map was dominated by the two great landmasses of Upper and Lower Caramine. The continent had once been in one piece but had been ripped harshly along the centre by a great land quake. To west was a series of small islands surrounding the heavily fortified Capital Island. To the south of that was the Great Academy. The eastern side of the map showed two other major islands, The Hammer and The Anvil, which housed the military and prison facilities respectively.

"First things first," Perin said, "where are we?" He had

only just realised that in relation to everything else he was completely clueless as to how far they had come or what they were near to. Occidens leaned over the table and stretched out with a groan, placing the tip of a stubby finger on the parchment.

"Here," she said, "give or take a few miles." Perin peered over her shoulder and saw that she had not been lying when she said they were dangerously close to Capital Island. They lay in the centre of the ocean between three points. The Great Academy lay south, Port Kennedia lay east and Capital Island lay north.

"When we first rescued you from the Academy," she said, pointing to it, "the plan was to stock up at Port Kennedia, which we did, and then slowly hug the coastline and try to sneak past Capital Island and round the north coast of Upper Caramine. It would be treacherous in itself, and long, but we thought we could keep it all quiet enough to get round. It would also have allowed me the time I thought I would need to train you."

"Where are we trying to get to?" Perin said, scratching his head. Occidens raised an eyebrow but smiled.

"You will find, dear boy, that the destination is almost always less important than the state of arrival. However, we have found that Port Antez is always a friendly port with little Committee interference."

Perin looked at the map and saw that the port Occidens was talking about was on the far side of Upper Caramine. It was unnervingly close to The Hammer and The Anvil but had a small island that almost completely shielded it from them.

"On that small island," Occidens explained, following his gaze, "is a watchtower that signals when official vessels are approaching. It gives plenty of time to scarper if required."

"So is that where you came from on your voyage to get me?" Occidens nodded. "Did you come round the north coast on your way here?"

"Ah," she said, "no, we came the south route past the chains." Perin's eyes glanced towards the south of the map. A land mass disappeared off the bottom end that was marked 'The Anchor', and there was a dotted line that ran across the ocean towards Lower Caramine. This was the established trade route between the eastern ocean and the west. Ships would approach the titanic Iron Chains, each link as large as a galleon. They would send an envoy to the shore that would state their business and arrange for the links to be dropped.

"How did you manage that?" Perin gaped.

"Rienta," Occidens replied simply. Perin understood; Rienta could have used a diplomatic turn of phrase to convince the guards that they were humble traders with goods to sell or drop off.

"I take it we couldn't go back that way?" Perin asked.

"That was never the plan even when Rienta was still here." She paused, lowering her head. "It would have been too risky – they would know to look for us after the commotion we caused at the Academy."

Perin thought for a moment, and accepted they couldn't go back that way. The north route would be too dangerous as the Committee would definitely now be on the lookout for them.

"What about the far east?" Perin speculated. "What is there beyond the edge of the map? Could we escape and find harbour? Friends?"

Occidens beamed at Perin and he concluded that he had found the answer. "We could escape that way!" she exclaimed. "But we'd be dead," she concluded with a frown. "But I am increasingly impressed by your creativity." Perin was downcast despite the compliment.

"Why? What's out there?"

Occidens paused and screwed up her eyes in concentration, considering how best to answer the question.

"The entire terrain of Caramine is set up to the

Committee's advantage. Don't you agree?"

"Well they've been in charge of things for a very long time – they've used the land to their advantage." Perin shrugged. Occidens shook her ancient head.

"You misunderstand them, dear boy. Don't you think everything on this map is just a little too neat?" She gestured at the map. "Capital Island, the Great Academy, The Anchor, The Anvil, The Hammer," she recited. "All a little convenient wouldn't you say?"

"So they named everything?" Perin said with confusion; he couldn't understand what Occidens was pushing at.

"You're halfway there," she said. "They didn't just *name* the islands."

"They created them?" Perin said, his eyes widening with realisation.

"That's right," Occidens nodded. "You see, when the Great Committee was first formed, they needed a seat of power. So they raised Capital Island from the ocean. Caramine was still one continent then and it was the source of population, food, resources, et cetera, as it is today. When the people saw what the sorcerers had done, they were terrified and decided to stop them. So they gathered their boats into a fleet and sailed for Capital Island. The Committee crushed that rebellion by waiting until the ships were in sight and then raising up other jagged crags and slivers of island around them to wreck and ruin the ships from underneath. The plan worked, which is why Capital Island is so well fortified."

Perin was entranced and aghast in equal measure. This was a version of history that had never been conveyed to him at the Great Academy. As far as he had known, geographical fact had never been questioned or queried.

"How do you know this?" he asked.

"Dear boy, haven't you fathomed how incredibly old both I and the Committee members are?" she said, exasperated. "With the exception of their young leader, the

Great Committee is the same then as it is now. They don't age and only magic can kill magic. I was there, dear boy!"

Perin stared open-mouthed at Occidens. "Did you fight in the battle?" She turned away and looked at her hands.

"No," she said slowly. "I had declared myself uninvolved at the time. I still wanted to believe that some of these sorcerers were good people. We had learned our craft together. It was this incident that roused me to action." Perin decided it was best not to continue with that particular line of conversation; he could tell that it upset Occidens to consider it.

"What has this got to do with what's in the far east?" he asked.

"After the rebellion was quashed," she said, ignoring Perin's question, "the Committee became extremely paranoid and created the chains to cut off attack from the south. Viri was convinced that strength of arms was the way to ensure an obedient populace so she raised The Hammer from the ocean. Seus considered the threat of punishment to be more useful and created The Anvil. It was Mistress Rumbrum, however, that had the most effective and yet most immoral approach. It was her idea that by controlling how children were raised, what they learned and what they were permitted to do afterwards would pay reliable dividends in the future. She created the Great Academy and started the process of removing children from their homes. No one could object because Viri's army of loyal zealots, entranced by the godlike power of magic, was terrifyingly present."

Perin was starting to realise just how insidious and evil the Committee was and how necessary it was to depose them. The only thing worse than the thought of children being torn from their parents was the idea that in only one generation of indoctrination, this would be considered normal!

"The stress on the continent," Occidens continued, "created a land quake that tore Caramine across its centre and that's how we came to have Upper and Lower Caramine. The death toll was catastrophic and subdued the population even further."

"I'm sorry," Perin said, "but I still don't know what the connection is between that and what lies beyond the borders of Caramine."

"The Committee have used their imagination to create," Occidens explained, "but also destroy." Perin still looked bemused. "The Committee have created so much open ocean around Caramine to the east, north and west by destroying the islands there, that any voyage in those directions is doomed to failure. We would run out of food and water before we found any other port."

Perin understood: the Great Committee had locked Caramine with an untraversable perimeter of sea. To the south was a barren continent of desert that couldn't support life either. Perin was at a loss for their best course of action.

"The teeth," came a rough voice from behind. Occidens and Perin turned round to see Stim, still sitting in the chair but looking slightly more awake than he had done. *Perhaps he slept a little,* Perin thought.

"Pardon?" said Occidens.

"We could go through the teeth," he said. Then, with what still looked like a great effort, he pulled himself up and walked across to the table. He reached out a calloused hand and traced a thin line between Upper and Lower Caramine. "The land quake," he said, "left a narrow passageway between the two that I know is completely undefended. We could sail right through."

"No, Stim," Occidens objected, "it may be undefended but we certainly could not just 'sail right through'. There is a reason it doesn't require a garrison to keep people away – because it's strewn with the wreckages of ships that have tried to navigate it. The rocks are razor sharp, the water is dangerously shallow and the corridor is barely wider than this ship in parts."

Stim smiled at her. "But we have you, your power and your shields – you could stand on the bow and defend us should we run into anything."

Occidens smiled and seemed to consider the feasibility of the suggestion before shaking her head. "I'm sorry," she said. "The power needed isn't the problem, but I would be required to watch and imagine too many things at once." Perin recalled Occidens after her last confrontation with the crew of the *Formalite'*. He suspected that she had lost confidence. The potential result of this would be paralysing for Occidens. If she couldn't picture herself as powerful, then she would cease to be so.

"You need to do this," Perin stated simply. "I'll help as best I can, but I don't think you need it. You are who this crew look up to now."

The truth was, Perin hated the idea of approaching the teeth. It seemed suicidal to him. He had to admit that he was getting used to coping with this feeling and the fact that it was so intimidating to Occidens had made it the necessary challenge for her to overcome. When they next came face to face with the Great Committee she would be needed at her full power and her full confidence.

Occidens looked toward Perin, and smiled thankfully at him. "For you, dear, anything."

"Great!" exclaimed Stim, straightening up as he did so. As he reached his full height he turned pale and swayed slightly on his feet. Perin ran to his side and put himself under Stim's arm.

"Stim, what is it, are you all right?" he asked. He thought he may have stood up too quickly and gotten dizzy. Particularly since he had been so tired when he sat down.

"A thought just occurred to me," Stim replied, staring off into the distance.

"What is it?" Occidens said, hobbling over to him.

"If we go through the teeth," Stim said, "I'll have to steer this bloody thing!" He clasped his hand to his head.

Perin couldn't help but laugh. Occidens seemed a little perturbed.

"Oh, it's all right for me to use marvellous and impressive magic to throw up shields and control the tides to guide us safely through, but you can't steer the damn wheel!"

It was absurdly funny to watch the shrunken and stooped old woman chastise the hulking bearded brute and Stim played the part of disciplined child with perfection. He caught Perin's eye without Occidens noticing and gave a sly knowing wink.

"Well, l do steer the ship quite well," he said, wringing his hands. "And if you're not up to your best…"

"Steering the ship?!" Occidens said in a flap. "There's no comparison! I will create an orb of energy around the hull that will deflect all bombardment! The world could end and we would still be safe – we'd be all that was left inside that bubble!"

The man's a genius, thought Perin. *Nothing breeds confidence like a little bit of competition.* He smiled back at Stim, who had a pouted lip in response.

"You're right," Stim said. "You are the supreme sorcerer and will keep us safe no matter what happens. I'll go and set course for the teeth."

With that he trudged slowly out of the door of Occidens' study with his head hung in mock shame as she shouted after him, "Well you just do that! And try not to get us lost on the way there so I have to get us out of another mess!"

Perin collapsed into the chair that Stim had vacated. He continued to laugh. Even though he knew they were heading into danger, and was still wrung out with grief over the captain, he couldn't help but feel confident and at home here with these people. Occidens returned from hectoring Stim from her doorway to find Perin laughing in the chair. She put her hands on her hips.

"What are you laughing at?" she said with indignation.

Perin could see in her face that this was all good fun for her too.

"Oh, I dunno," Perin said, "just the absurdity of the world!"

Occidens tried to look seriously at him, but she soon started to laugh heartily as well. It helped with the pain of losing Rienta and it helped with her confidence.

Job well done, Perin thought. *Job well done.*

CHAPTER EIGHTEEN

The spirits of the crew in general seemed to have lifted despite the obvious sense of loss. It could still be felt every time someone glanced up at the helm, where Stim now stood stoically, almost in imitation of the fallen captain. Although not quite at the levels of the initial despair, there was still a solemn quietness over the crew's motions, as if they were working in silent contemplation. Through it all, they carried out their duties efficiently. This, thought Perin, was exactly as Rienta would have wished it. He knew that it would fall to him to be the motivating factor for the crew. He walked up the stairs towards the helm and stood beside Stim, who had changed their course to head towards the teeth. This was not a mission that Perin felt should be kept quiet. The crew would be required to work together without the fear and shock of the terrain they were attempting to navigate playing against them. They would have to get all that out of their systems beforehand.

"Everyone gather round," he shouted over the noise of the wind and ocean. The crew turned in unison to look at him and, as one, made their way to the deck below the helm. Perin stepped in front of the wheel to make his announcement. He heard the telltale tap of Occidens' cane on the steps; she was also making her way up onto the helm. *Good*, thought Perin. Showing a united front between all three would inspire some confidence among the rest of the crew. He waited for Occidens to make her way beside them. The three stood stoically together, Perin and Occidens shoulder to shoulder and Stim behind the wheel towering over their shoulders.

"This," Perin said to the silenced crew, "is a brave and courageous band of men and women." He paused and allowed the crew to soak in a bit of the praise. "What we are about to attempt will surprise our enemies and strike fear into their hearts," the crew stirred with approval, "but it will also inspire everyone who hears of it and bring more to our cause!" A cheer began to rise up but Perin raised his arms to silence them.

"We are going to cut through Caramine by sailing through the teeth," he announced. A stunned silence held the crew in place. For a moment Perin was concerned that Occidens was keeping them locked from reaction with her mind, but when he glanced towards her he saw that she was nodding in agreement with Perin in silent support.

"Mr Stim will take the helm," he continued. "A better navigator you will never find. He could take this galleon through the eye of a needle." This inspired some nods from the assembled company.

"Lady Occidens will defend us with the use of her shields. The greatest sorcerer in all of Caramine and our defender can handle some jagged stones without any problem at all." More approval rang out from the crew, along with some applause. Perin turned to the old woman and saw that she was nodding appreciatively and winked at him in reply.

He drew in a slow breath. "I will be aiding Lady Occidens with the stones and the tides." He had begun to sweat and his mouth was growing dry. "Being a part of this crew and defending it is what inspires me, what makes my blood run faster and harder. I will use every ounce of my strength, both mental and physical, to get us through the rocks!" Applause turned into full-on cheering at Perin's impassioned speech. He waited patiently for it to subside before continuing quietly.

"Finally," he said, "there is each and every one of you." He opened his arms to indicate the whole crew. "Everything else will be for naught if the sail isn't tight, the cargo isn't held in place, and if every man is not at his best. I ask you, what would Captain Rienta want of you? Do this for her and everyone will remember that it was her crew that conquered the teeth." The tenuous composure that the crew had held broke. Some cried, some cheered and others embraced. Occidens leaned over towards Perin.

"Not bad, dear boy, not bad," she said. A sniff from behind signalled Stim's approval. Perin turned round to face him and Occidens also turned round so the three could have a more private conversation.

"How long till we get there?" Occidens asked.

"Not long," Stim replied. "Wind is favourable and I've got the engines running too."

"Should we go through on sails or engines?" Perin enquired.

"Engines," Stim said quickly. "Has to be – the sails would get cut to ribbons."

"Is the water deep enough and the gap wide enough for the engine-powered oars to work?" Perin asked.

"Now is not the time for ifs, wills and whys, dear boy," Occidens said. "We are into the realms of fantasy, which thankfully you and I have a degree of control over. The water will be deep enough because we will make it so, the gap will be wide enough because we will ensure it, and the sails," she looked towards Stim with irritation, "will stay perfectly intact as long as we can picture them that way. The truth is we will get through faster if we use both. So that's what I say we try to do."

Perin nodded; Stim sighed and nodded as well.

"Now the course is set," Stim said. "I suggest the three of us get some rest. We have a big day to confront tomorrow and we should be well rested."

"Thank the devils," announced Occidens. "I need a good sleep!" She headed towards the steps without another word, leaving Perin and Stim together.

"You better go too," Stim said to Perin.

"You've got the hard job," Perin replied, leaning over the wooden barrier to the deck below. He gestured for one of the crew to come up to the helm. Obediently a young crew hand came up nervously.

"Would you be so kind as to keep us on this course?" Perin asked. "I think it's important Mr Stim get his sleep for tomorrow."

"Of course, sir," the young crewman said with a nod. Perin knew that if he went down to his quarters to sleep then Stim would stay at his post all night as Rienta would have done, and that would lead to him half asleep at the helm the following day. He couldn't risk that. He reached up and patted the giant man on the shoulder.

"Off to bed, Stim," he said pleasantly but firmly. Stim looked hurt but nodded and walked down the steps with a stoop in his shoulders. Perin could see that he was still exhausted. In response Perin could feel the weight of his own shoulders finally getting the better of him, so he followed closely behind Stim and headed down below decks.

As he got to the final floor that housed his quarters he looked across and saw the closed door to Rienta's sanctuary. He almost felt that he could knock on the door and she would answer. He considered it for a moment but knew better. He wondered what would happen to her belongings. Perhaps there would be something of use to the crew. With a shake of his head, Perin decided that he couldn't quite face it. His muscles were failing and he had to go into his quarters. They were exactly as he had left them, although there was a new side of salted beef waiting for him. That could wait till tomorrow. He flopped onto his comfortable bed, not bothering to undress or get underneath the soft coverings. He simply fell into an exhausted, dreamless sleep.

Perin had no idea how long he had actually slept. It could have been anything from a few moments to a few days. He woke with a start, going from complete unconsciousness to poised and energetically awake. The sound that summoned him from slumber was a sharp rap on his door. *Too sharp to have been done with a hand.* He sprang from his bed, still fully clothed, and was at the door in a moment. As he swung it open Occidens stood on the threshold holding her cane.

She looked Perin up and down and then seemed to chuckle to herself.

"We're holding position just beyond the teeth, but the longer we stay here the more chance we will be spotted." She looked down again at Perin's slept-in clothes and sniffed the air. He hadn't washed since he had fled the *Muta.* "Not that it's required, but I do think we have enough time for you to freshen yourself up." She turned and headed back towards the stairs. Her progress was slow and as she reached the stairs Perin saw her hesitate while looking towards Rienta's room. Perin closed the door and gave her her contemplation in solitude.

There was a bowl of fresh water sitting on his dressing table. Perin was sure it hadn't been there before and Occidens had willed it into existence. It didn't matter; he stripped off quickly and started to wash himself off. Cold water and a fresh pair of clothes were a great restorative. Perin noticed that the clothes were distinctly loose-fitting. He was losing weight. *Not unexpected,* he thought. He certainly wasn't eating as much and these had been some of his most active days ever. He was hungry, however, so enjoyed a quick breakfast of a few bites of beef before leaving his room.

As he made his way upwards through the ship he noticed that the crew deck was deserted. That wasn't unheard of but was quite unusual. There was normally some sort of shift system that allowed the crew time to recuperate.

As Perin reached the top of the stairs and came out onto the deck his breath was taken from him. There was no light. The sun and majority of the blue sky had been blocked out by sheer and intimidating walls of stone that towered over the *Muta* on both sides. The sheer cliffs were far from smooth. Perin understood instantly why they had come to be known as the teeth. They were like razor blades that had been sharpened by the winds that whistled down the corridor. There were also chunks of splintered wood, dangerous in themselves, that were trapped in between two or more of the shards, looking like a piece of beef that had become lodged between teeth. The whole scene was terrifying. Perin swallowed hard and tried not to let his growing doubts about the plan show on his face. The crew that had been missing on the crew deck were all either working, standing by or taking in the magnitude of what they saw around them. Perin was heartened and impressed that he saw very little fear in their faces.

As he looked towards the rear of the ship he could see that they hadn't really entered the teeth fully; there was blue sky and clear ocean behind them. It looked very inviting in contrast to the terrifying, cold corridor they had in front. Stim stood at the helm. He did look well rested but his face bore the stress of what he was about to attempt. Occidens stood at the bow of the ship. She didn't show the stress of what was about to occur, but looked stoic about the venture.

A whistle sounded and the sail unfurled. A faint rumble in the deck beneath their feet told Perin that the engine oars had started as well. The whistling of the wind died away as it filled the sails and they entered the teeth at alarming speed.

The world became truly terrifying. Tooth and wreckage flew past at speed, any one of them sharp enough to impale a crewman, shred the sail, or rip the hull apart. Occidens raised her arms and a blue shimmer spread around the ship. Unlike her previous shields it then seemed to disappear. Perin momentarily panicked that Occidens had failed to defend the ship but within moments an ear-splitting crack could be heard overhead. As Perin and the rest of the crew looked up they saw a protruding spike being cracked and shaved by the invisible shield as if it were being ground down by some electrical charge. The deck was littered with gravel and dust from the sheared peak. Occidens' shield was working to perfection. For her part, she hadn't moved but kept her hands held high as the ship lurched forward.

The deck of the ship started to vibrate worryingly. At first Perin thought that there was a problem with the engines but as he approached the side of the ship he saw that the water level had dropped significantly and the bottom of the *Muta* was starting to rub against the floor of the canyon. Perin closed his eyes and pictured the wood underneath the shallow waters getting increasingly worn with each passing moment. Then he focused and pictured the water level rising, envisaging more water rushing in from the ocean behind them to fill this canyon and raise the *Muta* up from the canyon's bed. A wind caught him from behind and he opened his eyes and turned round. Water was rushing towards them from where they had come. It raised them up away from both the canyon floor and the lowest level of rocks that endangered the lower parts of the hull. The rush of water had increased the speed of the ship. There was another shower of gravel as the ship was raised into some of the upper spikes that were larger and, if anything, sharper.

Perin was covered with a layer of sweat, both because he was nervous and because the exertion of raising the water level had taken its toll. Occidens seemed to be holding steady. As Perin turned to see that Stim was okay he found a man possessed. Stim twirled the wheel of the helm one way then the other, catching it just at the moment he needed to avoid sending the *Muta* into too many rocks for Occidens' shields to deflect. Concentration was etched on his face but he was doing an excellent job. In fact, as Perin looked around he started to smile. They were winning; they were successfully navigating the teeth.

As the time passed and the stars started to appear in the sky above Perin realised what everyone else must have already known and he felt very foolish. *This journey is not a short one; this journey is not a sprint, it's a marathon.* This realisation caused the energy he had remaining in his body to flood out of his system even faster than the water was flowing across the hull of the ship.

He had to get some idea of how long this was going to take, if he would be allowed or able to eat or sleep. With slow deliberate steps he walked towards the helm. He took care to make sure that he didn't lose his concentration and he kept the water level inside the teeth high enough to keep the *Muta* moving.

As he approached the helm Stim smiled. Without taking his eyes off the horizon he shouted, "All right, Perin, going well so far." He sounded pleasant and fairly unconcerned. Perin's mouth had gone dry with the concentration. He swallowed and managed to stutter through the concentration.

"I don't know if I can do this." He looked at the deck and closed his eyes but quickly raised his head again when he felt the ship descend beneath his feet.

"What do you mean?" Stim said with a guffaw. "You *are* doing it, you're doing great…"

"Stim," Perin interrupted, "how long is this going to take?"

"Ah," Stim said with realisation. "It will probably take us about five days, maybe six." Perin's breath caught in his chest. Perhaps with Occidens' magical abilities and Stim's energised strength they could stay awake for six days, but Perin would collapse before that. They couldn't turn back now. He began to panic that he had sentenced the crew of the *Muta* to shipwreck when he eventually passed out.

"Stim," Perin croaked, "how can I keep this up for six days? I'm already exhausted and we aren't even at the end of day one!"

"Don't be silly, Perin," Stim said kindly. "After a good night's sleep and something to eat you—"

"A good night's sleep?!" Perin exploded. "Do you think we're going to come across a port in here? How can we stop for sleep?"

Stim looked at Perin with shock. Slowly his bearded mouth spread across his face into a wide grin and he began to laugh. Perin was confused, and started to feel angry but steadied himself when he felt the ship list downward and firmed his concentration once again. Stim grabbed the wheel a little tighter and snapped his eyes back to the horizon.

"What's so funny?" Perin asked testily.

"We are going to get some sleep, Perin," Stim replied.

"How?"

"Speak to Occidens. I don't really understand how it works."

Perin smiled and slowly turned to walk towards the bow where Occidens still stood with her arms raised, as she had done since they entered the teeth.

As he walked forward he was finding that his concentration was holding a little easier, like he was using a muscle that was getting stronger with repetitive use. It was, however, leaving him with a headache.

Occidens stood with her eyes closed in meditation. Perin didn't know if interrupting her would be appropriate. He was afraid that breaking her trance may shatter the shield she had erected around the *Muta*.

"Let me guess," the old woman said without opening

her eyes. The break in silence made Perin jump. "You are worried how we are going to keep up this pace?" She sounded unconcerned, almost bored. This calmed Perin a little.

"Well, to be honest, yes," he replied. "I don't think I can stay awake for six days." Occidens turned to face him, still keeping her arms raised above her head.

"You're probably right," she said. "Time to stop for the night."

There was an ear-splitting crack as Occidens turned her hands to face right. The cliffs on that side of the ship were cracking and crumbling away. Perin covered his ears to shield them from the noise and the *Muta* descended with the water level. Perin was in a state of utter confusion and couldn't re-establish his concentration to raise the levels. *We're going to hit the rocks.*

"Get down!" Perin screamed to the crew before dropping to the floor and covering his head to brace for the impact.

Nothing happened. The world went suddenly quiet but there was no crushing impact or sound of splintering or shattering wood. As Perin opened his eyes he couldn't believe what he saw.

Occidens had used the shield to carve out a semicircular cove in the teeth just big enough to comfortably contain the *Muta*. She had then raised the rocks around the other side of the ship, protecting it from the currents of the water. They were effectively docked. Perin stood staring with his mouth open at the perfectly made natural dock for the ship.

"Time for bed, I think," Occidens declared as if this was the most normal scenario on the continent. She pleasantly turned to face Perin and clapped her arm around his shoulders.

"To bed!" she repeated, this time a bit firmer. "You have a lot of work to do tomorrow. Can't have you falling asleep on us!" Without another word she turned on her heels and walked towards her study.

Perin still couldn't quite believe it; he stood silently for a few more moments, taking in the geographic reshaping he had just seen. After a while he really couldn't think of anything else to do other than go to bed.

The next four days followed this same pattern. After Occidens had dissolved the cove and allowed them to fall back into the rapid flowing waters of the teeth they would spend a day holding their course, maintaining the shield, and Perin would keep the water levels high.

On the sixth and final day of their journey, the routine had lost some of its exciting spectacle and Perin had mastered the art of holding the water level whilst enjoying some of his surroundings. As they had risen further up the canyon by the increasing water line more light had flooded the deck. Blue sky opened up above them and the sun beat down on them. It was a welcome change to the cold wind that still whistled through the canyon.

As quickly as the light had appeared, they were plunged into darkness. A black cloud spread across the sun forming out of nothing and rumbling with thunder. The temperature plummeted and made the sweat on Perin's skin go cold and clammy. Something was going wrong.

"What's going on!" Perin called to Occidens, who was still standing with her arms outstretched. She didn't answer and continued looking forward. Perin quickly made his way to the front of the ship so that he could ask her directly. As he approached her he passed several crew members. Now they showed fear and concern. "Stay at your posts," shouted Perin. "A little storm is nothing we can't overcome!"

As Perin reached Occidens and moved round in front of her he saw for the first time a look of fear in her eyes. A furious burst of rain started to fall from the sky onto them. He watched as Occidens' hair became wet and matted.

"Occidens, what is it?"

"It's her!" Occidens gasped. "Viri knows what we are trying to do, and knows that she can't follow so she's going to try and run us into the rocks with this storm."

"We'll see about that," Perin replied and looked up towards the cloud. He raised his hand and pictured the red lightning springing from his hand. It came forward just as he imagined and struck the growing cloud right at its centre. A clap of thunder rendered the crew momentarily deaf. Occidens winced and brought her hands to her ears for a moment.

The shield fell, there was a rush of air and an ominous shape appeared before them. A peak of rock, not yet shaved by Occidens' shield, was now heading towards them. With a rip that made Perin's heart sink it tore straight through the sail and the *Muta* started to sway. A ripped sail would make the manoeuvring of the ship even more difficult, even without the unnatural storm that now whipped around them. As Perin turned to check on Stim he saw the beast of a man struggling with the wheel and soaked through to the skin. His beard and hair were flattened against his skull and he kept shaking his head to get the water out of his eyes.

Perin's lightning bolt had been unsuccessful. The cloud still grew and was ominously rumbling overhead. Occidens had regained herself and re-established the shield but now that the *Muta* was handling more sluggishly it was colliding with more rocks and causing the shields to work much harder. Peak after peak sheared across the invisible shimmering force. Gravel and rain mixed together rained down on the crew.

"Take down the sail and get inside! Take cover!" Perin shouted at the crew, attempting to keep them as safe as he could. They lurched into action and withdrew the sail. Perin grabbed a crew member that was heading towards the lower decks. "You keep those engines running!" Without the sail they would need every metre those oars could get them.

As the deck cleared, the cloud above gave a concerning rumble. Perin looked up just in time to see a bolt of green lightning pierce the cloud and streak down towards the *Muta*. The bolt would normally have torn straight through the ship but instead it lit up the orb-like shield that Occidens had erected. Instead of the blue shimmer the rocks caused when they hit the shield the lightning created a green crackle and the bitter smell of burning ozone filled Perin's nostrils. The green crackle spread until it covered the top third of the orb. Perin looked towards Occidens, the wind sweeping her baggy clothes and wet hair around her. Her arms were stretched away from her and even from distance Perin could see her hands were shaking. A second green lightning bolt struck the same position as the first. The green electrical power splintered the shield. There was a flash and a blast knocked Perin to the ground. As he fell his shoulder crunched against the deck and a piercing pain spread across his side. He rolled away from the pain and saw that Stim had held his position and was still fighting with the wheel. Perin forced himself up and gasped. The shield was gone and Occidens lay lifeless at the bow of the boat. *Not again,* Perin thought, and the vision of Rienta tumbling over the side of the *Formalite'* pushed its way into his consciousness. As he looked at Occidens, desperate for her to move, hot tears started to stream down his face. Slowly he saw her roll over on the deck and Perin's heart jumped.

The *Muta* bucked to one side. A jagged peak had sheared through the front of the ship. Stim spun the wheel to get them away and to avoid running aground on it. Another peak appeared halfway through the opposite side of the deck with a wood-splintering crunch.

As Perin looked ahead he could see the end of the teeth. They had almost made it through, but there were still more than enough peaks to cut them to ribbons. The cloud above gave another ominous rumble and a streak of green lightning headed towards the undefended deck. Not just towards the deck but towards Occidens, who had just got back to her feet. Perin raised his hands and screamed:

"No!" Red energy burst from his hands and formed a cocoon around Occidens, absorbing the blast. Occidens put up her hands to defend herself before she realised she had already been given her defence. She turned towards Perin during the chaos from within the cocoon and smiled an exhausted smile at him. Perin smiled back.

Another lightning bolt struck one of the peaks above the ship. It splintered a huge section of rock overhead and it tumbled down towards the deck.

"Incoming!" bellowed Stim. The rock was heading towards the bow of the *Muta*. If it hit flush it would obliterate the ship. Perin held his shield over Occidens although she pointed wildly towards the falling rock. The trajectory the debris took was unnatural. For a second Perin could hear Viri's evil laughter on the wind. The rock was heading towards Occidens and Perin's shield. *This is all about her,* Perin realised. Although Viri's storm was assaulting the *Muta*, it was aiming for Occidens.

The rock collided with Perin's shield, the sphere of energy buckled and Occidens was violently knocked to the ground. The shield had succeeded in stopping the ship being obliterated by the rock. Perin imagined the wind throwing the rock back where it had come from, but this was too big a stretch. He did manage to guide it into the ocean beside them. The force of the wave pushed the *Muta* into the side of the canyon and the sound of poles splintering told Perin they had lost their oars on one side.

Stim spun the wheel in the opposite direction but only succeeded in dragging the other side of the ship along the canyon and stripping the other oars from the side of the *Muta* as they finally sailed out into clear water.

As Perin looked up the sky was clear. The water was calm. But everything on the *Muta* was in complete chaos. Perin looked through the splintered wood and wreckage towards Occidens. She wasn't moving or conscious. Perin leapt over the debris to get to her. Purple bruising had started to flower all over the left-hand side of her face and her left arm was at an unnatural angle and was most certainly broken. Perin was, however, extremely relieved that she was breathing. Stim appeared at his side.

"Well," he said, "that could have gone better!"

CHAPTER NINETEEN

Stim scooped up the limp old woman in his arms and turned towards her study. Perin felt truly helpless as he stood up and accompanied them.

"Is there anything I can do?" he asked.

Without looking down at him Stim replied, "Check on the *Muta* and her crew. I'll see to Occidens for the next while." Perin nodded and watched as Stim carried the unresponsive body into the study. As he approached the stairwell to go down into the bowels of the ship he could hear shouting and panic and crashing. He hurried down to check.

The engine room smelled of smoke. There was no fire but it was intensely hot. A sizzling sound was coming from the engine that must have worked as hard as it could until there were no oars left to row. Now it stood, fizzing hot and exhausted. There were gaps in the hull that had let water in from the storm and the waves of the sea. This had kept the room from catching fire but would also make it very hard to get things operational again. Light shone in through the punctures, creating a haze of smoke making it hard to see and uncomfortable to breathe. The oars themselves had all splintered, making it dangerous to cross the deck. In many ways the deck looked like a miniature version of the teeth itself, only here it was protruding barbs of sheared wood as opposed to rock and stone. Once Perin had checked that nothing was in immediate danger of bursting into flames he continued down towards the increasing commotion of shouting and crashing below.

The crew deck was a shambles. The hull had obviously taken more damage than had been obvious from above. The gashes towards the top of this level let in the light from outside. These were not the ones that concerned Perin at the moment. There were other streaks of broken wood towards the lower part of the deck that were below the water line. Water had been flowing inside the *Muta*. The deck was wet and crewmen slipped and fell as they scrambled to block whatever gaps they could find with whatever they could move. Crewmen's entire wardrobes of linen had been stuffed into smaller cracks, but as water still seeped through it became a useless measure. Trunks, hammocks and bedding had been used for larger breaches. The crew held many together themselves, as there was nothing to attach the material into position. A crewman came bounding up to Perin soaked to his skin. Much to his surprise, he had a jubilant look upon his face.

"You did it, young sir," he said in congratulations. "We made it through the teeth." He looked around and continued, "Perhaps by the skin of our own mind you, but we still made it!" Perin had to concede that this was one way of looking at it, but he was afraid the damage might be more extensive than these men knew. Successfully navigating the teeth was one thing, staying afloat afterwards would be quite another.

"Is there anything I can do to help you gentlemen down here?" Perin asked.

"No no, I think we have the matter in hand for the time being," he replied with remarkable confidence. "No one's been down to your level yet though, sir. Best you go check that." Perin nodded and headed back towards the stairwell to check the final level that housed his quarters and Rienta's.

There was running water everywhere. As Perin reached the foot of the stairwell he was ankle deep in water. He could feel from the chill on his skin that it was moving; the water was flowing in from somewhere. There was a leak that was slow enough not to have sunk the ship but large enough to sink her if left unchecked. He started to wade about in the freezing water trying to locate its source.

Once he did, the chill from the water spread up his spine and made his blood run cold. Water was leaking in from around the frame of the door that led to his quarters. The water was seeping in from chest height already. Perin knew he couldn't go back in the room. It would flood the lower deck in minutes and put the ship in real danger. He had known immediately what he had to do but he still hesitated. He looked towards the two levers that would eject his quarters, which would act as a safe house if he needed a place to hide. As he visualised the room filling up with the blue-black water he imagined it as a cancer growing on the hull of the ship threatening to drag them all down to the depths.

He leaned forward and grabbed the first lever. It took all of his strength but he managed to pull it downwards. A violent clunk followed and a large panel of wood swung downward to fill the void that the doorway to the room would leave. The room was now cut off from the *Muta*. The second lever would detach it.

Perin grabbed the second lever but it wouldn't budge. He lifted his feet off the ground using his entire weight but the mechanism was just too stiff.

"Don't worry, young sir," came a voice from behind him, "we're here to help ya." Perin turned round to see the same crewman from the crew deck and some of his colleagues. They carried buckets, blankets and other materials to plug leaks.

It took three of them, but with a great *shoom* the lever lowered and the sound of Perin's much-loved quarters sinking to the bottom of the ocean was undeniable. It was a sound Perin thought he would never forget. It was not that he had lost his belongings – he hadn't brought anything with him from the Academy other than what he was wearing. It was the fact that it had been home, that he had been welcomed and treated as more than a member of the crowd. It was hard to appreciate how special this could be when he had still been at the Academy. Everyone was treated with relatively little personal space or freedom in terms of their living conditions and this was considered the norm. That was perhaps the clearest of symbols to Perin. The room that had flooded, which he had just ejected into the depths, was a symbol of his liberty. He wiped the tears from his eyes and turned to face the crew who had come down to help.

"Can we work on getting the water cleared from this deck?" he asked. "We can't clear the captain's room until we can be sure opening the door won't create a minor flash flood."

"Aye, sir," replied the sailor who had led the helpers.

Perin left the men to their work and made his way back up the stairwell. The crew had done a serviceable job restoring a bit of order to both the engine and crew decks. In fact, given that they had no materials of note to work with, Perin thought that they had done an excellent job. He made a point of smiling and congratulating each crew member he passed for their hard work despite feeling rather desolate. Gradually he made his way towards Occidens' study on the main deck, his wallowing abating in concern for Occidens.

As he walked into the room he saw Stim leaning over the lounger with the old woman still unconscious lying on it. He was holding a cold rag to her head with one hand and held the old woman's hand with the other. He looked gravely concerned.

"How's she doing?"

"I'm not sure," Stim replied, tears in his eyes. His voice cracked as he spoke. "She's not babbling like she was last time, but I think she took a bad knock."

Perin forced a smile and tried to lift Stim's spirits. "She's not a young woman," he replied, "but she's a resilient old lady. I'm sure she'll be fine."

"That's the problem," Stim replied. "She's not the toughest of old ladies. She usually keeps herself healthy by using her magic and she heals herself with it if she needs to, but she's badly injured and I don't think she can this time." He started to sob. Perin stood silent for a moment before a thought struck him. *Only magic can kill magic,* he thought, *and it was my shield that hit her. This is my fault.* Stim didn't realise this or didn't want to say, but Perin was glad for either reason. His eyes filled with salty tears of remorse as he looked down on the broken woman with her purplish face and twisted arm.

"What if she doesn't wake up?" he heard himself say. Stim shrugged. Unexpectedly, it made Perin a little angry. It was all very well to try and raise Stim's spirits and to encourage and motivate the crew, but without Occidens Perin failed to see how they could get any further towards their overall mission. It was Perin who needed the support now. He was supposed to be the saviour and best chance, but without Occidens, or Rienta for that matter, to teach him how, he was nothing more than a rogue sorcerer with untempered abilities.

Abilities, thought Perin. *If Occidens was capable of healing herself with magic, why can't I heal her with my own powers?* It was a thought, but it was also a worry and a risk. Up until this point, Perin had only used his powers in a destructive way through control of elements and tides. This kind of gentler magic was not something he had ever really taken on before. *You created this mess,* he thought, *now you better take some steps to unmake it.*

He stepped forward towards the plush lounger. He

gestured for Stim to move aside and with a look of comprehension he moved away from her head, but still held on to her hand at her side. Perin kneeled down beside Occidens and closed his eyes. He pictured her lying there as she was, with her blossoming bruises and contorted limbs. He imagined the bruises sinking back into her head, being replaced with healthy pink flesh. He imagined her arm straightening and the bones inside resetting with a *click*—

Perin's eyes snapped open. The click had not sounded inside his head – he had heard it in the room. He looked down towards Occidens in amazement. The purplish bruise on her face was receding and becoming lighter and lighter until it died away completely. Just as Perin had pictured. Stim was watching in wide-eyed, breathless silence.

Her arm was a little more gruesome to watch; the skin was tightening to the elbow and forcibly straightening it out. It had a red glow around it as if it was being heated from within. As the arm became perfectly straight again the glow subsided and the skin started to loosen once more into the familiar wrinkles that had always lined Occidens' arm.

Stim and Perin stood for a few moments looking at the physically restored old woman, wondering if she was about to wake up. Her breathing had become easier and more comfortable now. It was as if she was just sleeping as opposed to being knocked out.

"Think of how she put up that shield," Stim said. "She's probably exhausted as well from all that effort. No wonder she needs to sleep."

"You think she'll be all right now then?" Perin asked. He was hopeful himself and when Stim grinned and nodded he relaxed a little bit. Stim clapped him on his shoulder so hard that Perin staggered a few steps.

"We're doing okay, kid," said Stim. "Once Occidens wakes up she'll know what to do and where to go and then we will get on with getting rid of those scumbags on Capital Island." Perin nodded. For all the discussion of this sort of thing, there had never been any talk of exactly how that was going to happen. This was another reason he needed Occidens fighting fit. The time had come for him to be brought in on the means of the plan and not just the ends. As he looked down at the peaceful old woman though, he realised that it wouldn't be just yet.

"We need to get this ship moving," Perin said. "The crew seem to have patched things up all right. However, I've lost my quarters, the engines are done and the sails are in shreds so I don't know how we are going to do this."

Stim looked at Perin for a moment before asking, "Any injuries to the crew?" To his shame this wasn't something that Perin had thought about, but when he considered it more closely he realised he hadn't seen anyone being tended to and there certainly weren't any bodies – he would have noticed that.

"A few cuts, scrapes and bruises, but they all seem to be doing okay," he replied.

"Good," said Stim, "we're gonna need them. If we're completely adrift, they will need to man the rowboats and tow us to safety. It will take some time and a lot of work, but I'm sure they will be up to it." Perin nodded. He had no doubt the crew would rise to the challenge. There were eight boats and it would take four people to man each one, meaning they would need thirty-two volunteers. The crew's complement, not including Occidens, Stim and himself, was forty. That would leave eight to man the *Muta* itself. It would be tight, but it could be done.

"Shall I go and get some volunteers?" Perin asked.

"No," said Stim, "I'll do it." He got up and placed Occidens' hand, which he had never let go, by her side. He headed towards the door and down to the lower decks.

"Occidens," Perin said, "I don't know if you can hear me, but I need you to be all right – not for me, but for this crew. They are good people. I don't know how you found them or brought them to you, but they deserve safety and success." Tears formed on his cheeks again. "I can't protect them, not like you can, not yet. I need your help to learn how to do that. So I need you to get better, and I need you to get up and tell me I'm being an idiot and teach me how to do the things you think I can do."

There was no reply. Occidens continued to lie still. She looked comfortable, peaceful and restored, but there was no other response. Perin sat down in the chair by the desk and tried to compose himself.

He wasn't sure how long he'd been there before Stim came back into the room.

"We're ready," he said. "The crew are in the boats. The bravest and strongest came forward immediately. Eight good men staying behind as well." Perin nodded and stood up from the desk and accompanied Stim out of the study. He looked back at Occidens, still unconscious on the lounger.

The *Muta* was surrounded by the flotilla of small boats that had launched to act as tugs to bring it to the nearest port.

"How far are they going to have to tow us?" asked Perin, realising it could be far enough to cause problems now they were on the eastern side of Caramine.

"Shouldn't be too bad," replied Stim. "If we were using the sails it would take us less than a day to get to Antez." That was the port just off the shore of North Caramine, Perin recalled. "But it's a bit too close to The Hammer and Anvil for my liking," Stim continued, "so I've got us going south a bit further to Port Graze. It's on its own island so there'll be fewer people, so less talking about what we're doing or the state we're in." Stim crossed his arms, clearly pleased with himself for his deductive reasoning. Perin understood it, but he may have chosen the opposite course of action. Port Antez was shielded by a small island in between Upper Caramine and the military island of The Hammer. They would have ample time to get out of harm's way if the cavalry for the Committee came calling. On the other hand, Port Graze to the south had a clear ocean all the way to the chains, making it a bit more accessible, and gave less chance to hide or escape. That said, there wasn't much else for it now.

The ropes that held the small boats to the *Muta* shook with tension. Very slowly, Perin could feel the ship start to move forward. Stim was standing at the bow of the ship, in almost exactly the same spot where Occidens had stood defending the ship during their journey through the teeth. He was holding a brass cone that amplified his voice when he shouted through the narrow end. He was giving the eight boats their rhythm to keep the *Muta* moving forward. Perin was enjoying the leisurely pace of the cruise until a bell started to sound from the crow's nest high above. It was too high to make out a voice from the occupying crew member. There was a system of bell rings to signify what the alarm was. Perin had not been on board long enough to know what these signals were. Stim was too busy with his work to have heard the bells.

A breathless crewman ran to Perin and with a nod said, "Young sir, we have a problem."

"Go on?" said Perin, nervously.

"A ship is approaching from the south-west, from the direction of the chains." he said. "A black ship. It's the *Formalite'*…"

CHAPTER TWENTY

How? Perin wondered. The *Formalite'* had been left a wreck after their last encounter. The sail had been on fire, the crew dispersed and they were still conducting repairs from the first assault. How had they managed to catch up with them so quickly? As Perin watched the black ship move steadily closer to them it struck him. Viri had known they were sailing through the teeth. She had sent her storm to soften them up and now she had sailed through the chains, which wouldn't have impeded her in any way, to make sure that they were finished.

As the ship grew larger on the horizon, he could tell it still wasn't in the finest shape. He could make out the mast of the ship, blackened and charged from Perin's assault, but it didn't seem to be holding a sail. *How's it moving?* he puzzled. The *Formalite'* didn't have any engines to speak of. As far as Perin knew they were unique to the *Muta*. The *Formalite'* did have oars, so the crew must be propelling the ship by hand. That would be slower than normal but still stronger and faster than the towing of the *Muta*.

Perin ran towards Stim, who still hadn't noticed they were being pursued. The sailors on the rowboats, being much lower down, hadn't been able to see the pursuing ship either. This was probably for the best, Perin thought;

if the crew panicked they would either row back to the *Muta*, stranding them again, or they would flee, pulling the *Muta* in different directions and possibly doing more damage. As Perin reached Stim he continued to shout out his rhythmic orders to keep the ships moving forward.

"Stim, we have a problem," Perin whispered to him.

"Forward!" bellowed Stim into the cylinder, before turning back to Perin. "What's wrong?" he asked, before roaring, "Again!"

"We're being followed."

"Row!" shouted Stim.

"It's the *Formalite*," Perin said with as much control as he could muster. Stim swore loudly into the brass cylinder. Perin thought he could hear laughter from the boats.

"Sorry!" was Stim's next bellowed statement to mark time. There was definitely laughter from the boats now.

"Is there any way we can pick up some more speed?" Perin asked. "The *Formalite* is in bad shape but it's rowing, so a bit faster than we are managing."

In between his shouts Stim managed to say, "I dunno. Any sign of Occidens?" The answer was no but Perin understood the suggestion: magic would either be required to help them escape, or help them in the confrontation that would be inevitable if the *Formalite* managed to catch them. *What can I do to help?* Perin thought to himself. He could possibly help them pick up some speed, but when Viri saw them pulling away she would probably be able to figure out how they had done it and follow suit. In fact, Perin was at a loss to understand why she hadn't already used her magic to increase their speed already. *Maybe it's something she isn't capable of.* That thought gave Perin a bit of cheer.

"I might be able to help us out a bit," Perin said.

"I think we'd all appreciate that," said Stim, still in between his shouts.

Perin left Stim at the bow of the ship and headed towards the stern. He made a point of trying to calm the crew members who had seen the *Formalite'* on the horizon. He was fairly convinced that he could increase the flow of the water around the *Muta*, giving both it and the tugs a bit of a boost. Hopefully enough to stay ahead of, and even lose, the *Formalite'*.

As he approached the stern, all he could see in front of him was the slowly growing image of the *Formalite'* like a black cancerous spot growing on the horizon. Perin looked down towards the water beneath the *Muta*. He closed his eyes and imagined the green-blue water slapping against the stern faster and harder, the water running more quickly beneath them, the currents increasing.

Perin could feel the wind in his hair slightly more fiercely. The deck creaked beneath his feet. He opened his eyes and saw that the water had increased in ferocity around them. He hoped it wouldn't be so different as to cause the crew in the boats any alarm. As they picked up speed, he closed his eyes again and imagined the wind pushing against the hull of the *Formalite'*. He imagined the wind crashing against the bow of the enemy ship and pushing back against it, making the rowers have to work harder to move forward in any way.

As Perin looked back at the pursuing ship, he couldn't help a smile from spreading across his face: the *Muta* was pulling away from the *Formalite'*. It was reducing on the horizon; they were going to lose them. As Perin made his way towards the bow to convey the news to Stim, there was a deep boom from the direction of the enemy ship. Perin's stomach gave a gut-churning tremor. As he turned round, he saw a black spot soaring through the air towards them.

A cannonball. But there was something unnatural about the arc of the shot. *Viri must be controlling the shots with her magic*, Perin realised, *but it's not very accurate*. The shot was too high in the sky; it wasn't going to cause any damage to the *Muta*. It was off course.

Screams brought Perin's attention back to the deck of

the *Muta*. He rushed forward to the bow of the ship where Stim was screaming at the boats.

"Stick with it, boys!" he roared. As Perin looked over the side he saw the wreckage of one of the boats. It had been blasted to smithereens by the cannonball. There was no sign of the crew of the small boat. They had either been dragged to the bottom by the impact itself, or knocked unconscious and sunk.

The remaining ships had panicked and the sailors were either trying to get back to the *Muta* or cut free of it. *Who can blame them?* thought Perin. Stim had tears in his eyes for the broken crew but he tried to keep the remaining ships in formation.

Another black circle streaked across the sky, and Perin tried to imagine it falling harmlessly into the ocean. Nothing happened. He was panicking and it was destroying his focus. The ball continued its arc, this time to the other side of the ship. Perin knew without looking from the sounds of screams and splintering wood that this shot had also hit home.

"Do we have any rear-facing cannons?" Perin asked quickly.

"No," said Stim. "The *Muta*'s strength is its speed – we stay ahead of the enemy."

"Well not for much longer if they pick off all of our lifeboats."

"To hells with the boats!" roared Stim, causing Perin to step back. "That's most of the crew out there – I've known them for years. Is there anything you can do to help?"

Perin stood open-mouthed. He had already tried and failed, but he didn't want to let Stim or the crew down. At the same time a third shot rocked the *Muta* as it exploded another of the lifeboats in a shower of splinters. This time it was one of the boats that was trying to get back aboard the ship.

"I don't think so," said Perin. He took the knife out of

Stim's belt and started to cut the ropes that held the small boats in place. "We have to let them go, and give them a chance." Stim's face fell, but he nodded. He reached across and with his bare hands started to snap the other ropes.

Once all five remaining boats were free Stim raised the brass cylinder to his mouth again to shout to the crew.

"Get outta here, boys – we'll deal with the scum!" He paused, tears streaming down his face. "Make for one of the ports – we'll meet you there." He threw the brass amplifier down in disgust and walked from the bow of the ship towards the helm. With one dejected move he spun the wheel to try and bring the *Muta* about. Very little happened; there was precious little momentum. At best they would be side on to the *Formalite'* and be able to fire a few cannon shots at them, but not enough to stop them. The *Formalite'* could sink them whenever they wanted.

As if in response to the idea three black dots streaked through the sky towards them.

"Incoming!" shouted Stim.

Perin closed his eyes but the screams and splinters of wood were too distant and lacked the impact to have hit the *Muta*. As he opened his eyes he was horrified to see that the *Formalite'* was still targeting the fleeing lifeboats. *No survivors,* thought Perin. *What does that achieve?* He then realised this was about showing Perin what happens when you cross Viri and the Great Committee. Fear and rage flooded Perin's veins.

There were two boats left. Perin could hear the panicked voices and frantic splashes as the crew aboard them desperately tried to flee.

"Those animals!" Stim screamed at the *Formalite'*. He pulled his linen white shirt, which billowed like a sizeable sail all of its own, over his shoulders and held it above his head, waving it from side to side!

"We surrender," he said in a panicked and sincere voice. It was a sad sight to watch. The power and strength in those muscles were useless in trying to avoid the culling of an entire life's worth of friends. They had spent so much time together they were probably more than friends. They were family.

There was a moment's pause. *Thank the Angels,* thought Perin, *they must have seen the surrender.* He gave a momentary sigh of relief, ready to face the *Formalite'* head on.

Two more booms shook the *Muta.* Perin and Stim watched helplessly as two more cannonballs streaked towards them. Stim let out a long piercing scream, as if his anger and venom could cause the balls to fall from the air. Perin could only watch in muted and resigned silence. He knew what was going to happen before it did. With two more sickening crunches the crew of the *Muta* were no more. Perin gazed over the side looking for any signs of life – a flailing survivor or a shout for help. There was nothing.

As he turned to look towards the oncoming *Formalite'* it had gotten much larger. *The cancer has spread,* he thought. *It might be too late to fight it off.* He was sure though that he would give it one incredible fight. He walked up beside Stim. The eight other members of the crew had armed themselves and joined them. They looked towards the *Formalite'* with disgust. They all had tears in their eyes. This had been a callous and unnecessary cull. They had announced their surrender.

"We're not done yet are we?" Perin asked. Stim stood beside him but had not taken his eyes from the growing ship now drawing up alongside them.

"Not by a long shot," the large man said slowly and deliberately. Ropes were slung from the larger *Formalite'* onto the deck of the *Muta*; they had grappling hooks on their ends which dug roughly into the deck. The ropes tightened and drew the *Muta* closer and closer to the *Formalite'*. Soon enough the hulls bumped together and the rope ladders were swung over the top of the *Formalite'* to the deck of the *Muta*.

The air changed; a cold wind blew around them. From

the deck of the enemy ship a green orb rose high into the air and lowered gently down onto the deck of the *Muta*. The orb disappeared and from within it Viri stood with her arms outstretched. She was accompanied by a number of her troops; Perin wasn't sure exactly how many there were, but the ten men that made up the crew of the *Muta* were severely outnumbered.

"Anyone left at home?" crowed Viri.

Something inside of Stim must have given way. With a roar he leapt towards Viri. She raised her hands and sent a green lightning bolt from her hands to the giant man. To Perin's surprise it didn't fry the flesh from Stim's shoulders. It bounced off his body, which momentarily glowed a light blue from somewhere underneath his skin. *He must still have some of Occidens' charge,* thought Perin.

Viri was clearly stunned at the ineffectiveness of her assault. Stim kept making his way towards her. Viri launched another volley, and it slowed the big man down but was ineffective in stopping him. Viri nodded towards her guards who rushed Stim as one. The crew of the *Muta* around Perin reacted equally swiftly; letting out a war cry they advanced to hold back the assault. Viri continued to volley shots at Stim. Perin knew that Occidens' magic wouldn't hold forever and decided he needed to step up. He looked at the woman with green fire in her eyes and imagined his own red lightning sparking from his hands and streaking towards her. As he looked down at his hands nothing was happening. *Not now,* Perin thought. He needed to be able to help or the crew wouldn't have any chance.

Stim continued to head forward but he was noticeably flagging. Viri's assault had become more concentrated and more vicious. Although Stim's skin still glowed blue when a bolt struck it, it was now leaving red scorch marks where the bolts had hit him. Stim fell to one knee just a few feet in front of Viri. She looked down at him and cackled. The soldiers that she had brought with her were containing the *Muta* crew members.

"Step away from my friends, you witch!" came a voice from behind them. Perin's heart leapt as he saw Occidens' climbing up the stairs from the main deck. Viri smiled cuelly at the old woman as if she was looking forward to the fight ahead.

"Occidens, you look even more than your usual half dead," Viri said, her voice dripping with sarcasm. She waved her hand at Stim and two electrical chains appeared around Stim's wrists, as if binding him to the deck.

"Oh but half dead is still a good distance away from dead," Occidens replied.

"I couldn't agree more," Viri beamed. The truth was that Occidens did look terrible; she was clearly still recovering and not at her full strength. She walked over towards Stim and patted him on the shoulder, bestowing it with a blue-white glow. Perin realised she was restoring his powers.

"That's enough of that, old woman," Viri said. "There's no need to make the brute any stronger than he already is."

"Oh it's okay," Occidens replied sweetly. "Just healing some of his burns. Now, beyond the boarding and torture of this crew, and what seems to be the senseless murder of a great number of loyal men and women, what are you here for? I presume you are intending to try again to kill Perin? Or abduct him?" She gestured towards Perin who stood up as tall as he could, despite feeling powerless and absolutely terrified.

"You must understand," said Occidens, "that I, this crew, and indeed Perin himself have absolutely no intention of allowing that to happen."

"Oh I'm sure that's certainly true," Viri replied. "You would fight tooth and nail to defend him, and rightly so — he is quite, quite important to you, and your plans." A horrible smile spread across her face. "I also have no doubt that that decrepit, ageing mind of yours is currently locked in a desperate creative process of defending him against every possibility I could think of." Perin glanced at

Occidens, and saw that there was probably truth in what Viri was saying. There was sweat running down the side of the old woman's face.

"I do have one query though," Viri said.

"What would that be," Occidens asked without the merest hint of actual enquiry in her voice.

"How can he be the saviour if there is no one to show him how?" Quick as a flash she stretched both her hands towards Occidens and green lightning flashed forward to hit the woman in the chest. Perin jumped back in fright but Occidens had barely budged. She teetered on her heels for a second and then fell backwards. Her eyes were still open and a blackened sizzling gap had appeared in her chest. In the blink of an eye, Perin's world had ended.

Stim's rage had broken him free of his shackles. It seemed that Occidens had not been entirely honest and had charged him up rather a lot more than restoring his bruises. In one shot he launched Viri into the air and back towards the *Formalite'*. Perin rushed forward to try and help Occidens in any way he could, but she was beyond help. He could hear Viri laughing above him, and as he looked up he saw the green orb had encased her again and was carrying her back towards the deck of her own ship. Stim was now throwing the *Formalite'*s crew overboard. They were not quite as quick to adapt as Viri had been and splashed into the water below.

Stim pushed Perin out of his way as he cradled the old woman in his arms and let out a blood-curdling scream that turned into a wail, and then into a sob. Seeing Stim reduced in this way broke Perin down as well. He dropped to his knees and took one of the old woman's hands. There was a clamminess, a waxiness that was setting in. Occidens was dead and there was no power that Perin could use to bring her back.

The *Formalite'* had started to row away and leave the wrecked *Muta* to starve and drift in their despair. Even if they found shore, Perin had no way to be of any use. He couldn't hope to fulfil the destiny that Occidens had laid before him if she was no longer here.

The hooks that held the *Formalite'* to the *Muta* were straining against the ship as it moved away. Two of the crew members cut the cords and the ship sailed into the distance. It was completely gone from view before Viri's laughter had receded from Perin's mind.

CHAPTER TWENTY-ONE

Stim was a broken man. Perin looked down on him as he sobbed uncontrollably. His shoulders heaved and his back curved around Occidens' broken body, forming a human shield around her. Perin stood stock-still as if his boots had rooted him to the ground. He realised that his shoulders were also shuddering, and his face was wet and his eyes burning with tears. He felt oddly removed from the world. He knew that things were happening around him but he wasn't truly registering them. It was almost as if the pace of the world had slowed to a crawl and although Perin continued to be aware of it, he was unable to intervene. It was a strange, sad experience.

He was aware of the remaining crew dealing with things in their own way. Some stood around Stim, as Perin was, forming a vigil around their fallen sorcerer. Some headed towards the side of the ship and yelled profanity or abuse at the departing *Formalite'*. A few had left the group and were pacing around without purpose, probably contemplating the scale of the loss. Rienta, Occidens and the vast majority of the crew were gone. It was impossible to comprehend, and it all led to one inescapable question. *What now?*

Perin couldn't help but close his eyes. He had

absolutely no idea how to answer this question. He felt as lost as the rest of the crew. However, he did have a strange feeling of resolve. He couldn't let Viri and the Great Committee win. He knew he couldn't fulfil everyone's dream of taking over the Great Committee any longer, but he could survive. Viri expected them to drift until they eventually succumbed to exhaustion and starvation. She knew they had no engines or rowing capacity – if they had they would have used that instead of the rowboats. The thought brought back the desperate screams of the crew members as they awaited the cannonballs headed towards them. Perin winced. It almost caused him physical pain. *No more,* he thought.

He leaned down and put his arm around Stim's giant shoulders, or as close to around his shoulders as his small arms would allow.

"Stim, come on, let's get you inside," he said with as much kindness as he could muster. The huge man rose without any comment or complaint. His head hung from his neck in a gesture of defeat and emotional exhaustion. Perin led him towards the stairs to bring him down to Occidens' study. Not ideal given the circumstances, Perin knew, but it was the closest room with the most privacy. Perin didn't want to leave the crew to fend for themselves but if Stim couldn't be brought back to some form of sense then the rest of the crew would have no chance.

As Stim trudged into Occidens' study he looked around and started to break down again. He threw his hands to his face to hide the scene from himself. Perin guided him towards a nearby chair and sat him down. He then made his way to Occidens' desk to see if he could find a relaxing drink that might calm him down. As he opened the drawer from which Occidens always drew her bottles he was able to make out the drinks they had enjoyed so far alongside other indescribable liquids he didn't recognise. He decided on Fire wine: Stim clearly had an enduring love for it and had lost his collection of vintages when they needed quick fuel for the engines. He withdrew the bottle and a glass. After a moment's hesitation he withdrew a second glass. Firewine burned like hell, and Perin was not a fan, but he felt he both needed and deserved a drink. Perhaps it would help him feel slightly better. He poured two generous measures, plus a little extra for Stim, and then made his way back over to the giant. He handed the large man the glass and then gaped as he threw it back in one go and held it out again for another. Perin looked at his own glass and decided it might be better off with Stim and handed it over. The second glass went the same way as the first. Perin took both glasses from Stim and walked them back over to the drawer. He replaced them with care, as Occidens would have done. He took a deep breath and turned round.

"Okay, Stim, what are we going to do?" He wanted to make sure Stim was given the clear message that this was not the end of things. He looked back at Perin with bloodshot eyes.

"I have no idea. I'm not the ideas man or the leader. Occidens was the brains, Rienta the leader. I was just the one who did the heavy lifting and kept the men in line." His eyes brimmed with tears again. "What the hell use am I now."

Perin had to make a snap decision on how to deal with Stim. *What would Rienta do?* he asked himself. In response he set his feet a bit wider apart and planted his stance. He clasped his hands behind his back and put on his most stern expression.

"Are you suggesting that others in this crew lack brains, lack the ability to lead?" As he heard the words escape his mouth he immediately regretted them. *Oh no, he's going to assume—*

"No, sir," Stim said, rising to his feet in a natural militaristic response. Perin wondered for the first time if Stim had ever served in the Committee's guard. *Probably not,* he thought. *He would stand out, and that's not the*

Committee's style. Perin started to pace in front of Stim. This was not what he had in mind. He hadn't intended to assume command. He had intended to convince Stim to do so.

"Wait a minute…" Perin said, "I'm not the best choice for—"

"You're the only choice, sir." Stim looked him in the eye. "You are the captain, Perin. I will follow your orders and so will…" he hesitated, "…what is left of this crew."

"How can you possibly think that?" Perin said, completely bemused. "I've never led anything before!"

"You've been leading this crew since you first walked on board. They serve at your pleasure," Stim stated simply. He then mirrored Perin's pose and put on his best Rienta impression. "Now, get on with it."

Perin had to smile. *Can I do this?* he wondered. He traced back his thoughts and actions since arriving on the *Muta*. He had always tried to consider the crew and show them kindness, but he didn't know if this translated into the kind of loyalty that Rienta had inspired. Stim obviously seemed to think so. The more he considered it the more he came to the conclusion that there really was no other option. Stim was too emotional to captain this ship.

He could feel himself straighten up: the decision was made. He was captain. *Gods help them all.*

"Okay then. First of all, let's identify the problem," he said with a measured tone. "We have lost our power and our tactical specialist." He paused, weighing up his next words. "These will be regained," he said firmly. "I don't know how yet, but that's a problem we will deal with as we go. Occidens and Rienta must have found their abilities and learned them. You and I will do the same."

Stim nodded in agreement. "Yes, sir."

Perin knew that it was important to inspire loyalty and morale in the crew. He would have to use words to do that, like Rienta had done. It was important to start here with Stim. In many ways he was the personification of the crew in general. Especially with the very few that were left.

"Our more pressing concern," Perin continued, "is that we find ourselves without a crew and without a workable ship. If we cannot deal with these things then nothing else will matter." Stim continued to stare straight ahead but he sniffed. The loss of all those friends still bore down heavily on him. "We can find new allies and effect repairs if we reach port. So getting us in motion is primary. I intend to go to the engine room and either fix those engines, or turn it back into a rowing room."

"We don't have the crew to row, sir," Stim said.

Idiot, Perin thought to himself. It would take at least twenty men to get a ship of this size moving. Rowing simply wasn't an option. Either the engines would have to start working, or they would have to get the sail intact.

"What is the state of the sail?" he asked.

"Mast is just about holding on, but the sail was ripped from top to tail in the teeth. It won't hold any air."

"Do we have any materials?"

"Nothing in stores but some food," Stim replied. "Not that we need it all now without a crew to feed." This gave Perin an idea. It was an unpleasant and stomach-turning idea. These were, however, desperate times.

"Those crew members don't need their belongings either," he said slowly. The look on Stim's face turned from confusion to comprehension to disgust.

"You want us to loot their bunks for scraps for the sail?" he spat. "That's cold—"

"That's practical," Perin interrupted. "I'm pretty sure that every member of the crew, if you were able to ask them now, would say they would want the rest of the crew to live and would therefore be happy to give up their belongings." He remembered them trying to repair the ship below decks. "In fact, I've seen it myself – they used their clothes, their trunks, their books and whatever they had to plug the holes in the hull that were made during our trip through the teeth."

"If their belongings are holding the ship together already, how can we use them for the sail?" Stim asked, a touch of petulance creeping into his voice. He did not like this idea.

"We are currently surrounded," Perin replied, "by driftwood from the lifeboats. Surely we can hook some of that in, use that to repair some of the breeches and then use the material the crew used to fill the gaps to repair the sail."

Stim stood in silence for a few moments. Perin suspected he was searching for a reason the plan would not work. As he suspected, Stim eventually gave up.

"You can tell the rest of the crew," he said, annoyance and defiance clear in his voice. He then turned to head out towards the deck. Perin decided to take a few moments to himself before he went out to join him. He needed a short time to himself to contemplate becoming the captain of the *Muta*. He walked around Occidens' study. He supposed he had use of it now. As he walked beside one of the bookshelves he ran his index finger across the dusty tomes. *Maybe the answer to controlling magic more reliably is in one of these books.* That would be a problem for a safer and quieter time though. At the moment getting the crew to port had to be the priority. *Spoken like a true captain.*

He walked out onto the deck to find the eight remaining crew standing side by side, facing him. Stim stood in front of them.

"Captain on deck," he shouted. The crew clicked their heels together. It lacked military precision, but this made it all the more endearing and Perin appreciated it. Despite attempting to make a stoic and dignified impression his mouth betrayed a grin.

"Gentlemen," he started, "I really don't know what to say. I'll try and lead you well." He paused. "Until you find someone better of course!" This got a laugh from the crew, but they were still raw from their losses. It was hard for some of them to laugh. One crew member stepped forward.

"Captain, we all donated one of the shirts from our backs and we have wrapped Lady Occidens on deck. What should we do with her…" he struggled to get the final words out, "remains?" Perin hadn't thought of this, but was heartened that the crew had also considered where to find materials and had come up with a similar solution to his own. The idea that the crew had donated some of their few remaining possessions to this respectful cause made Perin glow with pride and admiration for the brave few survivors.

"Unfortunately, we can't give her a proper pyre until we have a boat to put her in," he explained. "What I suggest is that we gather as much wood as we can from the water. Perhaps we can put together enough for a sizeable raft to send her on her way. We may also collect enough to effect some repairs." This seemed like a fair and palatable way to encourage the crew to get the materials needed to mend both the hull and the sail without using the word 'loot'. Since Stim had used it, Perin had felt slightly nauseated. It gave the impression of grave-robbing.

The crew busied themselves trying to fish in some of the debris. This was harder than it would have been if they'd still had even one lifeboat intact. Now, rope ladders needed to be lowered to the water level so the crew could swim to collect the driftwood. It had to be done in daylight and while there was no wind – soon the debris would be taken too far from the *Muta* by the water currents. Conditions were fine now but could change quickly. Six of the crew, including Stim, were doing this very physical work. Two more were in the stores preparing something for the crew to eat and one more was in the crow's nest keeping watch. Perin was left alone on deck. For a time he oversaw the operation to salvage the materials but his mind soon strayed to the knowledge that Occidens was enshrouded nearby. He had ensured that she had been moved inside her study and that cold-water tubes, normally used to keep food fresh, were laid alongside her. He decided to go and pay his private respects to her.

As he walked through the door of her study he shuddered. The sun was beating down outside, but this room was thoroughly cold. It was also rather macabre, with Occidens' shrouded figure lying on top of the table she had sat at with Perin several times.

"I don't know how to do what you did," he said. "I don't know how to be what you were, even less what you wanted me to be." He stopped for a moment. His self-pitying was not what Occidens would have wanted to hear. "But I will figure it all out," he said, smiling. "I could maybe use a hint, a few tips along the way though." He chuckled to himself. "As if you would give me any hints. You really weren't one for making things easy for me." He thought of his first day of 'training' and being thrown from the ship repeatedly. He remembered Rienta giving him some words of comfort. That made him smile. It seemed like a lifetime ago. It was truly incredible how quickly his life had changed. A month ago he had lived in a different world and never heard the names 'Rienta' or 'Occidens'. Now he wished they were both still here. Both would have agreed that wishing did not make things so, and he should dust himself off and get on.

With that in mind he walked back out into the sunlight. He was met with the smell of wet wood and seaweed, the source a sizeable pile of driftwood that had been salvaged so far. Another armful was thrown over the side of the boat and onto the deck, followed by Stim, his hair matted to his face by the water. If Perin didn't know better he would say that he looked like he was enjoying himself.

"Do you think we have enough?" Perin asked.

"Probably," Stim replied, shaking his head like a canine and splattering the deck with water. "But it will need a good amount of time to dry out, otherwise it will splinter when we try to do anything with it"

"Fair enough. Once all of the crew are back on board

tell them they've done good work." Seeing the disappointed look on Stim's face he added, "Although, it's better to be safe than sorry. Can you collect some more?" Stim looked relieved and jumped over the side of the ship, clasping his tree trunk legs to his chest. He landed with a dramatic splash not unlike the cannonballs had. Perin closed his eyes as he started to relive the assault of the *Formalite'*. He tried to block out the sounds his mind was replaying and ignore the sweat on his palms and the tears in his eyes. He clenched his fists and forced his eyes open and looked towards the horizon. As the tears cleared he could see blue skies and crystal ocean heading as far as the eye could see. He tried to measure his breaths in time with the gusts of wind passing to calm himself. He understood why Stim wanted to stay in the ocean. Recent events had left them all broken and they would all have to find a way to deal with that. *What's my way?* Perin thought to himself. He had no answer. He would have to figure it out as he went along. He had to get on with what needed to be done. He would simply find his own coping mechanism on the way.

As he turned away from the horizon he decided to check on the prospective damage to the ship. He wandered down each successive level, pleasantly surprised that the crew had largely held everything together.

Finally he reached the lowest level of the ship where Rienta and he had both had their quarters. The water, which had partially flooded the area, had been cleared. He approached her quarters, the captain's quarters – *his* quarters. He took a breath as he turned the handle and entered. Everything was identical to how it had been when he was last there. Rienta had her own collections of books and trinkets, and Perin realised there might be clues here to their next move as well. For the time being though Perin didn't feel he wanted to touch anything. Again, there would be time for that once they were moving.

He lay down for a few moments. It felt wrong to be in

this room. He knew that it was now his and that he would have to get used to that, but the idea of falling asleep here, of this room becoming his sanctuary as it had Rienta's, seemed wrong. It felt disrespectful. He didn't feel that way about Occidens' study. That was a sanctuary for magic, and he certainly had magic. His reluctance to be at ease in this room was to do with a lack of confidence as a leader of men. He knew it was something that should get easier, something that he needed to become comfortable with. He hoped it would happen fast, before he got anyone else killed.

With that in mind, he sat up. He couldn't rest and decided it was time to go and eat with his crew. Then they could get the ship repaired and limp in to port. By the time they got there, he would hopefully know what to do next and feel as if he was worthy to do it.

CHAPTER TWENTY-TWO

It would take at least a whole day for the wood to dry out. As frustrating as this was, Perin knew he, and the crew needed the rest. As they ate together, sitting on the deck with legs crossed like children, he hoped that a feeling of camaraderie would sprout up around the original crew to help pull them out of the dark thoughts of fallen friends. This would help heal wounds and create the support network he could tell they needed. Stim remained boisterous and bombastic but Perin could see that the merriment never reached his eyes. He saw one member of the crew saying a lot less than he used to and a third who lifted his glass a lot more. *I owe these people,* Perin thought. With any luck they would find a new crew in port, though he had no idea how he was going to convince them to join up. A big influx of new people was absolutely needed to keep the ship in working order, but such a rush of new blood threatened to flush out the old crew who had made the *Muta* a home as well as a ship. Perin couldn't let that happen. He stood up on shaky legs – they had all consumed a healthy amount of Occidens' drinks drawer – and raised his glass to the assembled company.

"I want to thank you for your efforts here today," he

slurred. "Tomorrow, I'm going to get those engines working," a cheer went up from the small group, and one fell backwards and started laughing, "but the job I have for the rest of you is less enjoyable." This silenced the small band. Stim looked at Perin, knowing what was coming, and he closed his eyes as if bracing for some form of impact. "We will need to find more materials to mend the ship, and we will need things we can barter and trade with when we reach port." The crew looked at him, puzzled. "I need you to respectfully go through the belongings of our fallen colleagues and put aside anything that could be useful or valuable."

He braced himself for the backlash and scorn that Stim seemed to hold for the idea. The faces in front of him now were certainly ashen, the joviality vanished in a flash to be replaced by the solemn memories of recent losses. One of the crew stood up. It was the same member who had led the repair operations below decks after they came through the teeth, and had helped clear the water around the lowest level. Perin was sad that he had never learned his name. It would seem rude now to ask.

"It would be an honour, sir," he said.

There was absolutely no point in attempting to hide the look of shock on Perin's face. This was not the response he had envisaged by any means. He had been prepared for everything from mutiny to dutiful obedience but he never considered it would be something the crew would consider an honour.

"I'm glad that's something you're comfortable with doing," he said carefully.

"I knew every member of this crew," the man replied, "I'm probably one of the longest serving members here. Every single one of them would want us to put their belongings to good use." Perin still looked bemused as he continued, "Going through their belongings is a chance to remember them all individually. It's a sign of respect and I'll be glad to do it." The remainder of the crew looked on and nodded. Perin swelled with pride at their attitude. *Stim is overly emotional,* he thought to himself.

"With that in mind, gentlemen," Perin said, "I think we have had our fill tonight." He gestured to the crewmen who had prepared the food. "Special thanks to our cooks who have restored the rest of us after a rather stressful time." A faint murmur of applause rippled round the small crowd. "Tomorrow, we will be revisiting the memories of some old friends while the wood dries out on deck. Then hopefully we can get this great ship up and running again!" A slightly more enthusiastic round of drunken applause rippled through. One of the men fell backward again. Perin thought it was time to take his leave. "I think I'll lead the charge to the bunks." He turned and headed towards the stairs. He wasn't even halfway towards them when a rough hand touched his shoulder. Perin turned to face Stim, whose eyes held nothing but apology and regret.

"I just wanted to say," he began, "I may not have been thinking straight when I said we shouldn't go through the crew's things." He hung his head and wrung his hands.

"Stim," Perin smiled, shaking his head, "the fact that you care that much about our crew is not a vice, even if it does cause problems. You're a good man with a good heart. There's no need to apologise for it." He clapped his hand to the top of Stim's arm, and then turned and headed down to the bottom deck. He heard Stim sniff as he went.

He entered Rienta's quarters and again felt like he couldn't touch anything. He sat down on the bed and removed his boots. Discarding them to the side he started to rub the soles of his feet, which had now become rougher even than Stim's hands. As he looked around the quarters he smiled at Rienta's efficiency. The chair by her desk looked hard but the desk itself was organised to within an inch of its existence. The bookcase was ordered in some way with an index book at the very beginning. Perin knew it would be complete and accurate without needing to open the cover to check. Amazingly, her table and chairs were still sitting perfectly in the room. *How?* Perin wondered. *We came through the teeth and an attack and it didn't send a thing in this room even an inch out of place.* Even beyond death Rienta seemed to have things here well in hand.

Perin fell back onto the bed, the air knocked out of him slightly by its firmness, but he soon recovered and fell into unconsciousness. His last thought before he drifted away into sleep was: *I must get those engines working.*

Perin was woken the next morning by the rock of the ship. He sighed slightly – he enjoyed the motion of the ship and its cradle-like effect. *Wait a second,* he thought. *Motion?* He sat bolt upright and threw the soft quilt away. The *Muta* was definitely moving. He could even hear the movement of the water on the other side of the bulkhead. *We've been attacked again and abducted,* was his first panicked impression. *Someone would have woke me,* he reasoned. He decided he would still have to find out what was going on. He threw off his clothes before realising the rest of his wardrobe had been ejected into the ocean with his quarters. Rienta was much taller than he was and, obviously, a woman. There was no way she would have anything that would fit Perin, but one even passing sniff at the stained and used clothes he had been wearing told him he would simply have to find something. Perhaps a pair of trousers that could be turned up or a blouse he could pin in so he didn't look like he had a bosom. He was also aware that turning up in Rienta's clothes on deck might be a bit on the nose for the still fragile sensibilities of the crew, and certainly for Stim. Needs must, however, so he had to have a look.

He approached the solid, dark chest of drawers and looked in the first drawer. He had no idea what some of these garments were for, so he closed it and moved on to the second. Skirts and blouses, nothing appropriate. He opened the third drawer and withdrew in shock.

His clothes sat in front of him. Folded neatly in the drawer. He had no idea how they had gotten from his quarters to Rienta's. More worrying still was that there was an envelope sitting on top of all the clothes. The handwriting was unmistakeable: this was a note left by Rienta. It simply read *Perin*. With his hands shaking he reached forward and picked the letter up. All thoughts of the *Muta* being abducted and towed to their doom had temporarily been driven from his mind as he sat down and unfolded the pages.

Dear Perin,

Put simply, if you are reading this note, then things are probably not going well. You have no other reason to be in my room, going through my things, unless I am seriously hurt or have been lost. I assume you have taken command. Your natural leadership and use of language make you the only choice. Stim is too emotional and Occidens is too hot-headed. You have my best wishes of luck with both of them.

I took the liberty of having some of your clothes put here. It is unlikely I have gone down without a fight and I would likely have forced you into that ejectable bunker we had for you. When we rescue you from it, it is unlikely we will have time for you to pack an overnight bag. Hence this precaution. I hope to be there to give you these belongings myself. If you are reading this, then that has clearly not been possible.

I would like to give you a piece of sincere and important advice about Occidens, which will become important if I am not there to keep her in check. She is thoroughly enamoured with herself and her own mysticism. She believed it was important for you to see her as all-powerful and all-knowing if you were to believe in magic. This is why she has not told you some basic facts about magic, its use and her history with it.

Occidens studied hard at magic. It did not come naturally. The progress you have made in a few days is truly stellar in comparison. She kept copious notes on her own progress. She does not wish to show you these, as they show up her own fallibility. They are not stored on the Muta. They are held in a secret archive somewhere in Caramine and they are maintained and added to by an archivist. I can't tell you where this archive is, other than it is in a secret cove that I have never seen on any of my maps. I also cannot tell you anything about the Archivist. Occidens does not wish to talk of it. You need to find a way to draw this information from her. I believe it is the only way for you to achieve true mastery of magic. I do wish I had been there to see that.

Good luck, Captain,
Rienta

Perin's hands shook as he looked at the note. He reread it twice. He didn't know if he should feel hope or despair. The idea that there was some resource that could still teach him how to use magic as efficiently as Occidens or the members of the Committee gave him butterflies in his stomach, but when he read the note, the one eventuality that was not mentioned was if Occidens was unable to give him the information. He had no idea how to find the cove. If it contained the information Rienta had written about then there was no chance the Great Committee knew about it – they would not allow the Archive to stand. So it must be exceptionally well hidden. Perin had no idea how he, with a derelict ship and no resources, would be able to track down this facility when the Great Committee with its fleet and four sorcerers could not.

Derelict, thought Perin, and his mind snapped back to the fact that this supposedly derelict ship appeared to be moving. He quickly gathered up the clothes from Rienta's drawer and hauled them on. He pulled on his boots and bolted from the room. As he ran up the stairs, he noticed that most of the crew were still in their bunks. *Perhaps the ship has been taken by pirates,* he thought, and slowed his pace to avoid giving some unknown assailant word of his presence. *Don't be an idiot,* Perin thought to himself, *what kind of pirate boards a derelict ship to mend it and sail it whilst leaving the crew asleep in their beds? Either a very clever or a very stupid pirate, nothing in between.* He quietly made his way up the rest of the stairs and poked his head out on deck. He burst into laughter.

Stim was lying underneath the sail on his back snoring louder than his voice had been when projected through the brass amplifier. The sail was back up having been sewn together through the night. Perin could make out britches, bloomers, shirts, ties and handkerchiefs all being used to join the patchwork sail down the tear. It was complete, even if it did look a little ridiculous, and it was holding. Stim had obviously worked through the night and was now exhausted, but they were moving.

He looked beyond the sail and saw the crew member from last night standing behind the wheel.

"What ho, Captain!" he yelled pleasantly. There was a glint from his smile as the light struck his gold tooth. "Not bad for a night's work eh!"

"You can say that again!" Perin yelled back. He knew he would have to risk the rudeness. "I'm so sorry, crewman, but I need to know your name!"

"Amic, sir," he shouted back, "and thank you for asking!" Perin smiled and started to walk towards the helm before Amic shouted again.

"Oy, Stim, captain on deck!" The hulking mass of hair and muscle grunted but did not wake up. "Stim, I said CAPTAIN ON DECK!" Stim's head shot up and he came forward into a sitting position as if rising from the dead. His hand shot to his forehead in a clumsy but endearing salute, not least because he had inadvertently slapped his own face.

"Ready for orders, Captain," he said sleepily.

"It's all right, Stim," Perin laughed, before adding, "As you were." With a sigh of relief Stim's head went back the way it had come and with a crash he was both back on the deck and fast asleep. It had clearly been a very difficult night's work. Perin made his way towards the helm where Amic was guiding the ship.

"I hope you don't mind all this, Captain," he said sheepishly. "After we spoke last night, the boys and I got to talking. We knew that you were gonna try and get the engines running, but we wanted to help you. The only way we could figure to do that was to get you to port as soon as possible. Now the wood wasn't dry, so it's still gonna be used to plug some of the holes." He gestured behind him and Perin could see and smell the wood. It did look drier than it had when it came out of the water, and probably by this evening it would be usable again. "We went through the belongings that weren't being used already and we found enough to mend the sail. So we did – I hope you don't mind."

Perin was overcome. "Mind?" he asked. "My dear Mr Amic, this is beyond my wildest dreams!" He had to restrain himself from throwing his hands round the crewman. "What's our heading?" Amic looked a bit more downcast at that.

"Now, sir, I know it's not the done thing for the crew to set their own heading, and we could have woken you, but we just seemed to want to keep it as a sort of surprise. We are heading for Port Antez. We are still far enough away to change it if it suits you."

"No," Perin replied. The *Muta* had been heading towards the more southerly Port Graze when the *Formalite'* had found them again. They had probably returned there. If the *Formalite'* knew the *Muta* was moving again, they wouldn't hesitate to sink them next time. Viri had made a strategic error by leaving them adrift and Perin was determined to make the most of it. "Can we get a new crew in Antez?" he asked. Amic blew air out between his lips.

"I reckon you can get a mercenary crew, but I wouldn't trust 'em." He rubbed his fingers together. "They follow money, sir, and the Committee are always gonna have more of that than we do." Perin's stomach formed a new knot. If they couldn't obtain a new crew how would they possibly be able to man the ship in the long term?

"Is there any way to get a genuine crew? How did you all join up before?"

"We were all young men," said Amic. "We didn't like how the world was going and we joined up on this great galleon with her powerful captain, strongman deckhand and in-house sorcerer." He spread his arms. "We were impressed, sir, and then once we were here we grew to love her!"

Perin smiled a sad smile. "Well we might not have Rienta or Occidens anymore, but we will inspire people again and they will come to learn to love the *Muta*, just as you did." This made Amic laugh.

"I'm glad to hear it, sir." He then started to chuckle again. Perin couldn't help thinking he was making a little bit of fun of him.

"Don't you think we can?" he asked, perhaps slightly indignantly.

"Oh, sir," Amic said, "please don't get me wrong, I think you can inspire a legion to join us, and Mr Stim could lift a house above his head, if he still has the charge in him." He started to laugh again. Perin's face fell as he realised that Stim probably did not have the power left in him, so it would fall to Perin to try to give Stim a boost of energy. This would be new and challenging. It didn't seem to be what Amic was laughing at though.

"So what's so funny then?"

"I'm afraid," Amic said, "I was just trying to imagine how I would have viewed the *Muta* if the grand old galleon had sailed proudly into port, all dressed to impress, held together by ladies' bloomers and sailors' britches!"

"Ah!" Perin hadn't thought of this, but Amic was quite right. Perhaps putting on an impressive display for the young sailors to make them desperate to join their crew would be a little more challenging than he had considered. It didn't stop both men indulging in a well-earned hearty laugh. It was so loud it almost matched Stim's snoring.

CHAPTER TWENTY-THREE

Perin allowed Stim a few hours to sleep. He spent the time in Occidens' study trying to find any clue as to the whereabouts of the Archive. A lot of the books in the study were written in Occidens' own handwriting. There were many descriptions of Occidens' exploits at the height of her powers but Perin could not find any mention of her early magic learning or career in the tomes. They were filled to the gunnels with eloquent writing of her many adventures but these all seemed to be since she had been onboard the *Muta*. There was no discussion of how she had come to be on board, never mind her magical studies.

The stories were still fabulous. Perin did not have time to sit and read them all, but he fully intended to do so once things had gotten a bit quieter: perhaps once he had found the Archive, and its relative safety.

He had found many maps. Occidens had clearly enjoyed drawing them in her spare time. She was a relatively skilled amateur cartographer. All of the maps were of Caramine, none as detailed as the largest one they had used to plan their journey through the teeth. They seemed to be mostly impressions of what Caramine may have looked like before the Committee raised the islands around the main landmass. These were probably attempts to imagine what the continent had looked like before these reformations. Occidens would have remembered what things had happened, but through the mists of time; what they looked like may have gotten lost. Other maps had different landmasses entirely, as if Occidens had imagined how the world could be recreated after the Great Committee had been deposed. These gave Perin hope for the future. He had given very little thought to what the world would look like after they were successful, *if* they were successful. He was sad that Occidens would never see it.

There was a knock on the study door and the light was blocked out by Stim standing in the doorway.

"Stim," Perin exclaimed, "you're up!" Stim looked sheepish but Perin's grin soon spread onto his face as well. "Thank you for what you did with the sail."

"I'm not sure if I can manage much more though," he said. "Occidens' last charge is wearing quite thin." He looked at his hands. "You don't think you could…?"

"That's what I wanted to talk to you about," Perin said. "I've been going through some of Occidens' books to see if I can figure out how she did what she did to charge up your powers." Stim looked hungrily towards him and at the books.

"And?" he asked hopefully.

"I'm afraid," Perin said slowly, "Occidens didn't really keep much in the way of records. These are largely stories of her adventures since coming here; they certainly aren't instruction manuals for how she did anything."

"No," Stim said dejectedly. "All the books with that kind of stuff will be in the Archive."

Perin stood looking at the massive man for a moment, open-mouthed.

"Sorry, what?" he asked.

"Occidens put all her records about magical learning in an archive with her friend," Stim said, almost as if he were describing the weather. "He's called 'the Archivist' – I thought you would know about that?"

"No I didn't," said Perin, "or rather, I did, but only because Rienta left it in a note for me. Do you know where this Archive is?"

Stim seemed rather conflicted as he looked back at Perin. "I don't know exactly where it is," he said carefully. "I know that Occidens never wanted anyone to know. One night when she was mad at Rienta she did let something slip, but I don't know if I should say."

"Stim, this is extremely important," Perin said. "Unless I can find some magical assistance, then I will never be reliable enough to take on the Great Committee."

"I'm not sure that the stuff in the Archive will be of any help to you," Stim said, as if trying to change the subject. "Occidens didn't keep an instruction manual, just records of her early magic experiments. She locked them away so that the Great Committee couldn't get them."

"Stim," Perin said, with an edge of steel in his voice, "you need to tell me what you know. After we get to Antez and get the ship repaired and a new crew, we are gonna need a mission, otherwise no one is going to have any reason to join up."

"I'm not sure," Stim said.

"You can give us that mission, you can give us that purpose. We need that purpose, we need that hope!" he implored.

"But Occidens didn't want—"

"Rienta did!" Perin interrupted. He could see the conflict on the big man's face but after a while he seemed convinced. Stim sagged at the shoulders a little before gesturing towards all the maps in the room.

"Do you notice anything identical about all of these maps?" Stim asked.

"Well none of them label the Archive on them. I've checked."

"No, they wouldn't," Stim said, "but it's on each and

every one of the maps. In fact it's the only position that never moves on any of them."

Perin looked at the maps in front of them. Many had similar attributes, and most had the central landmass of Caramine with different outlying islands, but there were one or two that had all the settlements spread out.

"The parchment is all the same…" Perin searched for an answer. Stim shrugged. "What?" Perin exclaimed. "You mean you don't actually know where it is?" Stim shook his head.

"That's what Occidens said," Stim explained. "That the Archive was hidden in plain sight and that it was the only point on the maps that did not change." Perin looked at the maps in front of him with truly no idea what each and every one of them had in common.

"Perhaps there is some marking in invisible ink that can only be seen when it is held up to the light," Perin suggested, to himself as much as to Stim. He knew that this was a method that had been used to transfer secret communications during military conflicts in the past.

"Possible," Stim said. It had clearly never occurred to him. Perin took hold of the map by both ends and took it to the door of the study. The sun was beating in through the doorway, providing a pleasant heat and as Perin held the paper up to the sun the map turned transparent with only the vague outline of the charcoal-drawn borders standing out, and the black mark of the compass. *The compass,* Perin realised. This was the point on the map that never changed. He quickly looked over the rest of the maps and the compass was in exactly the same position on each one. *This is it,* Perin thought, *this has to be it! The compass hides the Archive!*

"I've got it!" Perin told Stim. "I know where the Archive is. Thankfully it's on this side of Caramine so we don't need to try and get back to the west." Stim breathed a sigh of relief.

"So that deals with the 'where'," said Perin, "but I'm

afraid the 'how' still provides us with a bit of a problem. We need to get you all energised up," he said with a smile.

"Do you think you can do it?"

"I'm really not sure. The way magic works for me at the moment is that I can imagine something, and if I can picture it so clearly that it could be real, it sometimes becomes real. I'm not sure if I can do that to transfer power to you. I do need you to have it though, so that we can inspire the crew members to come and join us."

Stim smiled. "Yeah I remember, that's how we used to do it. Rienta would give a speech, I'd throw some stuff around and Occidens would shoot up some fireworks. It always did the trick."

Perin smiled in return. "Yeah, well I can give a speech," he said, "and I think I can manage some fireworks but I still need you to throw some stuff around. I just don't know how to give you that power."

Stim furrowed his brow in thought. "Can't you just imagine me as strong?"

"I've been trying that," said Perin, "but it doesn't seem to work that way. I already see you as strong, but it's about changing your potential as opposed to your physical presence."

"Huh?"

"In a way," Perin tried to explain, "it would be easier for me to imagine you having two extra arms than it would be to imagine you as having more strength. One is a physical change. What you are talking about is a change in your endurance, in your potential strength and abilities. I can't figure out how to do that."

"But I do change physically."

"How?" asked Perin, hoping this would lead to a new break in his experimentation.

"I'm taller, I'm grander, I'm…bigger!" said Stim. Perin slumped a little.

"No, Stim, you're not, you just feel that way because of the extra power." Like a lightning bolt the thought hit him.

"Wait a minute, that could be the key." He walked towards Stim. "Stim, I need you to describe to me how having that extra power makes you feel, with as much detail as you can." Stim looked a bit surprised but smiled, and Perin had the impression that this was something Stim might enjoy talking about.

"First of all," he said, "my breath swells up in my chest, until I'm all big and puffed out. I then continue to breath in and out, but my chest stays there, all strong and prominent. As the air shoots round my veins it burns my muscles a little as they twitch and tense and grow tight and responsive."

Perin had closed his eyes and imagined Stim feeling this way again. If he could do that perhaps the magical strength would come as a by-product. Stim continued, "My legs stand up straighter, my calves get tight and fill with energy like I could run a hundred miles. I have to stretch every muscle in my body outwards and I look towards the heavens and close my eyes. I can still see a blazing blue light through them as Occidens' power surrounds me. Then once the stretch is complete I bring my arms to my side and that's it done. I'm full of the power."

Perin opened his eyes to look at Stim, who was looking down at his own hands. He was shaking in disbelief. The faint blue glow that had enveloped his skin when Occidens had charged him up was just receding from his fingertips.

"Looks like you're all good to go," smiled Perin.

"But how?" said Stim in disbelief.

"I imagined that you felt the way you did before when you were all energised. That's really all it took."

Stim smiled and clapped Perin on the shoulder, which sent Perin falling to the floor with a crunch. Pain leapt up his shins; it wasn't serious, but it was extremely painful. He climbed back to his feet, but even the pain couldn't keep the smile from his face.

"I think if there was any doubt, we can be assured you are back to fighting fitness."

A bell sounded. Perin and Stim both looked up with a panicked expression until it was followed by a declaration from the crow's nest. "Port ahead."

"And not a moment too soon," Perin said, looking towards Stim. They had finally arrived at Port Antez. As they headed out towards the deck Perin could see they were approaching the cove that held the port.

Port Antez was nestled in the crook behind Antez Island that lay just to the east of Upper Caramine. This made it a perfect hideout for people who did not wish to be found. The lookout towers would watch the oceans for ships approaching The Hammer to the east coming round from the chains to the south. It was this way that the *Muta* had sailed, but it was certainly not a military ship or a threat in any way so was being allowed in with no impediment.

The crew had assembled on deck. They looked out towards the oncoming port, keen to arrive. Perin realised they were likely in desperate need of some shore leave.

"Gentleman," he shouted. "If we can secure the ship well enough, I'm quite happy for you all to take some time on your own to get some of your strength back." There was a murmur of content from the small company. "We have a plan for after we leave here. I don't know what will meet us when we reach our new destination so I would suggest that you all get as much rest as is humanly possible." The response was positive: the crew wanted a purpose, even if it did mean going into the unknown.

As the ship drew closer to port the smells started to assault the nostrils. The odour of fresh fish, baked bread and livestock and the sounds of a busy and thriving port would have made Perin a little nauseous before he began this journey. Now they were the smells of safe harbour. Perin could hear some laughter. The words of Amic returned to his ears and he imagined the ridicule that this sight must be causing on the docks. He knew he would have to do something about that.

The planks and rope ladders were lowered so that the crew could get down onto the gangway. Perin was aware that a crowd had formed to look at the peculiar ship with its makeshift sail. *Perfect,* Perin thought. The crowd had delivered themselves to him and he would have the opportunity to speak to everyone at the same time. He made his way to the top of the ramp so that he could see the whole assembled gathering. He was struck by how young he was in comparison to everyone else. This was less noticeable when he was on the *Muta* itself – Rienta and Occidens had been so old by comparison to everyone else that age didn't seem to matter – but here he would be trying to sound responsible and inspirational to a group of people who would likely think he was hardly out of diapers. This would be a tougher job than he'd expected. He raised his hands to silence the crowd.

"Thank you for welcoming us to your port," he boomed. "I don't mind telling you, there were times when I was afraid we would never make it. We are the remaining crew of the *Muta.*" That got a reaction. Passersby stopped in their tracks and onlookers started to view the ship as if it was something from a folk-tale or legend. As their eyes journeyed to the sail, some of them seemed to dismiss Perin's claims.

"Many of you will have heard of Captain Rienta, the inspirational leader of this band and extraordinary magical swordswoman." The attention was all back on Perin now – *that damn sail,* he thought to himself. "I am sorry to have to tell you that Captain Rienta was slain in defence of her crew by Mistress Viri of the Great Committee and the *Formalite'.*" There was a sharp intake of breath, particularly from the female members of the crowd. *It was entirely possible,* Perin thought, *that Rienta served as a role model to some of these women.*

"Please do not grieve for her," he continued. "As someone who knew her I can guarantee you that she would not have wanted your sympathy." He paused for dramatic effect. "She would have wanted your loyalty. She would have wanted you to join the cause and crew of the *Muta*."

The response to this was different was to his earlier speech to his crew. The reaction from the crowd of onlookers was one of bemusement and confusion. There was definitely also respect and curiosity, but he was far from having them convinced.

"You may be wondering why the *Muta* is in need of crew members." There was a clear murmur of agreement from the crowd. "The crew, including the great sorcerer Occidens, were slaughtered by the *Formalite'* even after the flag of surrender had been flown. They left us crippled and adrift in the ocean."

This time the ripple was one of fear. Perin was in danger of scaring his audience away. He had to be very careful. "And yet here we are, sad and shocked yes, but also composed and determined. This is a sign that not only has this attack failed, but that all attempts to break our spirit on our mission to liberty will fail."

That hit the spot: the crowd erupted in applause. Moving them to action rather than just gaining their support would be quite another matter though. "The *Formalite'* attacked and destroyed our lifeboats even though they were fleeing."

Through the shock and dismay of the crowd a voice could be heard above the shouting.

"So what did you do to fall foul of the Great Committee? Who are you anyway?" This was what Perin had been waiting for, a demand to prove himself, to present his credentials and then demonstrate why he was worth listening to. He took a deep breath. There would be no coming back from what he was about to do.

"My name is Perin," he stated. "I am the newest Sorcerer of Caramine." This was met with laughter. They did not believe him. Perin responded by looking up into the sky. The cloud above him turned black and rumbled with thunder and then, as he looked forward again, the cloud dissipated and left the sky blue once more. This silenced the crowd.

"I showed potential at the Great Academy. I was rewarded with imprisonment. Rienta and Occidens saved me, at great personal risk." The crowd were now hanging on his every word. "They saw potential in me and began my magical training. The Great Committee sent one of their own to stop them. Whether or not they succeed will be down to you." The crowd shuffled around uncomfortably. This was the time for Perin to elevate his speech to a grand climax.

"Occidens and Rienta believed that I could overthrow the Great Committee. They believed with a little bit of time and learning that I could take them on and make this a just and fair society again." You could hear a pin drop amongst the onlookers. "Whether or not that is true will depend upon you. This ship cannot sail without a crew. We are looking for as many good men and women as possible to come join us to take us forward into liberty and a future we can all be proud of." He paused. "You have until we are restocked and repaired to make your decision." He paused long enough for everyone to think he was finished before concluding, "In the meantime, for all our repairs and restocking needs, I would be grateful if you could direct your enquiries to Mr Stim."

Stim had been standing behind Perin out of sight this whole time. In one movement he jumped so high in the air it was as if he was flying. He had judged it just right. He eclipsed the sun momentarily, plunging the dock into darkness before landing on one knee directly in front of the astounded crowd. He then drew himself up to his full height, which was so tall even those standing at the very back of the group could see his face. He looked at everyone around him as if he had been totally oblivious to the fact that anything had happened.

"So," he said, "who's first?"

CHAPTER TWENTY-FOUR

After their dramatic announcement the port became a hive of activity. The usual traders and vendors rushed forward towards the ship to try and sell their wares to the *Muta*'s crew. As people selling everything from silk to socks advanced on the tiny crew, Perin was somewhat overwhelmed. He managed to hold back long enough to talk to Amic.

"Stim is getting us stocked up, can you get us repaired? We'll need new sails, new mast, new oars for the engines as well as replacing any broken beams."

"Aye, sir," Amic replied. "Do you want me to try and get a new quarters built for you that can be slotted back into the rear of the ship?" Perin hadn't considered this. It would give him the opportunity to leave Rienta's quarters and move back into his own space. When it came to it though, what were Rienta's quarters being saved for? Perhaps there was a better use for the ejection room.

"If you can replace it then yes, do it. I won't use it as quarters, but there's every chance we may have things on board we'd like to get rid of in a hurry if we were boarded." He was thinking of the Archive. If they found written materials that gave him a magical edge and brought them on board the *Muta* they would have to have a way of keeping them safe. Using the ejection room as a safe room would give them this option should they be boarded.

With that thought still going through his mind Perin managed to sneak out through the commotion onto the streets of Port Antez. It was his first chance at a change of scenery and some peaceful solitude in what seemed like a very long time. He immediately took a side street to escape the crowds and was soon walking along narrow cobbled streets with high buildings on both sides. Before long, all the sounds of the port had died away and Perin was blissfully alone.

The silence was deafening. The peacefulness overloaded Perin's senses and he found a secluded corner with no passersby twhere he could sit down and escape the world for a few moments. Antez was significantly warmer than the Great Academy had been. Perin knew that East Caramine had a generally hotter climate than the west, but he had obviously never experienced anything like this. The heat was pleasant, not in any way stifling. The bright sun overhead and cloudless skies created the illusion that everything was brighter and more vivid than it was in the west.

For a moment Perin considered running away from everything. He loved the *Muta* and her crew. He had come to believe in their mission. But it simply couldn't be denied that life would be simpler and perhaps a lot more pleasant if he managed to slip away and start a quiet life with none of the complications of political and magical revolution. He probably knew enough magic to set himself up a nice home with enough fertile land that he would never need to see another soul. As he stood on the quiet street and experienced the first solitude since this had all begun, he had to admit it was thoroughly tempting.

He snapped back to reality. Of course this was all ridiculous and he had no intention of following through on the daydream, but it was a comforting thought that life could be simpler. It could be quieter and easier. It was enjoyable to consider that once the world was reformed life would be very different. Perin had not really considered what his life would involve once their mission was completed. If he wasn't dead chances are he would be helping set up the new Caramine. *Probably not much time for solitude and peacefulness then*, he thought. *Maybe running away down these streets is a good idea.* A nice thought, but simply not part of Perin's destiny.

He looked around his little secluded hideaway. It was part of the residential area of Antez. The stone was white and served to bounce the light of the sun all around, making everything seem even warmer and clearer. High above him there were windows into the apartments or houses, the ledges bearing brightly coloured plants in purples, reds and yellows. Nothing was muted or subtle, and this made the world feel more vivid. Of all the places Perin had read about or seen this, he considered, was the closest to a paradise. If he reached an age where he could stand down from society, he would want to end his days here. *Another fanciful daydream*, he thought. When he considered Occidens and Rienta and even Viri, it seemed that any form of retirement or quiet in their advancing years was not what sorcerers tended towards.

He stood up, his feet slipping slightly on the cobbles beneath his feet. Looking down he could see that many years and countless feet had worn them smooth. He walked down one street, and then another, and then another. At first he enjoyed the fact that he could see and hear no other soul. He enjoyed that the smell and sounds of the market and the sea had faded into the distance. He took another turn and another, escaping even further into his own solitude.

It eventually occurred to him that he had no idea how to retrace his steps. There had been so many labyrinthine curves and choices of left and right that he had completely lost his bearings. The bottom fell from his stomach as he looked up to see if he could see anything of the skyline, but all he could see was blue sky. The buildings were too tall and the streets too narrow to allow him to see much else. Perin began to walk with more purpose, breathing more heavily as the panic set in. He was hoping to bump into someone or something that would give him any idea of directions. He knew if he were away too long then the crew of the *Muta*, particularly Stim, would also start to panic. This made Perin even more nervous as Stim panicking was likely to result in some erratic and unhelpful behaviour.

Perin realised how much a person relies on outside factors to guide them in daily life. The buildings blocked out the wind, so he couldn't use that to guide him. They blocked his vision of the hills that surrounded the port to at least give him an inclination as to what direction he should be travelling. There was no one to ask, or to follow to find his way back. He was thoroughly and completely lost.

A terrible thought occurred. *What if I inadvertently used magic when I thought about that quiet life of solitude?* Was it possible that Perin had in some accidental way conjured away the rest of Caramine so that he could spend the rest of his days in quiet solitude and contemplation? That dream immediately turned to a nightmare in Perin's mind. He started to walk faster down one street and then another, spinning wildly as he walked, desperate for some signal of his whereabouts or some human contact.

He came to a large circular courtyard. It was empty – there was still no one to speak to or ask for help. Identical-looking streets branched off from the square in all directions. In the centre of the square stood a simple fountain; three basins widening from top to bottom with water flowing from one to the other and then pooling in the bottom basin. The sound of the running water was welcoming. Although it was only a small comfort the knot in Perin's stomach eased ever so slightly. The cobbles in this circular square were painted yellow. Between that fact and the branching streets it reminded Perin very much of a child's drawing of the sun, a burning orb with its branches of light.

The sound of the running water made Perin realise he was thirsty. There were water jugs next to the fountain and he decided this must mean the water was safe to drink. He rushed forward. Leaning over the edge, he dipped his hands into the water and splashed it onto his face. Cupping his hands he then drank three hearty handfuls and sighed, feeling partially restored. He wiped his mouth on his shirt and then turned to see if there were any signs or symbols around that would point him back in the direction of the harbour. He was quite sure he had come some distance. There was now no hint of the smell of fish or spices they were able to smell from quite far out during the *Muta*'s approach. *I suppose,* Perin thought, *that had been open water. Perhaps these buildings would block the smell. They certainly block the wind.* The alternative was that Perin had strayed indescribably far from the port and he didn't want to think about that.

He looked up and was given some hope. The square had opened out so he could see the hills of Antez. The three watchtowers were visible. Each one in sturdy stone, they looked as though they may have sprouted naturally from the cliffs beneath. They were tall enough to see out into the ocean a good distance away. Each housed a bell, and then a thatched roof with layers of straw. This provided shade but could be ignited as a signal if there was no light. These three towers were what kept Antez safe. They were manned constantly and would sound if a suspect ship approached, to give people the opportunity to sail out of the port and make their escape. This had been described at the Great Academy in geography lessons. The students had been led to believe that Antez was a hive of crime and that the early warning system was perfect evidence for their transgressions. Now Perin found that not only did they make him feel safe but that they also gave him an approximate bearing. As the *Muta* had come into port these towers had been directly in front. The centre tower had been directly in line with the other two off at either side. Perin was now much closer to the towers, but off towards the left. If he walked onwards he would be getting further away from the port. Amazingly he seemed to have travelled in a general straight line and could now perhaps retrace his steps backwards.

He started to feel foolish for worrying and was grateful that no one else had been around to see it. Antez must have housed many people due to its secure location. A complex network of living spaces was bound to have sprung up. Reason also told him that the arrival of the *Muta* had caused quite a stir and the fact he hadn't seen or met anyone was easily explained: everyone who had been on the streets was probably at the docks either trading with or enquiring about the great galleon.

His journey back towards the port was extremely slow and tentative. With every turn he was careful to reaffirm in his mind where the hills had been and tried to move away from them whilst also travelling slightly back towards the centre. This was the trickiest part. If he just walked right whenever he could to try and centre himself he would probably overshoot his mark and get even more lost. He tried to approach it logically. *Three streets down, one to the right.* That should generally take him in the direction that he wanted to go. It wasn't that simple of course: some of the streets twisted and turned and put Perin in danger of turning full circle. Twice he had to double back and take a different street to avoid this from happening. Keeping track of it was quite mentally exhausting and the heat was finally taking its toll on him physically.

Suddenly he snapped his head upward and flared his nostrils with a deep sniff. Never had the smell of fish been so welcome. Perin smiled and quickened his pace as he started to be able to follow not just smells but voices as well. *So I didn't conjure them all away,* Perin thought to himself with a hint of a smile at his own ridiculousness. He knew the idea was silly and that he didn't have anywhere close to the power to do that. He stopped in his tracks. *Could the Great Committee do that?* he wondered. *They created so many of Caramine's islands and landmasses, could they just imagine the people they didn't want out of existence?* As he considered it, the answer was probably no. *If they could do that they wouldn't need a prison or an army. They wouldn't have needed to give chase after me either. They could just have stopped me.* Given how Antez had been portrayed at the Academy, they would probably have willed that out of existence as well if they could.

It was with this comforting thought that after another turn Perin ended up back on the main street towards the pier. It was bustling with activity and people all around. Perin couldn't help himself breaking into a large grin. He had been so silly to have gotten lost. It had given him some time on his own though which he thought he needed. He felt he was ready to get back to the *Muta*.

As he approached it, the hive of activity intensified. A mast, complete with new sail, was being erected. The sound of sawing wood told Perin that the central mast was being replaced right down into the bowels of the ship. It would be stronger than ever. At the rear of the ship a large winch with four sturdy ropes was moving what appeared to be a large wooden box into place. *The safe room,* Perin thought. He felt a pang of sadness as he considered his lost quarters, but he knew he had made the right decision. *Once we find the Archive, a room to store its secrets will be extremely useful.*

The rest of the hull of the *Muta* was hard to make out. There was such a sea of people clambering to get close. Many had carts to trade goods and supplies. Perin remembered that Stim and the crew were using the belongings of the old crew as currency to get what they needed. This must be hard for them. He would make sure that the crew had extra time tomorrow to recover and recuperate without today's frantic work.

As he approached the *Muta* itself his heart gave a flutter of pride. Perin had developed a feeling of attachment to the ship that before he arrived he would have considered absurd. He noticed that protruding from the hull and resting in the water were new oars. They had been successfully replaced and hopefully hooked up to the machinery. Perin started to move quicker. Stim was standing on the pier surrounded by ladies selling fruits, silks and ropes. He had his arms raised to his chest as if he were wading through waist-high water, as he towered above them all. He looked thoroughly harassed. When his eyes met Perin's he broke out into a broad grin and waved at him. Perin waved back and continued his way forward. He passed two or three of the *Muta*'s crew removing trunks and cases that belonged to the fallen crew members. Perin slowed his pace to a respectful walk and nodded to them as he walked past.

"Good work, men," he said deeply in as close an impression of Rienta as he could manage. The men gestured their heads in pleasant response.

As Perin walked up onto the deck of the ship the level of detail in the repair work impressed him. As he walked down the staircase and approached the engine deck he was amazed to find that it was as if nothing had ever happened. Not only had the new oars (in a dark menacing wood that suggested they may have been pilfered from a Great Committee vessel) been installed into the machinery, but all the splinters and shards of the previous oars had been removed. Standing next to the engine mechanism itself were three great canisters of a pink translucent liquid that moved with a slightly greater thickness than water. It gave off a deep woody smell. This was a new type of fuel.

"It burns slowly but over a long period," came a voice from the stairwell. Amic descended to join Perin. He had obviously tried to do some work on the engines himself as he was covered in black grease that was used to keep all the parts moving smoothly. "I thought that would be closer to what we needed out on the ocean." He tried to clean his hands with a rag that seemed to be as filthy as the hands he was trying to clean.

"How're the engines looking?" asked Perin. He assumed he would need to use some form of magical persuasion to coax them into life.

"As far as I can tell they should work," Amic said with a shrug. "Although we won't be able to test them till we get out of port." That was true enough. The engines would be nice, but if the sail was in working order they could get by without them, at least for a little while.

"How long will the other repairs take?" he asked.

"Well, the safe room is in place, the stocks have all been replenished and the sail is being fitted to the new mast as we speak." *Good grief,* Perin thought. *That's everything.*

"Sounds promising," said Perin cheerfully. "I assume the mast will be erected tomorrow."

"Yes, sir," Amic replied. "They won't do much more today, it's getting late."

Perin smiled. "Sounds like you have all had a hard day's work. I think you all deserve a night off."

Amic's toothy grin with his golden tooth spread from ear to ear. "I think that would be much appreciated, sir."

"Would you tell the men please?" he asked. "I would quite like to just have an early night if you don't mind."

"Of course, sir," he replied with a nod. "Though, if I may suggest, I think you should stay up to speak to Mr Stim. He would appreciate a word with you."

That sounded ominous but Perin was too tired and relieved to be back on board the *Muta*, an almost completely restored *Muta*, to be overly concerned.

"All right then," he replied. "Send him to the captain's quarters as soon as he can come. Then I can go to sleep."

"Very good, sir," laughed Amic. "I'll have one of the boys send down some food for you if there isn't already some in the room." He then hurried away back onto the main deck. Perin had another approving look around the engine deck and then made his way down towards the captain's quarters. He still couldn't quite bring himself to say *his* quarters, but he did know he had to break the habit of referring to it as Rienta's.

As he entered the comfortable room, there was already some meat and broth on the table so he helped himself to a mouthful of each and then sat in his chair. After a few minutes he realised that he had no idea how long it would take Stim to be able to prise himself away from the gaggle of merchants that had surrounded him on the pier. Perin decided that he could risk a lie down. No sooner had his head hit the pillow than he had fallen asleep, dead to the world.

It had been a dreamless sleep, no story or adventure playing through Perin's mind, and his world jumped back into focus with a heavy knock on the door. He knew it was Stim simply from the force of the knock but it didn't change the fact that he hadn't been expecting it. He scrambled sleepily to the door and pulled it open. He could only imagine what kind of dishevelled sight he must have presented. Stim, for his part, looked thoroughly uncomfortable. He seemed more interested in the doorframe than Perin. *Rienta didn't tend to have crew in or near her quarters,* Perin thought. This would probably have been a very strange experience for Stim. He decided that it might be best to walk and talk through the decks of the ship, rather than invite him in. He wanted Stim to be at ease. So Perin stepped forward, closed the door behind him and started to walk slowly towards the rear of the ship.

"Come and have a look at the new safe room with me," he said, "and what can I do for you?" Without turning back he heard Stim lock into step behind him and then appear at his side.

"Well, sir," he said sheepishly, "we have the new recruits on deck for your inspection." Perin was shocked, in the first instance that anyone had been found, but in the second instance that he would need to inspect them.

"Is something the matter with them?" he laughed.

"Well…" came the reluctant reply. Perin stopped and turned to face Stim head on.

"Stim," he said sharply, "what's the matter with the new recruits."

"You should come see for yourself," he finished and then headed up the stairwell. Perin sighed and followed him, having to almost run to keep up with the giant man's gait. He could take three of the steep stairs at once. By the time Perin reached the top he was out of breath and almost doubled over. He saw at once what Stim had been reluctant to tell him. These men and women were old. Unlike some of the older people he had met recently, they had not been maintained by magic. They lacked the vigour of the previous crew. Some walked with a stick, and another, smaller though not insignificant number, walked with two. *How on earth are they going to get around this ship?* thought Perin. The stairs he had just climbed would take hours for some of these people.

There were probably about twenty in total. It could have been worse: there could have been seventy. Perin had to decide very quickly how to deal with all this.

"I am very happy to see you all so eager to contribute to our mission," he lied. "Perhaps you would all be so kind as to tell Mr Stim what skills and abilities you can bring to us." He paused for a minute. He did not wish to judge these people too prematurely – they may have incredible skills, and he was reluctant to turn anyone willing away. At least as of yet.

One of the crowd stepped forward. He was relatively well dressed and even more well spoken. He had sharp features and wore spectacles. A slight stoop revealed a bald patch among his white hair.

"Good Captain," the old man said, "we are the Shufflers, a group of men and women who meet in private once a week to discuss the world before the Great Committee."

Perin smiled at the old man. This did not seem possible. Although these people were old, they were not that old. The learning he had received at the Academy had led him to believe that the Great Committee had ruled for at least several generations. Occidens had been remiss in not telling him exactly how long they had served for. With her magic restoration it could have been ten generations for all Perin really knew.

"When was that, sir?" Perin asked, as kindly as he could.

"In the time of our parents, good sir," came the reply. "We were the first generation to be taken from our homes and placed in the Great Academy." *Of course,* thought Perin. *If the first generation of Academy-goers were still alive they would remember having their whole lives ripped away from them.*

"For that, sir," he began, "you have my sympathy. Tell me, do you remember your parents?"

"Some of us do, sir," he explained, "others do not. It can all be very different just two or three years of birth apart. We are all united in one thing. We want the Great Committee to end. We may not look like much, and it may take some getting used to, but we can cook and clean, and load and fetch and carry, and if needs be fight. We want to do our bit."

Perin was immediately sold on the idea. These were the very people who had suffered the most from the Great Committee's reforms and he wouldn't stand in their way from joining the fight against them. The problem remained though that young, strong, armed men and women would be required to fill out the rest of the crew. The Shufflers would be a fine addition with regards history and perhaps even tactics, but he still required a crew of warriors.

"I would be delighted to have you join the crew," Perin announced. There was a respectful round of applause and the stamping of sticks on the deck to signal approval. "I do, however, still need a crew. Do you know of any strong backs and iron wills that would like to join up with us, or is everyone here of a younger generation just a lapdog of the Great Academy?" This led to another ripple of assent.

"I'm afraid, sir, that there are a great many who know no better than what the Committee has taught them," came the reply, "but there are those that would agree with what you have said. We have tried our best to foster those beliefs, but being too vocal would place both us and those that agree with us deep in The Anvil." A shudder ran through the crowd. "Most of those young and foolish enough to have fought your cause publicly have already found themselves there and I'm afraid many here who certainly agree with you are afraid of joining them."

"But you have decided to join us?"

"At our age, sir, a stay in The Anvil wouldn't last very long."

A large crack split through the air like thunder and everyone looked around. It had been so loud it had echoed throughout the harbour, making it impossible to tell which direction it had emanated from. Soon enough the screams could be heard from onshore. As Perin turned to look he saw that one of the watchtowers had collapsed, or was in the process of doing so. It fell downwards, each layer of bricks tumbling onto the next and overbearing it until it in turn fell onto the next.

With everyone's eyes on the first tower it was easy to see what happened to the second. A black dot streaked through the blue sky and crumpled into the side of the tower with another stomach-churning rumble and it too began its descent, sending dust clouds into the sky like fingers reaching up towards the sun.

All eyes were fixed on the third tower as everyone

waited for what seemed like the inevitable final shot. Instead a voice came booming, unnaturally amplified, from somewhere beyond the hills and out at sea.

"Citizens of Antez," the familiar voice proclaimed. "You are harbouring known fugitives from the justice of your Great Committee." *Viri,* thought Perin. The voice was unmistakeable and she was here causing untold fear just to flush out the *Muta.*

"These criminals," the voice continued, "were left to die on the high seas for attacking our flagship, which now waits on the other side of the island. We have tried to be reasonable, but have heard disturbing reports of complicity with their actions." *Oh no,* thought Perin. He had a terrible feeling he knew what was coming. Viri was going to punish the residents of the island for not giving them up immediately and obediently.

"This is not the first time that fugitives have been harboured in Antez. The Committee has shown you exceptional leniency over the years. I'm afraid I have taken the decision that there shall be no further clemency for your treason and retribution will have to be swift and final."

The third tower crumbled on the hillside. Without those buildings Antez's strategic value as a safe haven for all was gone. Perin didn't know how the *Formalite'* had avoided detection to get close enough to attack. He felt a resolve forming inside. *Enough is enough,* he thought. At that moment he decided to fight the *Formalite'* head on, even if he had to do so with only the Shufflers and the exhausted crew he already had.

"I have decided," Viri's voice said with a soft but cruel edge, "in my generous mercy, to afford you one final chance." Perin held his breath, having a good idea what was coming. "If you bring me the crew of the *Muta* bound, gagged and alive," she hesitated, "or alternatively, simply dead, then I will magnanimously not burn every man, woman, child and animal on Antez to cinders before sinking that festering ground beneath your feet back into the ocean where it belongs. You have one hour to decide."

An excruciating stunned silence was broken by a single voice.

"Well, that's certainly changed things." The voice was from Perin's side. It was Amic.

"Is there any chance the repairs are complete?" Perin asked hopefully.

"Would you believe it, Captain, they've just finished. The builders wanted to work through and get it done." Perin gave a sigh of relief but it was short-lived as a commotion on the pier brought Perin to look over the side of the boat. He had expected to see the residents of Antez clambering to get on board the *Muta* to run him through and carry his carcass on a silver platter to Viri's table. This was not exactly the case.

There was indeed a baying crowd angry and armed to the teeth. Stim had hurried down the gangplank to meet them, probably to fight them back. He now stood stunned, surrounded by a crew that didn't want to take the *Muta*, but wanted to join her. There were others whom Perin had never seen or met who had made a perimeter around the pier to hold back any attempt there may be to cause the ship or her crew harm. Perin wished he could speak to them. Then it occurred to him that he could. He closed his eyes and imagined his voice booming, filling the air around the pier so that everyone who had gathered could hear him. He opened his eyes, and as he spoke he heard his voice not just originating from within his own throat but emanating from the wind around him.

"Citizens of Antez," he thundered, the amplification adding bass to his voice and making him sound older, "there is no need to approach us with any violent or malicious intent." He paused and added, "Unless that intent is intended towards our enemies." A great roar of approval rose from the dockside and bolstered Perin's confidence. "I intend to go out to meet our enemy head on, but this time I do not intend to parley, or turn myself or my crew over. I intend to fight the *Formalite'*, I intend to win that fight and I intend to sink her to the ocean floor!"

The sea of humanity proved too strong for Stim to hold back. Men and women flooded onto the decks of the *Muta* and lined its sides. They all stood to attention and saluted Perin, unless they were carrying weapons of spades, trowels, clubs and in one inexplicable instance a large cured sausage. This was a spontaneous emotional response and Perin knew that once the cannons started to fire, the enthusiastic support could easily disappear, but there was little other option. For the time being, Perin had his crew and he intended to use them. Stim followed the crowd onto the deck looking thoroughly confused and a little sore that he had failed at his impromptu guard duties.

"Mr Stim," called Perin, "if you could meet me in the study we will come up with a plan of attack." Stim nodded and tried to wade through the crowd. "Mr Amic," he continued, the old man turning to face him, "set course for the *Formalite'* full sail! Please also show our new crew where the guns are. They're going to need them."

The atmosphere from the makeshift crew was buoyant as Perin led Stim into the study. He shut the door and noticed his hands were shaking with adrenaline. He turned to face his friend and said with a mix of humour and anxiety:

"So, we need a plan of attack…"

CHAPTER TWENTY-FIVE

Perin looked at the map, hoping that it would give him some clue as to a strategy. They were currently sailing round the southern side of Antez with the *Formalite'* on the east side with open water beyond that would eventually lead towards The Anvil and The Hammer. No help would come for the *Muta* in that direction. Not that any would come from the south, north or west either, but Perin knew he must keep an eye on the east as that would be where any reinforcements would come to help the *Formalite'*.

"Stim, I have no idea how to formulate a battle plan," Perin admitted. "I've read lots of past campaigns and historical accounts but I don't know how many of them are the Committee's fiction and if any of them really happened."

Perin was surprised to see that Stim was smiling. "In times like this," he said, "I tend to live life by one simple rule. 'What would Rienta do?'" He stopped talking, and stood as if he had provided Perin with the most profound answer of all time.

"I have no idea what Rienta would do!" Perin cried. "Something intelligent no doubt, something wonderful and surprising. I just don't know what that is."

Stim looked down at him a bit more gravely. "Well," he said, "why don't we do both?"

"Sorry, Stim, I don't wish to be rude, but what in hells' teeth are you talking about?" The adrenaline was causing Perin to talk very fast. He also felt he was starting to panic which did not help. Stim seemed to recognise the rush of blood that came with impending battle and seemed to avoid taking offence.

"You think we should do something from a historical battle," he explained, "and I think we should do what the captain would have done. So why don't we do what she did in a historical battle?" Once again he said this with a profound calm and almost sage-like wisdom. Perin didn't know whether it would be more appropriate to laugh or cry.

"Stim," he said shortly, "I don't have any records of historical battles that Rienta fought. All I have are Occidens' diaries and she focuses more on her own role in things than anyone else."

"But I was there," Stim replied simply. "I remember." *Good grief,* thought Perin, *he's right. Stim might actually have a good military mind by proxy if he can remember some of Rienta's strategies.*

"Well come on then," Perin said with a smile, "what do you think would be the best plan to put into action?"

"Well," said Stim, "I quite liked the plan we came up with to rescue you after you turned yourself in." He held up his hands and hurriedly added, "It didn't go completely to plan, mind, but this time I think we could get the job done." Perin had to think for a minute until he realised what Stim was suggesting.

"A boarding party?" he asked. "With you trying to capsize the *Formalite*?" Stim nodded and grinned. Perin blew out a long whistle. It was certainly bold.

"First of all, the last time you tried that, you weren't able to capsize the boat. Secondly, that mission got the captain killed. What makes you think we should try it again?"

"Different objective, sir," said Stim, suddenly becoming every inch the militaristic crewman. "Last time as a rescue mission, I was holding back for fear of hurting you. This time, if I can't capsize the bloody thing, I'll put a hole in the side of it big enough to sink it."

Perin nodded. He had to admit that that particularly useful difference in the plan had merit. He wasn't willing, though, for Stim to go out there without any form of backup.

"All right, you can take a small boat and try to get close enough to the *Formalite'* to sink her." He paused and allowed Stim to enjoy getting his own way. "It is daylight however, and there is no way they wouldn't see you coming, unless we can create a diversion." Stim's face fell slightly.

"It is true, sir, stealth is not one of my talents."

Perin laughed, "That's why we are still going to give the *Formalite'* what she wants. The *Muta* will engage her. We will sail in and out of her range, making attacks until they give chase. During this cat-and-mouse game, you should be able to sneak up on her, or if we keep it up long enough, use the cover of darkness to do it. The sun should be down in a few hours." This looked as though it worked for Stim. He had a smile on his face and had started massaging his knuckles alternately with both hands. His face soon fell though.

"What about Viri?" he asked. "When we attacked the *Formalite'* before, the reason that Rienta was there was to take on Viri," before adding, "stupid cow," not without affection.

Perin hadn't really considered this but it was a valid point. If Viri saw Stim coming, or was able to react before the *Formalite'* had been capsized, then she would probably be able to deal with Stim before any real damage was done. It was Perin who had distracted her before when Stim and Rienta had boarded. *I'll just have to do it again,* he thought.

This time, however, he had a different way of doing it, which would also help keep them ahead of the *Formalite'*. If Perin could amplify his voice and show Viri that he was still aboard the *Muta*, then her entire focus would be on pursuing the ship and not on Stim's approach.

"Leave Viri to me." He could see by the look on Stim's face that he wasn't satisfied with that. "I will keep her busy and distracted. You just focus on getting alongside that ship."

There was a knock on the door and a crewman entered that Perin did not recognise, obviously one of the Shufflers, judging by his age.

"Sorry to disturb you," he said with obvious reluctance, "but we have eyes on the *Formalite'*—"

"—which means they have eyes on us!" Perin stood and rushed towards the door, closely followed by Stim. They bustled past the stunned crewman, and the crash that followed them told Perin that Stim had accidentally knocked the poor man over.

The deck was still busy. There had been more volunteers than there were jobs to be done so some men and women simply lined the sides of the ship. They would perhaps become useful if and when close-quarters combat occurred. Perin would have liked to take time to get to know his new allies. The depth of their loyalty and service would be tested soon enough and it would have been helpful if he could have inspired a little personal loyalty, but as he looked out towards the approaching black ship on the horizon, he knew there was precious little time for that.

"Man your positions," he shouted as he made his way to the helm. Amic stood holding the wheel – he seemed anxious to give it up. He looked towards Stim, who would under most circumstances have been the natural choice to take over the manning of the helm. Perin stepped forward and took hold of the wheel himself. He then looked towards Stim and nodded. The huge man locked eyes with his friend and walked towards the rear of the boat which housed the new lifeboats. Perin tried to push the horrible memory of the last time the lifeboats had been manned out of his head. He was determined to use the *Muta* to defend Stim. He would not meet the same fate.

He closed his eyes and imagined his voice booming out over the ocean and reaching every corner of the *Formalite'* and striking fear into the chests of her crew.

"Mistress Viri," he announced in a voice so loud it made the wood underneath his feet vibrate. "I am here with the brave and proud crew of the *Muta*, in the name of its fallen captain Rienta, the sorcerer Occidens, and those in the crew who have fallen," he hesitated before adding, "and the equally proud and brave people of the Port of Antez who have joined us." He allowed his voice to echo and reverberate across the water and didn't continue until it had fallen away. A glance behind him showed that Stim was set in his rowboat and was lowering himself into the water. "You will no longer intimidate and terrorise the innocent people of these islands. I am here not to surrender, but to put an end to you."

Perin heard the rowboat splash gently into the water at the rear of the *Muta*. That was the cue he had been waiting for. He spun the wheel furiously and the ship began to turn so that its broadside was facing the oncoming *Formalite'*.

"Ready the guns!" he bellowed in his regular voice. The reply seemed to come from all around him as if the wind itself was speaking to him.

"You are a fool, Perin!" Viri's unnaturally shrill voice shrieked. It made Perin wince, and many of the crewmen on deck covered their ears. "My crew is more experienced, my ship better equipped and my own magic far exceeds yours." Her laugh was amplified to such a degree it sounded like thunder. "You are committing suicide in a way that will take all those men and women on your ship down to the depths of the ocean with you." The voice adopted a softness. It was like listening to a snake's hiss turned into speech and increased in volume a thousand times. "To those on the *Muta*, I suggest you remove Perin from command and deliver him to the *Formalite'*. All can yet be forgiven."

Perin had broken out in a cold sweat. He half expected the crew to turn on him. They had no real loyalty to him – they had run onto the ship in a moment of weakness brought on by the attack on their port. It could fade just as easily.

His breath caught in his chest as three of the better armed members of the crew proceeded up the stairs and approached him at the helm.

"Guns ready," said the first.

"Engines ready," said the second.

"Crew ready," said the third. Perin gave a sigh of relief and could feel his eyes filling with tears. The crew had been deaf to Viri's disingenuous pleas.

"I'm glad to hear it," said Perin. "The plan is for us to put on a bit of a show to distract the *Formalite'*, but that being said," he turned to the first crewman, "shoot those guns to kill." He turned to the second crewman: "Get the engines going – speed will be an absolute necessity, and please also make sure the sails are trimmed." Turning to the third crewman who had delivered news of the crew's readiness, he smiled at him. Judging by the apparent bald patch and liver spots he was one of the Shufflers. "Tell the crew I thank them for their readiness, and to be prepared to fight and do their duty. Today we take the first step to make Caramine free again."

The old man beamed at him with a toothless grin. "Aye, sir."

The three men quickly left the same way they had come, having made Perin feel a great deal better.

The feeling did not last for long as the *Formalite'* continued to head towards the *Muta*. It had not yet turned to face them broadside-to-broadside. This meant the enemy provided a smaller target. They were certainly within range though. The time had come.

"Cannons fire!" roared Perin, his voice amplified – he wanted the *Formalite'* crew to know what was coming. The air was filled with the sounds of exploding gunpowder, making the deck shake beneath Perin's feet. Great spurts of water erupted around the *Formalite'* where the cannonballs struck the ocean. One of the cannonballs had struck home on the deck of the *Formalite'*: a glancing blow on the left side. There was splintered wood and, if Perin wasn't mistaken, a small number of bodies now in the water. It didn't look like the Great Committee had a policy of saving their men who were lost overboard. The great ship had started to come about so that the guns of both ships would be facing one another. This would be Stim's cue to start rowing round from the far side of the *Muta* to try and sneak up alongside the *Formalite'*.

A thought occurred to Perin that he decided may aid Stim in his mission. He closed his eyes and pictured a cold and clammy mist rising off the water, enveloping both ships so that neither could see very far in front of themselves and certainly couldn't see each other. This should give the *Muta* some cover as well as allow Stim's approach to be undetected.

The wisps of low-lying cloud formed on the surface of the water and grew into great trenches of white smoke. It rose up the sides of the hulls of the ships and then poured over the deck. Within a minute, it had completely enveloped both vessels.

"Bring us about," Perin boomed with his amplified voice. Allowing the *Formalite'* to hear the commands would keep their focus on the *Muta*. He felt the ground beneath his feet start to tremble, and at first he thought it was some form of magical retribution from Viri, but he soon realised it was the engines starting to power up. The oars lowered themselves into the water – Perin couldn't see it, but he could hear it – and they started to move the ship forward.

Perin pictured in his mind the two ships diverging from each other, the *Muta* drawing away from the *Formalite'*. He started to turn the wheel. If he was lucky they could circle the ship and the enemy wouldn't have a good grasp on their position.

A cold wind blew through Perin and made him shiver. The sunlight had been partially blocked out by the fog, but this was a different kind of cold. The wind picked up further and Perin realised this was Viri's attempt at neutralising his fog.

"Fire the cannons!" shouted Perin. He wasn't sure that they were facing the *Formalite'* and he didn't want to give away his position but he wanted to keep Viri destabilised and maybe break her concentration. The boom of the cannons was followed by splashes. There was an absence of crunching of wood that would signify a direct hit. The *Muta* had given away its position without landing a shot on the enemy. That meant there was an increase in the chances of—

"Brace for impact!" Perin shouted just in time as the ship was rocked by a shot that hit off the bow of the ship. Screams told Perin that some had been injured and perhaps killed. He had to hold on to a nearby Shuffler to keep himself upright. The blow had knocked the ship onto a different course, but because of his own fog he had no idea what way they were now facing.

The wind was blowing up even faster and the fog was moving away around them – it would clear in moments. Perin decided this might be for the best, as at least this would give him knowledge of the *Formalite's* position and they could start up the assault anew.

As quickly as it had started, the wind dropped. The fog settled in the air and the biting cold in Perin's lungs subsided. *Perhaps Viri doesn't want to give away the tactical advantage I've given her*. He swore under his breath at his own mistake. He was about to whip the wind back up himself before Viri's voice came out of the clouds.

"Perin, enough of this." She sounded like a mother talking to an unruly child. "We have apprehended your pet giant. He will not be of any more help to you this day." Perin felt as if his heart had stopped beating in his chest, that the world had temporarily stopped turning. He had to force himself to breathe. Without Stim, the *Muta* did not have any sort of tactical advantage in this matchup. Effectively, the day was lost.

"You now have two choices," the voice continued. "If you turn yourself over to my custody, then I will send this large gentleman back to your ship and he can sail it away in whatever direction he pleases." Perin could almost hear Viri smiling even from this distance. "I will then kill you in as painful a way as I can imagine." A cold fear gripped the young man's chest. All talk of joining the Great Committee was gone. He was now a threat to be extinguished and that was all.

"If you do not hand yourself over," the voice continued, "then I will kill the giant now, and then kill you anyway. The choice is yours."

Perin closed his eyes. He had figured as much. In a strange way, he felt a cold, unfeeling resolve. He would no longer run from Viri, the *Formalite'* or the Great Committee, but he would also not allow Stim to die because he was unwilling to come forward. Perin closed his eyes and imagined the water swallowing up and dissolving the fog. He simply pictured in his mind's eye the swirling wisps of the cloud in reverse. When he opened his eyes, the fog was gone and he saw the *Formalite'* sat in the water not too far off the bow of the *Muta*. He imagined his voice filling the air again, but as he spoke it lacked the bass and conviction it had had before.

"I don't trust you, Viri. I will turn myself over to you, but I want you to meet me halfway and turn Stim over. An old-fashioned prisoner exchange." There were a few moments of silence, presumably as Viri considered her options.

"Agreed," came the amplified reply. *It's done*, Perin thought. As he walked towards the stairs to the deck Amic approached him, his demeanour very clear: he intended to talk Perin out of turning himself over.

Perin headed him off. "Amic, bring me a rowboat."

CHAPTER TWENTY-SIX

A stony silence had fallen over the crew. They stood, heads bowed, as Perin walked stoically towards the rowboat, trying not to betray his trepidation. His heart was pounding so hard in his chest he was sure it must be audible. The crew parted, forming a human corridor to pass through. Perin was touched by the display of respect and his eyes began to water. The crew had been untried and inexperienced but had not wavered in their devotion to the fight, even when Perin had assumed they would, and even when Viri had tempted them with clemency for compliance. He was sorry he hadn't had the opportunity to lead them for longer.

As he stepped into the rowboat, which might very well also act as his coffin, for the first time Perin considered what happened to a person after they died. The Great Academy had always taught that there was nothing. That a person was only here to serve the Great Committee and contribute to Caramine's health and success. They taught that this was the best legacy a person could leave behind them. Perin had been too young to really consider what seemed like such a far-off future, but now it seemed to be imminent. It focused his mind on the subject. *Will there be somewhere else after I die? Will my consciousness move onto another plane of existence?* He might see Occidens and Rienta again. They may have more grand adventures in some other world.

Perin nodded to the crew standing on either side of the rowboat and they lowered it into the water. They did this with a solemn dignity. Perin could hear some of the crew sobbing, or sniffing. *Incredible,* he thought to himself, *to inspire such depth of feeling in people who I don't know at all, and who only know me by a speech or two.*

Being lowered down in front of people that were already mourning him was an out-of-body experience. As he touched down into the water and started to drift, Perin almost felt he was being buried alive. He started to breathe hmore heavily. He closed his eyes and forced himself to take a slow deep breath, determined to face what was about to come with dignity. He looked at the oars with disdain. He did not like the idea of arriving with Viri gasping for air and drenched in sweat from the simple process of rowing the small boat. He briefly considered bringing someone with him to row the boat but realised quickly that it would make them vulnerable to capture too. This was a journey he had to undertake alone.

There was a splashing sound around the boat and he looked down to see something rippling under the surface of the water – some form of mammal moving around. Eyes appeared in the water, and a blue snout and pearl-white teeth broke the surface. *Smiling teeth,* Perin thought. It was a dolphin. Perin had drifted a sizeable distance away from the *Muta*. The animal wouldn't have come near if it had been too close to the large galleon, but its curiosity had gotten the better of the beautiful creature. Perin kneeled over and rubbed the animal's snout. It gave out a pleasurable noise, not unlike laughter. It made Perin smile. This was something he was glad to have done before what was about to happen on the *Formalite'*.

A jet of water hit him in the back of the head. This was followed by more of a cackle than a laugh, but this time from two animals. Perin spun round and another dolphin, darker in skin than the first, was smiling at him. Perin felt a fool but he smiled back. Such mirthful animals in such bleak circumstances couldn't help but raise his spirits. The first dolphin grabbed the oar, which was attached to the boat by a strong iron bolt, and started to pull. Perin stumbled, afraid the boat would tip, but the other dolphin grabbed the oar on the opposite side and joined in with the work. They were pulling the ship, towing it for Perin. He was amazed. *How did they know I needed help?* he wondered, amazed. *How do they know where to take me?* He had a slight moment of suspicion: the dolphins could have been bewitched by Viri to lead Perin to his death. For some reason he found it impossible to believe that these creatures could be corrupted by evil. *Perhaps they can sense my magic and have judged it to be good. Perhaps the animals of Caramine wish me well.* That made him smile and gave him comfort as he headed towards the *Formalite'*.

The black galleon grew in front of him. He could make out a similar rowboat to his own being lowered into the water. Even at this distance he could identify the large figure with bound hands and a head covered with some form of sack. *Stim.* At this distance he was the only reasonable possibility unless she had a giant of her own. *Now that's a thought that's going to fester,* Perin thought. Another form made their way onto the boat. It was Viri. She was too slight for Perin to make out any sort of features, but the way she held herself, with power and rigid authority was distinctive. He could see that there was now an added element to her stance. She stood in triumph, her back even firmer and more unyielding than it had been before. Perin sighed to himself in defeat.

The dolphins stopped pulling the boat. They let the oars fall into the water with a clunk, still held to the side of the boat by the iron. They then swam up the side of the boat and smiled their open-mouthed grins at Perin again.

"Thank you for your help," Perin said with the greatest sincerity. "I'll never forget it," before thinking, *I may not have time to.* "If I could ask one more favour of you?" He knew this was an inherently stupid thing to do, but he had become convinced that these animals could understand him. *Well,* he thought, *if magic works the way I think it does, then if I imagine that they can understand me, then they can.*

This notion seemed to be borne out when the laughter was matched by the slightest, almost imperceptible form of a nod from the creatures.

"Could you retreat to a safe distance – I don't want you to be in any form of danger – and then return to make sure that my friend gets to his ship safely." The happy chirping laughter that replied suggested that that wouldn't be a problem.

So the dolphins departed, disappearing underneath the surface of the water with a splash. Meanwhile the small rowboat containing the hooded Stim with his head held low and Viri, holding her frame in comparative victory, made Perin's flesh crawl. As it drew into ever-clearer focus, he realised that there were no oars to Viri's craft. It was being propelled by a current that existed only directly around the little rowboat. It sent out ripples in all directions, and when they started to reach Perin's craft they splashed up against the sides of his boat angrily and rocked it dangerously. Perin gripped the sides of the boat, causing his knuckles to turn white, but he was determined to look steady and resolute when Viri arrived. He would not give her the satisfaction of coming upon a scared little man.

When the boats finally drew alongside, the current died away and the ships sat in silence. The wind had dropped. Perin still knew the *Muta* was visible in the distance at his back. He wondered if they could still see him. He looked towards Viri. As their eyes locked, Perin felt nauseous. He fought to avoid showing this, resolutely holding her gaze with a stare of pure granite. She looked down at him hungrily and triumphant. She seemed to take an incredulous delight in Perin's show of resolve. *Something she can work on breaking,* Perin thought.

"This was the right decision," the woman said in a superior tone. Her voice roused Stim, who obviously couldn't see to know that Perin was only a few feet away.

"Perin!" he shouted, his voice muffled through the cloth hood. "What the hells are you doing? Get away from here!" Viri kicked him hard where his face would be underneath the cloth. Stim fell back and whimpered as he tried to bring his bound hands up to his face. Viri laughed a cold, hard cackle, before looking back towards Perin, his resolve broken and face showing signs of fury, fear and horror all at once.

"How did I do it?" Viri suggested to Perin mockingly. "How did I overcome the power of this great beast? I'll tell you, it was simple!" The glee in her face, as if sharing a wartime story of glory, made Perin's blood boil. "You see, what I wanted most in the world in that moment was to sap his strength – for the magic you, or Occidens I suppose, had imbued in him to be drained away so that I could overcome him." She cackled loudly and wickedly. "Which I did, but I thought, why stop there? And I drained even his human levels of strength until the poor fool could barely hold up his own arms. If I'd taken any more from him then his heart would have ceased to have the energy to beat. I could have done that but decided to use him to get you here. A fair trade wouldn't you say?"

Perin was horror-struck. *What must that have felt like for Stim?* he wondered. He remembered the giant needing a drink and a rest after his exertions before. Being powerless, weak and unable to exert physical strength had made Stim genuinely fearful. *Right now, he must be terrified.*

"The terms of our deal were that you let him go back to the *Muta* and let it sail away without any retribution," Perin said, as formally as he could. "Beyond that you can do whatever you like with me. I no longer care!"

This made Viri smile a wider smile than Perin had ever seen her make before. Her cheekbones were raised almost as high as her eyes and she seemed to lose her chin and cheeks as the entirety of her lower face gleamed with white fang-like teeth. It was horrific. *A smile of victory,* Perin thought. *To her, this is it, she has won and can return me to the Great Committee dead or alive and be treated as the conquering hero.*

"You're quite right of course," she said, looking down disdainfully at Stim. "Up," she commanded. Stim pushed and scrambled upwards to try and get to his feet, but he fell down as his legs couldn't support him, and he couldn't put his hands, which were still bound, out in front of him to stop himself clattering back to the deck of the small ship. Perin felt sick. A dark wet patch had started to grow on the rough sack around Stim's head. Viri's kick had obviously done quite serious damage. Seeing this she threw her head back and cackled mockingly. "Oaf!"

Perin imagined with all his might the cuts on Stim's face healing up of their own accord and the bruises receding back into his skin. The most likely thing that had happened was that Viri had broken his nose. Perin imagined it straightening forcibly, and the bones in his face realigning with a crack. Viri immediately stopped laughing as Stim screamed with pain. Viri looked not at the giant man, but to Perin, with fire in her eyes. The sound of the bones had been loud enough for her to hear. She knew what he had done.

"If you dare," she raged, "restore any of his magic abilities I will burst his heart in his chest!"

Before she could turn back to Stim to make a demonstration Perin quickly replied, "I was mending his nose, witch!" He was losing composure – not wise, but unavoidable. "He was in blinding pain. How did you expect him to get back to the *Muta* with the damage you did to him?"

"Slowly and painfully," Viri said simply. "But we must

get on with things." She turned and grabbed Stim by the arm and with unnatural strength that Perin thought must have been magically enhanced, she lifted Stim to his feet and threw him across the side of her boat and into Perin's. Stim's feet caught the side and he fell again with a thump, this time onto his shoulder. It would hurt like hell but hopefully nothing else was broken. Perin knelt down and tried to help him to a seated position, but he was a heavy mass. *She definitely enhanced her strength,* thought Perin. *Something else Viri has mastered. Something else to watch out for.*

Although it was a struggle, he got him seated. He reached for the canvas on his head.

"I think not," Viri interrupted. "My currents will take your oaf back to that rat-infested yacht of yours. He will stay bound and covered till then. I don't want to risk him coming back and causing a nuisance of himself again."

"It's not as if he can do you any harm!" Perin shouted.

"I take no more chances," Viri explained. "Now get onto this boat!" Perin held Stim by the shoulders for a second, the smell of the drying blood on the sack making him want to cry, but he had to show strength now, for Stim's sake.

"It's been an honour," he said. "Take good care of the *Muta* – you're her captain now."

"Perin, no," came the muffled and defeated voice from inside the sack, but Perin stood up and with a deliberate motion, stepped onto Viri's boat.

"Excellent," she said, and without any sign of outward concentration, the current returned and started to move the two ships in opposite directions. Perin sat down to keep himself steady, although Viri remained standing. She bore a wide stance that made her seem statuesque. Perin could hear Stim's sobs as they drifted apart. So could Viri, and each sob made her smile.

The short journey back to the *Formalite'* was conducted in silence. Perin wanted to lower his head as Stim had done, in dejection and defeat, but he would not allow Viri the satisfaction and resolutely kept his head high with an expression of defiance etched upon his face as if it was carved in marble.

As they approached the intimidating galleon a long walkway was lowered from the deck. It created a very gentle gradient compared to boarding a ship by climbing up the side of the hull. Perin couldn't fathom how it was physically possible. The length of the wood was almost as long as the mast. *Where is a plank of that size stored?* He looked out towards the oncoming plank and noticed that Viri had her eyes locked on the *Formalite'*. He could see the concentration on her face. This was her doing. As they drew closer, Perin could see that the wood was unnaturally rolling down the walkway, like a giant lizard's tongue unfurling. It was impressive, awe-inspiring magic. Perin had expected a degree of victorious pageantry from Viri, but he had thought it would probably be reserved for when she took either him, or at least his body, back to Capital Island. *I suppose,* he thought, *she has her crew like any other. Impress them and they will work harder for you.* He would be forced to play the part of humiliated enemy for them as well.

The wooden gangway finally reached the rowboat when it was still a good distance away from the hull of the *Formalite'*. Viri turned to Perin. The slightest gleam of sweat was forming on her head. This had been quite a task, but still, it didn't seem so much to exhaust the imperious old woman as it did invigorate her. She hadn't lost that evil victorious smile.

"Walk." Perin obeyed: he stood up and walked out onto the magically made walkway. It felt completely solid, despite not being supported by anything. The simple weight of the walkway itself should have both sheered it from the deck of the *Formalite'* and crushed the small rowboat.

Perin held his head up as he walked up the slight incline. He heard Viri step onto the walkway with him, a few steps behind. As he continued up the ramp the wood beneath him started to vibrate. He panicked, thinking that the hastily formed walkway was giving way. As he turned round, he saw that Viri was smirking at him. The wood of the boat had broken apart and was adding itself to the walkway as if it was being absorbed. The walkway had now begun to curl back upwards as they walked forward. Perin was in awe, as much as he tried not to show it. It had never occurred to him that the very ship itself could be a resource or that he could bend its matter and materials at will. If he had possessed this kind of imagination then mending the *Muta* after its confrontations with the *Formalite'* and their journey through the teeth would have been easy. He wondered if this was something Occidens was capable of, or if it was a unique talent of Viri's. *It certainly explains how the Formalite' was able to repair and catch up to the Muta so fast,* Perin realised.

He had clearly looked impressed when he saw what Viri was capable of. Her smirk spoke volumes. *She is showing me her powers are superior to my own. She is showing me the futility of rebellion.* These thoughts and impressions had crushed the wills and spirits of whole generations of the citizens of Caramine. Now they had come to Perin. He felt ashamed. Still, his head would not fall. If this was to be his last act of defiance, then he would make it complete.

He turned and continued to walk towards the deck of the *Formalite'*. He couldn't see over the side of the ship until he was almost upon it. He drew in a long breath and hoped he had taken in some courage with it as the scene opened out in front of him. The complete crew of the *Formalite'*, in the same black leather uniforms and helmets, lined almost every inch of the deck. A circular gap had been left around the end of the walkway, which turned seamlessly into a set of three steps as it reached the high side of the deck. Perin paused at the top of the steps and surveyed the crew. He was their captive, and he stood with his hands behind his back as if they were bound; indeed they may as well have been. He looked at them, simply as a man captured, not defeated or broken. Viri appeared at his back. Being much taller than Perin she towered over him and could also survey the crew. They waited on her command.

"Proud soldiers," she announced, "we got him!" She shrieked this last part in a tone Perin had never before heard from Viri: jubilation. She threw her hands in the air behind him and the crew erupted into cheering and adulation.

Perin knew there was a kind of applause and glorification that came from duty. There was always insincerity to that sort of applause. It had happened a lot at the Great Academy. Perin hadn't sensed it since joining the crew of the *Muta* and he didn't sense it now. The people around him loved Viri. They looked up to her with the same kind of devotion that those on the *Muta* had had for Occidens and Rienta. They had begun to chant her name. Viri stood with her arms raised and absorbed this for some time. *That's the difference,* thought Perin. *Rienta or Occidens would never have basked in glory. They did what was right and if people followed them then that was fine, but never the intention.*

Without warning, Viri raised her knee, connecting with Perin's lower back. He collapsed forward down the stairs and clattered hard onto the deck. He had managed to get his hands out in front of him and they screamed in pain. His knees hurt too, but his hands had definitely been cut. He got to his feet as quickly as he could and surveyed the damage. Sure enough, the skin had been taken from the palms of his hands and blood came forward from some splinters. *Painful,* thought Perin, *but nothing compared to what's surely going to come.*

The crew had erupted in delight at Perin's fall. He felt that he had misunderstood them. He had thought that they were merely bound by loyalty and had been led down a wrong path. *No,* he thought, *these are sadistic, merciless men and women. They've been selected to serve because of that.*

"The fool has given himself to us!" shrieked the jubilant witch. "What shall we do with him?"

"Burn him!" shouted one crew member.

"Boil him!" cackled another.

"Cut off his hair!" shouted a third.

"Cut off his hands!" cried another.

Soon enough there was a cacophony of suggestions, all of equal or greater unpleasantness than the last. It was as if someone had started an auction on punishment and a prize would be given to the one with the greatest suggestion. *Maybe that's exactly what's happening,* thought Perin.

"Enough!" cried Viri, bringing the bidding war to an end. The crew were instantly silenced. *Still some fear there, I think,* Perin concluded. "You are all exceptionally devoted warriors, and I commend your bloodlust," an evil chuckle rippled through the crew, "but you lack some of the basic intelligence required to truly achieve our desired goals."

She sounded as though she were a lecturer at the Great Academy, informing keen but slightly dim students in the way of the world. As such, the feckless oafs around her hung on her every word. Perin damned himself if he had ever looked like that.

"This boy gave himself up to save that oaf we apprehended." Disgusted mocking sounds came from the crew now, directed towards Perin. "Even now, my water currents have carried him back to that floating monstrosity on the horizon." Perin turned and saw that the *Muta* hadn't moved from its position. *What are they waiting for? Get the hells out of here.*

"He brought himself here to save the lives of his friend, and the other traitors that man that ship." More disgusted sounds from the crew. "What a fool." She turned towards the *Muta*.

"Viri," Perin declared with as much bravery as he could muster, "you shall leave the *Muta* and its crew alone. You have me, now do what you will with me." Viri released a shrill, mad cackle in response.

"Don't you realise, dear boy, that you have no power to stop me doing anything? I know your abilities, and their limitations. You cannot stop me, and you cannot stop this!"

She spun on the spot, her green skirts twirling around her, and threw her hands out in front of her. There was a crack, and the smell of burning atmosphere filled the deck. Green lightning erupted from her fingers and arced directly towards the *Muta*. It was more intense and more violent than Perin had seen before. It sparked and crackled as it travelled, the ocean below reflecting it with a wild glare that shone back up. Viri's face was green and monstrous with the light.

"No," Perin said calmly. He raised a single hand and in the distance the *Muta* was encased in an orb of red light, moments before the green lightning struck home. The surface of the orb glimmered like water and absorbed the lightning as though it were a pebble being dropped into the ocean. Viri was visibly shocked but kept up her assault. She brought her fingers closer to her palms. This seemed to intensify the beams. She was using every inch of her imagination to envisage the destruction of the *Muta* and the breaking of its shield. Perin knew the ship better and he had been thinking of nothing else but defending that ship with this orb of light since he had sat down aboard the lifeboat. His passion fed into his imagination and there was absolutely nothing that could break through his resolve. No doubt had entered his mind, and this made the field invulnerable and impenetrable.

Without breaking her gaze from the *Muta* Viri called to the crew behind her.

"Seize him! Kill him!" The crew moved forward to obey her. Some had time to withdraw their swords.

"No," said Perin a second time. Every single crew member fell to the deck unconscious. As Perin had stood at the edge of the gangway, he had taken in the crew, the shape and the pattern in which they stood. He had envisaged them all dropping like stones to the deck exactly where they stood from that moment. The only danger to the plan was the remorse he had begun to feel for them. That could potentially have weakened his resolve. Thankfully Viri had removed that feeling. He had sprung the trap perfectly.

The two of them were all that remained. The fallen crew had broken Viri's concentration. The lightning became less and less constant. It fizzled out in her hands and she whirled in anger at Perin.

"You wretch!" she shrieked. "You could have had this world at your feet!" She threw a bolt of lightning at Perin, but he waved his hand at it and it was diverted towards the helm of the ship, where it burst into flames. Viri looked astounded.

"How?" There was a new sound in her voice: *fear*. "Not even Occidens—"

"Occidens taught me a great deal about the rudiments of magic," Perin explained. "Imagination leads to the physical embodiment of what you imagine," he quoted. Viri looked at him with intrigued suspicion – she had heard these words before but clearly wondered where he was leading. Her hands were still outstretched. She could either attack or defend if needed. "What she did not teach me, and what I have found out for myself today," Perin continued, "is that there is one thing that will triumph over the imagination of someone else."

"Lies!" she shrieked, sending another bolt of lightning towards him. Perin closed his hand in front him and the charge fizzled out before it could reach him.

"I'm afraid not. Your magic is based on control, control of lightning, control of currents, control of people around you. Mine is not!"

"What else is there?" fumed Viri. "You're speaking nonsense!"

"The Great Committee is built upon the backs of

others! You have forced conformity on an entire continent." He gestured around as if to signify their surroundings. "My magic is based on the will of others. Unlike you, I do not seek to control or manipulate my surroundings based on my own will. I am using my power to grant the will of others. That's much easier, and a great deal more powerful!"

"I don't understand," Viri said, a tone of pleading and desperation creeping into her voice.

"You want the poor people in that ship to die," Perin spat. "Those brave, loyal, clever, dedicated and thoroughly free people. Your will is that they should die when you throw your lightning at them. Their will is to survive. My will is that their will should be granted. There are simply a great deal more of them than there are of you. The result is you can't touch them."

Filled with anger, Viri threw another furious bolt of lightning at Perin. He raised his hand and this time caught the lightning, gathering it into an orb. It changed from Viri's monstrous green to the red that was becoming associated with Perin's magic. He held the lightning in his hand as if it were a child's ball. He threw it up in the air lazily and caught it again. He threw it from hand to hand.

"That will not work on me anymore," he said coolly. His voice was cold – he had no sympathy for Viri, for the despicable crew, for the ship or what it stood for. A nervousness had crept onto Viri's face.

"Now that I know this can be done, the Committee will destroy you!" Viri spat. "We have followers of our own! We can control the will of hundreds of thousands, perhaps millions!"

"I'm afraid you have a problem there," Perin said without emotion or sympathy. "I think it is the will of those people, and certainly mine, that no one should ever have anything to fear from you, ever again."

He threw Viri's own lightning bolt high into the sky. It formed a small thundercloud, green at first but it turned dark and then grew red. This was all part of Perin's plan, and this was why he had to be alone. Magic could kill Viri, could destroy this ship and everyone on it, but he needed to be here to make sure it happened. He couldn't be the great hope of Caramine, he couldn't save the continent, but this witch, who had killed his friends and mentors, would not see another day, even though it meant him dying in the process.

The red lightning fell from the cloud and struck the *Formalite'*. First the bow was set on fire, then the mast. Then three strikes from separate points of the cloud streaked downwards directly towards Viri. She raised her hands to form a green electric shield but the force of will in the red electrical energy tore through it like shattered glass. Viri's limbs were thrown away from her body and she shook violently with the electrical energy. Her eyes were fixed open staring at Perin, and they flashed red now, not green, and they showed one thing above everything else. Surprise. This turned to fear and pain as they started to smoke. As she opened her mouth and more smoke spilled forward, she let out a scream as the lightning arced straight through her, desperate to be discharged into the ocean. The bolt ripped through Viri and the deck below to reach the depths. It ignited the gunpowder stored beneath for the cannons.

The *Formalite'* exploded in a cascade of red light, and a black mushroom cloud erupted in the sky, sending debris of both the ship and its crew into the air and the water.

CHAPTER TWENTY-SEVEN

Perin's eyes opened, but he couldn't see. He was staring into a bright light that took his vision time to adjust to. At first he thought it was the sun, but after a few moments he realised that it wasn't one large light, but several smaller ones. Six points of light to be exact, each connected by a tongue of tarnished silver. As his eyes adjusted he realised what it was: *a chandelier*. This struck Perin as odd. He was not sure whether he believed, or wanted to believe, in some form of continued existence after death, but he was fairly sure that if there was such a thing, it probably would not take the form of a rather unpolished and slightly rusting candelabra suspended from the ceiling. The only possible conclusion, surprisingly, was that he was still alive.

"He's awake!" came a cry from his side. Perin turned his head, which seemed to make the whole world spin, to face a man whose name he did not know. He did recognise him though: he had been one of the *Muta*'s new recruits. *I'm on the* Muta. Although it hurt his face he smiled. He was alive, and he was home. This led to so many questions, and chief among them was simply, *How?*

Perin was brought to sit bolt upright from a crashing

sound in front of him. Once the room had stopped spinning he realised that he had been laid on the table in the centre of Occidens' study with a firm pillow under his head. For an instant, he wondered where the crew had put her body. He trusted that they would have been respectful. The crashing he heard had come from Stim, who looked relatively well compared to how Perin felt. He had thrown the door open with such force it had come clear off its hinges and crashed into the cabinet of ornaments behind. Although the floor was now littered with the debris Stim looked as if he had either not noticed, or did not care.

"He's alive!" the large man shouted. He bounded towards him like an overgrown dog. He wrapped Perin up in his huge arms and gave him a monstrous bear hug. Perin laughed with as much breath as he had left in him but winced at the pain that fired through his joints and head.

"What happened?" Stim and Perin said in unison. Perin laughed but Stim looked as if he was going to cry with happiness.

"You first," said Stim, as he tried to compose himself. Perin needed a more comfortable position to tell his story and managed to shift himself round and off the table. The crewman he didn't know put his shoulder under Perin's arm and helped him to a more comfortable seat at the side of the room. He then filled a glass with amber liquid.

"For the pain," he said, and then bustled out of the room to give them some privacy. He needn't have bothered, but Perin was too tired to stop him.

Stim was looking at Perin unblinkingly, desperate for the story. So Perin began, with his explanation of using magic as a channel for other people's will as opposed to exerting your own will. He explained that if magic was used to selflessly grant the will of other people, and if several people's wills were aligned to want the same thing then the power created would be almost insurmountable. Stim didn't seem to fully understand, but made the right noises so that Perin could continue with the story. Perin then explained that he used the crew's will to live to defend them, and their collective animosity against Viri and her crew to defeat the *Formalite'*. He hesitated before explaining that his plan had not included his survival. He had very much expected to be killed in the blast with the rest of the *Formalite'*s crew. A thought struck him.

"Were there any more survivors?" Perin asked.

"Not one," said Stim resolutely. Perin thought of saying 'good' but decided that although the losses were necessary, he wouldn't indulge in bloodlust or triumph over people's deaths. They had been bad people who had done bad things and in war such actions were necessary, but he regretted that.

"So what happened?" Perin repeated, signalling that his story was finished and Stim's was supposed to start.

"Well," said the giant, "I did what I was supposed to. I rowed my little rowboat around the *Formalite'* out of sight as you fired cannons at each other." He made sound effects with his throat of the explosions. Stim's stories were very childlike and endearing. "I struggled a bit through the fog but I've known the *Muta* so long I know what her cannons sound like so I just headed towards the sound of the *Formalite'*s guns." Perin had wondered about that. In the heat of battle he had forgotten that Stim wouldn't have had the easiest time finding his target.

"When I tried to flip the boat," Stim continued, "that witch appeared on the deck above me and caught me in some awful spell." He had turned a little pale – this was a hard memory for him to relive, Perin knew. "The life drained out of me. Not only couldn't I flip the ship, I couldn't fight, I couldn't stand. I was totally at her mercy." He looked ashamed. Perin wanted to get up to put a supportive hand on his shoulder but still couldn't move under his own power. "When those beasts from her crew made their way onto my boat I couldn't even lift my hands to stop them from putting that bag on my head," he said with disgust. "Then I heard Viri tell the whole bleeding ocean that she had captured me," he hesitated, "and I heard you give yourself up." Tears had begun streaking down the poor man's face. They dropped with a small tap on the deck of the room. "If I'd had a knife at that moment I would have cut out my own heart to stop you."

A little melodramatic, Perin thought, *but probably not entirely untrue.*

"They bundled me into a rowboat, and I felt the rock of it leading us out towards you," Stim said. "I didn't know that Viri was the one in the boat when we left. The first I knew of that was when we got to you." He paused and brought his hand to his face, "And she gave me a good kicking."

"I tried to fix you up," Perin said quickly.

"I figured as much," Stim said with a slight grin. "My nose cracking back was almost as painful as the kick, but I was much better afterwards." He smiled. "Anyway, after I got myself all set up in your boat, it seemed to float itself back towards the *Muta*. They pulled me on board and we stood and watched the *Formalite'* for a while. Nothing much happened until that lightning bolt came flying outta their ship towards ours. We all thought we were goners till that shield came sprouting up around us." He gestured towards Perin, who knew all of this so far – it was from after the explosion that he was truly interested in, but Stim was clearly enjoying himself so he left him to his explanation. "Then the lightning stopped attacking us, and set their ship on fire," he said with dramatic flair, "then that thundercloud formed and ripped right through the filthy thing!"

Stim stood in silence for a few moments, as if this was the end of the story. Perin continued to look at him.

"And?!"

Stim jumped slightly as if he had just been reminded that Perin was there.

"Well," Stim said hesitantly, "we all thought you were

dead."

"I thought I was dead," added Perin. "Why did you hang around long enough to find out otherwise?"

Stim looked uncomfortable with this question. "You know how you wanted to use the belongings of the *Muta*'s old crew to make repairs and such?" Perin nodded. "Well I thought we might as well get as much from the wreckage of the *Formalite'* as we could. In case anything could be useful, you know?"

Perin nodded and smiled. He wasn't surprised that Stim was uncomfortable in admitting this, considering how against the idea of salvage he had been even when it was from the *Muta*'s own crew for their use. Stim was the captain when the *Formalite'* had exploded. *In fact he still is, I suppose,* thought Perin. So it had been his choice and, as far as Perin was concerned, he had taken it well.

"Well done, Captain," Perin said with a smile. "Did you find anything useful?" he asked, before adding, "Apart from me?"

"That's just it," Stim said excitedly. "We found you first, on our way towards the wreckage. You were in a state. Badly beat up and unconscious. You floated towards us." Perin's expression was blank, Stim looked at him with confusion. "Don't you understand?" he asked. "You floated *towards* us?" He shook his hands exasperatedly at Perin. "Against the current!" *Oh,* thought Perin, *that's new. Perhaps I was able to control the currents as Viri did.* But he had been completely unconscious and there was no one else's will at work other than his own.

"How?" asked Perin, who was now looking at him with a cheeky grin.

"As far as the crew knows, that's it," he said. "You are merely an incredible sorcerer with a will so strong that it can control the oceans even when you're unconscious!" He was obviously very excited about this.

"But you know what really happened?" Perin enquired.

"Indeed I do," Stim said proudly. "I was the one who

got down in the boat to rescue you. You weren't being held up by the water, you were being held up by a couple of—"

"Dolphins!" Perin realised at once. The smile faded from Stim's face, and Perin felt a little bad for stealing his moment, but at least now he understood.

"Why would they help you though? They're usually awfully shy creatures. They certainly made a run for it as soon as I had you out the water."

"I have no idea," said Perin. "That's another thing we can try to find out from the Archive." He suddenly realised he had no idea where they were at the moment, or how long he had been unconscious. He decided to start with the first question.

"Where are we anyway?" This caught Stim off guard, but he smiled.

"On our way to the compass point now. It's the only part of the map that isn't really drawn to scale, so it'll take some time to find out exactly where to go. We're still not completely sure that we will find the Archive there."

Funnily enough, this thought had never occurred to Perin. As soon as they had discovered that all the compass points were in the same place on the maps, he had been sure that it was the solution. Strangely, even with Stim's doubt, he still felt convinced.

"So what has happened since you got me back on board?" he continued, deciding not to labour the point.

"Well," Stim sighed, "we salvaged some good strong thick wood from the *Formalite'*. So much we were almost bursting. We used that to reinforce the hull. It should take more than one cannonball to get through the two woods. We got some cloth, ammunition and bounty. We mounted many of the spears we found from the crew onto the fore and aft so that we won't get rammed, and if *we* do any ramming it'll hurt like hell." He looked gleeful.

"Wait a minute, wait a minute," Perin interrupted. "You've completely refit the *Muta* using the wreckage of the *Formalite*?"

"That's right. We put in to port and got her all fixed up."

"How long was I out, Stim?" Perin realised it was clearly longer than a few hours, or even days.

"About six weeks."

"Six weeks! That's not possible!" Perin cried. "A man can't live without food and water for that long."

"We've been nursing you. We put sponges soaked in water, milk and the like to sustain you. The other bits ain't important – let's just say you were well taken care of. We knew you would come back."

Perin was astounded. First of all that he had been what could now be described as comatose for a month and a half, but also that the crew had stepped up to nurse him.

"Amazing," was all he could really muster himself to say. "Have we been attacked or anything dramatic in the time I've been out?"

"Oh there's been drama," Stim said proudly, "but we've been the ones creating it this time."

"What do you mean?"

"Everyone who came through the port thinks you have strong enough magic to continue even after you're unconscious. They also know you killed Viri and blew up the *Formalite*."

"Hopefully that will inspire them a little," Perin mused. Stim burst out into a broad laugh that had a touch of hysteria to it.

"Perin, it's done more than inspire them!" he said with glee. "Both ports this side of the chains have declared open rebellion against the Great Committee – they won't stock their ships and will fire on any that approach. They've declared themselves 'free ports'."

Not possible, Perin thought. First he was stunned, and this moved on to shock at how quickly things had escalated and finally he started to laugh with a similar hysteria to Stim. *We're winning!*

"Has the Committee come forward with any retribution yet? Can those ports defend themselves?" he asked.

"Antez is armed to the teeth!" Stim exclaimed. "They've mounted three giant cannons where the watchtowers used to be. They can almost reach The Hammer and Anvil themselves. Nothing can sail towards them without being blown to smithereens. Not only that, but they can take out any ship as it approaches The Anvil. The prison is cut off from the rest of Caramine." *That could be of strategic value,* Perin thought. "Amic stayed there and took command to make sure it stays safe. To be honest though," Stim continued, "the Committee isn't rushing to fight – between you being the newest Sorcerer of Caramine, and the *Muta* being probably the most well armed vessel ever constructed, they are still smarting a bit."

"Viri was the head of their armies," Perin explained. "It will take them some time to figure out what to do next without them. We will need to figure out what we are going to do next a little quicker."

"Any ideas on that score?" Stim asked. Perin drank the amber liquid, which was revealed as Firewine, and for once he enjoyed it. *Perhaps I'm getting older,* he thought.

"Slow down, Stim," he said. "I didn't expect to be alive right now, never mind wake up over a month later in a completely different world!" He was truly at a loss. All he could think to do was to fall back on his original plan and gut instinct. "I think we are headed on the right course, both figuratively and physically."

He took another drink of the Firewine, emptying the glass, and decided to stand up. It was going to hurt whenever he did it so he may as well grasp that particular bull by the horns. He wanted the crew to see him at least alive, if not yet well.

He was correct: it did hurt like hell. He stood upright on his legs, his muscles screaming in pain from disuse as well as from any lingering injury. He tried to imagine the pain ebbing out of his body, as though his pain and injury had taken liquid form and was evaporating or perhaps even running off him like water from glass. This was only partially successful. The throbbing in his head had divided his attention and made it hard to concentrate. He was unable to fully submerge himself into his imagination. He was able to walk and move around without looking like he was in pain, which would have to do for now.

He made his way, slowly at first, to the door, and with each step he felt a little better. As he headed for the light that shone in from the door, Stim rose from his chair with concern etched onto his face. He was clearly ready to catch Perin should he stumble or fall. *Gods let him always be there to do that,* thought Perin, *because it's going to get bumpier from here on in.*

As he reached the door he could tell that word of his emergence had already spread like a dry hedge fire through the crew. There is a particular kind of quiet created by people waiting for something. That was what Perin could hear now. As he walked out into the sun and enjoyed the warmth on his skin he was greeted by every member of the expanded crew. They lined every available space on the deck and faced him, standing to perfect attention, but with wide grins on their faces. Perin felt grateful to be among them.

What a ship! Perin thought. The *Muta*'s warm wooden panels were still recognisable but beyond them, Perin could see that Stim had not exaggerated the refit they had undergone. Beyond the panels that had always existed there were dark wooden panels that used to belong to the *Formalite'*. They had been carved and shaped to match the hull of the *Muta*. At regular intervals the dark wooden panel on the outside would be hinged, acting as a covering panel from behind which a soldier could take cover and fire during an attack. The reason for this was obvious: each of these protruding panels had a crossbow and fully stocked quiver attached to it. Boarding the ship would now be very difficult.

There were other armaments and defences. Perin couldn't understand what they were all intended for from first glance. He found that they very much changed the feel of the ship, but not the ship itself. *It's still the* Muta, *just like I would still be Perin if you put me in a new suit of armour.* He thought this was actually the perfect analogy. The *Muta* was indeed the same ship at heart, but simply had a new suit of armour to wear that would make her stronger and faster. Perin was aware that she might have lost one of her more important attributes because of all of these added extras. *I doubt she can still be the fastest ship in Caramine anymore. Not with all this extra weight.*

The crew were watching him when the silence was broken by a crew member that couldn't be distinguished through the throng in front of him.

"Perin, Perin, Perin," he chanted rhythmically. More members of the crew around him soon joined. It wasn't a war cry. It was a cheer of pride and hope. Perin's eyes started to fill as the whole crew joined in, stamping their feet in time with their voices. After a much longer time than Perin would have expected this to last he realised that they weren't going to stop without his intervention, so he raised his arms to silence them.

"Thank you, one and all, for taking care of me," he said. "We have, together, struck a blow for Caramine; a blow for freedom against the Great Committee." A cheer rang from the crew.

"As we head forward towards our destination, and a greater understanding of the magic that we wield, I thank you for your help and service." He really didn't know what else to say. *That's a first,* Perin thought. He couldn't be sure, but he thought that voice in his head might have been a combination of both Rienta and Occidens.

"Our mission so far has not been without casualties." The silence of the crew listening became instantly sombre.

"Our previous leader and Sorcerer of Caramine, Occidens, remains the inspiration for our mission. Whatever I am able to accomplish, I do in her name." Instead of a cheer this time, a respectful round of applause rang round the crew. *Many of them didn't know who Occidens was,* Perin realised. *That was the original crew.*

"She led the original crew of the *Muta* for a large number of years. A crew that was brave, strong and resolute. They maintained hope, before there was hope to be maintained. They waited and planned for what is happening now. Most are not here to see it and shall never be forgotten." More applause, and some whistles and stamps from the remaining crew who remembered who Perin was talking about.

"That brings me to the captain of the *Muta*. Rienta was the greatest inspiration to that crew. It would never occur to any of them to second guess or countermand her orders. She simply inspired us all. She also saved my life and gave her own in the process. Despite not having magic of her own, it is her loss I feel most strongly. She had a magic that transcended sorcery. She could bring people to their feet. Inspire them to cooperation through her will, personality and explanation. Occidens had the power, but Rienta created the means and will to make her vision a reality. I may carry out this mission in Occidens' name and rightly so, but I have the physical faculties and abilities to do so because of Rienta." Now the crowd did cheer. Whereas Occidens would have stayed very much in the background whenever the *Muta* came to port, Perin thought that Rienta would likely be a presence and many would remember her. This seemed to be true. "I ask all of you as you go forward to think to yourself, 'What would Rienta do?' If we stick to that mantra we won't go far wrong. Thank you, and continue on with your duties." One final cheer rose up from the crew.

Perin turned to Stim, that ever-present force that backed him wherever he went and whatever he did.

"Well, Stim, do you have any idea what Rienta would do now?"

"You know," Stim smiled, "I was just going to ask you that!"

CHAPTER TWENTY-EIGHT

It took another two days of nothing but open blue water rolling past the warship before a small outcropping of rocks appeared on the horizon. To call it an island would have been generous.

"Land ahead," came the call from the crow's nest, and Perin jumped up from his chair. His limbs still ached an objection but he was able to ignore them much more easily now. He rushed onto the deck to see what the commotion was.

All crew on deck were looking ahead. Many had to squint to be able to make out the small dot heading towards them. Stim was manning the helm and after peering through a telescope to locate it, he altered the course slightly so that the approach would be dead on. Sure enough, there was a small landmass heading towards them. It seemed to grow not lengthways, but vertically as they approached.

Once they got nearer the reason for this was quite clear. The rocks were quite narrow for an island. Two ships of the *Muta*'s size if placed side by side would be the whole width. The cliffs were too tall to be able to discern how long the island was. The other side was simply not visible.

Small rock formations in the centre of the ocean tended to be rounded and smooth, worn down by generations of waves and winds. That was not the case with this structure. Sharp cliffs surrounded it that were almost identical to those found in the teeth. Those had survived because of their relative shelter in the narrow passage. Perin was at a loss to think of any natural means that would have maintained the shape of this island. *Unless it's magic,* he thought. His heart started to race and his breath quickened in his chest.

There was a danger here. Having access to magic had a side effect that Perin did not like. It was very easy to fall into the trap of explaining everything you did not immediately understand as a potential work of sorcery. It was understandable, but over time could lead to ignorance, and magic was more powerful the more you knew. He remembered that Occidens had been unable to fix the engines as she had little comprehension of how they worked. Perin was determined that this would not be a weakness of his own. He decided that although he suspected magic could be the cause he would continue an investigation of the island without it being assumed. Part of the analytical mind he had been provided by the Great Committee was still immensely valuable, and deep down Perin relished the opportunity to use it against them.

Investigation of the island directly would prove rather tricky. There was no dock or port that could be seen. It did not seem to be a very large island, but there was only one way to know for sure. Perin made his way up to the helm and stood beside Stim.

"Take us around the island," he said. "If there is a dock or entranceway we need to find it."

"Aye, Captain," replied Stim. He turned the wheel so that they were no longer heading directly for the island itself but circling it. Perin stood for a few minutes as they sailed round the port side of the outcropping. There was something strange about the pattern of the rocks. There was almost uniformity to their lack of uniformity. Like the way some ornate rooms are decorated with complicated wallpapers that are designed to have no discernible pattern, but if you look at it in the correct way you can tell where the joins between the pieces are and where the pattern matches up.

"Slow us down," Perin said to Stim urgently, "I want to look at these rocks more closely as we go past them. There's something very strange about them." Stim nodded and ordered that the sails be lowered. The engines had been turned off on their approach. The water current itself should do most of the work.

The strangest thing occurred. The water current at first did take them around the island, which was much longer than Perin had thought. Then the ship began to turn. Stim grabbed the wheel and tried to pull the ship back into position parallel with the ragged coast but the water flow had changed. It was not heading directly towards the rocks and taking the *Muta* with it. Perin looked out over the side of the boat towards where the water was taking them but no waves crashed on the rocks. The current just seemed to disappear against the stone. This could not be a natural phenomenon. *That settles it,* thought Perin. *Magic, definitely.*

The question remained, was it magic with intent to harm, or with intent to help? Clearly the initial response would be to harm. The current was dragging the ship towards the rocks. The new reinforcements that had been built into the hull may avoid it being obliterated entirely but it could still be run aground. There were no trees, buildings or shelter of any kind on those rocks. Running aground would be a death sentence.

"We'll have to start the engines!" Stim yelled, as his muscled arms strained against the wheel, trying to keep the ship away from the rocks. There was something thoroughly peculiar about the whole scenario. Particularly the fact that the water was not crashing onto the rocks. Perin wanted to buy some more time to figure things out, but looking at Stim, he could see that wasn't an option… or was it?

"Let the ship face the rocks," Perin said to Stim.

"What?!" the large man yelled. "Are you crazy? We'll be smashed to splinters!"

"Trust me," Perin said simply. Stim looked at him, with exasperated worry, but he complied. The deck rocked under their feet, and the *Muta* was now turning into the current. They would soon be heading face-on to the rocks.

"Lower the sail!" Perin shouted. The crew looked up at him, thoroughly terrified that they were heading for the rocks. The wind was blowing across the side of the ship now and would not do them any good, but they complied. The sail lowered and flapped unhelpfully in the wind. The rocks were growing closer.

Perin closed his eyes and pictured the wind blowing across the island towards the front of the *Muta*. He pictured every member of the crew willing the ship backwards and the sails filling and pushing the ship away from the island, acting as a counterpoint to the current. Perin imagined the feeling of that wind pushing against him. He felt the cold air wash over his face, making the sweat of fear feel like ice on his skin. He opened his eyes and saw that the wind had changed. The sail was blowing in full reverse. Their progress towards the shore had halted and they were now stationary, facing the strange point on the island where the water made no impression on the rocks. He turned towards Stim, who looked impressed but still nervous. His muscles flexed in readiness to grab the wheel again and try and steer them away from the rocks.

"We need to look closer at this spot," Perin said. "There's something strange about it and how it reacts with the water."

"Closer?" Stim exclaimed. "I think we are already plenty close enough."

"We'll hold this position," Perin assured him, "but I'm sure the entrance to the Archive is nearby. It might even be here."

"We could take boats," Stim said, trying to be helpful, "but those waters look pretty choppy. They could be smashed up on the rocks themselves." Perin agreed. There was also no form of incline. Even if a small ship made its way to the rock face then its crew would not be able to disembark anywhere helpful.

The ship lurched forward. The current had increased, more so than the wind and sails were compensating for.

"What the hells?" said Perin. Stim swore as the rocks grew closer to them. Perin closed his eyes to try and imagine the winds increasing to compensate. He felt them blowing across his face and almost knocking him down with their force, but still the *Muta* crept forward. The best he could do was slow it down.

"I can't stop it," Perin said, "I can't stop the ship." He was truly amazed. Whatever magic was controlling these currents was powerful enough to overcome not just his will but also the will of the whole crew. They all wanted to survive and they all wanted to avoid colliding with the rocks. Perin had tapped into this will through his own powers but still the ship moved forward. That meant whatever force was pushing them forward and controlling these currents was more powerful than Viri had been.

Perin was scared. He considered telling the crew to man the cannons and prepare for an assault. The force causing this had to be close, had to see them and how they were reacting. He still couldn't comprehend what was going on. He had to think fast – if he couldn't stop the ship he'd need to find another solution. The answer came to him from the part of the mind that always projected the most ridiculous ideas. This was also the creative portion of the mind, and was one that Perin was learning to listen to more, regardless of having been taught to dismiss it.

If I can't stop the ship from moving, then I will just have to move the island. It was a ridiculous notion, which would obviously prove impossible, but he didn't see what other choice he had. He closed his eyes and imagined the cliffs retreating, the jagged edges and rough stone moving back from the water.

The noise was astounding. With unexpected ease the cliffs receded back. Perin's eyes shot open. His magical will prodding at the rocks had been like a giant key turning in an unseen lock. The waters gushed and flooded backwards into the chasm that was being created in the centre directly facing the *Muta.* The cliffs ground against one another as a slit that had been invisible to the eye before appeared as two rock doors slid backwards, pushing the other cliffs out of their way. The wind died away, as did the current, allowing the *Muta* to simply sit in the water facing the entranceway that had been created. As light made its way through the giant doorway and lit the chasm beyond, what was revealed made Perin's heart leap.

The island was hollow.

The inner cavern held a hidden dock inside. It was not like the ports that Perin had seen so far: first of all, there were no people to be seen. There were buildings, as though there had been or could be a small village of people. The houses were of strange shapes and not of any determinate size.

"Take us in, Mr Stim," Perin said determinedly.

"Aye, sir," the big man replied with a grin.

The entire crew had gathered on deck, drawn by the commotion. They stared open-mouthed as they sailed into this hidden city floating in the centre of unnamed, unexplored waters. As they passed the threshold into the small, enclosed cavern they could finally appreciate the size of the island. The *Muta* had to turn quite sharply to avoid crashing into the other side, but the water's current was gentle and seemed designed to help ships along the inside of the structure. The island was long and thin, and once the *Muta* had turned so that it sailed along this corridor of enclosed stone the sound of grinding rocks returned and the entranceway closed behind them. Natural light was cut off but was maintained inside the structure by giant candelabra with fires of red, gold, green, purple, blue, yellow and even black burning in the various arms. It cast a mystical light across the cavern.

The roof itself had been ground smooth, and stars had been painted onto it. This was clearly an ancient structure that had been built up and worked on for generations. The *Muta* came to a gentle stop and Perin signalled that the crew at the side of the ship should tie it off against the dock and ready to disembark. This was rather more complicated than usual without anyone to help from the dockside of the port. The crew had to lower themselves with the ropes down the side of the ship and then tie them to the heavy stone bollards that dotted the walkways. A plank was then lowered from the deck to allow prepare to disembark.

Perin and Stim made their way to the gangway. The rest of the crew stood awaiting orders. Perin could see in their faces that they were keen to get out and explore this strange and unusual small floating town but Perin was slightly more wary. He was still concerned there could be some sort of trap at work here. Magic had not only made him powerful, it had given him an inbuilt suspicion of when things seemed to go well.

"We'll go first," he announced to the crew, gesturing to himself and Stim.

"That won't be necessary," came a voice that Perin had never heard before. It was well spoken and seemed thoroughly comfortable in its surroundings. It was then that Perin heard sharp footfalls and realised that someone was walking up the gangway towards the *Muta*.

A well-dressed man in a formal suit with a colourful flower attached to his lapel greeted him with a warm smile. He stood at the top of the gangway as if deliberately revealing himself to them with dramatic flair.

"I am the Archivist," he announced, "and you must be the newest Sorcerer of Caramine and the great hope that Occidens set forth to find."

Perin stood looking at the man, whose smile glinted in the unnatural light.

"I also imagine, given the hesitation and resistance you showed to entering, that the dear old lady has," he hesitated but did not lose his smile, "gone on to greater things," he concluded kindly.

"That's right," Perin said, with a tone of seriousness. "My name is Perin." He left this statement open to try and get some explanation of who this man was, and perhaps even a confirmation of where they were.

"That's a nice name," came the eccentric reply. *He's not going to be directly helpful,* thought Perin.

"Sorry to be so blunt," Perin explained, "but who are you and where are we?"

"I believe I am who you expect me to be and you are where you want to be," came the thoroughly unhelpful and maddening reply. Perin knew he was going to have to take the lead.

"You are the Archivist and this is the Archive," Perin stated. The man beamed and threw his arms out wide.

"Wonderful!" he exclaimed. "Welcome, welcome, welcome!" He almost jumped up and down as he repeated this. He walked forward and clapped Perin on the shoulder.

"Sorry to be so unhelpful," the old man said, "but you see the Archive is not a library. I may very well be able to confirm your theories and provide your answers, but you must find those answers yourself. Simply handing out information without making people discover it for themselves is what created the Great Committee and what I think you have taken issue with."

That made a strange sort of sense to Perin, and he thought he might react quite well to that sort of relationship. He couldn't help but smile at the Archivist –

he was an eccentric who had clearly spent much time alone, but was still thoroughly entertaining.

"I am hoping," the old man continued, "that you might be able to fill in some gaps in my own knowledge. I get no news here, so my archive has become far from current."

"I'm sure we can help you with that," Perin said, and he realised the crew were watching this exchange dumbfounded. "Do you mind if my crew take shelter in one of your buildings?" The Archivist looked at him rather oddly.

"Dear boy, these buildings belong to you and your crew. This is your archive. This is your city!"

There was a pause as everyone – Perin, Stim and the rest of the crew – absorbed that statement. They now not only had a ship at their disposal, but a small city as their base of operations.

"In that case," Perin said slowly, "while the crew make themselves at home," *quite literally,* he thought, "perhaps you could give me and Mr Stim here a tour and show us the resources you have at your disposal."

"I would be delighted," said the old man with a smile and he turned and walked down the gangway without any further hesitation. Perin had not meant quite so immediately but he nodded towards Stim and they hurried after him.

The width of the island was restrictive enough that there was only really the main thoroughfare on either side of the water to be seen. There was everything you would expect a small town to hold. A tavern, a shoe shop, a tailor, an ironmonger and all other forms of trades were represented.

"Who works in these establishments?" Perin asked.

"You do," replied the Archivist, "and your crew. The island was designed so that it could be totally self-sufficient with a small community, just like that of your ship. To be honest, life may be a little easier now you are here."

"How so?" Stim asked. The Archivist stopped and

pointed at the far end of the island, the opposite end from the way they were walking, where the buildings seemed to thin out and become a large garden.

"Over there we have the gardens where we have all manner of fruit, vegetables and spices. It is also where the cows, sheep, pigs, horses and other animals are free to eat, roam and reproduce as nature intended. I am a perfectly reasonable gardener and that is how I have fed myself, but I am a thoroughly incompetent butcher and therefore haven't had a piece of meat since Occidens departed. Perhaps one of your crew will be better suited to that." Perin knew that a few certainly would be. There were at least two men who had been butchers by trade on Antez before joining up.

"Couldn't you use magic to prepare the food?" Perin asked, thinking of how the salted beef had continually magically appeared until Occidens had died. The Archivist stopped again and looked at him in a curious manner.

"I don't have magic, dear boy. The island is maintained by magic, but the island itself was imbued with magic. I have access to some of it, and it is tuned in to my will, but I can't really control it or how it works. If you like, I will explain my role in all of this when we reach the main hub. That may make things more clear to you, and give you an idea of how to move forward." As he talked he wrung his hands together, weaving his old fingers. They seemed unnaturally long.

They made their way further along the street until a large structure appeared that marked the end of the island. It was a grand white structure with pillars holding up a great mezzanine. It had a rounded front and in golden letters above the entranceway read THE ARCHIVE. Having lived here for some time the Archivist felt no need to stand and look at it and continued inside. It was hugely impressive to Perin and Stim and they could not help but slow their pace to take in the opulent marble and beautiful gold lettering on the building.

Perin realised the Archivist was quite far in front of them as both he and Stim had been drinking in the sight of the grand structure. They hurried to catch up and walked inside the large double wooden doors.

The Archivist was sitting at the head of a long table as if he had been there the whole time. He was surrounded by shelf upon shelf of books. They lined the walls and stretched all the way up to the ceiling. Great ladders led up to the roof and could be wheeled along the walls.

"Welcome to the Archive," the old man said. "You can refer to me as the Archivist and I will be your guide through the information you see before you." This had the sound of a prepared speech and Perin and Stim sat down to hear the rest of it.

"In the days before the Great Committee, I was in charge of keeping the records of magical study and for disseminating them to people who showed magical ability. That is where the bulk of these manuscripts come from. They are records on magic from everyone who has studied or attempted to study the subject. They also catalogue the history of magic and how it grew from the gift of Caramine to its curse as the four sorcerers of the Great Committee took control of the continent." Perin found he was leaning forward and listening intently. The Archivist was looking off into the distance and not making eye contact with either man. It was as if he were speaking to someone who was not there.

"This facility was raised from the ocean by the sorcerer Occidens to house all the information that could be saved from the time when the Committee ceased direct magical instruction for all who showed potential. I agreed to stay here as the Archivist, so that a future sorcerer of potential could benefit from my experiences, and to atone for the mistakes I made in passing on information on the practice of magic to those that did not deserve it."

Perin realised the sadness of this man's position. He had given the knowledge to become sorcerers to the

Committee, who had used it to bring society to its knees. To be in charge of the old way of education and for it to be subsumed by the Committee's new clinical form must have been very painful.

"I stand ready to aid you in any way I can," the Archivist continued. "Now, if I may ask you a question, what is your mission here?"

"To bring down the Great Committee," Perin said. "To restore magic's place as a force for good in Caramine and to liberate all its citizens so they may live their life with free will in peace."

Now the Archivist met his eyes – they flashed with sincere joy and his mouth broke into a wide grin again.

"Oh," he said, "is that all? Then let's begin."

EPILOGUE ONE

Capital Island was dark. The waves that crashed upon its ragged shores were black and the winds that drove them howled like an animal in terrible pain. News of Viri's death had reached the island two hours ago and the storm had risen up around the island, cutting it off from all ships that may wish to approach. The ship that had brought the news had been wrecked against the rocks as it had tried to depart.

This could all be surveyed from the tower that housed the Great Committee in the centre of the island. The tower was long and smooth, carved out of expensive black marble. The argument for its smoothness had been that it would be impossible to scale by attackers. In truth it was simply a sign of opulence and power. It was an unnecessary building. The only floor that had any rooms on it was the one at the top. Four triangular apartments made up the domains of the four sorcerers. From here there was nothing but a long stairwell that led down into the depths of the island below street level that was the war room and bunker where the meetings would be held. It was here that the four remaining members of the

Committee sat. Their wrath gathered outside, causing havoc to the poor people who were the rest of the population of the small island. The Committee only tolerated a small population for a defensive garrison and those to cater to their needs.

Although the small table they sat at was round, there could be no question to any onlookers, if such things were ever allowed, as to who was in charge of the Committee. In a slightly more ornate chair, with more distance between it and the other three chairs, one of which stood empty, was a black-haired young man. His hair was slick against his head and his eyes a deep shade of grey. His face bore the marks and lines of someone who had spent most of their life sneering at others, and the natural position of his nose was slightly turned up. He dug his hands into the arms of his chair as his eyes bore into the other two members of the Committee. This was Master Ibrum, the chairman of the Great Committee.

"Armies in chaos," he said, "The Anvil cut off from Lower Caramine and the chains," he continued, "our flagship sunk, and Mistress Viri killed." The thunder raged outside as if to highlight his anger. "Would either of you two like to put forward an explanation as to how a child has accomplished this? Or even better," his voice raised to a growling roar, "what you suggest doing about it?"

The two much older ladies jumped at his raised voice.

"The Anvil may be cut off," said Mistress Seus, "but it is still secure. Reinforcements from The Hammer are still available for deployment there. It is in no imminent danger." She was a small, smiling woman and thoroughly round, but her smile was not kind. It was a dangerous smile that seemed to hide evil intentions that could never be truly discerned. She wore flowing flower-covered robes that contrasted with the stark greys of the room as well as Ibrum's plain black robes. "I suggest we hold out there until more ships can be sent round from the east around Upper Caramine to make up a large enough force to rout the insurgency."

"That will take months!" screamed Ibrum. "Who knows what untold damage the *Muta* can do in the meantime, what they might learn or who they might recruit."

"It sounds to me," said the cool and efficient voice of Mistress Rubrum, "that you have a particular person or group of persons in mind with that statement." Her voice betrayed no fear of Ibrum. He may have made Seus nervous, but Rubrum seemed to take it all in her stride. "If you tell us what it is you are afraid of, then I will endeavour to find you a solution."

"I fear nothing," fumed Ibrum, "but I am justified in anger when one of our number has been killed. For the first time ever we have a vacancy on this Committee."

"That's not strictly true, dear," said Seus tentatively. "After all, you weren't here at the start—"

"That's not the point," Ibrum interrupted angrily. "The point is, they must be stopped and as quickly as possible."

"Well," Rubrum continued, "Seus is right, we can send reinforcements over Upper Caramine. Yes it will take time, but outnumbering our foes is the only option. I will increase the emphasis on military training to the Great Academy and we should be able to gain troops from there. How is our support holding up at home?" She turned to Seus.

"Lower Caramine continues to remain loyal," she said. "We should be able to get some willing recruits from there. Obviously the staff at the Great Academy are our own people, as are those on The Anvil. There is some wavering dissent on Upper Caramine but nothing we cannot bring back on side. Particularly with a show of force passing across their borders."

"I'm glad you think so," said Ibrum, "because you're going with them!"

"What? Me?" came the startled reply from the short fat woman, her jowls shaking nervously. "Surely Rubrum is more suited to that sort of confrontational—"

"Viri excelled at confrontation," said Ibrum simply, "and she is dead. Rubrum will be needed to oversee the changes at the Academy. You are the best at making a show to the peasants and making them feel loved and wanted. I want you to peddle those lies for all they're worth and fill our warships with willing recruits." The woman nodded, but Rubrum did not seem appeased.

"What exactly do you think this Perin and his crew are doing?" she asked.

"With Occidens dead," Ibrum replied, "they will be looking for some further source of information. My best guess is that they have the Archivist stashed away somewhere and have gone to find him. If he is still alive then those damned books of his exist as well," he looked at the two women with more concern, "containing every word and thought all of us have ever had when we were learning our craft."

"Well we can't have that," said Rubrum. "Do you have any idea where they would have him hiding?"

"You knew the old woman better than me," Ibrum snapped, "and you have access to the Great Academy and all its books and knowledge. You find out and come back to me with some ideas. We must stop the Archivist from helping Perin."

"Why?" asked Seus. "Let's be honest, the information he gave you convinced you to come with us on our plan to reform Caramine – perhaps it will be the same for this Perin."

"Don't be stupid, woman!" Ibrum spat. "He has already killed the head of our armies. He is more powerful than I was at this point. Though I shall never admit it again. He has already decided on his course."

"He is more powerful than you?" Rubrum repeated with a beautiful and vicious smile. "Quite the admission."

"The dead are no stronger than anyone else," Ibrum amended, "and I intend for Perin to be dead soon, along with all his other followers."

"I certainly hope so!" Rubrum said. "This does seem likely to be one of those them-or-us situations. So what do you intend to do while we are rearming and responding to these threats?"

"Once you find the Archivist and his tomes, kill him and send for me. I will pore through those books and become more powerful than Perin could ever imagine. Then I will sink that ship of his and boil every spoonful of his blood whilst it is still in his veins, one drop at a time."

This seemed to satisfy Rubrum, and Seus had seemed distracted since being put at the head of the force being sent to recapture the ports of eastern Caramine.

"If that's all," Rubrum concluded, "then let's get to bed. Tomorrow we will deal with Perin and the *Muta* and soon it will be as if they never existed."

The chairs scraped on the hard stone floor, and the candles that lined the walls extinguished themselves until all that was left was the sound of the storm continuing to thunder on outside.

EPILOGUE TWO

One of the Great Committee's weaknesses was the contempt they held for other people. Capital Island had been set up to serve them but it had also been constructed to limit and reduce their interaction with people as much as possible. As such, there were dozens of secret avenues and hidden passages that enabled servants, cleaners, cooks and guards to move about the tower without having to be seen by, let alone communicate with, the four members. The Committee room was no exception to this. Underneath the room, amongst the pipes, with dripping water and stagnant pools for company, someone listened to their meeting. She was exceptionally keen of hearing, and fairly adept at avoiding detection.

She listened to the voices. Ibrum was emotional and, to her mind, slightly unhinged. Seus was a coward, but covered up her evil with a simpering voice. Rubrum was the most dangerous. The calculating calm and cool evil would always be more of a threat than the other two. At least that was how she saw it.

Perin was in danger. That wasn't new. They had probably guessed right about the Archivist as well. These were not un-resourceful or stupid people. They could not be underestimated. She had to get to Perin first. They had made it to the east side of Caramine. That was good. They had probably gone through the teeth. They seemed to have caused merry hells when they got there and Perin had obviously managed to dispatch Viri. That was a shockingly good start.

A network of caves led from the hiding spot underneath the Committee room down into the catacombs of Capital Island. They were used primarily for drainage these days, but could also serve as an escape tunnel should the sorcerers wish to flee attack. What could come out of these tunnels could also come in. The network had provided her with entry to steal food, bandages and supplies she needed to repair her rowboat. She had hidden it in one of the more secluded parts of the cave system and it was here she was heading to now.

She was not the first to reach it. She could see a lantern light glowing amongst her belongings being held at eye level for someone to get a look around. As quietly as she could muster she drew her sword. She was forced to do so with her unnatural arm. Her shoulder was still below peak efficiency. Even using her bad arm she had never met a swordsman or woman that she could not best.

She approached as stealthily as she could with catlike steps and efficiency. It was a guard, or a sentry, probably on a routine patrol who had simply come across the wrong boat at the wrong time. As she reached striking distance she made a deliberate sound to make the man jump. To his credit as a soldier he did not – he whirled round whilst unsheathing his sword and brought it clanging together with her own. His sword snapped where the two blades met.

"What the—" he started.

"My name is Rienta," the woman stated, "captain of the *Muta*, and you have two choices. So I ask you, would you like to be free or dead?"

To be continued
in
The War of Caramine

ACKNOWLEDGMENTS

I would like to take this opportunity to thank my extremely patient and supportive family, particularly my mum, Helen, brother, Adam and partner, Fiona. Their support has kept me going through this project but has also provided the healthy dose of skepticism that I need to remain realistic.

The rest of my extended family, My Grandmother, Aunt and Cousin - over many meals and conversations have provided that incredible optimism and positivity that really makes a person feel they are capable of anything.

Tone Julskjaer, who designed the front cover, the Map of Caramine and some concept artwork for me. She has really brought this world to life. She has been a delight to work with at every step of the process. This is one book I am happy to have judged by its cover!

Helen Hart and the editorial team at Silverwood Books have done a great job with this and I can't recommend them highly enough. Peter Harrison did a last beta-read and proof-read for me, thank goodness for his keen eye!

Finally, I would like to express my sincere thanks for your support in reading this novel. This is my first published work, signifying the start of, hopefully, a positive literary adventure. I would be most grateful if I could ask a few more things of you. The biggest challenge for a new author is to make enough noise to be heard. A mention of this book on social media would be much appreciated. A follow on Twitter, (@lukesband) Goodreads or YouTube would be of great help, as would a review on Amazon. Thank you once again.

29040330R00193

Printed in Poland
by Amazon Fulfillment
Poland Sp. z o.o., Wrocław